AN IRRESISTIBLE, WIDE-CANVAS STORY

JEWEL OF THE SEAS is a totally enthralling novel about Julia Howard, a woman as headstrong and untameable as the sea she loved—and as unforgettable to the men who loved her . . .

Jason Thatcher feared and hated the sea, yet he followed it in hopes of awakening and keeping the woman he wanted in Julia.

David Baxter was the rugged captain of Julia's own ship, but that was not enough. He wanted to possess Julia, and to sail the rolling waves of the sea with her forever.

Stephen Logan, Harvard-educated, didn't want the land any more than Julia did—but his love for Julia threatened the only other love he had ever known!

JEWEL OF THE SEAS is the epic story of America when America was young, and when a woman like Julia could dare to fulfill her dreams.

ing the set of a

Crossing the

D0818282

JEWEL OF THE SEAS

ELLEN ARGO

A KANGAROO BOOK
PUBLISHED BY POCKET BOOKS NEW YORK

POCKET BOOKS, a Simon & Schuster division of
GULF & WESTERN CORPORATION
1230 Avenue of the Americas, New York, N.Y. 10020

Copyright © 1977 by Ellen Argo

Published by arrangement with G. P. Putnam's Sons.
Library of Congress Catalog Card Number: 77-3180

All rights reserved, including the right to reproduce
this book or portions thereof in any form whatsoever.
For information address G. P. Putnam's Sons,
200 Madison Avenue, New York, N.Y. 10016

ISBN: 0-671-81845-7

First Pocket Books printing September, 1978

Trademarks registered in the United States and other countries.

Printed in the U.S.A.

ACKNOWLEDGMENTS

For their gracious assistance in my research and verification of the land and its people, I wish to thank Mrs. Anson H. Howes of the Dennis Historical Society, Dennis, Massachusetts; Mr. and Mrs. Henry H. Sears, Mr. and Mrs. Dean Sears, and Mr. Robert Eldred, Jr., of East Dennis, Massachusetts. In matters relating to the ships, the staff of the Mystic Seaport Museum at Mystic, Connecticut, was most courteous and helpful, as were Mr. Francis D. Wright, Jr., and Mr. Laurence Hartge of Annapolis, Maryland. Most of all, I only wish that I could thank so many of the elder generation of East Dennis and Dennis, particularly Mr. Benjamin Walker, who enchanted the small child I once was with tales of the days of which I now write. Unfortunately, these friends have, themselves, set sail for another country.

For my handsome, winsome Johnny

Chapter One

1827-1830

BLUE POOLS LAY SCATTERED over the beach like fragments of broken sky. Beyond the first stretch of water, the bar emerged, its rippled surface bared to the hot, high sun. Seagulls, quiet for once, lazily patrolled its length with one eye cocked for fish left stranded by the receding tide. Busily pecking at the water's edge, sandpipers darted amongst them.

A small girl, her black curls wet and tangled, knelt beside one of the tide pools. She had been trying to coax a hermit crab out of his whelk's shell home with a piece of jade-green seaweed, but now she paused and let the seaweed slip from her hand. She looked out beyond the pools and sand and gulls, beyond the white sails of fishing schooners and coastal packets that skimmed the Bay. Farther out lay the real objects of her interest.

The ships. They were still there. The ships with their towering stacks of white canvas, more beautiful than birds in flight, lovelier than the clouds that sailed the summer sky: square-rigged East Indiamen, barkentines, brigs. Some homeward bound with their rich cargoes of spices, fruit, brocade, and tea. Others, embarking on a new voyage, beat

1

their way northeastward to clear the treacherous rocky shoals off Provincetown at the tip of Cape Cod.

Ships like the *Flying Mist* that had been her home for the first few years of her life. She had been born in the captain's cabin, been rocked to sleep in her own small bunk, and had played on the wooden decks. She remembered the feel of the sea wind in her hair, the taste of salt spray on her lips, the rhythm of waves beneath her feet. She longed to be out there once more past all sight of land. Out there where the air was clean and clear and where nothing broke the horizon but an occasional ship or spouting whale. So intent was she on those distant sails she wasn't aware of the man's approach until he spoke.

"Julia, it's noon. Time for dinner."

She looked up then, tilting her head back until she could see her father's face. His coarse black hair was blown back from his weathered forehead by the breeze off the Bay. Looking down at his small daughter, his deep blue eyes, which could harden or flash with anger beneath their bushy brows, were gentle. His strong, clean-shaven chin and firm lips were softened by a smile.

"I'm not hungry."

"You will be by the time we get home."

Ignoring her salt-wet dress and sandy legs, he scooped her up. She squirmed in his arms in an attempt to get down, but he was already walking rapidly up the beach toward the bare, twisted path that lay between the high dunes. She knew by the set of his chin that it was useless to try to escape his strong arms and she relaxed, her head resting against his shoulder. She took a deep breath and inhaled the rich, mingled odors of fresh-cut oak, tar, and sweat that clung to his shirt after his morning's work.

"Can I come back after dinner, Papa?" she asked, her sapphire eyes willing him to say yes.

He smiled down at her with eyes that so nearly matched her own. "We'll see. Depends on what your mother has to say."

"But I *want* to come back."

"I know, but your mother might want you home for a while."

"Don't *you* want me to come?"

"Of course, I do," he said as he strode through the shipyard, now fast emptying of men on their way to the midday meal. Tools lay abandoned on the ground. Gleaming in the sun, the frames of the new ship stood lonely. Uncle Josiah was leaning his spare body against the doorframe of the office, while he puffed on his pipe.

"See you found her," he said laconically. There was no love for either child or man to be found in his narrow brown eyes or in his bony, sallow face.

"Julia's not hard to find. She's always near."

"Still don't think a shipyard's place for a girl. Dangerous. Been playing in the water, too. Tide's more dangerous yet."

"The tide's no danger to *this* one." She heard her father's voice harden. "You forget she was born at sea. She's the sea's own and it will never harm her."

"Superstition!" Uncle Josiah spat. "That's heathenism, and you tempt the Lord in your pride, Benjamin."

"You may be right, Josiah, but the girl comes with me, and *I* run this yard." Her father walked over to the hitching post, where his horse, Baron, stood patiently waiting. He swung Julia up into the saddle, then turned back to face his brother. "It's time you understood that, Josiah."

"I'm part owner of this yard!" Josiah pointed his pipe at Benjamin. "A fact you seem to be forgetting."

"I'm not forgetting anything!" There was menace in Benjamin's voice as he approached Josiah. "I'm not forgetting the condition this yard was in when I came home after Papa's death. A shambles! I'm not forgetting that most of the men wouldn't work for you, and those who would were worthless. I'm not forgetting that you had only one small fishing schooner building, and that would have been better used as firewood. And I'm *not* forgetting how you took the money I sent home to Papa to invest for me and threw it away on worthless schemes, hoping to make a profit for yourself.

"You may be part owner of this yard, Josiah, but it's the smallest part; say those sheds over there, the old railway, and part of the marsh belongs to you. That's about what you own. The rest is mine, and I have the papers to prove it, complete with your signature.

"If it wasn't that Papa built this yard with pride and if Lydia wasn't so poorly, I'd sell my share . . . most of this place, Josiah . . . and go back to sea."

"Pah!" Josiah twisted his mouth as though he'd bit on something sharp. "You'll never go back to sea. After losing that boy of yours overboard, you lost your nerve. Who'd trust you with a ship?"

"Anyone! I'm still one of the best masters around. And you . . . you're scared of the sea. I remember when you went. Thirteen or thereabouts you were, and when you come home, you wouldn't set foot in a dory. Don't know that you have to this day. You spend your time preaching sin and heresy and try to steal your own brother's money. You sneer at men who go to sea as not facing up to life on shore . . . because you're a yellow-bellied coward."

Benjamin strode to his horse and swung up behind Julie. Then he stared down at his brother. "Just remember I *could* sell this yard . . . and then what would you do, Josiah?"

Her uncle stared back at him, contempt narrowing his eyes and twisting his thin lips. Shoving his cap farther back on his straight brown hair, he exposed the white line of skin above his weathered face. Then he whirled around in anger, stamped into the office, and slammed the door behind him.

As they trotted out of the yard, Julia glanced up over her shoulder at her father's face. It was stony, his cheeks flushed and his blue eyes bleak. He had looked like that on board ship when he had trouble with Mr. Tompkins, who was mate for a while.

"Papa?"

"Don't worry, Julia." His face was still angry, but his voice was gentle. "You'll come back this afternoon and tomorrow, too." He slowed Baron down to a walk as they neared the path over the marsh. "And as long as I choose thereafter," he added so softly she could hardly hear his words.

"Uncle Josiah doesn't like me, does he?"

"It isn't you, darling. It's me he doesn't like. Josiah's a jealous and a bitter man."

"Why?"

He held her closer for a moment and ruffled her dark curls. "For the same reason you're sometimes jealous of Sarah and Amelia. I have some things he doesn't have."

"What doesn't he have?" she persisted.

"Well, for one thing, he doesn't have any pretty little girls of his own." No point in going into other reasons with a child.

"He won't try to take me away from you?" She remembered how, only last week, Sarah, in a fit of jealousy, had taken her favorite doll and broken it.

He laughed and she could feel his big body relax. "No, he can't do that. You're my very own child. No one can take you away from me." He squeezed her. "And no one ever will."

"Why can't we go to sea again?" she asked after a moment, as she looked at the birds rising out of the green salt grass on either side of the raised path, but saw a white bow wave flashing in the sun and porpoise playing beside the ship. Life had seemed so much easier then. There had been storms, but they were honest storms. On land, she could never completely understand what was going on. Uncle Josiah. Aunt Harriet. Even her mother had changed since they'd come ashore to live. Or had her mother changed before that? Puckering her brow, she tried to remember.

"There are a lot of reasons, sweetheart. When you're older, I'll explain them all to you."

"But I *want* to go."

"We'll go back someday, Julie. Someday." His voice sounded softly far away as though he had left her.

"Promise?"

"It's a promise I can't make, Julie. It's a dream I'll try to make come true. But it won't be for a long time."

He understood the child's disappointment and longing because they were echoes of his own. If only he could find something to give her that would make her forget her first home. Perhaps if he were to tell her what he was trying to give himself, it would help.

"I've been thinking, Julie, that even if we can't go to sea, we can build a ship. The perfect ship. She'll go faster around the world than any ship ever built, and she'll be more beautiful."

"Can I help you build her?"

"Of course. I couldn't do it without you." He paused, thinking of that ship, his own creation, rising on the ways. Damned if he wasn't going to do it.

"And we'll name her after you," he said.

"Julia?"

"No. The *Jewel*. The *Jewel of the Seas*."

"And once she's built, can we go to sea on her?"

"I don't know. I hope so." He smiled. "Don't tell anyone, but I think we will."

They came to the highway and, bound together in their silent thoughts of the sea, they rode under its cool green arch of trees. As they rounded a sharp bend in the road, the large white house suddenly appeared. It stood proudly back from the road with its black shutters and wide, trellised porches, guarded by tall horse chestnuts and elms, surrounded by solid chinked stone walls. One of the good things about the land was the house, Julia thought; the house with its large, airy rooms and sunlight. They turned in when they reached the wide oystershell drive. Julia always enjoyed the clinking, crunching sound the horse's hooves made on the crushed shells. At the carriage house door, her father swung off the horse, lifted her down, and handed the reins to old Ezra, who helped around the place.

When she heard the sound of hooves, Lydia came out onto the porch that ran the length of the kitchen and dining room. Pushing her heavy blond hair back from her face with a delicate hand, she watched them dismount. Now she called to them.

"Benjamin. Don't bring the child in the house like that. Sand all over her. Take her round to the pantry door. I put some buckets out on the back porch for you to wash up.

"And no shells in the house," she added, looking at Julia.

"I don't have any, Mama."

"Well, that's a small blessing. Though you look like you've brought half the beach home. Look at your dress. And your hair!"

Julia opened her mouth to reply, but her father took her firmly by the hand. "Come, Julia. The sooner we wash up, the sooner we eat." He smiled at Lydia. "Smells like a good dinner from here."

He pulled Julia with him around the carriage house, past the cherry trees by its side and the row of stables and storerooms that stood directly behind it. She smiled up at the three towering spruce trees that marched half the length of the house. Somewhere she had heard that the

Indians had planted them, and they seemed like the Indians themselves to her, straight and proud and true. Their dried needles felt crisp and slippery under her bare feet. She bent to pick up a pine cone, but her father tugged at her hand.

"Come, Julia. Don't dawdle."

She obediently followed him up the shallow steps onto the wide back porch. It was cool and crisply scented by the trees.

Benjamin went to the long deal table against the wall and poured water into the two basins that stood waiting for them. Julia reached for the washcloth beside her basin, dropped it into the water, then smeared it over her face. The cool, fresh water was delicious on her sunny, salty skin. She threw the soaking cloth onto the table, stretched up on her toes, and plunged her face into the basin, blowing bubbles underwater.

"Julia!" Her father pulled her up by a handful of curls. "Not that way. You know better. Take off your dress and petticoat and hang them over the rail."

He watched as she struggled with the buttons and squirmed out of her clothes.

"Now off with your pantalettes."

While she wiggled out of them, he picked up a large sponge and dunked it in the bowl. Squeezing it over her, he rinsed away the sand that clung to her skin. The cool water and the warm breeze were sweet on her bare body. She stood still, savoring their touch. Then she shut her eyes tight and lifted her face to him. He squeezed the sponge slowly over her finely arched eyebrows, her rosy cheeks, and red lips. Like watering a flower, he thought.

"Now take your washcloth and give yourself a good soaping."

As she washed, she watched him strip off his shirt and expose his broad shoulders and the taut chest covered with springing black curls. Vigorously lathering, he hummed a song the while.

"Papa, you're pretty."

He looked down at her in surprise, then threw back his head in laughter. "You're a minx. And right young, too."

She couldn't understand why he was laughing, but then

7

she often didn't. She only knew that she had amused him, and that pleased her.

"Will I look like you when I grow up?"

"No, sweetheart. You know you're going to be a lady like Mama."

"Why?"

"Because God wills it," he said flatly, and she knew he didn't want to talk about it anymore. "Now come here and let me rinse you off."

She was subdued as she submitted to her second shower.

"Not perfect, but I expect you'll do."

"Benjamin!" Her mother was framed in the doorway. "That child's naked as a jay bird! And with Ezra around, too." She hurried out and wrapped a large, soft towel around Julia.

"There's nothing but purity and sweetness in a little girl's body, just as the Lord made her, Lydia. As for Ezra, seems I remember he had three, four little girls of his own. Doubt it's anything new to him."

"It's not decent!"

"Well, be that as it may, there's only one way to keep sand out of the house, and that's my way."

"Run up and put your clothes on," her mother said to Julia.

As soon as the child had disappeared, she turned back to her husband. Her face softened as she handed him a fresh shirt. He still looked like the young man she had married, and yet things were so different now. When she spoke, her voice was sad and gentle. "Benjy, it's bad enough having her down at the shipyard all the time, but you can't bring her up as though she were a boy. She's got to start learning to be maidenly."

"At the age of seven?" He laughed and, leaning over, he gave her a light kiss. "Let her be a child. Soon enough she'll have to wear long skirts and stays, learn to house-keep and flirt with boys. She's healthy and she's happy. Let her be, Lydia."

"Seven is none too soon to start."

"'*Tis* too young, Lydia. And that's that. You bring up the others the way you want. I'll decide what's best for Julia."

She laid her hand on his arm. "Nathaniel's dead, Benjy,

and you can't ask her to replace him. You can't turn a girl into a son."

"No. That I can't," he said, buttoning up his shirt. "Wouldn't if I could. She's fine just as she is. But I won't have her turned into something she ain't. I won't have her spirit broken nor will I forbid her the sea. 'Twould break her heart."

"As it's breaking yours?"

"Don't be a goose." He turned abruptly away from her, picked up his coat, and entered the house.

Her green eyes misted as she watched him and she once again pushed the weight of her hair back from her forehead. I'm not a goose, Benjy, she thought. 'Tis the truth. But you'll get over it. I won't let you go. Never! The sea won't take you from me. Not like it took my father and my son. Not while there's breath left in my body.

She gathered up the clothes from the rail and shook them out on the sweet spruce needles. She looked around for shoes and stockings, then remembered seeing Julia walk around the house barefooted.

"Benjamin!" She hurried into the house. "Where's Julia's shoes and stockings?"

She found him in the whitewashed, wood-beamed dining room, fingering a small amber Buddha. His face had that lost, yearning look that she'd seen more and more frequently in the past few months. It appeared whenever he thought of his voyages and his youth.

"Benjamin! Julia's shoes," Lydia repeated sharply. She had to bring him back quickly from that world she feared and hated.

He put the Buddha down and looked at her absently. "Oh, I forgot them. They're down at the shipyard."

"Really! That's too much. Last pair she had, one was lost in the sand."

"That's why I took them off before she went down to play on the beach. Doesn't matter. We'll get them when we go back after dinner."

"You're not taking her back this afternoon?"

"I am. To spite Josiah if nothing else."

"Had another row?"

"Nothing out of the ordinary. Happens most every day."

"I don't know why you two can't get along."

9

"Lydia." His eyes were serious in their question. "Do you *like* Josiah? Really like him?"

"No, can't say I particularly do. But he's *your* brother. Surely you two can be friends. At least work peaceful together."

"If the Lord ever made two men more unlike than Josh and me, then I never met them." Suddenly he laughed. "Sometimes I do wonder what Mother was up to when Father was at sea."

"Benjamin! Your mother was the soul of propriety. A fine, religious woman. How you can cast aspersions on her, your own mother, when she's dead and gone, is more than I can say."

" 'Twas only a joke, Lydia."

"Not a very funny one."

He shrugged and went to stand by the empty fireplace. "We can't seem to get on today. Why don't you tell Maryanne to dish up?"

"I'm sorry, Benjy. I know you've got a lot on your mind and I don't mean to dispute you." She looked at him pleadingly as she sat in the carved walnut chair he held for her.

Benjamin seated himself at the head of the table, and as he unfolded his damask napkin, he studied his wife's face. She looked tired, the lines around her mouth etched deeper than he remembered seeing them yesterday. When they had first left the ship, she had picked up rapidly. Month by month, her beauty had freshened, but now she seemed to be fading again.

"It's all right," he said. "I understand. You're trying to do too much. Lie down after dinner and get a good rest this afternoon. Remember Doctor Willett said you mustn't overtire yourself."

The horse's sides felt hot and sticky under ten-year-old Julia's bare legs as she headed him over the dunes to the beach. Come to think of it, she felt hot and sticky, too. It was September, but seemed more like August. Maybe summer won't end this year, she thought hopefully. Maybe it'll go on and on till spring.

She let the horse pick his way through the sharp grass along the top of the dunes. The tide was high this afternoon, she noted. High and peaceful with only beckoning fingers of foam reaching up on the sand. Perfect.

"Come on, Baron." She kicked the horse and guided him down a path between the dunes, then up the beach over the scattered sea wrack to a cascade of boulders and rocks that reached far out into the water, where they protected and limited this stretch of sand. Here she slithered from his back and looped the reins around a tall piece of embedded driftwood.

She glanced around. Only the seagulls, the terns, and small swishing waves broke the silence of the afternoon. The clam beds safely hidden by the tide, the sand picked clean earlier in the day of any treasures the sea might yield, the people had gone. The few fishing boats were standing well offshore. Farther out the larger vessels mutely crossed each other's wakes. No sound of shouted commands, of rattling lines, fluttering sails, or creaking spars reached the beach. It was safe.

She quickly pulled off her dress and tossed it on a flat, grey boulder. Freed of its confinement, she shook out her hair and stretched her arms upward to embrace the sky. Mama would kill me if she knew I'd gone off without a petticoat, she thought, but it does make things simpler.

Wearing only her chemise and pantalettes, she raced down the beach, swerving around patches of pebbles, and plunged into the water. She could feel it streaming along her body, flowing through her hair, its liquid pressure caressing her, buoying her up. Here she was weightless, light as the strands of seaweed that floated on its surface.

Savoring its taste, she licked the salt from her lips. Then she dove and swam along the sandy bottom. Occasionally she picked up a shell. When she could hold her breath no longer, she shot up to the surface, and the sun and sparkling waves exploded around her. She threw her gathered shells, one by one, as far as she could out to sea.

Trying to time her rhythm to theirs, she played porpoise with the gentle waves. She plunged down under their crests, rose up in their troughs, and laughed when she missed and received a mouthful of water instead of air. When she tired of this, she took several deep breaths and dove far, far down. She swam underwater for as long as she could, counting the seconds. When she finally popped to the surface, she shook her streaming hair away from her face. Better than last time. Best yet! Exhilarated, she struck out for the open sea.

She didn't know how long she had been swimming when she noticed the color of the water had changed. She looked at the sun. Later than she'd thought. She'd better get back fast. Papa would be upset if Baron wasn't at the yard when he was ready to go home.

The sun was lower in the sky and the tide was ebbing when she finally reached shore. Standing up, she felt the pebbled bottom under her feet. She picked her way gingerly through the shallows, then ran up the sand to the rocks where the horse stood waiting. He whickered an impatient greeting.

She wrung out her hair and pulled her dress on over her wet chemise and pantalettes. Releasing Baron from the driftwood stake, she used a rock to climb on his back. Then she guided him down to the hard-packed sand near the water's edge.

"Come on, boy! Let's go!" She kicked him with her heels, urging him on faster and faster. The horse welcomed the exercise and stretched out his strong legs, going as fast as a large-hooved Cape horse could in the pebbled sand. A seagull, soaring overhead, swooped down above them, gave a mocking laugh, and headed out to sea.

At the top of a tall dune, she checked the horse and wheeled him around to face out over the Bay. The ships were there, scattered on the horizon all the way to Provincetown. The whalers, the deep-sea merchantmen, were sailing away from Boston Harbor on their way to the Indies, France, the South Seas, the Mediterranean.

Longing to be aboard, Julia watched them and sighed. The boys were going one by one when they turned eleven or twelve. Some of them didn't even want to go. It's not fair, she thought. She turned the horse abruptly away and let him find his own path until they came to Sesuit Road.

When Julia met Benjamin on the road, she felt guilty. He looked tired and she was sure he didn't appreciate having to walk home.

"Hello, Papa," she said as she reined in and slid off the horse's back.

"Wondered when you'd get around to bringing my horse back."

"Are you mad at me, Papa?" Her sapphire eyes darkened with apprehension.

"No, I'm not mad at you. It's been a long day, and I'd just as soon walk home." He took the reins from her and looked at her torn, wet dress. "You're going to have to face your mother, you know, and I'm not going to help you this time."

"You *sure* you're not mad at me?" she asked as they started walking up the dusty sand road.

"No, but you're going to have to start standing on your own two feet and facing up to your own actions."

"Long as *you're* not mad at me, it's all right then."

"Where's your lunch pail?"

"Up the road under the old elm tree."

"Why didn't you tell me about Uncle Josiah yelling at you on the road in front of the schoolhouse yesterday?"

"Didn't want to worry you. Besides, I don't care what he says."

"Don't you care what other people think? Out in public like that?"

"Not 'specially. They know me, and they know Uncle Josiah, and they're going to have to take their pick."

"You didn't feel bad at all? You didn't cry?" He looked down at her curiously.

"Not till I got down to the beach where no one could see me. Maybe I cried a little then. I told the sea about it, and she said I wasn't to let it matter. There's bigger things in the world than Uncle Josiah and what people think."

"Julia! The sea isn't a person. You shouldn't think that. It can't talk to anyone."

"She does to me." Julia reached up and took his hand. "She talks to you, too, doesn't she, Papa? Sometimes I've seen you listening."

"I'm not listening to the sea. I'm listening to my own thoughts. That's all you're doing, too."

"Then why do I hear things I've never thought and nobody ever told me before? And why do you have to go down to the beach or out sailing to hear your own thoughts?"

"It's a good clean place to think. No clutter of other minds."

"On the *Flying Mist,* there were a lot of other minds, and she talked to me then. She's always talked to me," Julia said firmly.

"Always?" He smiled.

"Always!"

"Well, I hope she told you what you're going to say to your mama. There's the elm. Go get your pail."

Lydia, sitting in a rocking chair on the porch outside the parlor, was watching the road when they rounded the bend. As soon as they reached the house, she called out, "Julia, come here. I want to talk to you." She didn't seem too happy.

Julia threw her father a pleading glance, but taking the horse around the side of the house, he pointedly ignored her. She went slowly to her mother.

"Sarah brought me a note from Miss Coombs this afternoon. Seems you weren't in school today."

"Yes, Mama."

"Is that all you have to say? Where were you?"

" 'Twas early when I left the house. I remembered you talking about blackberries yesterday, saying how good they'd taste, so I thought I'd pick you some. Here they are." She thrust her lunch pail at her mother.

Lydia took it, but didn't look into it. She kept staring at Julia, her green eyes narrowed. "And then what?"

"Well, the best ones were at the top of Scargo Hill." She glanced at her mother uncertainly. "When I got there, it was noon. Too late to go to school."

She decided she'd better not tell her mother about climbing the trees and what a glorious view you got from there. All the marshes and rivers and ponds. The villages with their neatly steepled churches. The rolling hills. The way the bay shaded off from crystal green along the foaming shore, growing darker and darker till it was almost blue. The ships looking like toys out there. Not as good as going up a mast, but you could pretend it was.

"And when did you go swimming, and when did you go to the shipyard?" Her mother looked pointedly at Julia's bedraggled dress.

14

"Well." Julia looked down at the ground. "That was later."

"Benjamin!" Lydia called as he rounded the house. "Did you know Julia skipped school today? Not just the afternoon like she sometimes does, but a whole day."

"That does get serious." He frowned at her. "Was it because of Uncle Josiah?"

She hesitated. It would be easy to say it was, but she had to tell the truth. "No," she said.

"Then I'd like to hear the reason. You know you've got to go to school. How else are you going to learn anything?"

"I know everything."

"Hardly."

"Well, I know everything Miss Coombs was going to say today. And if I don't, I'll find out tomorrow. She goes so *slow*."

"I'll have a talk with Miss Coombs. Depending on what she says, maybe I'll put you to studying a few things she don't."

"With the palm of your hand or a good leather belt," Lydia said.

"Don't pay to beat girls," he said.

"Some it does and some it don't. You bring her up enough like a boy, makes no difference, seems to me. Besides, it's about time she put her hand to helping around the house."

"But I help Papa at the shipyard, don't I, Papa?"

"You plan on being a sawyer or a caulker when you grow up?"

"No! Papa's not a sawyer or a caulker. He designs vessels and runs the yard. I'm going to do that or else be the captain of a big ship like Papa *used* to be."

"You see, Benjamin? You stuff that child's head full of nonsense."

" 'Tisn't all nonsense. Julie could be a big help to me when she's older."

"Oh?" Her mother laughed, but it wasn't pleasant. "I can see Josiah now, letting a girl work down there, even puttering around. She'd be more nuisance than help. Besides, no daughter of mine is going to do anything so unseemly. 'Twould create a scandal."

"Josiah will do what I tell him," her father said sharply. "As for Julia, she could help me out in the office. There's plenty of paper work she could relieve me of. That is," he said, looking straight at Julia, "if she goes to school and learns a lot more than the 'everything' she knows now."

"Oh, Papa! Do you mean it?" Julia ran to him and threw her arms around him. "Do you really mean it?" Her eyes were sparkling as she looked up at him.

"Maybe." He couldn't resist a small smile.

"Well, if you do, I won't miss a single minute of school."

"Benjamin . . ." Lydia began.

"Run along and get washed up, Julia," her father said hastily.

When she had gone, Lydia turned on him in real anger.

"Benjamin, I've said it before, and I'll say it again. You can't turn that girl into a son."

"No, but I often think Nathaniel would have been a lot like her if we hadn't lost him. I've no sons to follow me, Lydia, and you know there won't be one. Since Julia's smart as a whip, there's no reason she can't learn to run the yard eventually. Carry on after I'm gone. Not if she has proper training."

"You think the men will do what she says?"

"If she's good enough, and she will be, they'll respect her. And if they gradually get used to her being around now, they'll do what she tells them when it's time for her to take charge."

"Precious little you know about men."

"A lot more than you do, sweetheart, being one myself."

"Besides," Lydia tried another tack, "in a few years, she'll be getting married."

"Maybe."

"Not maybe. That's sure. She's too pretty for the boys to leave alone. I've already seen them watching her, especially when she flips those long black curls and flashes those big blue eyes. Everyone spoils her now. Just you wait."

"Now, Lydia," he said, putting his arm around her still slender waist. "You're right pretty and I don't see it's done you any harm."

"But I was brought up proper, like I'm bringing up Sarah and Amelia. I learned to cook and sew and tend house instead of running wild through the woods, swimming and idling around a shipyard."

"Yes, Amelia and Sarah will make good wives for some lucky men. But the man that gets Julia is going to get something special. He's going to have to be pretty special, too."

"If she keeps on the way she's going, no man's going to be able to handle her . . . nor want to, neither."

"Be a good thing if she did scare most of them off. But she won't scare off the right man. Not that she'd settle for anything less than the best. That's what I'm going to get for Julia."

"If I know you, Benjy, there never will be anyone special enough for her. You'll never give her up. You'll bring her up like a man in woman's skirts. Most likely die an old maid if you have your way."

"No. When he comes, I'll give her up. 'Twill be the only way to keep her. You don't understand the child, Lydia. She's like a bird. The tighter you try to hold her, the farther away from you she'll fly. But if you pet her lightly, rouse her curiosity, and love her without trying to put a cage round her, she'll never leave you. Not in her heart."

Chapter Two

1833

BENJAMIN STUDIED THE WHITENING sky, then climbed the dunes behind the shipyard to watch the way of the waves. The wind was backing round to the east. Rain and fog would be coming. For the past week, the weather had been clear with a warm hint of spring in the air, but he didn't like the looks of it now.

"Bad weather." Daniel Sears came limping up the dune to stand beside him. "Good thing the schooner's all but finished."

"Yes." Benjamin glanced at the wiry, dark-haired young foreman. "We're ready for the March tide, but I wonder how we'll stand come fall."

Daniel nodded. "Having only two tides a year high enough to launch on does make it hard."

"Almost impossible, but the *Belle of Canton has* to be finished come September. I promised Will Thacher. Besides, we'll lose a packet of money if that railway's tied up an extra six months." He watched the green waves flattening out, toppling over their own white crests, and shook his head. "No help for it, Daniel. We're going to have to let some of the other work sit for a while and put most of the men to work on the *Belle*."

18

"There's some won't like it, Captain Howard."

Benjamin knew Daniel was thinking of their customers, men from the nearby townships as well as from Dennis. Near enough so they could come often to inspect their vessels, and with eyesight far too keen.

"They'll just have to wait. All the winter sickness held us up."

Jamming his hands deep in his pockets, Daniel frowned and nodded.

Benjamin turned to look back at the shipyard. The *Belle of Canton* lay, half-planked, on the largest railway, her frames gleaming whitely in the winter sun. On the smaller railway, near the golden marsh, was the nearly finished schooner. Already the lines for her replacement, a brigantine, were laid on the mold loft floor. Across the road and up the hill among the green fir trees, several smaller craft were in various stages of construction. He ran his hand through his vigorous black hair, then scratched his head.

"Lot of work there, Daniel. Think we'll get it done on time?"

"Can't do no more than try." Daniel bit off a ragged thumbnail.

"Maybe we're growing too fast," Benjamin said. He'd more than doubled the business in the seven years he'd been home. The fame of the Howard Shipyard was growing, and inquiries had come from as far away as New York. He had almost two hundred men working for him now and needed more.

"We're going to have to advertise for more men," he said to Daniel, who still stood beside him in companionable silence.

"Hard to find good men," Daniel said skeptically.

"I know. We'll have to train them. Promote the best we have. Put more apprentices and green men under them."

"Might work, but training takes time. Might slow us down."

"No. I won't let it and neither will you."

"I'll try." Daniel shrugged. "Best be getting back."

Benjamin watched him go limping down the soft sand hill. Daniel's leg had been twisted by a fall from the mast of a fishing schooner while up on the Grand Banks when he was only fifteen. He'd lived, but he'd never be able to go back to sea. The fall hadn't changed his love for ships, though. Hadn't slowed him down, neither.

A good man, Benjamin thought affectionately. Been with him from the start, and he could trust him. That was the first promotion. Give Daniel some of his, Benjamin's, own responsibilities. Young, but he showed a lot of promise.

Lord knows, he needed promising young men. They were hard to come by in New England nowadays. With each outgoing tide, they sailed to fill the seas and harbors of the world. Where was he going to find them? Where were the men who would love a ship and yet be content to stay ashore and work for wages rather than shares?

Benjamin idly plucked a tall sea oat. Then he strode down the soft dunes and across the shipyard to the sandy road, where he could see the run of the hull of the *Belle.* Nice lines and they'd come out of his head. Still wasn't the ship he wanted to build. Will Thacher had insisted on the apple-cheeked bow where Benjamin dreamed of a sweet curve. She was better, though. Coming closer to *the* ship.

As he gazed at her, the unpainted, unfinished hull grew before his eyes into completion. He saw her running free before a wind with all her sails set and flying, her bow lifting in a joyous rhythm to meet the sea. He was on the quarterdeck again and felt the rise and fall of his own ship beneath his feet. He watched the helmsman steady the wheel. He heard the mate shout out his orders.

"She's beautiful, isn't she, Papa?"

And suddenly, Benjamin was back on shore with the trees and rocks and a landbound, lifeless ship. The sounds of the caulkers, the blacksmith, and the sawyers surrounded him, and his twelve-year-old daughter stood before him.

"Yes, she is that. Why aren't you in school, Julie?"

"School's over for the day. Can I help you now?"

"All your schoolwork done?"

"Yes."

"All right, then." He took one last look at the *Belle.* "Come along to the office. We've got a lot of orders to get out. Been figuring what we'll need for next season."

They entered the small building that served as an office. It was drafty but warm with the potbellied stove radiating its heat, and it smelled of dust and ink and old paper.

Julia threw her red mittens and her books on the tall oak

desk and went directly to the stove, wiggling her fingers above it. They had grown cold and numb during the long walk from the schoolhouse.

Benjamin sat on one of the tall stools beside the desk and picked up a sheaf of papers. He watched her patiently for a moment. Her long black hair, which she refused to braid, was wind-tangled, and her cheeks glowing from the cold made her eyes beneath their black brows seem more brilliantly blue and her winter skin whiter.

Not a child and not a woman, she possessed a little of each, yet was conscious of neither. She was by turns clumsy and graceful as she learned slowly to handle this tall body, which had grown several inches in the past year. Already she was taller than most boys her age and painfully aware of it. The girls seemed dainty and feminine beside her. Seeming to prefer the company of adults, she shunned them all. Benjamin knew that she was often lonely, but there was nothing he could do about it. She would have to find her own way.

"I want you to do something special for me, Julie," he said.

"What is it, Papa?"

"I want you to start thinking."

She looked at him in surprise. "But I always think."

"Oh, you think about your penmanship and how not to make inkblots. You think about the proper form of a business letter. But that's not really thinking. That's only imitating what you've seen me do. Now I want you to start using the brain God gave you."

"Well, what kind of thinking did you have in mind?" She raised her chin and looked at him with eyes that held a cool challenge.

He was tempted to swat her across the bottom. There were times when Julia and her damned pride could be positively exasperating.

"Real thinking," he said levelly, keeping his eyes as cool as hers. "See these papers? There's a list here of all the supplies we'll need next season. The dates when we'll need them are beside each item. Now you order them."

She left the stove and came to take the sheaf of papers from him. She glanced at the first page. "You forgot to put the suppliers' names in."

21

"I didn't forget. That's what you're going to do. Another thing's missing. The shipping date. All you've got there is the date they have to be in the yard."

She sighed and hoisted herself up on a tall stool next to him. She laid the papers on the desk. "All right. You don't have to tell me I don't know everything. Just exactly what do you want me to do?"

He smiled. She'd learn yet.

"You've written plenty of letters for me in the past year. Did a good job of it, too. Good enough so's I think you're ready for the next step. Are you?"

"I guess so." She listened to the wood crackling in the stove. It reminded her of the sound of halyards creaking in a breeze. The lifeless papers before her had nothing to do with ships or the sea.

"Julia?"

"Yes, Papa," she sighed her disappointment.

"Are you listening to me?"

"Yes, Papa."

He pushed his chair away from the desk and went to look out the uncurtained, multipaned window. Julia watched him as he stood silently with his back to her. Through the window, she could see the fog already rolling in. The sounds of hammer, saw, and anvil were muffled by its presence.

"Julia, I'm beginning to wonder if your mother wasn't right when she said a shipyard was no place for a girl." His large shoulders sagged as he stared out the window.

"Oh, no, Papa!"

He looked so lonely. Was he going to send her home?

"Up till now, you've been willing to learn." His face was sad when he turned to look at her. "Suddenly you don't care. What's happened?"

"I don't know." She glanced down at the papers on the desk, avoiding his eyes.

"Must be something."

"Well . . ." She lifted her chin and looked directly at him. "*This* isn't learning how to build ships! I sit in here, copying letter after letter, while the *real* work is going on out there." She nodded at the window. "I'm not learning anything cooped up in here."

"You're not? Come here. I want to show you something."

She slowly got down off her stool and went to stand beside him.

"Look out there. What do you see?"

"The fog."

"What else?"

"The shipyard."

"What makes a shipyard?"

She shrugged and glanced at him with eyes that were uncertain. What kind of game was he playing now?

"The ships?"

"And . . . ?"

"The buildings. The men."

"Look at the sawpit."

She looked over at the sawyers. The curling fog shrouded them like ghosts as they straddled the big timbers. They pushed slowly up and down on the tillers of the giant saws.

"What are they working on?" Benjamin asked.

"I'm not sure."

"Planks for the *Belle of Canton.*"

"Well, if I never get out, how could I know that?"

"What are they making them from?" he asked, ignoring her question.

"White oak."

"Right. How did the oak get here?"

"You ordered it. It came by packet."

"And without the oak, the tar, the oakum, the cotton, the oil, and the nails; without the saws, the bellows, the planes, and the hammers that we order, where would this shipyard be?"

"I guess it wouldn't be."

"That's right. No orders, no shipyard. No dories, long-boats, or ships. No buildings. No men. Nothing. Just the sand and salt grass, water and rocks. The only life you'd see would be birds and crabs; maybe a few fish in the creek."

She stared out the window. The mist swirled around the building, thickening and blotting out the world beyond.

"But if there were no shipyard, we could go to sea."

"On what? You need a vessel. It's got to be built."

"But you're not building our ship. You're building them for others."

"Just practicing on them so, when we get around to the

Jewel, she'll be perfect. You do want to help me build her, don't you?"

She sighed and blew moisture on the glass. She traced a crooked "J. H." on it. "I just don't believe in her anymore, Papa. You've been talking about her ever since I can remember, but those vessels out there don't even look like your models."

"No. They don't." He left her side to pace the room. It was really too small for anyone his size to pace in, but he had never lost the habit of the quarterdeck.

After a few moments, he said in a low voice, "Julia, you've *got* to believe in her. If you don't, how can I?"

"Oh, Papa!" She flew to him and threw her arms around him. "I'll believe in her. Truly I will. And I'll learn whatever you want me to learn."

He held her close for a moment, smelling her fresh child's fragrance, then released her. "Even if it means you're cooped up in the office?"

"Well . . . yes. But when spring comes . . ."

"When spring comes, I'll find something for you to do outside. *After* all the ordering's done."

"All right, Papa." She went to the desk and picked up the dry sheaf of papers. She glanced at them for a moment, then looked up at him with a gamin smile. "But we'd better hurry. Spring's almost here."

Benjamin grinned back at her and shook his head. He often wondered at the tie that bound him and this one particular child so close. Whatever it was, it was special. Despite all else, in this, he was blessed.

Once, when they were young and their love so achingly new, he'd thought he and Lydia would be so bound. Safe. Happy. Close together. For some reason, though, it hadn't happened. 'Twasn't her fault. She'd tried. So had he. Yet it hadn't happened. He still loved her as she loved him, but over the years, they'd drifted farther and farther apart.

Lydia was still a beautiful woman with her long golden hair and her slanted sea-green eyes. It just made it harder, though. He would sit and look at her by evening firelight when she thought he was reading the paper. Then he would go to his lonely bed apart from her at night.

But he couldn't take any chances. Not after nearly losing her at Amelia's birth. When Doctor Willett said another child would surely kill her, he'd made his resolve. Stuck by it, too.

'Twould have been easier to take if he could have gone back to sea. He was still only thirty-eight, and no one held a sailor accountable for his actions in foreign ports. His few visits to the colorful ladies of Boston hadn't satisfied him. There was too much guilt attached, worrying about word getting back to Lydia.

Still, there was the yard, the ships . . . and Julia. He turned around and picked up a half-model that was lying on a shelf. He ran his fingers over the sleek hull. He'd build her yet. Despite what everyone said, he knew he wasn't wrong. That bow would slice through the water like a knife. She'd clip days off the record and still carry her full share of cargo.

Low cumulus clouds prophesying summer were driven northward by the warm south wind. Fragments of their white reflections chased across the horseshoe curves of Sesuit Creek. Fish jumped in the water, attracting a flock of screaming gulls.

As they swung their ringing hammers in an easy, practiced rhythm, the shirt-sleeved caulkers complained of unseasonable heat so early in June. Beside them, wisps of oakum and cotton hung from the ship's seams like the straggled grey beard of an old man. The hot, rich odor of boiling pitch mingled with the clammy, marshy smell of low tide.

Apprentices ran back and forth between the vessels and the blacksmith, sawpits, caulkers' and carpenters' shops. Men were shouting, hammering, sawing, pounding, cursing. Men were everywhere on the lowland and on the hill.

Captain William Thacher strode down Sesuit Road into this scene of seeming turmoil, which was really the efficient operation of a well-run shipyard. He paused for a moment as he sighted his ship. There she was. The *Belle of Canton*. High and proud on the ways. The first sight of a rare and wonderful thing.

After he was satisfied that she really existed, he looked around the yard until he spotted Benjamin Howard checking the set of a knee on the frames of a smaller vessel.

Crossing the yard, William shouted in a voice that could

carry over the clatter of sails and the roar of wind and waves, "She looks right fine, Ben!"

Benjamin shook his head in annoyance and looked up, impatient at any interruption. Then he realized it was his old shipmate and Lydia's cousin. Big, burly, blond as a Viking, Will walked the earth as he did the decks of his ship. He was master of all.

Benjamin's frown turned into a broad grin. He dropped the wooden battens he was holding and ran across the yard to meet Will halfway.

"You old sea dog!" Benjamin said, managing to pound his friend on the back despite the vigor of Will's powerful embrace. "I didn't expect to see you for two, three more weeks!"

"Well, I sold the *Sally Anne* sooner than I expected. Didn't seem to be much point in hanging round Boston any longer. Went on home to Brewster for a few days, but I couldn't take it." His grin changed with unexpected swiftness to a wry smile that barely held back the tears. "The house was empty, Ben, full of echoes. With Margaret gone and both Jason and Samuel at sea, there's nothing for me there now."

Benjamin gave Will's shoulder a final pat. "I'm sorry about Margaret, Will. 'Twas quite a blow to Lydia and me. We didn't even know she was ill."

"Thanks, Ben. They tell me she wasn't ill long."

"Lot of sickness around here last winter."

"So I hear, but never expected it of Margaret." William stared at his ship, but saw neither the ship nor the creek beyond. "Strange because she was always such a healthy woman. Even after the boys were born, she was up and doing mighty fast."

Benjamin ran his hand through his sawdust-speckled hair. "I remember. Had more energy than any other two women put together."

"She was coming to sea with me again, Ben." Will's normally booming voice was muffled with unspent grief. "On the *Belle of Canton*. With Samuel off to sea, there didn't seem any need for her to stay home. Margaret named the ship, you know. Said she was finally going to see China."

"Figured that might be the cause when you specified the master's cabin. 'Twas too fancy for one man alone."

"Yes. 'Tis. But that's how it's going to be."

You won't be alone long, Benjamin thought, as he looked sympathetically at his big handsome friend. He clapped William on the shoulder.

"Come on now and take a look at the *Belle*. See what you think. I know you're dying to check her out and make all kind of changes."

"Not today, Ben. Tomorrow." He squared his shoulders. "Well, tomorrow, I'll point out all the mistakes you've made."

"You going to stay up all night thinking up flaws?"

"Maybe. If you don't give me a comfortable bed. I left my bags at your house. Thought I'd stay with you a spell. Hope you don't mind. When I woke up this morning, I knew I had to get out of Brewster."

"'Course, I don't mind!" Benjamin's face lit up with the blue-eyed grin that could still charm men and women alike. "I'm delighted. It'll give us a chance to do some real gamming. We've got plenty of room and there's always a place for you. Wish I'd thought of it first."

"Well, I don't like to put Lydia out, though I must say she gave me a right warm welcome. Where's Josiah?"

"Oh, he's around somewhere, most likely stirring up trouble. Rather do that than work."

"Still a problem to you, is he?"

"Aye. For the time being. He owns part of the yard, so there's not much I can do about it."

"Not unless you can afford to buy him out."

"Can't yet, but I'm working on it."

"Good." William stared absently beyond the shipyard toward the inlet. "Look, Ben, I think I'll take a walk down to the beach. Just give a shout when you're ready to go home."

"I'll do that. Be about an hour or so."

Benjamin watched his friend stride off to the dunes and felt helpless. He remembered their first voyage together. William, being a couple of years older and more experienced, had been kind to the twelve-year-old Benjamin. On that first voyage, Benjamin had been, by turns, gloriously happy and miserably homesick, and Will had helped him over those first few hard months.

Later, as masters of their own ships, they had met, some-

27

times at sea, sometimes in foreign ports, rarely at home, until Benjamin was forced to leave the sea. Still, the friendship had remained deep and enduring through all the years.

William strode the hard-packed sand without really noticing where he was going as he tried to walk off some of the grief that overwhelmed him when he thought of his plump, dark-haired, rosy Margaret. He still found it hard to believe she was gone.

He had stopped to light his pipe when a flurry in the water caught his attention. A young girl, clad only in chemise and pantalettes, was rising from the sea. She raised her arms and flung her dripping long black hair away from her face with both hands.

"And who might you be?" he asked. "A mermaid?"

"Close enough," she said, standing with her hands on hips that were half hidden by the water. She scrutinized him carefully, noting the rough golden beard that matched his thick, unruly hair; the clear, tanned skin that set off his green eyes; the proud set of his broad shoulders. There was something vaguely familiar about him.

"And who might you be? Neptune?"

"Close enough," he gravely mimicked her.

"Then what are you doing, standing up there on the beach with all those clothes on?" she demanded. "Why aren't you in the water? And where's your trident?"

"I am surveying my kingdom," he replied with a lordly air. "Don't you find my sea a bit cold for you so early in the year?"

"Don't see any ice floes," she answered, seriously scanning the water around her. Then she lifted her chin in an imperious gesture. "And now, if you would be good enough to remove yourself from my beach, I will come up, let my tail grow into legs, and get dressed."

He threw back his head and roared with laughter, the first true laughter that had come since he'd heard of Margaret's death. Then he gave her a courtly bow. "Your servant, *madame*."

He was still chuckling when he topped the dunes and strode down into the shipyard.

Benjamin looked up in surprise at his friend, who only a short while ago had seemed so wrapped in misery. Will

28

had never had what you'd call a mercurial temperament. Sound and steady, he'd always been. Had Margaret's death unhinged him?

"What's so funny?" he asked.

"I just met a mermaid." William shook his blond head in delight. "Never met one at sea despite all the tales I've heard of them. But here, right on your beach, one just appeared out of the water and talked to me. Right sassy she was, too."

"William . . ." Had his friend suddenly gone mad?

"I'm not crazy, Ben, if that's what you're thinking. I really did meet one! In fact, she's coming over the dunes right now. Let me introduce you."

"Introduce me, hell! That's my daughter Julia."

"Really? That's even better." William chuckled again. "Haven't seen her since she was a wee girl, but I should have noticed the resemblance between you two. Not just in the face. That's close enough, but she's every bit as saucy as you were at that age."

"I was not!"

"Were too. You weren't much older than that when you put some flying fish in the mate's bunk. Remember how you got out of it, too. Turned his anger to laughter . . . and he wasn't exactly what I'd call a laughing man."

Benjamin grinned at the memory.

"Julia," he called. "Come here."

She came skipping across the yard to him, the wetness of her chemise showing through her plaid dress.

"I want to introduce you to one of my oldest friends."

"But we've already met, Papa." Her eyes were sparkling with mischief. "He's Neptune."

"Well . . ." He glanced quizzically at William, who was having a hard time keeping his face straight. "He may be that, but he's also Captain William Thacher, your mother's second cousin. Will, this is my daughter Julia."

"I'm most honored to meet you," William said as he bowed formally once again. "I wasn't aware that mermaids had names. But then again, I suppose they must. How else would they keep themselves straight?"

"Of course we have names," she said with regal dignity. "And have you ever played at being a siren, sitting on

29

those deadly rocks, combing your long black hair, singing and luring poor sailor lads to their death?"

"That comes later."

William looked her up and down in a most embarrassing way.

"Yes," he said seriously, "I believe it does."

Benjamin didn't care for the turn this game was taking. Julia was too young for such nonsense. Will ought to know better.

"Julia, go into the office and dry your hair," he said. "Comb it, too. You can't go home to your mother looking like that. She'd skin us both."

"All right, Papa," she said, a merry child once more, and skipped off to the office.

William studied his friend's face while Ben, in turn, watched Julia's retreating back.

"You love that child too much, Ben," he said.

"Does it show?" Benjamin raised one bushy eyebrow.

"Too much. Children grow up and leave you. Boys to the sea and girls to their husbands."

"I know. She'll be thirteen next month. I hate birthdays."

"You can't hold her, Ben. Not that one. I can see why you'd want to, though. She's enchanting."

"She's special." Benjamin watched as Julia shut the office door behind her. "And she loves the sea. Loves ships almost as much. It's only natural."

"Natural? Maybe now, but she won't later. Women never do." Even Margaret, though she'd been willing enough to come with him.

"No. She won't change. She was born at sea. It's been her nursery, cradle, playground. Sometimes I think she's half fish." He smiled. "She's the sea's own child."

"Don't tempt fate, Ben." William was deadly serious. "I mean it. You give your child to the sea, and the sea will take her. It always claims its own."

"No, I don't think so. They seem to have an understanding. She talks to it."

William shrugged. "A lot of us do. Talk to it, laugh at it, curse it. If I were you, Ben, I wouldn't encourage her fancies. They could be dangerous."

"Reckon you're right. But I notice you got drawn into

one of them. Neptune, indeed!" He threw back his head in laughter.

"Oh, come now, Ben. I was just amusing the child."

"Oh, I'm sure of that," Benjamin said. Smiling wickedly at his friend, he clapped him on the shoulder. "It's getting late. We'll lock up and get on home."

Although first dark was just upon them when they approached the house, the lamps had been lit, and the vertical panes of glass that lined each side of the front door glowed with a welcome warmth. Benjamin threw open the door and the smell of rich, succulent food—lobsters and clams, cornbread and fresh garden peas—flowed out to meet them.

Upon hearing their footsteps in the hall, Lydia came out of the adjacent parlor. Tonight she wore a full-skirted green silk dress in honor of their guest. It made her eyes glow a deeper, richer green, and the low-cut bodice enhanced the sweep of a neck that seemed too fragile to bear the weight of her coiled golden hair.

She shot a questioning look at Julia, whose hair was curling damply over her shoulders and down her back. The child's plaid dress was wet where her undergarments touched it.

Julia smiled sweetly at her mother. It was a tactic that sometimes worked.

"Well, Lydia, you see I brought them back to you." William gave his cousin a hug that threatened not only her carefully arranged hair, but her dress as well.

"William, you'll never grow up," she laughed. She didn't mind if William mussed her up a bit. She'd always been exceedingly fond of this big bluff cousin of hers and knew that he had never learned gentler ways.

"You haven't done much in the way of growing up, yourself, miss." He held her away and looked admiringly down at her hair, face, neckline, and gown. "Still don't look a day over sixteen."

"And you're still the worst liar I ever met," she reprimanded him, but it was obvious from the glow in her cheeks that she enjoyed it. "Your room's ready for you, William. Ezra took your bags up, and there's a nice fire going if you want to wash up before dinner. It's the front room upstairs right over the parlor."

"Yes, come along, Will," Benjamin said, putting his arm around his friend's shoulders. "I'll show you the way."

As the men went up the steep carpeted stairs, Julia turned to her mother. "Mama, that's *my* room! Why does it always have to be mine?"

"Hush! If you've got one of the best rooms in the house, then you'll just have to give it up when we have company. You know that. You'll sleep with Sarah."

"Oh, no! Not with Sarah, Mama." Julia pulled on a damp lock of hair. "She kicks and turns all night. Let me sleep with Amelia."

"No. You'd keep the child, and me, too, awake half the night, telling her tales that have more fancy than truth to them."

"I won't!"

"You will. You do it every time you're alone with Amelia. Maryanne has already moved your things into Sarah's room, and that's where you'll sleep. Now go wash up. And try to look decent for dinner!" Her mother's lips were set in a very determined line.

"Yes, Mama." Julia started slowly up the narrow stairs, her shoulders stiff and her chin held high.

"Julia, come back here a minute."

She returned even more slowly, her pride still showing through and her eyes ignoring her mother's.

"Julia." Lydia took her daughter's face gently in her hand, forcing her to look at her. "You do know I love you, don't you, child?"

"I guess so." Julia tried to evade her mother's soft but penetrating look.

"I do, child. I really do. Maybe I don't show it enough."

Lydia's eyes were calmly searching her daughter's face, but her voice was strangely wistful. Julia could feel her mother's hurt and hugged her.

"I know, Mamma. It's all right. You're just busy with Sarah and Amelia. They take a lot more doing for than I do. They're younger."

"Yes, Julia." Her mother held her closely. "They're

younger." But, she added to herself, they don't take more doing for.

Where Julia came home with stained, torn clothing, their dresses remained relatively whole. While Julia was off at the shipyard or roaming the woods and dunes, they played with their friends or stayed home and tried to learn the duties she taught them.

Not that they were angels, by any means. Sarah could sulk for days and Amelia's rare displays of temper were a wonder to behold. Still and all, they were easier to understand than this one, who was filled with blazing sunlight and deep shadows.

She sighed and kissed Julia on the cheek. "You go on up and get ready for dinner now."

The whitewashed, wood-beamed dining room was softly lit by tall silver candelabra that flickered above the linen-draped table and the large walnut sideboard. On the mantel, two single candles flanked each side of the hand-painted clock that ticked below the portrait of Benjamin's father. A fire crackling on the hearth added its glow as well as heat that was still welcome in the evening, no matter how warm the day. Pink roses, their shading deepened by the rich salt air, gave color to the white and silver table. In front of each place, there was a tissue-wrapped package.

Amelia, her freshly brushed blond curls swinging forward, was the first to pounce on hers. "Oh, Mama, look!" she cried with all the dancing, dimpled delight of an eight-year-old.

"Not till we've said grace, 'Melia," her mother reproved her.

Amelia looked reproachfully at her mother, but put the package back on the table.

Benjamin glanced around, then bowed his head. "O Lord, we are gathered here to thank You for Your bounty. We thank You for the food You have granted us and for the joy of Your days. We thank You for bringing William home safely to us and pray that You will guard and grant Your grace to all those who are still upon Your seas." Out of the corner of his eye, he could see Amelia wiggling with suppressed excitement. He decided to make it short. "Amen."

"Amen. Can I open it now, Mama?" Amelia asked without taking a breath.

Lydia smiled indulgently at her youngest daughter. It was hard not to smile at Amelia. "Yes. You may open it now."

Amelia, aware that her mother was watching, untied the ribbon carefully and laid it aside as she had been taught, but when it came to the tissue, she ripped it off, exposing a small box. It was green and pink with Chinese lettering, and it had that spicy, pungent smell that came only with gifts from the Orient. She opened the box and lifted the square of tissue that lay on top.

"Oh, Mama! An elephant!" She handed the ivory figure to her mother. "Isn't he pretty?"

"He's beautiful." Lydia ran her finger over the finely carved lines. "You must take very good care of him. He's not for playing with. He's for looking at." She handed the carving back to her daughter. "Now thank Cousin William."

Amelia laid the elephant carefully in its box. Then she jumped up and ran around the table. She threw her arms around William's neck and planted a kiss on his beard. "Thank you, Cousin William!"

"You're more than welcome," he chuckled.

"I'll take good care of him," she said earnestly. "What's his name?"

"Now let me think." William felt the warmth of her small body and examined her round face, her long pale-blond curls, and her big china-blue eyes. "As I recollect, the little Chinese girl who owned him told me it was Pen Loo."

"Won't she miss him?" Amelia looked concerned.

"Well, she had a whole herd of elephants. Now, Pen Loo was her favorite, you understand." William smiled at the child who leaned so trustingly against him. "But when I told her about you and how you didn't have a single elephant, she said I must bring you the very best. And that was Pen Loo."

"Did she look like me?" Amelia was caught up in his story.

"No. She had short black hair and her eyes were black as midnight, too. But she did have a dimple in her cheek, almost exactly like yours." He couldn't resist touching it.

"Really?"

"Really. And she had a giggle just like yours, too."

Amelia giggled in appreciation and her dimple deepened. Then she slipped from under his arm to run back to her place.

Sarah had watched all this with grey-eyed patience, but as soon as Amelia was seated, she smoothed her light brown hair and daintily picked up the package that lay in front of her.

"It *is* my turn now, isn't it?" she asked her mother.

"Yes, you may open yours next."

Sarah lowered her black lashes and smiled the secret smile that always came when she got her way. It seemed secret because Sarah smiled at Sarah, including no one else. She slowly unwrapped the package, folded the ribbons and tissue with care, and savored the moment. When she could no longer delay opening the long, flat box, she found an intricately carved sandalwood fan. It was touched here and there with small delicately painted flowers and birds.

She opened it wide and ran her slender finger down its ribs. Then she raised it to her face, looking at William over its arch with grey eyes that seemed far too old for her ten years.

"Thank you, Cousin William." Lowering the fan, she smiled at him.

"That's lovely, Sarah," Julia said. "May I see it?"

Sarah glanced coolly at her sister, who sat beside Cousin William. "Later, perhaps. Aren't you going to open your present?"

"Of course." Julia picked it up.

Julia's package was smaller than hers, which pleased Sarah, but when the amber beads spilled out, flowing like burgundy against the white tissue, she immediately became dissatisfied with her fan. It wasn't fair. Just because Julia was older, she always got the best things. Someday, she promised herself, when we're both grown up, everything I have will be better than Julia's.

Julia fondled the beads, letting their coolness spill through her fingers. Then in her first, unconscious act of coquetry, she turned smiling to William. "Thank you, Cousin William. Will you put them on for me?" She handed him the beads, swept her curling black hair up with both hands, and bent her long, slender neck toward him.

He clasped them for her, his fingers lingering on the warm white skin. Suddenly aware of Lydia's eyes fixed on him, he withdrew his hands, leaned away from the girl, and pretended to admire the effect.

"They're a little old for Julia now," Lydia said in a clear, firm voice, "but she'll appreciate them much more when she's older. Meanwhile, I'll put them away for her."

"It's just a trinket, Lydia," William said quietly.

"Oh, Mama, let me wear them now!"

"Tonight. But they're not meant to be worn with a child's clothes, Julia. They're for a lady's dress."

"Yes, Mama," Julia said, determined to wear them at every opportunity.

"Aren't you going to open your package, Mama?" Amelia asked.

"Of course." Lydia smiled at her cousin, then deftly undid the tissue and opened the brocade-covered box. She drew out a smooth jade pendant hung on a slender golden chain. Large as a robin's egg, it dangled from her fingers like a teardrop.

"William, this is too much!"

"No, Lydia. It matches your eyes. When I saw it, I knew 'twas meant for you," he said gruffly.

"I truly do thank you," she said, as she lightly touched his arm.

While she was gazing into its sea-green depths, Benjamin opened his large, bulky package to find a finely carved ivory junk.

"This does take me back, Will. Do you remember our first voyage?"

"I remember."

"Life was so new then. Everything for the first time. Days like mirrors on the China Sea while we watched the junks and sampans fishing, wondering if any of them were pirates. How long ago it seems."

" 'Twas a long time past." William worried a piece of lobster out of its shell. "We thought the life hard and full of cares. We didn't realize how young and free we were."

36

"No. That we didn't. But the responsibilities don't seem to weigh too heavily on *your* shoulders, Will. Tell us about your voyage." Benjamin buttered his spoonbread, then raised an eyebrow at his friend. "And no more lies than you can avoid in the telling."

"Lie?" William grinned and stroked his golden beard. "Why would I lie when, once you put to sea, more of the fantastic actually happens than most men would credit?"

"Sounds like you're warming up for a whopper."

"Now, I wouldn't do that, would I?" William winked at Amelia. "Actually, it was a good trip . . . until we ran into the pirates."

"Pirates?" Amelia stared round-eyed at Cousin William.

"Aye. Pirates, they were. We'd had uncommon good luck till then. A fine crew aboard. No troublemakers, for once. All sails set and the wind astern, just where the *Sally Anne* likes it best. I was certain we had our way won through the Straights of Sunda and would be making our way up the Pearl River to Whampoa in record time. But towards evening, the wind dropped off and left us flat becalmed."

"Were you near land?" Julia asked.

"In those straits, you're never far from some pesky island. Then the pirates came pouring out of the creeks in twelve of their heathen boats almost before we'd lost headway. Screaming like banshees, they were. 'Twas't long before they had us surrounded."

"Oh, no! What did they look like?" Julia had forgotten her dinner and was leaning toward William, chin in her hands and elbows on the table. Her deep blue eyes were sparkling with excitement.

"Devils!" William narrowed his eyes and lowered his voice. "Clad only in a few dirty rags and their imagination."

"They sound dreadful." Sarah shuddered daintily.

"They were, but we thought we were holding our own. Had men stationed along the rails and up on the ratlines, shooting down on them at a good rate. Somehow, though, a thirteenth boat snuck up astern of us."

"Oh, no!" Julia and Amelia said together.

"Oh, yes. The devils came swarming up over the taffrail. Murdered two of my best men before we knew what had happened."

"That's hard," Benjamin said.

"Aye. Both Cape lads." William was silent for a moment. Then he picked up his fork as though the tale were over.

"But what happened then, Cousin William?" Amelia asked. "Did they take you prisoner?"

"Prisoner?" He laid down the fork and looked at her with mock indignation. "I should say not! Didn't take long before we'd killed off the lot of them. Picked off a right good number from the other boats to boot."

"But how did you get away?" Julia asked.

"Luck, that's how. When the moon rose, it brought the wind with it. Soft at first, but stronger all the time. It filled our sails, we picked up our heels and were off. Left them in our wake."

"Talk of pirates and murder isn't fit conversation for the table, Will." Lydia frowned at her cousin. "Girls, eat your dinner."

"Oh, Lydia, the girls have heard it all before," Benjamin said.

"Not at dinner. Surely you've more pleasant tales to tell, Will."

"Not much to tell, really." William picked up his fork once more and began to eat. "Good dinner, Lydia. Best I've had in many a day."

"Come now, Will." Benjamin wouldn't leave him alone. "Tell us about Cape Horn. How was your passage?"

"None too bad. Though, of course, it's never what you'd call a pleasure ride. Took about two weeks. No loss of men or rigging."

"And you had good air and perfect weather the whole way out and the whole way home?" Benjamin said skeptically.

"Well, we did run into a typhoon in the Pacific, but it didn't amount to much. Carried off a couple of longboats. That's all."

"You make it sound a mite too easy," Ben challenged his friend.

"Oh, you know what it's like, Ben." William glanced pointedly at Lydia. "No use boring you with details."

"No mutiny? No desertions?"

"Desertion, yes. Had a little trouble in the Sandwich

Isles." He attacked his spoonbread with a great show of relish.

"Well?"

William grinned and laid down his fork. He knew that Ben would never let him rest easy until he had every detail of the voyage. Not that he was reluctant to tell it, but Lydia, seated at his left, lovely though she was, was a sea anchor that held him back.

"Two of my men disappeared. Homeward bound, too! That surprised me. Might be expected on the way out. For a while, I even suspected they might've been killed."

"Were they?" Amelia asked, ignoring her mother's warning look.

"No, no. They were on friendly terms with the natives. Each of them had a pretty vahine there. We spent two days searching through the villages along the coast, but they must've headed for the hills."

"Aren't the hills dangerous?" Julia asked.

"Not to those who know them. I suspect they had guides. You see, the two girls were missing, too."

"That pretty well explains it," Benjamin chuckled.

"Aye. It's a great temptation to a poor sailor lad. Life's too easy. Food falls off the trees into your hands. Bananas, papayas, coconuts, guava, breadfruit. Fish practically jumping out of blue lagoons begging you to eat them. Plenty of fresh water in the rivers that come cascading down from those tall, cloud-wreathed mountains. Lush and green everywhere you look. Beautiful. Truly beautiful." William munched on a clam fritter while he thought about it.

"Oh," Julia sighed. "It sounds like Paradise."

"Reckon it's the closest thing to it you'll ever find on earth," William agreed.

"Someday I'm going to go there," she said with enthusiasm, pushing her hair back from her flushed face. "Aren't we, Papa?"

"Well . . ." Benjamin, aware that Lydia's eyes were fixed on him, carefully cut up a piece of lobster. "I don't know about that. Maybe someday you will."

"But you promised!"

"I never promised to take you to the Sandwich Isles."

"Julia," William said, trying to ease the tensions he

39

could feel were growing steadily stronger, "after dinner, we'll get out some charts, and I'll tell you all about my voyage. That'll be almost as good as going."

"Oh, would you?"

"Certainly."

"But it really won't be as good as actually going."

"Well, maybe someday, after you've grown up, I'll take you on a voyage as my very special guest."

"That would be marvelous. When?"

"Never," said Lydia. "You are not going to sea, so just get that idea out of your mind. Tell me, William," she said as she turned to her cousin. "How are the boys and where are they?"

"Well, I haven't seen either one of them for quite a spell. You know how 'tis. When I'm ashore, they're not, or t'other way around." William loosened the bottom button of his waistcoat and settled more comfortably in his chair. "They were good about writing to their mother, though, and there were a couple of letters waiting for me when I got home."

"Are they at sea?" Julia asked enviously.

"Aye. Jason's on the *Fair Wind* with Captain Ross out in the West Indies. He's sixteen now, and according to his last letter, sounds like he'll be promoted to second mate right soon. He'll do all right."

"And Samuel?" Lydia asked.

"Only been at sea a year. Hard to tell about him yet. Sounded a mite homesick in his letters, but weren't we all at thirteen? Besides, the last one he wrote was about six months ago. He'll have shaped up by now."

"I'm glad all mine are girls," Lydia said. "You send away a boy of twelve or thirteen, then barely get a glimpse of him again till he's a grown man . . . if you ever do."

"Samuel's just my age," Julia said dreamily, "and he's already been at sea a year."

"Julia," Lydia said sharply. "Sit up straight and eat your dinner."

Chapter Three

1833

SEPTEMBER AND ALREADY THE air was turning cool. Yesterday it had been warm enough to swim, but the first nor'wester of autumn had blown through during the night, brushing the Cape in its passage. Across the marsh, the first flicker of flame in the trees and the first tinge of gold in the salt grass shone sharp and clear.

Julia hurried over the dike path. She hardly noticed the whirling sails of the tall grey windmills as they busily pumped saltwater in from the sea. Nor did she see the vats of drying salt that were banked alongside the path and edges of the marsh.

All afternoon, she had watched the clock on the schoolhouse wall tick off the long, slow minutes. Now she was free.

Free to race to the shipyard and see if Cousin William had arrived today. She wanted to hear all about his trip to Boston; about the masts and spars he'd ordered; about where the rigging was to be done; about the cargoes he had lined up for the first voyage of the *Belle of Canton*. Most of all, she wanted to see Cousin William. She'd missed his hearty laughter and his improbable tales.

The sound of bells ringing the hour floated down from

41

the village and Julia began to run. Red-winged blackbirds and marsh wrens flew up out of the reeds as she rushed by, their wings whirring in protest.

At the shipyard, the door to the office was open, but when she went into the room, she found it empty. She tossed her books and lunch pail on a chair next to the cold iron stove and went back out into the noise and pandemonium of the yard.

"Daniel," she called when she saw the wiry foreman limping toward the sawpit. "Has Captain Thacher come?"

"He's here." Daniel glanced briefly at Julia in passing.

"Where?" She hurried after him.

"Up on the ship with your pa." Daniel was much too distracted by the complaints of a master sawyer to pay attention to the girl.

"Thanks, Daniel." Julia changed course and headed for the railway by Sesuit Creek where the *Belle* sat ready for her launching.

As she prepared to mount the scaffolding beside the gleaming black hull, she saw Uncle Josiah watching her from across the road. She gave a shrug and hoisted her skirts above her knees anyway. Let him call her wicked, but there was no other way to climb a rickety ladder if you were unlucky enough to be wearing skirts.

"Papa," she called as she dropped lightly over the oak rail onto the fresh-scrubbed deck. "Where are you?"

"Down here in the saloon," he answered, his voice distant and echoing through the empty ship.

Julia went aft and ran down the companionway. The autumn sun poured golden light through the stern windows of the cabin and sawdust motes glimmered in the air. The two men were seated at the gimbaled table, their heads close together. Cousin William was studying a sketch her father was drawing.

"There's my favorite mermaid," William said, looking up at Julia with his infectious grin. "School out?"

"Yes. Oh, I'm glad you're back, Cousin William." She gave him a kiss on his ruddy cheek.

"Now that's what I call a proper welcome. Makes coming back worthwhile." He hugged her to him for a moment, then released her.

Julia went to lean against her father's chair. She looked over his shoulder. "What are you doing?"

"Trying to figure where we can put in some more shelves for this cantankerous old man," Benjamin said.

"*More* shelves? What for?"

"Books," Cousin William said, pulling his pipe out of his jacket pocket. "What about over there on the starboard bulkhead, Ben?" He pointed with the stem of his pipe.

"Might squeeze in a couple of small ones," Benjamin agreed. "Won't hold much, though."

They heard Daniel's limping footsteps in the companionway and he appeared at the cabin door. "Captain Howard, can you spare me a minute? We've run into a snag on the brigantine."

"Sure you need my help? Can't handle it yourself?" Benjamin knew he'd been pushing Daniel hard, but 'twas the only way to train him.

"Yes, sir. I do." Daniel stood firm.

"Very well," Benjamin sighed and pushed himself up out of the chair. "If you'll excuse me, Will, I'll be right back."

"Take your time," William said. "I'm not going anywhere . . . and neither is this ship till you've got her right."

Benjamin cocked an eyebrow and grinned mockingly. "She's right now and you know it. You just can't let her alone." He followed Daniel down the passageway.

When they had gone, William looked at Julia. "Just as well. Been wanting to ask your advice about something."

"*My* advice?"

"Yes. Has to do with this saloon." William gestured around it with his pipe. "It's not quite right. Can't put my finger on it, but ladies always know how to make a man comfortable."

"I think it's perfect the way it is." Julia looked admiringly at the scrolled walnut paneling, the gleaming brass lamps that hung from the overhead, the polished oak of the gimbaled table. "Maybe a lady would think different, but I'm not one."

" 'Twon't be long before you are."

"Never! Not if I can help it!" The vehemence in her voice surprised William. "I can't help growing up, but I'm not going to be a lady." Her chin was set at its obstinate best.

"What's wrong with being a lady?"

"Everything. I wouldn't mind if I could still be me. Then it might even be fun. But they'll try to change me."

"Don't appear to me they've had much success so far." William puffed on his pipe. His face was serious, but his eyes were twinkling. "What would you do if you could grow up the way you want?"

"First of all, I'd go to sea."

"That figures. How do you plan on getting there?"

"As a supercargo. No one'd take me on as a sailor, but I'm learning about business." She threw herself into a chair opposite him, leaned on the table, and clasped her hands tightly before her. The intensity of her dream made her cheeks glow brighter and her indigo eyes sparkled under the delicately arched black brows. "I'd sign on a ship that was bound on a long voyage. I'd sail all the seas and go to all the places you and Papa talk about."

"Can't say I ever heard of a woman supercargo." William tapped his pipe into a large clamshell. "Doubt there ever will be one 'less the world turns inside out and stands on its head."

"I know." Julia slouched back in her chair. Her eyes had lost their sparkle. "There's absolutely nothing interesting in this world for a woman to do. You see! I told you that, once I grow up, I won't be able to be me anymore."

"*That* I doubt," William chuckled. "There's other ways of going to sea, you know."

"How?" Julia sat up straight, her blue eyes intensely expectant.

"As the wife of a shipmaster."

"Oh." Her face fell. "You have to get married to do that."

"Certainly. And someday you'll want to get married."

"I don't think so." With the tip of her finger, she outlined the reflection of her face on the table. "Anyway, I don't want to go to sea as a useless female. I want to help sail the ship."

"If you married the right man, he might let you."

"Never seen one yet as would. Except Papa." She looked up sharply, straight into his eyes. "Would you?"

The question demanded an honest answer. William squirmed inwardly under her clear gaze. "Well . . . I wouldn't trust just any woman. But one who's learned business and navigation . . . one who's smart as you are. Reckon I would."

"All right." Julia watched the sunlight flickering gold on his beard and smiled. "Then I'll marry you when I grow up. 'Twouldn't be like really getting married. We're already related."

"Well, that would be my pleasure," he said, "but I won't hold you to it. You look around at all the likely lads before you make up your mind."

"Oh, I will," she said airily. "Haven't seen one that would suit me yet, but maybe I will."

"You will."

"Besides, maybe long before that, we'll build our own ship and Papa will take me to sea. Maybe someday, Mama will let us go."

"Don't count on it," Benjamin said, appearing in the doorway. "Julia, there's work laid out for you in the office. Best get to it."

"Now?" She was enjoying this conversation with Cousin William. Besides, she still hadn't heard about his trip down to Boston.

"Now!" Her father's voice brooked no discussion. Julia wondered what had happened to the brigantine to upset him. On the way to the office, she'd have to stop by and find out.

"All right, Papa." She pushed back her chair and went to the door. "But don't forget what you promised, Cousin William," she called back over her shoulder.

When he was sure she'd gone, Benjamin whipped her chair around and sat down. "Will, I want to talk to you. I overheard part of your conversation with Julie."

He leaned on the table with his hands clasped in almost the same pose that Julia had assumed earlier, but Benjamin's blue eyes were angry and his voice cold. "Don't go putting any ideas of marriage into her head. She's way too young, and she'll *always* be too young for you. Understand me, Will?"

"Why, we were just joking, Ben. Didn't mean nothing." William stroked his beard uneasily.

"Didn't it?" Benjamin's eyes were unrelenting.

"No, 'course not." William kept his voice as casual as possible. He'd seen Ben riled up before.

Benjamin sat back in his chair. "Maybe it meant nothing to you, but it meant something to Julie."

"Julie? Why, she's just a child," William said soothingly.

"You're right." Benjamin's voice was still cold and hostile. "She is a child. Treat her like one. Don't go putting any ideas of marriage in her head."

William, though steady of temper, would allow himself to be pushed only so far. He put his pipe down in the clamshell with a clatter. "Now, you want to know something, Ben? I don't think you're mad at me. I think what scares the hell out of you is the idea of Julie marrying and leaving you someday. Marrying anybody. Ever."

"That's nonsense!"

"No, 'tisn't. You've given me something to chew on. Here's something for you. When she's not many years older, say three or four, the first captain that comes walking into this shipyard and offers to take her to sea, she'll marry. Not the second. The first."

"Bah! Julie's got more sense than that!" Benjamin said, but uneasiness had crept in to mingle with the anger in his eyes.

"Nope." William knew he had the advantage now, and he pressed on. "Young or old, handsome or ugly, rich or poor, she'll go."

"Not if I have anything to say about it!"

"You won't. You won't be able to stop her. You've brought her up, filling her head with ships and the sea. Given her more freedom than most girls have. Taught her more than a girl needs to know.

"She's headstrong, Ben. Like you. When she wants to go, she'll go. Not you nor anyone else will be able to stop her. You better just start praying that, when he comes, he'll be young, a decent lad from a good family. That's all I've got to say." He got up and put his pipe into his jacket pocket. "Except that I'm leaving this evening."

"Wait." Benjamin slouched back and looked down at his boots. "We've been friends a long time. Shouldn't part like this."

" 'Tisn't my choice," William said gruffly.

"Then for God's sake, sit down!" Benjamin still didn't

look up, but he lowered his voice. "There may be some truth in what you say."

"There is."

"Might be in what I say, too. This isn't the first time we've had a difference of opinion. Probably won't be the last."

"Likely not."

"Then sit down and let me go over to the office and fetch a bottle of brandy. With its help, maybe we can talk this out."

William walked stiffly back and sat down. When Benjamin looked up, he smiled. Benjamin smiled ruefully back at him.

"When was the first time, Ben?"

"Seems to me it was coming round Cape Horn. Had something to do with whose watch was quicker at reefing."

"Never did settle that one, did we?"

"Oh, *I* think we did." Benjamin grinned at him.

"Well, that's something else we'll have to discuss over that bottle of brandy. It better be a good one."

Benjamin pushed back his chair, stood up and stretched. "It is. The best."

On the day of the launching, when the high autumn tide came racing up Sesuit Creek, they were ready for it. In East Dennis, it was a holiday. A day different from all other days. One that happened only twice a year, and the *Belle of Canton* was the largest ship ever to be launched from the Howard Shipyard. The saltworks lay neglected, the fishing boats were in, and the shipyard was filled with people. The overflow lined the land and the docks on the opposite shore.

The south wind whipped the gaily colored flags that were strung between the buildings. It fluttered the bunting that hung on the docks and on the ship. White tablecloths draped over rough planks, ready for the feast that would follow, had to be weighted down with clean stones.

The *Belle* sat proudly on the ways, her black hull gleaming, her white waist straight and clean, her copper-clad bottom glittering in the sun. At her bowsprit, the figurehead of a dainty Chinese princess lifted her face, as though in eagerness to meet the sea.

Julia, held fast by her mother's eye, waited impatiently beside Sarah and Amelia. She would rather be with her father, checking over the last-minute details, but her mother said her new blue silk dress would be ruined. Bother the dress!

She looked up and caught Cousin William's eye. He winked at her.

"Don't you want to be over there with Papa?" she asked him.

"Not I. My turn'll come soon enough. Until she's launched, she's your father's problem. Once she floats, she's mine."

She looked at his dark blue tailcoat, the brass buttons sparkling in the sun. "Do you get a new coat every time you get a new ship?"

"'Tisn't that often a man gets a new ship. Have to do the lady proud, you know." He nodded at the figurehead.

"You'll ruin it on the trip to Boston."

"Oh, I'll change once we get out in the Bay. Won't be long now." He pointed at the banks of the creek.

Dusting his hands, Benjamin came toward them and went to stand beside the Reverend Lamson. He shouted for silence. Almost immediately, the noise of the crowd dwindled, giving way to a murmuring rustle that was all but hidden under the sounds of the incoming tide and the shrieking gulls. The moment had finally arrived!

"Go ahead, Reverend," he said.

The minister, gaunt in his rusty black suit, his white hair ruffled by the wind, opened his Bible. After clearing his throat, he called out in his best pulpit voice:

"Now, don't go gettin' impatient. I know you're here for the launching and not a sermon, but it's our bounden duty to pray that God look down with favor on this launching and on this vessel. We pray that her voyages will be bountiful and that the men who sail on her will be kept safe in His hands. Safe in their *souls* as well as their bodies." He paused and looked pointedly around at the crowd, which included a good number of seafaring men.

"We pray that she may find favoring currents and fair winds." He glanced down at the Bible in his hands. " 'The wind goeth toward the south and turneth about unto the north; it whirleth about continually; and the wind returneth again to his circuits. All rivers run into the sea; yet the sea is not full; unto the place from whence the rivers come; thither they return again.' "

He paused again and shut his Bible before sweeping the crowd with his eyes. "And just as the wind and the rivers return to their origin, so we pray that this ship will return safely to us; return to the place where the rivers run."

Benjamin, who had been watching the rising water, tapped the minister on the arm. The Reverend Lamson glanced at Benjamin, saw the look in his eyes, and called out a hasty, "Amen."

The tide had reached a marked crevice on the large black boulder up the creek. Now Benjamin signaled the men who stood waiting near the ship. They were the strongest men in the shipyard, and they stepped proudly up to her sides. In the heat of Indian summer, they had stripped to the waist, and they carried their heavy steel-faced mallets lightly.

Standing in pairs on either side of the ship, they inserted iron wedges into the large blocks that cradled the *Belle* on her ways. Strong muscles rippled in their backs and arms as they swung their weighted mallets. The crowd watched with bated breath. As the first blocks under the stern were sundered and fell away, there were loud cries of encouragement. Tension mounted as the men worked their way forward, block by block, toward the bow.

When only one pair remained, a hush fell on the crowd. Anything could happen now. This was when legs were broken, arms crushed, or worse. The men struck their final blows. The blocks shattered. Throwing away their mallets, the men ran from the ship to safety.

The *Belle* quivered for a split second, as though she weren't sure of her freedom. A few creakings and the railway shuddered. A final explosive crack. She began to slide down the ways. Faster and faster she went until she plunged into the water, throwing up a wave that drenched some of the crowd.

"Sits well in the water, Ben," Captain William Thacher said as he looked at his new command with a critical eye.

"No more than I expected." Benjamin removed his tall beaver hat and mopped his brow with a large white handkerchief.

"She's alive!" Julia said, hardly able to contain her excitement.

"Not yet," William chuckled. "With that jury rig in her, all she can do is limp down to Boston. Wait till you see her fully rigged. Her masts and spars in. All her sails set and flying. Let her get a taste of the wind. Then she'll *really* be alive."

"That she will." Benjamin nodded his agreement.

"Best be on our way." William glanced out at the water where pilot boats were securing the *Belle* with lines. "I'll just say goodbye."

After he had gone around the shipyard, shaking hands with the men who'd built his ship, he returned to the shore and paused to take one more look at her. Josiah, who had stayed safely out of harm's way during the launching, joined them. Dressed in an elegant pearl-grey suit that hung oddly on his lanky frame, he was now taking full credit as one of the owners of the shipyard.

William saw him approach and turned to shake hands with him. "Josiah, thanks for all your help."

Then he turned to shake hands with Benjamin. "Sure I can't convince you to come along with me? You could teach me a few of the tricks you've built into her."

"I'd like to, but I can't." Benjamin gestured toward the half-planked brigantine sitting on the other railway. "Got too much to do. Tomorrow we start laying the keel for the next ship."

"You *are* coming down to Boston when we start rigging?" William was anxious to be gone, but this point had to be settled first.

"Send word when I'm needed. I'll be there." Though the ship was launched, Benjamin's responsibilities toward her had not ended. He would have to go to Boston and advise William on the fitting out. Well, it was as good an excuse as any to get away from home for a while. Even Lydia couldn't quarrel with that.

"I'll write you." William turned to Lydia, whose fair face and golden hair were shaded by a green parasol. "Goodbye, Lydia." He leaned down to kiss her cheek. "Stay as pretty as you are."

"And you keep out of trouble!" Lydia answered. Her chin was starting to quiver. "Come back safe to us."

"Never knew trouble to keep me from coming home safe before, did you?" he laughed at her.

"No. Not yet." She tried to smile through the mist that was forming in her eyes.

"Well, God willing, it won't this time." He abruptly turned away. Lydia and the sea! Next thing you knew, she'd be weeping.

He bent over Sarah's light brown hair and kissed her on the forehead. When she returned his kiss, there was a surprising warmth to her lips. Her black eyelashes fluttered modestly down over her grey eyes. Eleven years old? She was too young for that!

He quickly stooped and picked up Amelia. At least with this one, there were no problems. Not yet. He rumpled her pale blond hair, and she rubbed her face against his beard like a kitten.

"Be a good girl while I'm gone," he said, holding her plump body tightly to him, "and I'll try to find something special to bring you when I come home again."

"I will." Amelia smiled at him gaily. Her cornflower-blue eyes twinkled and her dimple deepened. "And if you see that little Chinese girl, tell her thank you for Pen Loo."

"I'll be sure to do that. Julia." Still holding onto the safety of Amelia, he stretched out his hand to the older girl. "Goodbye. I'll think of you often when I'm at sea."

"Goodbye, Cousin William," Julia said, her eyes a deep indigo blue and wistful. "I wish I could go at least as far as Boston with you."

"Not this time. Maybe next." He touched her chin lightly. "When you're a grown-up lady. Remember? Besides," he added gruffly as he turned away from her, "won't be much to see this time."

He gave Amelia another quick squeeze and set her down on the sand. Picking up his bag and throwing it into the waiting skiff, he swiftly climbed in after it.

As soon as the captain was on board, the crew went into action. Sails were bent on the jury rig, shore lines were cast off, and the pilot boats set off before the wind, hauling the ship behind them. Those left on shore watched the *Belle* as she slowly floated down the creek on her way to meet the Bay and her first sight of the sea.

Once she had cleared the mouth of the creek and

vanished around the bend, workmen and their families gathered at tables now covered with platters of food. Picnic baskets appeared as the rest of the crowd settled down to the meal that would precede the music and dancing.

Julia ignored them and headed for the dunes, where she could watch the ship make her way down the Bay. She wasn't hungry.

Josiah saw her go and nudged Sarah, who was standing beside him. "That's one time she didn't get her way," he said slyly.

"Who?" Sarah smiled up at her uncle. She didn't care what the rest of the family thought. She liked Uncle Josiah.

"Who else would I be talking about?" He tilted his hat back on his head and grinned at her. "Your sister Julia."

"No, she didn't, did she?" Sarah said, her smile deepening into delighted agreement.

"Tried hard enough. Followed Will Thacher all over the yard. You should have seen her. Shameless! Bet she did the same at home."

"Yes. She did." Sarah looked thoughtful.

"Well, Miss Julia's just beginning to find out things don't always go her way. Unless I'm powerful wrong, she's not going to get her way much longer. The Lord don't countenance her kind of wickedness."

"Do you really think so, Uncle Josiah?" Sarah opened her eyes admiringly wide. She had recently discovered it had a wonderful effect on men.

"Know so," he said with a malicious chuckle. "Goin' to be right interesting. And we'll be right there to see it."

As Julia stood on the seaward face of the dunes, nothing could have been further from her mind than Sarah and Uncle Josiah. All her wishes were centered on the ship that was slowly diminishing in the distance. Someday, she was thinking, someday . . .

"I'm always sorry to see a ship leave, too," Benjamin said.

Julia jumped. She hadn't heard her father's step on the sand. He held his tall beaver hat in one hand and the wind ruffled his hair.

"There's sorrow, but there's joy in it, too." He put an arm around her shoulders and stood beside her to watch the progress of the *Belle*. "When you build a vessel, you build a part of yourself into her. When she sails away, a part of yourself goes with her."

"There's no joy in that," she said, staring out across the Bay.

"Of course, there is." He hugged her closer to him. "There's nothing more useless than a landlocked ship. We built her to go to sea, and she looks happy to be on her way. That's the joy of it. We built a good ship."

"I suppose so," Julia said impatiently, "but I didn't have that much to do with building her. I wanted to sail on her."

"You know that's not possible."

"I know." She watched the tide beginning to ebb, leaving broken shells and small pebbles tangled with seaweed in its wake.

"I know something that *is* possible, though," Benjamin said.

"What?"

"For you to build something."

"Our ship? At last?" She looked up at him, her eyes filled with hopeful anticipation.

"Nope. Afraid not." He avoided her eyes. "Still haven't been able to sell anyone on the idea."

"I don't know why you have to sell anyone on the idea. She'll be our ship. Why can't we just build her for ourselves?"

He withdrew his arm from around her shoulder and stuck his hands in his pockets. "Can't afford it," he said abruptly.

"But I thought we were rich."

"Rich? Where'd you get an idea like that?"

"I don't know. You own half the shipyard. That's more than most people have."

"I've got more bills than most people have, too. Most of our money's tied up in that yard. We've made a lot of improvements, hired a lot of men. The rest of it . . ." He pointed out to the far distant sea, where clouds of sails appeared and disappeared over the horizon. "It's out there. Tied up in other men's ships."

She shrugged. "You can sell your shares in those."

"I could, but it still wouldn't be enough to build the kind of ship we want. Maybe in a couple of years . . ."

"Years! It's always years." She impatiently pulled off her straw bonnet and let the breeze take her hair.

"I know. It's hard, the waiting." His voice was so low, she could hardly hear him over the sound of the waves. She looked up and saw the lines deepen in his face.

"Hard for you, too, Papa?"

"Yes. Though maybe not as hard as it is for you. As we get older, we learn patience."

"That's one thing I'll *never* learn! You never get anything if you're too patient." She flung her head back and tilted her chin at a stubborn angle.

"Perhaps." He ran his hand over his windblown hair, smoothing it back. "I did have something in mind for you, though."

"If it isn't a ship, I don't want it."

"Would you settle for a boat?"

"A boat?" She impatiently swung her bonnet back and forth by its blue satin ribbons.

"Yes. You can help build it." He began to pace along the ridge of the dunes. "It'll take a while, but I figure we could have it ready by next July. In time for your fourteenth birthday."

"Papa, a boat isn't a ship."

"Well, maybe it wasn't such a good idea, after all." He watched the *Belle* and the schooners. The wind was slackening, and they were moving more slowly now. "Somewhere I got the idea you wanted to learn more about sailing; figured you wanted to learn how to build a ship. Seems I was wrong. All you want to do is dream."

"No, I don't! I mean, I do."

"Well, then?"

"Well, would it be my boat? Could I do what I liked with it? With no one to tell me different?"

"That's about what I had in mind."

"Then I'll take it."

Lord, where did the girl get her airs? he wondered. But all he said was, "Going to have to build it first."

"What's it going to be like?"

"What do you want?"

"Oh . . ." She paused and thought a moment. Her eyes

swept the water and the craft scattered across it. "Not too big. One I can handle alone. Has to have a sail. Have to be able to row it, too. Just in case there's no wind."

"You're beginning to sound like a customer. Here's what I had in mind." He knelt on one knee and began to draw in the soft sand. Julia knelt beside him, careless of her blue silk skirt.

"Now what I think you want is a small fishing dory."

"Fishing!"

"Hold on a minute!" He continued to draw. "Now, she'd have a mast step here, oarlocks would go here and here." He punched the sand with his finger. "You could scull her from the transom, too."

"Will she be lapstraked?" she asked, becoming interested.

He nodded. "And made out of the finest oak and birch and spruce money can buy."

"Will you make a half-model for me?"

"No. You're going to do that."

"How?" She pushed a half-buried clamshell deeper into the sand.

"Go up the hill and take the lines off the best dory up there. We don't usually bother with a model for a dory, but you might as well learn." He looked at her levelly. "If you think you can, that is."

"Of course, I can!" She looked up, her eyes half-hidden by her tangled hair, but he could see the indignation in them.

"All right, then. Let's get to work." He stood up and brushed the sand from his knee. "Now you're not to tell anyone about this, do you understand?"

"Not even Mama?" She scrambled up and shook her skirts, blowing sand all over him.

"Especially not Mama."

As they walked down the back of the dune into the shipyard, the fiddles were already scraping away and the flutes trilling along with them. On the mold loft floor, the dancing had begun.

"Go find Daniel for me. Tell him I want a word with him," Benjamin told Julia. "I'm going over and see if anyone saved us a bite to eat."

When Julia returned with Daniel in tow, she found her father seated on a nail keg, careless of his best clothes. On a flat board beside him, there were two plates of food and a couple of mugs; one of milk and the other looking suspiciously like rum.

"I won't keep you away from the dancing long, Daniel," Benjamin said and immediately wished he hadn't. He was so used to Daniel's limp, he often forgot the man had a crippled leg.

"That's all right, Captain Howard," Daniel said with a grin. He understood the reason for his employer's embarrassment. A lot of people made the same mistake. He didn't mind. He knew he was more of a man than many who had two sound legs. There was no reason to pity Daniel. "I was just tryin' to figure which lady I'd favor."

"There are some right pert ones around today. I can understand how a man might have trouble choosing." Benjamin picked a chicken leg off the nearest plate. "I want to thank you, Daniel. Without you, I doubt we'd have been ready for launching in time. You'll find a bonus come next payday, but I wanted to tell you personally how much I appreciate it."

"No need. Today made it worthwhile."

"Well, I hope so. There's just one other thing I wanted to speak to you about."

"Sir?" Daniel glanced toward the crowd gathered at the mold loft doors.

"We got an order today. A small one, but it's got to be perfect." Benjamin bit into the chicken leg and chewed on it for a moment. "Want some chicken?" He gestured at the plates on the board.

"I've already eaten, thank you." Daniel wished Captain Howard would get on with it. He'd spotted a certain girl from over Yarmouth Port way he wanted to get better acquainted with, and he was afraid that, by the time he got back, someone else would have spotted her, too.

"Well, about this order," Benjamin continued. "It's the first one I've gotten from this customer. A fishing dory, about twelve, thirteen feet long."

"'*Tis* a small order."

"May be, but it can lead to bigger things. Some of the most important things in this yard's future might come out of that little boat. So it has to be right. Understand?"

"Aye."

56

"Got plenty of time. It doesn't have to be delivered till July. Gives us ten months. But it's got to be perfect. Top-grade wood. First-class fittings. Put our best men on it."

"The best men won't like being put on a dory, sir. They'll think it beneath them. They take pride in their work and the vessels they build."

"That's as it should be. But you explain how important this particular boat is. I think," he paused to take another bite, "when they see who comes to take delivery, they'll be right pleased."

"Papa, don't forget to tell Daniel about me," Julia, who had been standing by, put in.

"Oh, yes. Almost forgot. It's time Miss Julia learned more about shipbuilding. This is a good opportunity for her to learn. The men are to teach her as they go along. No work's to be done on it unless she's on hand. Saturdays. After school."

"The days are gettin' shorter," Daniel said. "Won't be able to go very fast."

"I know," Benjamin said impatiently. "I *said* it doesn't have to be ready till July. We'll get started on it tomorrow."

"Yes, sir." Daniel grinned at Julia and she wondered if he had guessed their secret. "Is that all, Captain Howard?"

"Yes, that's all, Daniel. Go on back to that young lady I've seen you eyeing."

Chapter Four

1836

TRELLISED VINES SHADED THE large kitchen, captured the mid-morning sun in their leaves and filtered it. The room was saturated with a green underwater light. Locusts were singing in the trees. Had been since dawn. Another hot day.

Too hot for making preserves, Lydia thought. She patted her damp face with a linen towel and pinned her heavy silver-gold hair more securely away from her forehead. Still, when the blueberries were ripe, that was when you had to can them, heat or no.

She glanced over at the wide deal table where Julia sat patiently sorting through the berries in a large china bowl. Despite the mass of blue-black hair that curled around her face and down her shoulders past her waist, her daughter seemed oblivious to the heat. Land, the girl was slow! It was obvious from that dreamy look in her eyes that her thoughts were on something besides berries. Lydia wished that she had one of the maids helping her instead of Julia. Even Sarah or Amelia would be better.

No. Benjamin let her have Julia three mornings a week, and those three mornings were all the time Lydia had to teach Julia how to run a house. There were other things, too, a girl must know before she became a woman. And with her sixteenth birthday only a couple of weeks away, Julia was fast approaching that stage.

It was a mother's duty to instruct her daughter, and Lydia never shirked her duty. Even if it meant taking twice as long to make preserves.

When Julia finished school last year, Lydia hoped it meant she'd have more time with her, but Benjamin didn't see it that way. Said the shipyard came first. Lydia hadn't even fought the idea very hard. She still didn't approve of a girl working down there with all those men. She had just plain given up.

Lydia measured some sugar and poured it over the berry juice.

It was too hot for talking this morning, but Lydia wondered what Julia was thinking about. Boys, maybe? They'd been coming around for a couple of years now to ask Julia to go berrying with them, to go for a sail. At one time, it had amused her. How many excuses could a boy find to hang around when he should have been off at his chores?

Julia treated them as friends, though rather distantly. She didn't seem to have any real friends unless you counted the men down at the shipyard. Could the girl really be as unaware as she seemed? Didn't she suspect the real reason for the boys' interest? With Julia, you never knew. She kept a lot of things hidden where no one could reach them.

Lydia sighed and reached for the jelly bag. Somehow it didn't seem very amusing anymore. Land, when would Julia have that batch of berries ready?

She walked over to the deal table and peered into the bowl, but it wasn't the berries she saw. It was Julia's hands!

Like Lydia's own, they were slender with long, tapering fingers, but there the resemblance ended. Instead of the white, well-manicured hands of a young girl, they were hard and callused, with short, ragged nails. Lydia was shocked. They looked like the hands of a boy! Something had to be done . . . immediately.

And not only there.

She looked closely at Julia, who was unaware of her mother's scrutiny. Although her hands went on picking through the purple berries automatically, Julia was wondering if she could find a private spot to swim before she went on down to the shipyard.

Lydia continued her inventory. Salt wind and summer sun had done their work and turned Julia's white skin to a light tan. As usual, her hair was loose and curling untidily. Her high, full breasts were straining against the tight bodice of the faded blue-grey dress, and the hem was far too short. Lydia frowned at the black-stockinged leg it exposed.

"Julia," she said in a vexed voice. "You've got to give that dress to Sarah. You've outgrown it."

"Oh, it's all right." Julia pushed her hair back with berry-stained fingers and wondered at her mother's sudden outburst. "Sarah wouldn't wear it, anyway."

"No, it's too tight." Lydia eyed the faded material speculatively. "If nothing else, it can be cut down for Amelia. None of your dresses fit you proper anymore. We'll have to buy some material and make you up some new ones."

"Oh, Mama, these will do," Julia said impatiently, knowing full well who would have to do all the stitching. She simply didn't have time for it. "Long skirts and loose material would just get in my way down at the yard."

"Well, you'll have to learn how to handle them. You can't go around looking like that. It'll create a scandal."

"Oh, Mama!" Julia looked down into the bowl before her and set her chin. She ran her fingers through the blueberries.

"And another thing." Lydia sat down in a chair next to Julia and studied her daughter's face. It was beginning to get that stubborn look, but Lydia pressed on. "You've *got* to stay out of the sun."

"Stay out of the sun!" Julia looked up then, directly at her mother. Anger was beginning to darken the blue of her eyes.

"Yes. You're too old to run around looking like an Indian."

"I can't." Julia's voice was firm. In this, at least, she knew she was right. "I *have* to be out in the sun down at the yard. Ask Papa."

"I don't have to ask your papa anything," Lydia said, "but I do know you can wear a bonnet and gloves. Otherwise, you'll ruin your complexion. Boys like girls who have pretty white skin. Yours would be fair enough if you'd give it half a chance."

Julia sighed and went back to her berry picking. She could just see herself working down at the yard decked out in a bonnet and gloves. She could hear the men sniggering now.

"I'm not a porcelain doll like Sarah, Mama. I'm me," she said. Then her eyes lit up with an impish sparkle. "Besides, I haven't noticed it keeping any boys away. Wouldn't mind if it did put some of them off." She flipped her hair across her shoulder with that arrogant toss of her head that so annoyed her mother.

"You're getting vain, Julia," Lydia said in a low, warning voice, "and that's a sin. Don't you forget it."

"I am not vain! Can I help it if they follow me around?"

"And you like it." Lydia's green eyes narrowed. "You walk around like the Queen of Sheba with her subjects trailing after her. Well, they'll not stand still for that long. They'll go find themselves sweeter, nicer girls."

"Good!" Julia pushed back her chair and carried the bowl of berries to the sink to rinse them. "At least, they run after *me*. I'm not chasing *them*. Not like Sarah does."

"Sarah?" Lydia looked at Julia's back in surprise. "Sarah never chased a boy in her life."

"Oh, no?" Julia swirled around to face her mother. She leaned back against the sink heedless of her faded dress. "The minute anything in pants comes near Sarah, she's fluttering her lashes over those soft grey eyes of hers. Looking so helpless and appealing. She swishes her skirts and tells them what big strong men they are."

"I don't believe it," Lydia said flatly.

"Well, you'd better." Julia's eyes were seriously intent on her mother. "She watches from the porch upstairs to see who's coming down the road. Then when they come around the curve, she's sitting under the chestnut tree, pretty as you please, with her skirts spread out just so."

"Not Sarah."

"Yes, Sarah. And that's not all, Mama." Julia pushed her damp sleeves up above her elbows. "She's starting to wander over to the shipyard in the afternoon. She just drifts around, asking for an admiring look. Believe me, she gets them, too."

Lydia cut Julia short. "You sure you're not jealous because your sister's showing an interest in your precious shipyard?"

"Jealous? Of Sarah?" Julia laughed mockingly. "Sarah's not interested in the shipyard. Sarah's interested in men."

"Not at her age." Lydia shook her head. "Thirteen?"

"I was interested in boys when I was thirteen."

"I don't believe it."

"Well, I was, but I didn't carry on the way Sarah does. I still don't."

"You're imagining things, Julia. Your father hasn't mentioned it."

"Probably hasn't noticed yet. He *does* have other things to think about."

"Well"—Lydia got up and went to the stove—"I'll keep an eye on her. If I find any truth in what you say, I'll have a talk with her. But if I don't, miss"—she turned to look sternly at Julia—"you're the one that will hear from me."

"I'm not worried, Mama," Julia said with an imperceptible smile. "You just watch."

Lydia stirred one of the steaming pots, letting the rich, sweet fragrance fill the air when she took off the lid. She frowned as she checked the sauce.

"You know, Julia, you really should start thinking of boys more seriously. You're nearly sixteen now, and the best ones always get caught young. There are some fine young men around who'd come courting if you'd give them half a chance."

"Landlubbers. All the best men are at sea . . . where they belong." Julia vigorously pumped water over the berries in the sink.

"Just because a man has an honest occupation ashore don't mean he's less a man. There's some I know of who'll inherit a good business. They'd be safe at home with you, not roaming all over the world." Lydia dropped the jelly from the spoon. Almost done.

"Look at Aaron Martin," she continued. "He's a nice-looking lad. Got a pleasant manner. He'll inherit his father's saltworks, too, someday. If you'd encourage him, I think you could have him. I've seen him eyeing you in church when he should have been listening to the sermon."

"Oh, Aaron!" Julia poured the berries into a large pot.

"He's so dull. If I ever marry, it'll be to a sea captain. I'm just waiting for one to come along and ask me."

"You and your sea!" her mother said in exasperation, slamming the lid on the big kettle. "You'll learn, Julia. You go ahead and marry your captain, and you'll learn to hate the sea. Wait! You just wait. It'll take those you love away from *you*, too. You're no exception. No woman is."

"It won't take him away from *me*," Julia laughed. "I'm going with him. You don't think I'm going to sit home and wait patiently while the men are out there having all the fun, do you?"

"You'll wait," Lydia said grimly, "but not patiently. Painfully, you'll wait. Wondering whether the sea will give back what you've loaned it. Oh, yes, you'll wait. And you'll hate it."

"No!"

"Yes. When I was your age, I thought I liked the sea, too, but I certainly wasn't as daft about it as you are. I went with your father, and believe me, *that* was no joy ride." Lydia banged the long iron ladle down on the table. "You brag on being born at sea. Well, just remember, miss, I had to be there, too. You weren't borne by any mermaid.

"Then it started to take away from me." Her voice sounded strained, and the lines around her mouth and green eyes deepened. She walked across the room and sat down in the tall rocking chair that faced out toward the green salt marsh.

"First it was my father," she said, and there was pain in her eyes as she looked out the window. "Then Nathaniel, my own sweet, darling boy. A few months later, it was my brother George. I only had one father. One son. One brother. It took them all. 'Twould have taken your father, too, if I hadn't put my foot down.

"They say the sea is a woman," she mused in a lower tone, rocking slowly back and forth. "Sometimes I wonder. Would a woman be so cruel to another woman? I don't know. But it does like the men. It takes them away from you and doesn't give them back. First it claims their hearts, then their bodies. I've heard of women like that. I guess it has to be female."

"Oh Mama!" Julia dried her hands on her skirt and ran

to kneel on the floor beside her mother. "Don't grieve so. It breaks my heart."

"Child," Lydia said, stroking the thick black curls, "if only I could save you some of the grief I've had. I don't want you to live through the same miseries. It doesn't make sense. Generation after generation. Mother and daughter, mother and daughter, endlessly. Sometimes we should stop and learn. Somewhere this chain should be broken."

"Mama, I'm sorry." Julia hugged her. "I'd do as you say if I could. I just can't. I wish I could, but the sea's always there, calling me."

"Oh, Julia."

"I've looked at the boys, the young men around here. Really I have, Mama. Sometimes I can even fool myself into believing that I could marry one of them. You know how it is. You like the way one walks or another looks or maybe it's a voice that's special. But then some sailor comes home, and I forget the others."

"Often I don't even like the sailor, but they all carry a special magic perched on their shoulders. They've been to sea." She thought of them, sailing down that blue-green path of sunlight, stormlight, black nights, phosphorus, stars, gales, and hurricanes. "They've rounded Cape of Good Hope or Cape Horn, and *that* takes a man. They've seen ice floes and tropic birds. Smelled oranges in the ports of Spain and spices in the streets of Canton." Her eyes were shining with the glory of it all.

"Mama, how can I stay home and settle for someone like Aaron Martin? I'd be so miserable."

"I know, child," Lydia sighed. She looked away from Julia's glowing face and stared out over the marsh that led to the sea. One hand was still entangled by the thick curls of her kneeling daughter.

"It's in your blood. It's come down to you through all the generations. Down through your father's side. Down through mine. Usually it calls the men, and they have no choice but to follow it. I expect you'll go, too. But God spare you the trouble it brings."

Julia searched her mother's face. How tired she looked.

"Mama, why don't you go up and rest? I'll finish the preserves."

"I will soon, but I've more to say. Bide your time, Julie. Don't go marrying the first shipmaster that asks you. You can have your pick. Wait till the right one comes along."

Julia smiled. "You just said the best ones always go first."

"That's different. I was talking about the young men around here. Sailors grow up and rise up at sea. They've not the time for marriage quite so young."

"All right, Mama. I'll look them over." Then her eyes filled with gamin laughter. "You sure you're not telling me to wait just so you can keep me home with you? Might end up an old maid that way."

"You?" Lydia's face relaxed into a smile and she seemed younger. "I don't reckon any of my daughters will end up old maids, especially if what you told me about Sarah is true. But you'll be the first to go."

A few days later, they got word that Captain William Thacher would be home in the late summer.

When Julia heard he was coming, she was filled with a bubbling excitement that she tried hard to hide. She still thought of him as Neptune with his sea-green eyes and his thick golden beard. She was sixteen now and she remembered his promise.

Would he consider her grown-up enough yet? She went upstairs to her mother's room and surveyed herself carefully in the tall pier glass. Pressing her dress close, she ran her hands over her body, turning and twisting to get a better view. After the first astonishment at the changes that had come a couple of years ago, she had ignored the developments that had followed. Now she saw how small her uncorseted waist was compared to her hips and noticed how her breasts swelled out above it. Her height helped, too.

Then she pulled her hair back and examined her face. She looked awfully young for a man like Cousin William. Would he think she was still a child?

Taking some hairpins from the enameled box on her mother's dressing table, she tried coiling her hair up on top of her head. It did make her look older. She took her hands away and her hair tumbled down. She tried again. This time it stayed up, but it looked so lopsided and clumsy. How did women ever manage it? She was repinning it for the sixth time when she heard a snicker from the doorway.

"Can't make a silk purse out of a sow's ear, Julia," Sarah said.

Julia whirled on her in an embarrassed fury. "No one asked you! Get out of here!"

"This isn't your room. It's Mama's. I've got as much right to be here as you have." Sarah folded her arms and leaned against the doorjamb.

"You! You're always sneaking around, spying and prying."

"You're a fine one to talk after what you told Mama about me."

"What do you mean?"

"Oh? What else have you told her?" Sarah raised her black eyebrows. Below them, her grey eyes were hostile. "I mean when you lied to her about me chasing boys."

Julia laughed. "That was no lie."

"Well, it's none of your business. Now she's forbidden me to go over to the shipyard anymore."

"And a good thing, too."

"What are you trying to do to me, Julia?" Sarah approached her like a cat with unsheathed claws. "Just exactly what are you trying to do? You've taken Papa. He doesn't even see me anymore. It's always Julia this and Julia that. Now you're trying to turn Mama against me. Don't you think I need someone to love me, too? Someone who thinks I'm special?"

"Oh, Sarah." Julia was shocked by the lost look that mingled with the anger on her sister's face. "I never meant to take anything away from you."

"Well, if you didn't, you've done a fine job of it, anyway." Sarah's eyes were desolately bleak. In all their lives together, Julia had never seen them quite like this before.

"Sarah," Julia repeated. She put out an arm to comfort her sister.

Sarah backed away, her whole body rigid. "Don't touch me! I don't want your pity! I hate you!" She turned and ran from the room.

Julia started to follow. Then, hearing her sister's bedroom

door slam shut, she returned to the pier glass and stared at herself.

Have I done that? Can it be true? Have I turned Mama against her? Have I taken so much of Papa's love he doesn't have any left for Sarah?

But it can't be! It just can't be.

But Sarah thinks it is.

She sat down on her mother's bed.

What can I do now? If I talk to Mama, Sarah will think I'm tattling on her again. Papa's so busy, I can't bother him. Besides, I don't think he'd really understand this time. I can't help her. She won't let me come near her. She never really has. Not like Amelia.

I just don't know what to do.

She got up, took the remaining pins out of her falling hair and tossed them carelessly on the dresser. Then she went downstairs and quietly left the house. There was only one place to go. Only one person who ever really listened to her. She went to the sea.

But while the sea comforted her that evening, it offered her no immediate solution, and Julia remained troubled. She went sailing in the early mornings before her work had begun and sought the beach in the evenings after the day was over. She watched sunrises and sunsets and still found no answer.

Benjamin and Lydia both noticed her troubled preoccupation. Each approached her separately, but she would tell them nothing. They worried about it alone and together, but could come to no conclusion.

It was after an evening spent wandering beside a low tide that Julia, her dress bedraggled and her hair windswept, returned home to discover Cousin William had arrived. Even before she reached the front porch, she could hear his hearty voice booming out like surf on the rocks. Horrified, she swept back her unruly hair. What would he think of her looking like this?

She could tell he was in the parlor, so she decided to slip quietly in at the dining room door. She would go up the back steps and tidy herself before he saw her.

But no sooner had she stepped through the open door

than William and her father came into the dining room to fetch the crystal decanter that stood on the sideboard.

"Julia! My mermaid!" Cousin William swept her up and gave her a hearty kiss. "Let me look at you." He held her away from him. "Well, you've grown, but you've still got the taste of the sea on you. Have you been down playing with your starfish and seahorses? Jason," he called over his shoulder. "Jason, come here and meet your cousin Julia."

The tall young man who appeared in the doorway could not have been more unlike his father except for his height and the color of his eyes. His straight hair was almost as black as Julia's own. He was clean-shaven, though his sideburns were long, and there was a bright flush on his lean, high cheekbones. While his shoulders were broad, he appeared slender beside his father's bulk.

William clapped him across the back and steered him over to her. "Julia, this is my eldest son and your cousin. Jason, this is a mermaid. You'll not meet many of those."

She held out her hand. "I'm pleased to meet you, Jason."

"I'm honored," he said formally. His voice was softly husky and strong, but his green eyes twinkled as his father's were apt to do. "Are you really a mermaid?"

"Only on rare occasions."

"You look as though you'd just come up from the sea." His expression was both admiring and amused.

"Well, yes and no." She withdrew her hand from his warm one. "I'm a little windblown. If you'll excuse me, I'll go up and change."

"But you'll be back?" The amusement had gone and only the admiration remained.

"Yes." She smiled at him. "I'll be back."

As the door swung shut behind her, William said, "Jason, if you'll go entertain our hostess and young cousins, I'd like a word alone with our host."

When they were alone, William frowned as he looked at Benjamin. "Julia seemed troubled when she came in. Is something bothering her?"

"Yes." Benjamin looked worried. "And we don't know what it is. She won't confide in Lydia or me. Maybe you can find out."

"How long's it been going on?"

"A few weeks."

"I'll see what I can do. You still got that crazy idea about Julia running the yard?"

"She'll have to. I have no sons." Benjamin picked up the amber Buddha and stroked it with his fingers, enjoying the sensual smoothness of the stone. "You're fortunate in your two boys, Will."

"Yes, I am." William realized that his voice sounded a little too smug. "But you wouldn't trade me either one or both put together for Julia."

"No, I wouldn't." The Buddha glowed red as he turned it in his hands. Cherry blossoms, gongs, spices, and pretty dark-haired girls. He and Will had been younger than Will's son when he had bought it. "That Jason of yours is a likely looking lad, though."

"I think so. Doing well, too." William glanced in the direction of the parlor. "He'll be sailing soon with Captain Avery on the *Katy Saunders*. Just turned nineteen and already first mate. Wouldn't surprise me to see him make master after this voyage. I'm right proud of him. I only wish Margaret could have lived to see him grown up and become a man."

"Well, she probably knows." Benjamin put the amber Buddha down on the sideboard. He suddenly felt depressed. Time. Where had it gone?

"I'm sure of it." William looked at his friend's face, which reflected his own sadness. Perhaps he had been wrong in coming here. Ben probably had troubles enough without his adding to them. "Hope you don't mind my bringing Jason with me. By luck, I arrived in Boston just a few days after his ship docked."

"No. We're glad to have him. And Samuel? How's he doing?"

"Coming right along. He's like his mother. Nothing can keep him down for long. Bounces right back and knows how to make the most of life. I saw him aboard the *Gitana* off Cape St. Roque about a year ago. Samuel's already second mate. Captain Kelley and I had a long chat about him, and Kelley thinks he'll go far. Says he's shown a keen eye for trading."

"Good, good. Well, let's go in the parlor before Lydia

comes out here and accuses me of monopolizing her favorite cousin."

When Julia entered the parlor, both William and Jason stood up. It was the first time a man had risen for her. Maybe I really am growing up, she thought.

"Come sit with me, Julie," Amelia called. She was on the floor on the far side of the room. The firelight had turned her pale blond hair to silver, and her large powder-blue eyes were sparkling with delight. "See what Cousin William brought me!"

"What is it, Amelia?" Amelia's happiness was always infectious, and Julia started across the room to her.

"Don't you want to see what I've brought you, Julie?" Cousin William's voice made her pause.

"Of course, but let me look at Amelia's first." She stopped in front of the fire and looked up at him. In the brighter light of the parlor, he looked older than she had realized. Older and sadder. She smiled at him. "Then I can spend the rest of the evening enjoying mine."

She settled down on the floor beside Amelia.

Lydia frowned. It was time Julia learned what chairs were for.

"Look, Julia." Amelia's dimples were in full play. "The same Chinese girl who sent me Pen Loo sent me this tiger. Isn't he marvelous? Look at his teeth." She had brought the elephant down from her room and had placed the two ivory figures side by side.

"They look like they're friends already," Julia said.

"Oh, yes. Quite good friends." Given the slightest excuse, Amelia's imagination was apt to take over. "In fact, they knew each other back in China. They're very happy to be together again."

"Isn't that wonderful." Julia raised her head to smile at Cousin William. "They're just . . ." And she was aware of Jason sitting across the room watching her, looking at her in a way no one had ever looked before. "They're just lovely, Cousin William," she faltered, embarrassingly aware of the blush that was flooding her face and of those clear green eyes across the room. Eyes that seemed able to penetrate into her secret self.

70

"You about ready for your present now, Julie?" William was impatient for her to see it.

"Oh, yes, of course." She was glad of the distraction.

"Well, it was too big to wrap, so I'll have to fetch it."

He stepped through the door to her father's study. In a moment, he was back with a full-scale model of a ship in his hands; every sail set, every line in place, even the belaying pins in their tiny sockets.

"Cousin William!" Julia jumped up from the floor and went to examine it.

"It's the *Belle of Canton,*" he said. "Since you couldn't sail on her, I brought her to you."

"Oh!" Julia took the ship from him and settled down on the floor directly in front of the fire, where she could study all the intricately worked details. "Even the figurehead! She's there, leading the way."

"Julia!" Lydia reprimanded her. "Aren't you going to thank Cousin William?"

"Oh! Yes, of course. Thank you, Cousin William. I'm sorry. I was just too excited, I guess."

"There's more than one way to say thank you," William chuckled. "And I do believe yours is the best. Words are only a nuisance. Often don't mean too much."

"Sometimes words can mean too much," Julia said softly. "Sometimes they can hurt most terribly."

"Yes, they can," he agreed. Her tone alerted him. Perhaps the girl would tell him what was bothering her.

Benjamin picked it up, too. Words. Had someone said something about Julia? Something vicious? Had she overheard it? Or had someone spiteful, like Josiah, said it to her face?

But what could anyone say that would hurt her so deeply? She never seemed to care for the opinion of most people, only that of those she loved. And with them, it really did matter to her. She, who seemed the most invulnerable of his children, was actually the most vulnerable of all. Perhaps she would confide in William. He hoped so.

However, it did make him think he'd better get Josiah out of the shipyard. 'Twouldn't be easy to get the shares away from him. Have to figure out something. The trouble his brother made for him, he could handle, but the trouble he was capable of causing Julia was something else.

The next morning, William and Jason accompanied Julia and her father down to the shipyard. Rain had fallen during the night, and the clean, washed scent of trees and grass and brush mingled with the rich, sweet odor of damp sand. The familiar hills and fields and marshes looked freshly made as though the world had just been born. It was a morning made for joy.

As she walked beside Jason over the narrow footpath behind her father and Cousin William, Julia wondered at her soaring spirits, but there was too much happiness for questions. The world was young and she was young. It was enough.

"Do you really work at your father's shipyard? Or is it just an excuse to get out of the house?" Jason asked, distracting her attention from the red-winged blackbirds that sang and fluttered amongst the reeds beside the path.

It was a question that always came up with strangers, and Julia hated it. It made her feel like a freak. Just because she was a girl! No one would ask a boy such a question. It took a bit of the brightness out of her morning. However, Jason's voice was deep and gentle, not mocking like some.

"I work there," she answered. "It's not just an excuse."

"What do you do?" He noticed how the blue of her eyes had changed with the morning's light from nighttime indigo to peacock blue.

She, in turn, examined his face. Though he held it serious, he seemed to be making quite an effort to keep it that way. Julia was sure she could see the shadow of a twinkle in his clear green eyes, a quiver to his peaked eyebrows, as though they wanted to rise, and a slight lift to the corners of his mouth. The early morning sun glinted brown-gold highlights on his black hair. My, he's handsome, she thought. She almost forgave him his questions and the amusement she sensed behind them.

Still.

She looked across the marsh that was green with summer, its creek winding blue as the sky, past the grey windmills and white salt vats, to the clustered village on the far hill.

"I do the ordering," she said quietly. "Pay the bills. Keep the accounts. Spend a lot of time out in the yard, learning the proper way to build a vessel."

"What good will that ever do you?"

This time it was definitely a challenge.

"What good!" She rose to it, and her cheeks flushed with indignation. "How will I ever be able to run the yard if I can't judge a piece of timber, know how to splice a rope, understand how paint must be mixed and laid on? I have to know good joinery from bad, a well-caulked seam from a poor one. Everything."

"*You* are going to run the yard?"

"Yes. *I* am going to run the yard." Pulling off her hat and shaking her head, she freed her blue-black hair to the morning wind. It was the first time Jason had seen that stubborn lift to her dainty chin, the straightening of her already straight shoulders. Angry, she seemed even more beautiful than she had last night by firelight.

"Why?" He was fascinated by her, fascinated by the eyes that were now once again darkening to the blue of indigo, fascinated by her anger.

"It's really very simple," she said caustically. "There's no one *else* to do it."

Jason shook his head.

"Seems strange work for a girl."

"Maybe. But it's my work."

"Do you like it?"

"I love it."

"Doesn't it frighten you?"

"*Frighten* me? What?"

"The responsibility. The future."

"No. Why should it?"

"It's an awful lot for a woman to handle."

"Does the idea of being master of a ship someday frighten you?" She looked up at his lean, high-boned face, staring defiantly into his green eyes until the amusement left them. "I suppose that's what you're aiming for."

"No. Of course, it doesn't frighten me," he said.

"Well? What's the difference?"

Jason smiled, but this time gently, no longer laughing at

73

her. She was so lovely he didn't really want her to be angry with him.

"You're a girl," he said. And she certainly was. "Don't you ever think about getting married? How are you going to run a house and a shipyard, both?"

She shrugged.

"I can do anything I set my mind to," she said.

"I'm sure you can," he said, and her anger relaxed a little of its hold.

Jason wondered whether running the shipyard was her idea or her father's. He knew something about fathers.

"And what you've set your mind on is running a shipyard? That's what you really want to do?"

She walked on a moment in silence. Her father and Cousin William had rounded the bend of the road just ahead. She and Jason were alone for a moment. He didn't really seem to be taunting her. In his last questions she had sensed real interest in her, Julia, and a strange sympathy. He really seemed to care.

"I'll tell you what I really want." She paused to pick a wild daisy growing beside the sandy road.

"What?" He stopped beside her and looked down at her profile, which was half-hidden by her long, curling hair.

"I want to go to sea." She looked up at him, her wide eyes trusting him with her secret.

He glanced away from her, sharply startled, and then walked on, making no comment. Julia felt defensive. She wished now she hadn't confided in him.

"Well, that may sound silly to you, but I'm going to do it," she said defiantly.

"How?"

"There are ways. I'm just studying on the best way to do it."

"You'll never do it," he said flatly.

"Oh, yes, I will." She tossed her head and swung her hair behind her shoulders. "I'm determined, and when I'm determined, I always get what I want."

"So far."

"Yes. So far and I always will."

"And you're going to sea."

Julia couldn't read the narrowed eyes beneath those

74

peaked black brows. His high-planed face, like his voice, was without expression.

"Yes, I'm going to sea."

"Who's going to run your shipyard then?"

"Papa." She glanced up at a grey, shingled windmill. Its sails were turning slowly under the soft south wind. "I used to think he was going to build a ship for us and take me to sea someday. He said he was. But now, I don't think he ever will."

"And when he retires?" Jason persisted.

"He won't retire for a long time yet. I'll go to sea till he needs me. Then I'll come home again."

"You have everything planned so neat and tidy." His voice was harshly bitter now. "You don't know what the sea's like. Maybe you think it's a picnic, but it's not."

"I do *so* know. I was born at sea."

"That was a long time ago. I bet you don't remember it, not the worst of it."

"Yes, I do."

"I doubt it. Even if you did, you would have been tucked safe in the cabin below. Your father wouldn't have let you up on deck."

"I can take it."

"It's rough, it's cruel, and it's lonely."

"I don't care."

"You will."

"Then why do you go to sea if it's rough and cruel and lonely?"

"I don't know." He stopped when they reached the top of the hill. From here, they could see the Bay and the white sails of merchantmen, fishing sloops, schooners, and whalers, their wakes crossing, crossing, eternally crossing.

"I often wonder," he said. "Sometimes I blame my father for shipping me out when I was only eleven. Sometimes I blame my mother for letting him. Then I blame myself for not leaving it."

"If you feel that way about it, why *don't* you leave it?" Julia looked at him curiously. Harsh lines had appeared beside his mouth and the muscles in his jaw stood out prominently. He looked older than his nineteen years.

"There's nothing for me ashore." His voice was harsh as he reached up with a long arm and snapped a pine cone from a nearby tree. "I'll keep going to sea until I die. I know that. And I hate it."

"Hate it? The sea?" She, too, watched the horizon-bound ships, their clouds of white sails pulling at her, calling her. The longing, which never left her, deepened. "I love it."

When he didn't answer, she looked up at him. "Are you afraid of it?"

"Sometimes. Anyone who isn't afraid of it at one time or other is a fool."

"And the other times?"

"The other times?" He tossed the pine cone up and caught it in his hand. "Sometimes it's beautiful. With the wind on the quarter. The sails all setting perfectly. The bow wave curling green and white. Is that what you mean?"

"Yes."

"That's when I hate it most of all," he said vehemently.

"Why?" The violence in his voice startled her.

"Because I know the sea. I know that, beneath that beautiful surface, there's nothing but treachery and evil, waiting to trap a man."

"We should trade places," Julia said. "You should be me. Stay ashore and build ships. I should be you and go to sea."

"No," he said moodily. "I'm not content on land."

"Then you *are* happy at sea?"

"Not happy. It's just where I belong."

"And yet you hate it?"

"Yes."

"I don't understand."

"And you won't till you've spent eight years out there. Eight years!" He flung the pine cone over the bank. "It seems more like eight lifetimes."

"You certainly are strange," she said. And he was. She knew a lot of men who hated the sea, but they didn't say that was where they belonged. They made their fortunes quick as they could and left it. Others didn't even bother to wait for their fortunes. They just left. Like some of the men in the shipyard and some in the saltworks.

"Perhaps," Jason said. They started walking down the hill to the shipyard. "But my father's even stranger. After all these years, he still loves the sea. I think he loves it most when it does its worst. Says he like a good fight. Likes to win."

"And you don't?"

"No. After a bad storm, I'm just worn out, disgusted, drained. It's terrible. Worse if someone's been lost overboard or injured."

"Does your father know how you feel?" She could see Cousin William now, standing and talking with her father beside the new packet they were building.

"No. I don't want him to know. He's proud of me. Thinks I'm just like him."

"Maybe when you're master of your own ship, you'll feel different."

"Maybe."

They walked on and entered the bustle of the shipyard in silence. The brightness of the morning was gone. It would be just another workday for Julia.

Jason felt it, too.

"Look," he said as they neared the office. "Let's forget about the sea. It feels so good to have land under my feet. While I'm here, will you show me around?"

She looked at him, puzzled. After their conversation, she hadn't expected he'd want to spend much time with her.

"Will you?" The bitterness on his face had been replaced by a gentle yearning. It was hard to resist him.

"All right. What do you want to see?"

"Oh, the woods and fields. I'd like to explore them. With you. It'd be a memory I could take back with me. Something to think on when all I can see are stars and black sky and black water. Something for the long night watches."

"We could go up Scargo Hill," she said thoughtfully. "If you climb a tree, you can see all over the Cape from there."

"You don't climb trees!" His voice was lightly mocking again.

"I certainly do!"

"When was the last time you climbed one?"

"Why, it was only . . ." She tried to think back. "Only about a year or so ago." Could it be that long?

"Julie, Julie, you're growing up. Only children climb trees." He looked younger when he smiled. His green eyes were lit with teasing laughter.

"Want to bet?"

"Yes."

"Then I'll show you."

She led the way across the yard to the shore of Sesuit Creek, where her father and Cousin William were deep in conversation.

"Papa, can I have the afternoon off so I can take Jason up Scargo Hill? I want to show him the view."

"Well, I guess if you have to." Benjamin turned to William and winked. "That's the trouble of having relatives working for you. They always want special favors."

Chapter Five

1836

As SOON AFTER DINNER as they could escape, Jason and Julia left the house. Avoiding the road, they walked through fields that still held the sweet warmth of summer, though fall was on the way. Bees buzzed frantically about them in search of the last crops of honey; and the mingled scents of clover and poverty grass, bayberry, bearberry, wild plum, and woodbine rose all around them.

Jason, released from the sights and sounds of the sea, the interminable talk of ships and voyages, walked gaily beside her, still a boy with his youth regained. He would pause to pluck a leaf from a wild azalea, and crushing it between his fingers, would raise it to his nose to sniff its acrid, sweet aroma. Then an almost blissful look would suffuse his face. Or he would gather a handful of pungent, waxy grey bayberries to roll in his hand and eventually stuff into his pocket. He delighted in the thornbriars and the black alders that grew on the edges of the marsh. Occasionally when they passed a granite boulder, he would trail his fingers along its rough crevices. He seemed as happy here in the midst of land as Julia was when she walked the tideline between sand and sea.

"You really miss it, don't you?" she asked, watching him pick a blackberry the birds had missed.

"What?" He popped the berry into his mouth.

"The land."

"Yes. I miss the land and the woods and the sight of a pretty girl." The smile he gave her was young and free, his green eyes clear and candid beneath their dark peaked brows.

"And yet you've seen so many lands. They must be more beautiful than this."

"It's a long time between them. Most of what you see is water. For weeks and months at a time, nothing but water. And I'll tell you something pretty Julie." He took her hand to help her across a rock-strewn stream. "There's no place more beautiful than this."

She laughed. "I can't believe that."

"It's true. The place where you're born, where you've grown up; it's the most beautiful place in the world. When we're homeward bound, even before I can sight the Cape, I can smell it. I can smell this." He waved his free hand around, including the hills and trees and the rough pasture in his gesture. "Then I know I'm home."

Julia enjoyed Jason's pleasure in the land, but after they had forded the stream, she became slowly aware of a disturbing undercurrent that threaded through the afternoon. Once he had taken her hand to help her across the rocks, he had not let it go. He kept it firmly in his. She didn't understand why it distressed her so. Distressed and delighted.

When they reached the foot of Scargo Hill, she could bear it no longer. She took advantage of a sudden turn in the path and pulled away from him. She ran up the sandy path ahead of him. Jason, with his long legs, quickly caught up with her.

"Hey, slow down," he said. "We're not racing anyone."

He reached for her hand, but she snatched it away.

"No, don't," she said.

"Why not?"

"I don't know."

He stepped in front of her then, blocking the way.

"Don't you, pretty Julie?" He put his arm around her and tilted her chin up to meet his gaze. His flickering green eyes held light amusement and something deeper, denser, rather frightening.

She tried to pull away, but he held her fast.

"Let me go, Jason."

"Why?"

"Because I said so."

He smiled, but the amusement had faded when he leaned down to kiss her lightly on the lips. It was so unexpected she didn't have time to duck. His lips were warm and gentle and the smell of his skin richly clean.

"Who are you afraid of, Julie? Me? Or yourself?" he asked when he lifted his lips from hers, for he had felt her instinctive response in the kiss.

"I'm not afraid." But she was. "I thought you wanted to see Scargo Hill."

"I do." He released her.

She picked up her skirts and hurried up the hill, but he easily caught up with her.

After a few moments, he said, "You don't have to run away from me, Julie. I'm sorry if I upset you."

"You didn't."

"It's just that I like you very much."

"I know."

"And you'll forgive me?"

She slowed her step and looked up at him, expecting to find that amused twinkle she was beginning to dislike very much. Instead, his eyes were sober and his mouth was set in a straight line, emphasizing the hollows under his high cheekbones. The boyishness was gone and he looked as disciplined as he had at the shipyard this morning.

"Yes. I'll forgive you."

"Is that the first time anyone ever kissed you like that?"

"I don't want to talk about it."

"Is it?"

"Yes."

"Then I really am sorry."

"It's all right."

"How far is it to the top of the hill?"

"Not far."

The path narrowed and he dropped behind to follow her. She could still feel his lips on hers, and she pressed them tight together to stop the tingling. A kiss had never affected her this way before, but then the light brush of her mother's lips, the firm, fleeting contact of her father's were not the same thing. She knew it was wrong, but she yearned for him to do it again. She sensed a certain danger . . . as well as pleasure . . . in the company of this cousin who was still a stranger. And the danger lay not just in him but within herself.

Deciding it was best to go home, she glanced back over her shoulder. He was walking with his hands jammed in his pockets, looking down at the needle-strewn ground. He was frowning and all his earlier, joyful exuberance was gone. He looked lonely and sad, not dangerous at all.

"Jason."

"Yes?" He looked up at her, and there was such a lost forlornness in his face.

"Why don't you walk beside me?"

"The path is too narrow."

"No, it isn't." She held her hand out to him. "Not if we walk close together."

He caught her hand and joy came flooding back to his face.

"But don't try to kiss me again."

"I won't." He matched his step to hers. "Not until you want me to."

They walked silently up the hill, and Julia wondered if she hadn't done the wrong thing in offering him her hand. Even his touch was different from any other touch.

Blue jays and sparrows were calling in the trees, and the pungent smell of pine mingled with the heathery, sandy smell of the earth. Julia was aware of these things as she had never been before. She wondered if, because Jason held her hand, she was seeing things through his eyes, smelling them and hearing them as he did.

When they reached the top, Julia paused in the clearing.

"We're here?" Jason asked.

"Yes. We're here."

"I'm sorry."

"Why?"

"Because I wanted to keep walking up that hill with you forever."

"Oh." Julia didn't really know what to say. "Well, it's even nicer here at the top."

"I hope so." He was looking at her again with that terrible intensity that both flattered and upset her.

"It is," she said. "Come on. I'll show you the lake."

She dropped his hand and scrambled through the underbrush. Jason followed quickly behind her.

"There it is," she said, stepping between two pine trees. She pointed at the large oblong of blue far below them. "Scargo Lake."

"Fresh water?"

"Yes. They cut ice there in winter."

"Are there any fish?"

"Lots of them. In fact, there's a story about the fish and the lake and the hill. Would you like to hear it?"

He was leaning against one of the scrub pines, his arms folded in front of him, looking down the hill.

"If you want to tell me," he said.

Julia sat down on a fallen log and clasped her hands in her lap. Out of the corner of her eye, she could see the beaches, the Bay, the arms of sand and rock reaching out from the coves, beckoning the passing ships, but she ignored them and concentrated on the lake.

"It was a long time ago, when the Indians still lived here," she began. "There was a princess named Scargo, and her father, Sagam, was chief of the Nobscusset tribe."

Jason sat down on the log next to her and stretched his long legs out before him. His attention was intensely focused on Julia and not on the lake below. The hill and trees and birds and brush were to him only a setting for the dark-haired girl beside him. Julia glanced at him, then looked quickly away.

"When Scargo was born, her mother died," Julia continued, "and Sagam was broken-hearted because she had been beautiful and he loved her. But he still had his little daughter, Scargo, who was the image of her mother, and Sagam swore he would never let her heart be broken the way his had been."

A breeze had sprung up, blowing Julia's hair around her face in a blue-black cloud. As she pushed it back, Jason caught one of her curls and wound it around his finger.

"Was she as beautiful as you are?" he asked.

"More. Much more."

"That's not possible."

"Well, she was. In fact, as she grew up, she became more and more beautiful, and suitors from all the tribes of the Cape came to court her. But she fell in love with only one, the strongest, handsomest, staunchest brave of them all."

"Did he love her?" Jason now had two of her curls in his possession.

"Of course, he did."

"And they were married and lived happily ever after." His clear green eyes were teasing.

"No." Julia frowned and edged a little bit away from Jason. "Just before they were to be married, the brave was sent on a long, dangerous journey by his chief."

"That hardly seems fair."

Julia looked at him and noticed for the first time two thin white scars on his face. One ran up beside his right eye and passed through his peaked black eyebrow to his forehead. The other slanted across his left cheek. She wanted to trace them with her finger, to ask him how he had gotten them, but she continued her story.

"And he had to go. But before he left, he took a large pumpkin and carved it out. He filled it with fresh water and put some little perch and trout into it. Then he gave it to Scargo and told her that, as long as the fish lived, he would live, too."

"Did he?" Jason moved down the log, closer to her. Julia caught her breath.

"I'm not sure I'm going to tell you. Are you interested in me or the story?"

"Both."

"Well, don't come any closer."

"I won't," he said, but his eyes said that he lied. "What happened next?"

"He went away and the fish grew bigger. Scargo missed him, but as long as the fish lived, she knew he lived, too." Julia bit her lip. She could feel the warmth of Jason's lean body so close to hers. It was hard to concentrate on the story.

"After he'd been gone a long time," she continued, "the fish got too big for the pumpkin. So Scargo went down to a stream of fresh water that flowed near her tepee and dug a pond for them. They seemed happy there and got bigger and bigger."

"That's always a good sign," Jason said.

Julia looked at him and realized he now had a whole handful of her hair and was twining it round and round his fingers.

"Are you trying to scalp me?"

"No. I'm just borrowing it."

"Well, you can just give it back."

"Now? I can see Scargo much better when I hold it. Besides, it keeps it out of your face."

"Well, all right, but don't take any more. You have enough."

"You were telling me about Scargo."

"Are you sure you want to hear it?"

"Definitely. I want to know what happened to the brave and his fish."

Julia looked at him skeptically, but his face was completely serious and intent. Intent on what? she wondered.

"Well, everything went all right till summer came and with it a drought. Then the pond began to dry up and the fish started dying. So Scargo tried to deepen her pond. She dug all day everyday until her hands were raw, but she couldn't get enough water to keep the fish from dying."

"Sounds bad. As though the brave's not going to make it."

"It *was* bad. Scargo was afraid he was going to die, and so was her father. Then Sagam swore once again he wouldn't let her heart be broken. So he called in all his tribe, and when they were assembled, he told them they had to dig a large pond for Princess Scargo's fish. An arrow shot in each direction would determine its size, and Scargo was to choose the biggest, strongest brave she could find. So she chose the biggest, strongest brave she could find."

"Naturally." Jason was now so close his arm was touching her shoulder. She looked up and saw a yearning in his green eyes.

"He shot the arrows," Julia went on quickly, "farther than any arrows had ever been shot before, one to each point of the compass. But Scargo thought one arrow had fallen short, so that night she stole out of her tent and moved it. That's why the lake is longer, you see."

"Were her eyes as blue as yours?" Jason asked.

"No. She was an Indian. They were brown."

"Too bad."

"Why?"

"Because then you could say her eyes were as deep and blue as the waters of the lake. Like yours." He slid an arm around her waist. When she looked up, he was smiling. She knew she should tell him to take his arm away, but he looked so happy. Besides, she had to admit she rather liked the feel of it there.

"Is the story over?" he asked.

"No. The drought continued, and the Indians dug and dug with their clamshells all through the summer. They piled the sand up here. That's how they made Scargo Hill. But the fish kept dying. Come fall, Scargo had only a few left. With fall, though, the rains came and filled up the hole the Indians had dug, and Scargo put her perch and trout into the new lake. They're still there today. Thousands of them."

Julia leaned her head back against Jason's shoulder and gazed out over the lake. It was so comfortable and seemed so natural. She felt terribly lazy.

"So the fish are still alive. But what happened to Scargo and her brave?" Jason asked, holding her closer, his chin brushing against the top of her head.

"She's still here, waiting. On a moonlight night, you can see her standing right here, watching over her fish."

"And the brave never came back?"

"He's still coming." Julia looked at the lower hills that rolled on beyond the lake, with all their varied greens of late summer. Here and there a tinge of color appeared where a tree was preparing for fall.

Jason gently brushed her hair away from her face.

"And you, Julie? Will you keep my fish alive for me?"

She looked up at him, understanding and yet not sure.

"Will you?"

His green eyes almost seemed to slant upward over his flushed cheeks. They were warm and so intense she felt as though she were falling through them, becoming part of what lay beyond and beneath them. As he bent his head, she lifted her face and lips to him. She closed her eyes in a sweet ecstasy of soft lips and strong arms. Her breath was filled with his, and the hard, fast pounding of his heart matched her own.

When they slowly parted, she looked at him, bewildered.

"Oh, Julie." His voice was no more than a husky whisper. "Keep my fish for me. Wait for me to come back."

"No, no! I can't." She jumped up from the log, but he was as quick as she. He caught her arm.

"Julia, I'm asking you to marry me."

"I know. Let me go," she said, jerking her arm away from him and running through the brush, which caught at her skirt.

"Julia, I'm sorry," he called close behind her, but she ran on, ducking through a low screen of trees and taking a secret path few knew about.

Halfway down the hill, she found a group of bushes that provided what had been one of her favorite hiding spots when she was younger. She crawled into the center of them and sat down. Putting her hands to her flaming cheeks, she tried to cool them.

Then slowly, she tried to understand what had happened. It had been so fast, not at all the way she'd imagined a man would court her. How could she have let it happen? But it had seemed so natural.

She wasn't even sure how she felt about him. She liked him. But the way he had talked about the sea? He was awfully handsome. And she shivered as she thought how strong his arms had felt around her, how gentle his lips and so warm. She wanted to be with him again, to have him hold her, but she was afraid of him. Afraid of the hot trembling of her own body.

How could she ever face him again? How would she explain it to her parents when she arrived home without him? She couldn't possibly tell them what had happened. Of course, he may have gone on home ahead of her. Or was he looking for her?

She listened, but heard nothing except the wind in the tops of the pines and the screeching protest of a blue jay. Slowly she got to her feet and tried to straighten her hair and dress as well as she could. She was tempted to go down to the beach, but there was no use putting it off. She'd figure out something by the time she got home.

But when she reached the road, Jason was there, waiting for her.

"Julie!" he said when he saw her emerging from the trees. "I would have come searching for you, but I didn't know where to look."

"There's no need," she said, looking down at the sandy path so that she could avoid those penetrating eyes.

"But I wanted to talk to you. I *have* to talk to you."

"There's nothing to talk about."

"There is." He moved closer, but when she backed away, he stopped and spread his outstretched hands toward her. "I'm sorry. I was wrong, but I guess I just couldn't help myself. You're so beautiful and . . . and I do love you."

She looked at his hands and then up at his face. The high bones of his cheeks and the lines beside his mouth stood out sharply in the light of late afternoon. He looked older, much older, and yet his green eyes looked young with pleading pain.

"You hardly know me," she said.

"I know you, Julie. Please don't be angry. I want you so much. You're the only girl I've ever wanted to marry."

"You're only a mate," she said, looking away from him again.

"But I'll be a master soon . . . in a couple of years. I'll take you to sea with me then, Julie," he promised.

"Don't ask me any more, Jason. Please! Just don't ask." She wanted to run from him again, but he was blocking the road.

"Well, will you show me some more sights, then?" he asked quietly. "If I promise not to touch you again?"

"It's getting late. We have to get on home."

"Tomorrow?"

"I have to work tomorrow." She turned her back on him and looked up the hill. The sun would soon be setting.

"You're saying you don't want to be with me anymore."

She clenched her hands together and held her breath. Why? Why did he frighten her so? He was really gentle and kind, and she guessed that he was as upset as she was.

"I . . . I'm not saying that," she said. "I just . . . just . . . I don't know. Give me time, Jason."

"Then you might say yes?" There was an uplift of hope in his voice.

"I'm not saying anything of the sort."

She turned and looked up at him and saw again the pain in his eyes that she couldn't handle. She quickly darted past him and started walking down the road at a fast pace, which he easily matched.

That evening, she ignored Jason and concentrated her attentions on Cousin William and his sea stories. But even when he was in the most exciting part of a tale, her mind would wander back to the afternoon. Then she would look up to find Jason's eyes on her. She excused herself, saying that she was tired, and went to bed early, but after Sarah had come to bed with her, she lay awake and tried to understand why she longed so for Jason, why she still felt the tingling touch of his lips on hers.

For several days, she was able to avoid Jason by pretending to be immersed in her work at the shipyard, but often she would forget what she was doing and then she would find that her eyes had involuntarily sought him out.

Jason, though he watched her in return, left her alone with her thoughts.

Then one evening in the shadowless time of twilight, when she and her father and Cousin William were returning home from the shipyard, they met Jason and Sarah on the road.

Julia, even from afar, could see that they were laughing and talking easily, as though they had been old friends. She continued to walk beside her father, but she felt as though her entire body, from her lips to her feet, was numb. Each step was an effort and she wondered if she could take another one.

Had Jason kissed Sarah, too? Up on Scargo Hill? Or had they chosen another spot? But Sarah was too young for Jason. She had just turned fourteen. But she looked older.

But Jason had proposed to *her,* Julia. How could he so easily forget? He probably hadn't meant it. Besides, she hadn't agreed. She had no right to him. But she wanted him. He wasn't Sarah's. He was hers.

"Hello," Sarah said gaily as she met them. "Jason and I have been having the nicest walk. I've been showing him all the sights."

"Well, that's grand," Cousin William said and looked at

his son, who had suddenly become silent. "There's nothing like a good walk before supper."

"Oh, we've been walking all afternoon," Sarah said. "Of course, we sat down a few times to give ourselves a rest. Jason's been telling me all about the exciting times he's had at sea. It must be marvelous to be a man and have all those adventures."

"They're not that exciting," Jason said quietly.

"Oh, but they are. It's just that you're so used to leading an exciting life you don't realize how it sounds to stay-at-homes like us."

Julia looked down at a patch of poverty grass by the side of the road. She didn't want to see Sarah's sparkling eyes or fluttering eyelashes, but she was very much aware that Jason was looking at her, Julia. As they walked on down the road together, Jason managed to walk next to her. He said little, but she could hear Sarah chattering away on his other side.

Well, if it was Sarah he preferred, she thought angrily, let him have her. She quickened her step and caught up with her father.

The next morning, she was at the shipyard at dawn. Sleep hadn't come easily during the night, and when she had finally dozed off, her dreams had been restlessly filled with Jason. A light breeze had sprung up with the coming of day, and its coolness whispered against her skin. There wouldn't be many such days left, she thought as she untied the bowline of her dory. Already the mornings were colder.

"Do you have room for a passenger?"

It was Jason's voice. She froze for a moment. Heard, without seeing him, his husky voice had a special magically compelling quality of its own. She turned and looked up at him. He gave her a smile that was no smile, for his eyes were too serious.

"Are you sure you wouldn't rather be with Sarah?" she asked acidly and then wondered why she had said that. She wanted to be with him. Why was she trying to drive him away?

"No. I wanted to see you," he said quietly.

"You followed me," she accused him.

"Yes, I did. I wanted to know where you went so early every morning."

"Now you know." She slipped the final loop of the line off the piling, giving it all of her attention.

"That's a nice boat," he said, looking down at the lap-straked dory.

"It should be. I built it."

"You're still angry with me, aren't you?" he said, looking back at her with eyes that seemed to be trying to read her every secret.

"No," she answered coldly. "Why should I be? It's just a habit with you, kissing every girl who comes along."

"That's not true, Julie, and you know it's not."

"Then what about Sarah?" She looked up at the sail that was slatting in the breeze.

"What about Sarah?"

"You kissed her, too."

"I did not. She's just a little girl."

"You two certainly looked as though you were having a good time."

"I got tired of hanging around the shipyard when you wouldn't even speak to me. Then Sarah offered to show me around, and I went with her."

"No reason why you shouldn't."

He took the line from her hand. "You get in and I'll shove off."

"Maybe I've changed my mind. Maybe I'm not going sailing after all."

"Stop being so stubborn, Julia. You know you came down here for a sail. If you don't want me along, I won't insist."

Without looking at him, she stepped into the boat. "You can come if you want to." All of her attention was focused on the sheet as she uncoiled it.

The dory rocked forward under his weight as he climbed in. Sitting on the midship thwart, he faced aft, even though he had trouble finding room for his long legs.

"Are you mad at me because I kissed you or are you mad at me because of Sarah?" he asked as they tacked across the creek.

"I haven't made up my mind yet," she said, pushing the

91

tiller hard over, "and if you don't keep down, you're going to have an aching head."

"Are you going to teach me how to sail, pretty Julie?" he asked as he ducked under the swinging boom. His green eyes were teasing now.

"The way you talked about the sea, you might need a few lessons," she said, forgiving him for everything, for anything.

"So that's it! Well, I promise I'll never say anything derogatory about the sea again. I should have known better than to speak to a mermaid that way."

"Would you like to take it?" she asked as they sailed out the inlet into the Bay.

"Are you sure you trust me?"

"I'm just checking you out. After all, I'm not going to go around the world with a man who doesn't know how to sail."

"Oh, I can sail, pretty Julie," he said as they simultaneously changed places in the small dory. He sheeted in the sail and set the boat on a new course. "It's the only thing I can do, but I do it well." Then he suddenly realized the full import of her words. "Did you mean that about sailing around the world with me?"

"I said I'm checking you out." She kept a straight face, but he could see that her eyes were lightening to a sapphire blue. He was beginning to be able to read the signs.

"Well? What do you think?"

She studied the set of the sail, then looked at the angle of the waves as they met the bow.

"You've got the makings," she said.

"Of what—a sailor, or a husband?" His eyes were narrowed against the rising sun as he watched the wind moving across the water.

Julia thought about it. Again everything seemed to be moving too fast. "A sailor," she said. "The rest takes more time."

"I don't have much time, Julia. I'm going back to sea soon and I won't be home for a couple of years."

"I know," she said quietly, studying his face. He would go back to sea, and in every port there would be another pretty girl. She had overheard men talking, and she knew that, for someone as goodlooking as Jason, the girls would not be hard to find.

"Can we talk about it later?" she asked.

"As long as there is a later," he said, grinning at her. Then he turned his attention to a sudden shift of the wind.

Julia watched him. His long, lean body seemed completely relaxed in the stern of the boat, yet he was alert to every puff of breeze that traveled over the water, anticipating with precision the exact moment to take advantage of it. The dory, quivering and alive, as though one with the water and the wind, had never sailed so well as it did under Jason's expert handling. Julia could feel the boat singing under her, the waves singing with the hard diamond light of early morning, the breeze singing through her hair. The unity she had often felt with sail and sea was greater than it had ever been before, for Jason was a part of her completion.

She smiled at him with quiet joy, and when he smiled back, she knew that he was the one, the one who had been coming all of her life.

During the next few afternoons, they roamed the fields and hills, the villages, and the shore together. One morning, they rode over to Brewster. While Jason laid flowers on his mother's grave, Julia, wandering through the cemetery, looked at the tombstones and their inscriptions. So many were so young, she thought. How much living can you do in such a short time?

Then she looked across the green grass to where Jason stood, his head bowed above the flowers, and she understood so much more. Why he rushed into things, into life. Why he savored each moment they spent wandering. Why he looked at each tree, each flower as though he had never seen one before.

"Would you like to see the house?" he asked when she rejoined him. "It's not far."

"Yes," she said quietly. "I'd like to see it."

The low, rambling, grey-shingled house looked desolate with its shutters up and its flower beds containing only a few neglected roses. Jason pulled a key from his pocket.

"Would you like to go in?"

Julia glanced at the large brass key, shining in the palm

of his hand. "You planned on coming here when we left home?"

"Yes. I wanted to show it to you. It will be mine someday."

Because of the shuttered windows, it was dark when he opened the door, and Julia hesitated on the doorstep. Jason pulled her into a small entrance hall and said, "Wait here, I'll get a light."

As Julia stood waiting for him, she looked around the small room with its short flight of steps leading to the encased stairway. She knew why he wanted her to see the house. If she married him, this would be her home. What would it be like to open this door and walk in, knowing every room, the contents of every cupboard and drawer?

"I want you to be able to see everything," Jason said, when he returned with a candle in a brass holder.

He nodded at the closed door at their left and said, "That's my parents' room. We won't go in there, but come see if you like the parlor." He held out his free hand and she took it.

There was something sad about the dust sheets over the furniture and the smell of mustiness in the air. As she followed him through the parlor and the dining room that lay behind it, Julia tried to visualize the house when it was alive and filled with voices and people. The kitchen was more cheerful with its stone fireplace and the pots and pans that still hung from the walls.

"The pantry and summer kitchen are out there," he said, nodding at a door in the far wall and putting the candle on the table. "Then there are two bedrooms upstairs. One of them mine and the other Samuel's.

"What do you think of it?" he asked, slipping his arm around her waist. It was hard to read his face in the flickering shadows thrown by the candle, but she could hear the anxiety in his voice.

"I think it's very nice," she said noncommittally.

"I know it's not as large as *your* family's."

"That doesn't matter. It would probably be very comfortable if we were to open the shutters and let some fresh air blow in for a while."

"Julie, I wanted so very much for you to like it."

"I do." She reached up and lightly touched the scar that slanted across his left cheek. "How did that happen?"

"I got hit by a belaying pin when I was about fourteen."

"On purpose?" she asked, horrified. "Did someone hit you?"

"Yes, the second mate." Then when he saw the look on her face, he added, "Those things happen, Julie. You should know that."

Yes, she thought, I should, but she ached for the boy who had had his cheek laid open by a man's anger. She traced the line that ran through his eyebrow to his forehead.

"And this? Was it the same man?"

"No. That happened about a year later. A block got loose in a storm. I just happened to be in the wrong place."

"It could have blinded you!"

"But it didn't." He took her hand away from his face and kissed her fingers. "Does it really bother you so much?"

"I don't like the thought of your being hurt," she said softly.

"You know how to keep me from harm, Julie," he whispered and his arm tightened around her as he bent to kiss her.

She started to turn her face away, but then she found she couldn't and her lips were seeking his as eagerly as his sought hers. His arms were strong about her, holding her safe, and the mustiness of the house was dispelled by his clean, rich scent. It was a private world where they fit together and belonged together. Nothing evil could touch them in this close embrace.

"Those fish, Julie," he said huskily as he drew his lips away from hers. "You *have* to keep them for me."

"I will." She reached up and ran her fingers through his coarse black hair, feeling it spring up under her touch. "But you mustn't keep me waiting as long as her brave has kept Scargo."

"I won't. I promise." His voice was stronger now, but even by candlelight she could see his face was passionately pale and serious. "It will only be a couple of years."

"And then you'll be master of your own ship?"

"I hope so."

"And you'll take me with you?"

"Yes." He tenderly kissed her brow, her nose, her eyelids. "I'd never leave you behind."

Julia smiled with the contentment of a cat and nestled her head against a hollow in his shoulder. It seemed to have been made for just that purpose. Jason brushed her hair back and held her face close to him, feeling the softness of her cheek through his long fingers.

"Maybe you'll teach me to love the sea," he said. "Maybe it takes a mermaid."

"I'm not really," she whispered.

"I'm not sure you're not." He ran his fingers lightly over her skin, memorizing the feel of her nose and chin, her cheeks and her eyebrows. "You must be magic or you couldn't bewitch me so."

It was dusk when they returned to the house. Everyone was home and gathered in the parlor. William was entertaining them with one of his sea stories as Julia and Jason entered the room.

He was stopped short by the radiance of their two faces.

"Did you have a nice day?" he asked.

"Yes," his son answered. "We went over to Brewster and then up Scargo Hill to see the sunset over the lake."

"Oh, yes. Good fishing there," William said and wondered just what kind of fishing had been going on.

"Good afternoon for it," Benjamin said and, saddened, thought, so this is the one. I only hope he's good enough for her. Too early. Too young. Perhaps he's just the first.

"Yes, sir, it was a fine afternoon," Jason replied.

"It was just glorious!" Julia said, unable to contain her elation.

Sarah watched them silently and thought, so she's gotten *him*, too. I might have known.

"You looked flushed, darling. You'd better run up and change for supper," Lydia said and thought, so she's finally growing up. Now she'll forget the shipyard and settle down, even if it is with a sailor.

"Did you bring home any berries?" Amelia asked, thinking nothing except how pretty Julie looked.

"No. We didn't look for any, Amelia. You're right, Mama. I'll go on upstairs right now."

"And don't mess up my room!" Sarah said sharply.

"I won't, Sarah." Julia was too happy to remember her worry over her sister, and in her joy, she loved the whole world, even Sarah.

After supper, as they left the table, Jason asked Benjamin if he could speak to him privately.

"Of course, of course," Benjamin answered jovially, though he had a sinking feeling that he knew exactly what the lad had in mind. "Come into my study. We can talk there."

After Jason had tensely settled himself in the chair, Benjamin asked, "What's on your mind?"

"It's Julia, sir."

"What about Julia?"

"I would like your permission to marry her."

"And how does Julia feel about this?"

"Well, she hasn't told me she'd marry me, not in so many words, but I believe she will."

"What makes you think so?" Benjamin touched his fingers together and studied their tips.

"Well, sir, I just do."

"What was going on over at Brewster and up on Scargo Hill today?" Benjamin lowered his hands and leaned forward, all the captain now, interrogating one of his mates.

"Oh, nothing wrong, sir. Believe me. I wouldn't hurt Julia. I want to take care of her."

"Tell me again, then. What makes you think she'll marry you?"

"Well, sir." Jason forced himself not to fidget under Benjamin's close scrutiny. "She said she'd go to sea with me."

"Didn't know you were a master. Thought you were a mate."

"I am, sir. But she said when I got my own ship, she'd come with me."

"Julia'd say that to anyone who asked her to go to sea. Don't mean she's in love with them or wants to marry them. She's just sea-crazy."

"I know, sir, but it was more than that. She . . . she said she'd wait for me." He looked down at the flowered carpet.

"We're talking about a young girl, Jason, a very young

girl," Benjamin said gently, not wanting to be too hard on the lad.

"Yes, sir."

"Do you know how old she is?"

"Seventeen?"

"No. Just turned sixteen. Too young to be thinking about marriage."

"A lot of girls marry at sixteen. My own mother did."

"Maybe some do. But not Julia. She's not ready for it."

"Well, sir, we love each other. I'd take good care of her."

"As I recollect, you're sailing next month."

"Yes, sir."

"Then how do you propose to take care of her? You on one side of the globe and she on the other?"

"We wouldn't have to be married right now, sir. Not till I come home again. Just as long as I know she's waiting for me."

"A couple of years?"

"Yes, sir."

"And what makes you think Julie wouldn't meet some other young man she fancied more in the meantime?"

"I don't know. But I don't believe she would."

"And what makes you so sure you'll be master next time out?"

Jason drew himself up straight and met Benjamin's look with strength and sureness. "Because I'm a good mate, and I'll make a good captain."

Benjamin chuckled. "Well, on that score, damned if I don't believe you."

Then he became grave again. "But I won't have my Julie tied down this young, not even by a betrothal. She doesn't know her own mind yet. Yesterday she was still a child. Today it looks like she's done a little growing up, thanks to you. But you're the first young man she's shown any interest in, and I think she'd better spend a little time looking over the field."

"But I love her, sir."

"I'm sure you do. It's pretty hard not to. I love her, myself. I'm just saying she doesn't know her own mind yet. She's my daughter, and I have to protect her."

"I think I have very good prospects, sir, and my family's not badly off."

"I probably know more about your father's finances than you do. I'm not saying you're not a very eligible young man. If it was a year or two from now, I'd probably say yes right off, but it's not a year or two from now. It's now."

He got up and put his hand on Jason's tense shoulder. "Look, son, you're both young with long lives ahead of you. There's no need to rush into this. When you come back after this voyage, we'll discuss the matter further. You have my permission to court her meantime. But nothing out of bounds. You understand me?"

"Yes, sir, I do. I'll be mighty careful. You see, sir," he said earnestly, "I really do love her."

"Right. Long as you understand. Now let's join the rest of the family. No need to mention this to anyone."

"Yes, sir."

But, of course, when they entered the parlor, everyone had a pretty good idea what they'd been talking about, and everyone studied the two men's faces. Both, with long years of training at sea, remained expressionless and completely unreadable.

Julia, who had risen and come halfway across the room when the study door opened, stopped and looked at them, puzzled. Papa, she knew, had put on a mask purposefully. But Jason! He should look either happy or unhappy, one. Yet he looked just like Papa.

Jason saw her look of bewilderment and he smiled at her.

"Would you like to take a walk and look at the stars?" he asked and was rewarded by seeing her expression change to joy.

"I'd think you'd have done enough walking for one day," her mother said.

"It's all right, Lydia," Benjamin said. "They won't go far or be long. Am I right, Jason?"

"Yes, sir. Just around the house."

Julia flashed her father a smile and ran to get her shawl. Jason followed more slowly, and as the front door clicked shut behind them, he took her hand.

"Oh, Jason, what did Papa say?"

"Well, he said I can't ask you to marry me."

"Oh, no!" Clutching his hand more tightly, she whirled

around to look up at him and tried to fathom his face in the shadows.

"But you do still want to?"

"Of course, I do!" he said fervently.

"Then we'll get married anyway. Papa can't stop us."

Jason pulled her under one of the big horse chestnuts by the road. He tilted her face and looked down at her lovely features, chiseled white by moonlight.

"I love you, Julie," he said earnestly.

"I know," she sighed. "I love you, too."

"But we can't get married right now. Not without your father's approval."

"Why not?"

"A number of reasons. First, you're under age. No minister would marry us without his permission."

"Oh, I bet I could find one."

"No. Oh, my darling." He pulled her tightly to him and, leaning down, buried his face in her billowing, sweet hair. "We can't."

When he straightened up, she could see, even by moonlight, that his eyes were wet with held-back tears. "I'm sailing soon, and if you ran away from your family, you'd be all alone in Brewster. I can't take you with me. Not yet."

"I can take care of myself."

"Oh, no, my sweet, no." He stroked her hair. "I couldn't bear to be at sea, knowing you were all alone with no one to take care of you. You must stay here."

"Well, Papa would take me back. I know he would."

"We can't take the chance, Julie."

"Well, either you want to marry me or you don't! Which is it?" she demanded and she drew back from him.

"You know I want to marry you. You just don't know how much. How *very* much."

"Well, I'll go convince Papa. He always does what I want." She turned to go, but he caught her and drew her close to him once more.

"Julie, I don't think it'll do any good. He was pretty determined. But he did say that, when I come home again, he'd probably agree."

"That's years from now!"

"I know. Oh, how I know. Don't you think that every single day, every single night, of those years I'm not going to be thinking of you and wondering if you've forgotten me? Wondering if you've found someone else? Decided that you love them more?"

"Jason! How can you think such a thing of me?"

"It's a long time, Julie, and there will be plenty of men coming around for you to pick from."

"Oh, Jason, never. There's no one else in the world like you. I've seen plenty of men, but never one like you. I couldn't love anyone else. I just couldn't."

"Nor could I."

"But let me go talk to Papa. I bet I can convince him."

"Not tonight. Stay with me awhile."

"It has to be tonight. We don't have much time." She pulled away from him and ran into the house.

Jason reached down and picked up one of the fallen chestnuts. He peeled it aimlessly. Perhaps she could convince her father. He had to agree with Benjamin. Julia was young to be married. Little more than a child, and yet he couldn't bear the thought of not securing her for his own before he sailed. Married, he would be sure that she was here waiting for him. Single and warm and beautiful, how could he know?

He wandered up in back of the house to the cutting garden that was dying back with the knowledge of coming winter. It was here, amongst the moonlight-grey withering flowers, that his father found him.

"You 'bout ready to tell me what's going on?" William asked gruffly.

"Hello, Papa," Jason said, tearing the petals off a dead marigold.

"Well?"

"I asked Cousin Benjamin if I could marry Julia."

"I suspicioned as much. Why didn't you consult with me first?"

"Didn't seem to be any need. I knew you'd approve."

"Naturally. But I could have given you a little advice on how to handle the matter. You seem to have botched it up for a fair."

"I have to grow up, Papa. I *have* grown up, and I've had to do it without your advice."

"Best way to do it. But damn it, this is a ticklish situation, and I've had a bit more experience than you have. Even you'll have to grant me that."

"Yes, sir."

"I gather the answer is no."

"Yes, sir."

"Well, while you've been mooning around out here, Julia came tearing in the house, mad as a hatter, and got her father closeted in the study. Couldn't hear what was said, but their voices were loud enough. Then she came tearing back out, slammed the door, and ran upstairs. Slammed that door, too."

"Oh." Jason crumbled the flower in his fist.

"You say you've grown up. I'm not so consarned sure of it. Letting a woman fight your battles for you!"

"Well, maybe I feel her father's partly right. Julie's awful young yet."

"In other words, you don't know whether you want her or not!"

"Of course, I want her!" Jason threw the flower away from him.

"Well, you don't act like it."

"She's just turned sixteen."

"Old enough!"

"I'm not sure."

"You're not sure of what, for God's sake?"

"That she's old enough."

"She's old enough! It's you I'm not so sure is old enough. If you want her, go get her. If you don't, leave her alone. You'll not get two chances at a girl like Julie. The only reason why you got the one chance is because you came along at the right moment."

"Then maybe it isn't right for me to take her. If it *is* just the moment and not because she truly loves me."

"Jason, you're being a fool! When I was your age, I fought for your mother. Do you think her father was willing to let me have her? Me, a poor boy, who'd, by luck, risen to be first mate? That's all I was when we were married, and she was only sixteen, too."

"Julie's still partly a child. Her father was right in that."

"Damn it, Jason!" William pounded his fist in his hand. "What you know about women would fill a thimble. Men take a long time in growing. A woman can grow up in one day, one night, or one afternoon. That's all the time it takes them."

"I guess you're right. I'll talk to her father again."

"Don't talk! Demand!" William stomped off toward the house, muttering to himself. If Jason lost Julia, 'twas his own damned fault. Serve him right. And if he wasn't man enough to fight for the girl, then he wasn't man enough to marry her, either. How do you tell your son that? 'Twould take a strong man to handle that one. She was no ordinary, docile lass. He wished he were twenty years younger. By God, he'd have the girl and no disputing that. He was still more a man than his son would ever be.

Chapter Six

1836

THE NEXT MORNING AT the breakfast table, Julia was subdued. Her cheeks were pale under her tan and dark shadows made her deep blue eyes seem larger than ever.

Her black hair was bound back by a blue ribbon, and she had taken greater pains than usual with her dress. She seemed almost as neat as Sarah. It made everyone a little uneasy.

Benjamin kept a steady flow of conversation going, but when he addressed Julia, she would answer only in monosyllables. After a while, he gave up and talked around her. But out of the corner of his eye, he watched as she picked at her food. For all her quiet manner, he knew that, underneath, she was smoldering. He was waiting for the explosion.

After breakfast he rose from the table and said, as he did almost every morning, "Well, time to be off to the yard, Julie."

"I'm not going," she said, turning her face away from him and staring out the window at the hills and fields beyond.

"And how's the work to get done?" He stood beside her

chair. If she was going to explode, might as well get it over with.

"Same way it always gets done when I'm not there," she said stiffly, refusing to turn her head to look at him.

Benjamin shrugged. He guessed she hadn't reached boiling point yet. "Reckon you deserve a vacation. If you feel like it later, come on down."

When he received no answer, he went into the front hall and reached for his coat. The early mornings were growing colder.

"You coming, Will? Jason?" he asked.

"I am," William said, taking his coat from the rack, "but I think Jason has some other plans for the morning." He followed Benjamin out of the house.

The air was crisp and sweet with autumn, and overnight, the trees had begun to flame. A rime of frost had appeared on the poverty grass, and patches of wild cranberries formed crimson pools around the edge of the marsh.

The two men, bundled in their warm coats, strode vigorously over the path across the marsh.

William saw no reason in postponing anything that could be met head on. "Ben," he said in his usual blunt manner, "I want to talk to you about Jason and Julie."

"I said last night all that's to be said." Benjamin's bushy black eyebrows were drawn together in a frown, and his chin was set as rigidly as the rocks in the far fields.

William studied his friend's face, but he wasn't about to be put off by Ben's stubbornness.

"And I think you're wrong," he said. "You remember what I told you years ago? That the first one that came along and offered Julie the sea, she'd follow?"

"I remember." Benjamin's lips were hard and tight.

"Well, he's come."

"And you brought him."

"Yes, I brought him." William watched a flight of ducks rise from a shallow pool in the marsh. " 'Twasn't with that intention, really."

"No?"

"Don't think so. Maybe 'twas in the back of my mind somewheres, but if so, I wasn't aware of it."

"Well, you can just take him away again." Benjamin's face was growing darker by the moment.

"It's out of my hands, now. And yours, too."

"The hell it is. I'm her father, and you're his father, and it's very much in our hands."

"Nope." William stroked his rough golden beard. "Time for that's past. Your Julie's grown up now. Sooner or later, you're going to have to let her go. Best be with a good lad like Jason, who'll treat her right and provide for her, than with some stranger you know nothing about."

"No!" Benjamin fumed. "She's too young."

"She's of the age when it happens."

"No," Benjamin repeated. "If they're of the same mind later on, that's another matter. *But not now.* I told them both as much last night. Your son seems to have sense enough to agree with me. Which is more than I can say for you."

"And in the meantime, while you're waiting for 'later,' she'll run off with that stranger. He'll take her straight away from you, Ben."

"I won't permit it. And I won't permit this, either. They hardly know each other. It's just their youth and hot blood."

"I think they know each other well enough," William said slowly. "After all, who ever really does know the woman he marries until the deed is done?"

"*I* knew." Benjamin was stonily stubborn.

"Did you, Ben?" William asked gently.

Glancing at his friend, Benjamin wondered how much William guessed about his relations with Lydia. Probably too much.

"All the more reason to be sure," he said.

"Can't be. I brought you a fine young man. He's my son and I'm proud of him. Not every father can say as much."

"Didn't say he wasn't."

"And they're related," William persisted. "Not close enough to be troublesome. Just close enough to be comfortable."

"I'm not objecting to that." Benjamin quickened his pace.

"He's got everything Julia wants and, I would think, everything even you could ask. Handsome enough to provide you with some good-looking grandchildren. Handy enough with a ship. When he takes Julie to sea with him, you won't have to worry about her safety. Smart enough

106

to build his own fortune. She'll be well provided for. And later on, he'll inherit a right good sum from me."

"The answer is still no."

When they reached the top of the hill, both men paused to look at the shipyard below, which was just beginning to come to life in the early morning sun.

"You don't want to let her go," William said, "and I don't blame you. But think on this. If they're married now, he can't take her with him. When he sails, she'll come back home. You won't be losing her for a few years yet."

"I'll not have her tied down so young. Maybe even a child to come when she's no more than a child herself."

"Sometimes they come and sometimes they don't. Besides, I never saw a child that did any harm. Might even be a boy you could raise to run the shipyard."

"The shipyard belongs to Julia," Benjamin said, starting down the hill. "She's still got a lot to learn, but no one, man or woman, will ever run it better than she."

"Ben, you'll drive her away from you if you keep on like this."

"No." Benjamin's tone moderated. "Not my Julie."

"You saw her this morning."

"She'll get over it."

"I'm not so sure about that. Trouble is you're both stubborn. Up to now, you've mostly agreed. Haven't had occasion to run head on into each other. This time it's different." William watched the screaming gulls following a fishing schooner into Sesuit Creek. "It's your own fault, Ben. You've encouraged her to be headstrong."

"I taught her to stand on her own feet and think for herself."

"That's what I mean, and that's exactly what she's doing. I'm not saying you were wrong, Ben. I'm just warning you. Don't turn her against you."

"I've said all I'm going to say, Will. Now do you want to see that new packet we're building or do you want to go on back home? I'll not discuss the matter further."

William grunted and followed Benjamin into the yard. "Packet it is, then."

As soon as the men had left, Lydia began her morning chores: directing the maids and her daughters, setting the house to rights. Feeling in the way in the house and useless in the gardens, Jason wandered about uncomfortably. He wished he had gone to the shipyard, but his father's warning had been clear enough. He was to stay away.

Lydia, noticing him through one of the windows, took pity on his aimless wandering. She liked her young cousin well enough and thought him a good match for Julia. The sooner the girl was wed, the better, as far as she was concerned. Otherwise there'd be trouble. She'd had enough worry over her these past few weeks.

She went into the study, which her daughter was supposed to be dusting. She found her staring out the window instead.

"Julie, why don't you go out and entertain Jason? Might pack a lunch and have a picnic later."

Julia dropped the feather duster and hugged her mother. "Oh, thank you, Mama. At least *you* understand." Leaving her mother to pick up the duster, she dashed out of the door.

Lydia shook her head as she watched her go and smiled to herself. It didn't seem so long ago that she, as young and lovely as Julia, had gone running out of another door to meet her handsome Benjamin coming up the path. What had happened to them, she wondered, those two young lovers? Somehow, they had disappeared, just evaporated over the years. Once in a while, she caught glimpses of her youthful, ardent husband, but he rarely appeared anymore. I suppose that is the way of life, she thought, and someday Julia will be standing in my place.

Well, she thought, flicking with the duster at the desk, it's a pity we must lose that blissful joy as we grow older, but there's a lot of comfort in it. At least, there's always our daughters to follow us. Oh, the trouble ahead for that child, though.

She shook her head and firmly turned her back on the past. She was no longer a young girl, but a matron now with a large house to run. She went out the study door to resume her duties.

Julia, released into sunlight, pulled the ribbon from her hair and picked up her long, full skirts, which were such a bother. She ran up the hill to the grape arbor. All morning, she had been constantly aware of Jason and had watched his wanderings. She had had a pretty good idea of where he was every single minute. And oh, how she had longed to go to him.

She saw him from the distance, half-hidden by the shadowy grape leaves. She paused.

"Jason," she called, "Jason, I'm free!" She pulled her skirts higher to clear the long grass and flew to meet him as he ran toward her.

"Oh, sweetheart," he said as they met and embraced.

She laughed in pure joy and exhilaration, her deep blue eyes sparkling, her cheeks flushed, and her cloud of black hair curling and floating behind her as she looked up at him.

He looked in wonder at this beauty that was his. His! He would not let her father or anyone else keep her from him!

"Jason." She looked hungrily at his lean, high-boned face, the strong cleft jaw, and the peaked black eyebrows that accented those beloved green eyes.

"I know. Oh, my Julie." He leaned down to meet her lips, gently at first, then stronger and stronger.

They felt all the world fall away from them as their breaths became one, the pulsing of their hearts one. There was no space to separate them. His arm and her back, his hand and her breast, their legs pressed together, were all one in a blending of glorious perfection. This was completion, and they were achingly aware that, until this moment, neither of them had been a truly complete person. Together they were one.

Eternities later, Jason released her lips.

"Oh, my Julie." His voice was husky and his eyes shone in wonder.

"Don't stop. Oh, don't stop," she pleaded. She was trembling.

"I must." His hand shook as he stroked her hair and pulled her head to his chest. "I must."

"No," she said, reaching up to pull his face down to hers.

"Julie . . ." The muscles in his jaw tightened in a tremendous effort of will. "Julie, you don't know where this leads."

"I do!"

"No!" He grasped her so tightly she couldn't breathe

and then suddenly let her go. He turned away from her and his shoulders were shaking. "You don't know."

She swung around in front of him and looked at him. Feeling rejection, she implored, "Jason."

He looked away from her at the rolling, wild, stone-walled fields beyond. "Julie, sweetheart," he said hoarsely. "I'm afraid of myself. Afraid for you. I only have so much control."

"It doesn't matter." Her eyes were blazing as blue as the sky overhead.

"It does." He took her hand, then instantly dropped it as though it burned him. "It can't happen till we're wed. Come on. Let's walk."

She reached for his hand, but he stopped her.

"Not yet. Wait a while. If you touch me now, I don't know what will happen."

"All right, Jason," she said, shaken but subdued by the force of his words.

He strode up the hill, over small rocks and through the brush. Julia followed, trying to match his long stride, the thorny bushes and tall weeds tearing at her skirts, holding her back. He was going away from her, leaving her.

"Jason, Jason. Wait for me!" she gasped.

He looked back to see her struggling through the brush.

"I'm sorry, sweet," he said contritely and turned back to help extricate her skirt from a thorny bush. He dropped to one knee beside her as he worked her hem loose, and she looked down at him, at his bent and rough black hair that fell across his forehead. Her heart seemed to turn over in her breast and leave her breathless.

When he had worked her free and stood up, he looked at her ruefully. "Are you all right?"

"Yes," she laughed, trying to catch her breath. "You don't realize what long legs you have."

"Come," he said, taking her hand. "Let's sit here." He led her to a large, flat granite boulder, put his arm around her, and sat down beside her.

She leaned her head against his shoulder. Closing her eyes, she felt as though she were floating with the sun on her face, the warmth of the granite beneath her, and the strength of Jason's arms around her.

Jason looked down at her, so trusting, so vulnerable, in

his arms, and he was doubly determined to have her for his wife. No other man should ever touch her. No one else would ever care for her so tenderly as he.

Whatever the price, they would be married before he sailed. His father would help them. He had to. He had almost implied as much last night. Maybe he could talk Cousin Benjamin around. If not . . . If not, what?

He felt the helplessness of his situation. Bound to the sea with few friends left on land, where could he turn? If Benjamin refused and cast Julia out, how could he leave her? He looked at a grove of scrub pines far up the hill. Well, so be it. If he must, he would leave the sea and find some sort of work ashore. But what could he, who had spent his life at sea, do ashore? Could he make enough to take care of her? For himself, it didn't matter, but Julie . . . She must have the best.

"Why are you looking so angry, Jason?" Julia had opened her eyes and was staring at him.

"Because we must be married. Now. And I can find no way if your father refuses."

"There's always a way."

He smiled at her beautiful innocence. "Life's not always so simple, sweetheart."

"It is if you make it that way." She reached up and touched his hair. "If you think things are going to get in your way, they will, but if you don't let them, they shrivel up and blow away. The thing to do is to know what you want and then go get it."

"That's a little ruthless, Julie. You have to think of other people."

"No! I never shall. I come first. No," she corrected herself softly, "we come first."

"Perhaps you're right."

"I know I'm right. It's easier to think out by the water. Mama said we could take a picnic lunch. Let's go over to the beach and have it there."

"It's getting cold on the sand this time of year."

"Oh, no. It's a lovely day. And we can always find shelter in the dunes if the wind comes up. I want to show you my favorite place."

"I want to see all your favorite places." He pulled her up

111

with him as he rose. "Let's go and find them. Someday, I'll show you all of mine."

"At sea?"

"No, not at sea. There've been a few in foreign ports, but mostly they're over in Brewster, though it's been a long time since I've seen them."

As they entered the kitchen through the back door, Lydia glanced quickly at each of them. Their eyes were sparkling and their cheeks flushed. She knew instantly what had been happening. At first, she was alarmed. Then she thought, well, if it goes any further, they'll have to wed. Might be for the best. Benjamin won't be able to stand in their way then.

"I've had Maryanne pack you a lunch," she said, indicating a wicker basket sitting on the large deal table.

"Oh, thank you, Mama," Julia said. "I was going to do that."

"You'd only have been in the way. Now go along and enjoy it. There won't be many such days left. Winter is coming."

Winter is coming, Julia thought and shivered, and Jason's leaving.

The beach was warm and the Bay calm with just a light, southerly breeze riffling its surface. As they climbed to the top of the dune, they could see, in the far distance, several merchant ships heading northeast to the ocean.

"Perhaps it wasn't such a good idea to come here," she said.

Jason had followed her glance as he had followed her thoughts.

"Perhaps not. But I'm glad to see it. When I'm out there"—he nodded toward the ships—"I'll be able to picture you here on the sand, waiting for me."

"I'll be here, I guess, or somewhere. But I'll be waiting."

Jason set the hamper at the foot of a dune, and they walked down to the hard-packed sand near the water's edge.

"We're going to have to work this out, Julie." He frowned down at a wet heap of seaweed tangled with crab shells and whelk's eggs lying on the sand.

Julia thought how exactly his eyes matched the fresh

seaweed, clear and green with the sun sparkling on it. "Let's walk awhile," she said. "It helps."

"I don't know whether we can convince your father to give his consent or not." He picked up a water-washed stone and skimmed it out over the surface. "What do you think?"

"I don't know. I don't understand him. He's always given me everything I ever wanted. This is the first time he's ever denied me. Even when Mama's said no, he's always said yes. Now I think Mama's on our side but Papa isn't. It's very confusing."

"He says you're too young." Jason captured one of her long curls and wrapped it around his finger. "That seems to be the main problem."

"Well, I was. But I'm not anymore." She smiled up at him. "Not since you came."

"He doesn't see it that way. That's why he wants us to wait."

"Well, I won't."

"Nor I," he said fervently. "If we're not married before the *Katy Saunders* sails, I won't be on board. I'll stay here with you."

"But you can't, Jason!" She was appalled. "You can't do that. I won't let you."

"There'll be another ship one day."

"They're not so easily come by if you break your word. You promised to sail on her, so you must."

"There are other things besides ships."

"No! Papa gave up the sea for Mama, and he's been miserable ever since. I simply won't let you do it."

"He doesn't look so miserable to me."

She caught his hand, and he slowed his steps to match her shorter ones as they walked along the yielding sand.

"Well, he is," she said. "I've seen him watch each ship he's built when it's gone down the Bay to Boston. He stands on the dunes, sometimes even in the middle of the day, and he watches them out there, coming and going without him. All the captains come down to the shipyard when they get home. They tell him about their voyages, and I see that lost, longing look on his face. I won't let that happen to you."

"I'm not your father. I might be happier ashore."

"No. Never. If you don't go now, you'll never be master of your own ship, and then you'll never be able to take me to sea with you."

He looked at her curiously. "That means a lot to you, doesn't it, Julie?"

"It means everything."

And if I weren't at least a first mate with good prospects of becoming a master, would you ever have loved me? he wondered. But he knew better than to ask that question. He was afraid he knew what the answer would be.

Here, walking at the water's edge, with the breeze riffling the black tendrils that framed her face, she looked more alive, more beautiful than ever. She belongs here, he thought. Or out there. He envisioned her standing on a quarterdeck with the sea wind whipping around her. A mermaid his father had called her. He didn't know, but whatever she was, she was linked in some fashion with that large, cruel, rolling body of water. If he tried to break that link, he would lose her. To keep her love, he had to go to sea. Forever? he wondered. And he knew the answer to that, too.

He sighed. "Well, if I'm to sail on the *Katy*, then we'll have to do something fast. There's not much time."

"How long?"

"Three weeks."

"So soon?"

"Yes."

"Well, I'll just have to talk to Papa again tonight. Somehow I've got to make him understand."

"And if he doesn't?"

"I don't know," she sighed. "I guess we'll just have to run away and get married somewhere. We'll have to find a preacher who'll believe I'm old enough to marry without my father's consent."

"That won't be easy." He watched a wave ripple its foam along the sand. "It might be impossible."

"Then we'll just go away so we can be alone together until you sail."

"No. That we won't do," he said firmly, squeezing her hand. "I won't let you be shamed that way."

"There's no shame in love."

"There is in some people's eyes, and I'm not going to have them looking at you with their ugly thoughts. I'll never let anything evil touch you."

They walked on in silence with gulls calling overhead and the sandpipers hopping a few short steps ahead of them until they reached the boulders and rocks that limited the beach.

"My father might help us," Jason said as they sat down on a large grey stone.

"Do you think so?" Julia asked hopefully.

"I don't know. He and I had a long talk last night. I think he might."

"I'm awfully fond of your father."

"He feels the same way about you."

"Well, if we can't talk Papa around tonight, then maybe you'd better ask him. We're going to need all the help we can get."

"What about your mother?" Jason asked.

"I don't think so." Julia pushed her hair back behind her shoulders. "It's better not to let her know anything. She might tell Papa. Even if she doesn't, there's not much she can do."

Jason turned her hand over in his and studied her long, tapering fingers. He noticed the cuts and the ragged nails, but they only endeared her to him.

"If my mother were still alive," he said, "you could have stayed with her while I'm gone. She would have loved you and taken care of you."

"You miss her, don't you?"

"Yes, very much. Especially now." He closed his hand tightly around hers. "Julie, I just don't want to leave you alone."

"I probably won't be alone." She leaned her forehead against his upper arm. "No matter how angry Papa is, he'll probably let me come home."

"We'll have to think about what we'll do if he doesn't." He put his arm around her. "Of course, you can live in our house. It's not all that far away, and it's sitting there empty. But I hate to think of you all alone there."

"I won't be alone. Not in your house. And not while I know you're somewhere out there thinking about me."

That night, though Julia stormed and raged, Benjamin

thundered back and remained adamant. First Jason and then William entered the study to back her up, but even those three strong wills combined could not shake Benjamin. He ended the tempest by shouting, "I'll not discuss the matter further," and went slamming out of the house. Probably over to the shipyard, Julia guessed.

The three left in the study looked at each other silently for a moment. Then William said, "Well, Ben never was a man to be blown off his course once he'd set his mind to it."

"Guess we'll just have to tack around him," Jason said.

"And how do you plan to do that?"

"We'll go down to Boston, Julie and me, and find some preacher who'll marry us."

"Just going to run off like that?" William stroked his golden beard thoughtfully. "Without making any plans?"

"Cousin William, you've got to help us," Julia appealed to him.

"And what makes you think I'll help you go against your father? He's my friend, you know. Been friends a long time."

"You've got to help us. You're my friend, too."

"So no matter what I do, I lose a friend?"

"No. But I might not think so kindly of you in the future."

"And you, Jason? If I don't help you, I lose a son?"

"No, sir. But last night, you were mightily upset because I didn't ask your advice. I'm asking it now."

"Well, since you put it that way . . ."

"That's exactly the way I'm putting it," Jason said firmly. He surprised even himself. He had never spoken to his father in that tone before.

William smiled in approval. That was more like it.

"Please, Cousin William," Julia said.

"Had a long talk with your father on the way to the yard this morning. Didn't think he'd give in tonight, but it didn't hurt to try."

"And he's not going to," Julia said.

"No. Been mulling this whole thing over in my mind all day."

"You have?" Julia's voice was hopeful. "You've thought of something?"

"Reckon I have. After all, it's not every day you get a chance of having a mermaid in the family."

"I wish I was. Then maybe I could do something about it."

"You said you'd thought of something," Jason reminded his father.

"Yes. Here's the way I see it. Jason, you and I are going to be leaving in the morning. Don't think we'll be very welcome after tonight."

"Oh, no," Julia wailed. "You can't."

"Now, just let me finish." William patted her shoulder. "We're not going far. Just over to Brewster. From there, I'll make the arrangements."

"Let me come with you."

"No. You've got some packing to do. Not too much. Don't want to arouse anyone's suspicions. We can get you more later. Just a small bundle you can carry on your horse."

"I can do that tonight."

"With Sarah buzzing around? Wait till tomorrow when we've gone."

"Do you think the minister over in Brewster will marry us?" Jason asked.

"No, I don't. Too close to home. I think we'll have to take the packet down to Boston. I'm not sure yet. Julia, you know that big elm tree up the road?"

"Near Scargo Hill Road?"

"That's the one. I'll send you word tomorrow evening. You'll find it under the rock beside that tree. The way I figure it, you'll leave here the next morning. Wait till your father leaves for the yard. Then saddle up and ride to the landing in Yarmouth Port. We'll be waiting for you there."

"Yarmouth Port?" Jason said. "Why not take the packet from Brewster?"

William pulled out his pipe and filled it. "Because the minute Ben gets wind that Julia's gone, he's going to be over in Brewster looking for her. We're goin' in the opposite direction."

"I'd better come for Julie," Jason said.

"Nope. Someone might see you together and go running to Ben." He lit his pipe. "You know the way?" he asked Julia.

"Yes. I've been there before. Oh, Cousin William!" She got up and hugged him. "I knew you'd help us. You're wonderful."

"Ha! If I was twenty years younger, I'd show you just how wonderful." He puffed on his pipe and winked at her. "But I guess I'll just have to leave that to Jason here. Now we'd best break this up before that sister of yours comes sneaking around listening at the door."

"Oh, Sarah wouldn't . . ."

"Oh, yes, Sarah would. That's another thing. You've got to put on a good act. Don't let anyone even guess what you're planning. Go right on acting mad."

"That's pretty hard to do. I'm so excited!"

"You better do it. Think how it would be if Jason was really going away and you wasn't going to see him again for a couple of years. That ought to put you in the proper frame of mind. Pretend it's the truth, even to yourself."

"I couldn't. I might believe it."

"You could never really believe it, sweetheart." Jason put his arm around her. "But Papa's right. Try to believe it until you're on your way to meet me."

"It'll be such a long time," Julia said wistfully.

"A whole day." William grinned mockingly at her. He went to the door to the parlor. "You two say your farewells while I go check on Sarah. I want to say goodbye to your mother, too. Might not see her again for quite a spell."

When he entered the parlor, Lydia and Sarah were sitting, sewing, before the fire. Sarah looked sullen and Lydia was keeping a sharp eye on her.

"Can I go to bed now, Mama?" she asked when she saw Cousin William coming through the door.

"Not yet." Lydia glanced at William with a question in her eyes. "I don't know what's come over you, wanting to go to bed so early."

"I told you. I don't feel well," Sarah said pettishly.

"Then lie down on the couch," her mother said, knowing full well that, Sarah's room being directly over the study, the girl would try to hear every word that was said in that room.

"Julia and Jason are saying goodbye," William said,

settling down on the love seat next to his cousin. "We'll be leaving first thing in the morning, Lydia."

"There's no call to do that." Lydia laid her sewing down on her lap.

"Yes, I think there is. Ben won't take kindly to us staying on. Not now. I'm sorry for it, but we must go."

"But where will you go?" Lydia frowned in her concern.

"Home. It's about time I made my peace with Margaret's death. I want to see to her grave and make sure her house is in good order before I sail. Then I'll have to go down to Boston to see about the *Belle*. There's a lot to be done."

"Oh, William. I'm so sorry for all this."

"There's nothing to be sorry for." He patted her hand. "Those two have met. Now we'll all have to bide our time. Tell me. Do you look favorably on the match?"

"Yes, I do. He's a fine young man."

"He should be. He's Margaret's son."

"And yours," she said affectionately with a smile for her handsome cousin.

"I only hope Julia will wait for him," he said, looking into the fire as though he might find the future there. "She's impetuous."

"Not so much impetuous as tempestuous," Lydia sighed. "I reckon she'll wait."

They heard the study door that led to the dining room open. Lydia called out, "Julia, you sleep with Amelia tonight. Sarah's not feeling well."

"All right, Mama," Julia called back as she and Jason went to the foot of the stairs.

Lydia waited until their footsteps parted overhead, making for their separate rooms. "You can go to bed now, Sarah."

"I don't think I want to anymore."

"I said, *go to bed*."

"Yes, Mama." Sarah slowly put away her needlework. She gave both her mother and Cousin William a searching look with her black-fringed grey eyes before she left the room.

After she had gone up the stairs, Lydia turned to William. "You'll take good care of her, Will?"

"What?" His surprise was real.

119

"I asked if you'd take good care of her."

"You know?"

"I guessed."

"I'll take good care of her . . . and so will Jason."

"Then I'll sleep better nights."

Chapter Seven

1836

AFTER THE STAGECOACH HAD come pounding up the sandy road and taken Jason and Cousin William away with it, Julia found it hard to settle down. She wandered through the house, then up the path, then changed her mind and strolled over to the shipyard, but when she saw her father at a distance, she turned back.

Returning home, she went up to her room, shut the door, and looked through her wardrobe. It was hard to figure what she would take with her. A small bundle, Cousin William had said, but she couldn't decide just what she'd need. She gathered a few things together and laid them on her bed. Too much. They'd never fit in a small bundle. Those dresses would be nice in Boston, but she'd never get them there. She put them away and got out some simpler ones. But she couldn't wear those in the city! If only she knew for sure where they were going.

Frustrated, she put everything away. The afternoon was wearing on. Perhaps word had come from Cousin William. Then she'd know better what to do. She ran down the stairs and out of the house. She had to see if the message had arrived.

She hastened down the road to where the old elm tree

stood peacefully brilliant in its autumn gold. She went around to its other side, where the rock lay nestled in the poverty grass. Just as she was about to lift it, she caught a flicker of movement and a flash of pink in the bushes around the curve in the direction of the house. Sarah!

Julia sauntered past the elm to a pine tree and picked up a large cone from the ground. Then she returned to the road and strolled in the direction of the beach. That should discourage her sister. Sarah wasn't much for the sea. Never had been. Always complained about the sand in her shoes and the wind tangling her hair.

Before she reached the path to the beach, though, she thought, what if Sarah stays by the elm? What if she's there when someone tries to put my letter under the rock? She turned and hurried back, arriving breathless.

There was no sign of her sister, but still she didn't dare lift the rock. She spread her skirts and sat down on it. The minutes ticked by. Sarah might still be about, but all Julia could hear was a light breeze rustling through the treetops. Sarah must have gone home. Julia had just decided to chance it when her sister stepped around the curve.

"You can sit and wait forever, but he's gone," Sarah jeered. "Must not have wanted you very much or he would have found some way to make Papa give his consent." She laughed tauntingly, her grey eyes flickering with malice. "And while you're sitting here, turning to stone, you can think of all the pretty girls he'll be meeting."

Julia resolutely ignored her sister and stared across the road at the marsh that shone greenish-gold in the autumn sunlight.

"You plan on waiting here all the years he's gone?" Sarah moved to stand directly in front of Julia, blocking her view.

"Sarah, go away," Julia said quietly.

"It's a public road. I can walk it same as you."

"Well, go walk it."

"No. I like it here."

"Then stay here!" Julia said, her patience at an end. She got up from the rock and dusted her skirts. "I'm going home."

"Guess I might as well come along, too."

"Suit yourself."

Lydia saw her two daughters walking down the road together, Sarah's neatly bound light brown hair shining with golden highlights and Julia's loose black hair sparkling with blue fire. Sarah, in her immaculate pink dress, seemed from the distance older than her taller sister. It had something to do with the way she walked and held herself, so quiet and self-contained. And from Julia's fast, loose stride, you could tell she was annoyed. Just the way her blue skirts swirled the sand into a cloud behind her was a warning signal.

Lydia pushed back her heavy golden hair and sighed. Why was Sarah that way? Why couldn't she leave Julia alone?

She looked around the warm, sunny kitchen and gathered together a loaf of fresh bread, a jar of preserves, and part of a cold chicken. Putting them in a wicker basket, she covered them with a white cloth. She was ready when her daughters entered the house.

"Sarah," she said, "I want you to run an errand for me. Take these provisions over to old Mrs. Elsie Meekins. I'm concerned she isn't eating right. And while you're there, read some from the Bible for her."

"Why can't Julia do it?" Sarah asked petulantly.

"Because Mrs. Meekins is right fond of you. Just the other day, she was telling me what a comfort you are to her. Poor old soul. I worry about her."

As Lydia had planned, Sarah became entranced with her own importance. She smoothed her already smooth hair and her eyes smiled that inward, secret smile.

"I know," she said complacently. "She's always telling me she just doesn't know how she'd be able to go on without my visits."

Sarah picked up the basket and headed down the road toward the village.

"Well, that ought to keep her awhile," Lydia said to Julia. "Once Miss Elsie starts talking, Sarah won't be able to leave for quite a spell. You can get on with whatever you were doing."

"Thanks, Mama," Julia said, subdued, wondering how much her mother knew. She felt it safer not to ask, though. Whatever, she didn't think her mother would give her away.

She left the house and returned to the golden elm, whose shadows were lengthening with the coming of evening. She looked up and down the sandy road. There was no one in sight. It was safe. The flat grey rock looked different, as though someone had moved it. She held her breath as she lifted it. Sure enough, there was a white envelope under it.

Picking it up quickly, she let the rock fall back. Then she studied the envelope. It was sealed with red wax. She couldn't make out the impression left in the wax, but on the other side, it was addressed to "Miss Julia Howard" in a strange hand.

That surprised her. She had seen Cousin William's writing on letters he sometimes sent her parents when he was at sea. It wasn't his.

She tucked the letter into the bodice of her dress and climbed through the tangled low brush, past some scrub pines and bayberry bushes to a hidden, secret glade. It was safe. No one had ever disturbed her here. She wasn't even sure whether anybody else knew about it.

She settled down on a fallen log and took the letter out of her bodice. She held it for a moment in her hand. Her whole future lay in that envelope. She was almost afraid to open it. Now that it was here, did she really want it? Yesterday seemed far away and Jason seemed a stranger.

Summoning her courage, she broke the seal and opened it. Her eyes went immediately to the bottom of the page. There, in bold, black strokes, was the name "Jason Thacher."

Her heart leapt when she read it. Once again, she could see those eyes green as seaweed, smiling in amused tenderness, clouded with worry. She could see his dark hair, and the scar that intersected his eyebrow; the high, slanting cheekbones and the set of his clean-shaven chin.

He was no stranger. He was her love.

And his hands had touched this paper. The bold, slanting script was his. She stroked the paper with her fingers, thinking of his long, hard ones.

Then she read the letter.

DEAR JULIA, MY SWEET, MY LOVE,

Papa has decided the preacher here won't do, so

we're going on to Boston. There's a hitch in our plans, though, because the packet from Yarmouth Port will sail earlier than expected. You'll have to leave the house before your father goes to the yard if you're to get there in time. Leave the house before anyone is up, and go direct to the landing. Don't take a chance on the back roads at night. You might get lost. We'll be waiting for you there. I miss you so much already, my sweet Julie. I can't bear to think of the months to come when we will be parted for so long a time.

Your devoted and loving,
JASON THACHER

That was a hitch! Julie thought. She'd have to leave well before sunrise if she were to elude the entire household. And she'd be missed at breakfast. It wasn't going to work.

Yes, it was! It had to!

She'd leave a note in the kitchen, saying she'd gone down to the beach. 'Twouldn't be the first time. She'd done it before. Shouldn't surprise anyone. It would be a few hours before anyone thought to look for her. Time enough to get safely away.

Once again in her bedroom, Julia tried to pack a few things. The large wool shawl. Plain but warm. She'd need it under her cloak on the packet. One extra dress. Her best one. A few undergarments. The amber beads Cousin William had given her.

She was startled when her bedroom door quietly opened and her mother came into the room. There was pain in Lydia's misty green eyes, but no disapproval.

"Mind you have your brush and comb, and take some soap," she said, closing the door behind her. "They don't always provide it at the inns."

Julia could feel the heat rising to her cheeks.

"Mama, I . . ."

"Never mind," Lydia said firmly. "I don't want to know anything. Then I can't lie about it."

"But, Mama . . ." Julia dropped the amber beads onto the shawl.

"No. Don't say anything." Lydia leaned her golden head back against the door, the knob still in her hand. She could see so clearly the repressed joy underlying Julia's embarrassment. "Just listen. After dinner, I'm going to fix a packet of food. It'll be on the top shelf of the right-hand cupboard in the kitchen. It'll be handy next time you go down to the beach and miss your breakfast. And mind you take your warm cloak. When you go riding down there at all hours, I worry about you catching cold."

"Thank you, Mama." Julia wanted to run to her mother and throw her arms around her, *really* thanking her, but something in Lydia's face held her back.

"Send word when you can." Lydia opened the door and turned away from her eldest daughter. She suddenly realized how much she would miss those sparkling blue eyes, the sight of a cloud of blue-black hair whipping around a corner. Shutting the door quickly behind her, she went to her room with the tears running silently down her face. Then she knelt beside her bed and prayed.

It was dark when Julia wakened from a restless sleep. She lit her candle and saw it was four-thirty. She'd have to hurry. Hastily, she washed and dressed and took her bundle from the wardrobe. After smoothing the quilt over the bed, she silently opened her door and crept down the front steps in darkness that was punctured only by moonlight.

She tiptoed through the sleeping house to the kitchen, carefully skirting furniture she knew lay in her way. On the top cupboard shelf she found the packet of food her mother had promised and tucked it into her bundle. Then she remembered the note she'd written saying she'd gone to the beach. Well, it was really no lie. She *was* going to a beach . . . in Yarmouth Port. She laid the note on the large deal table and anchored it with the sugar bowl.

Now she had to return from the kitchen, through the dark pantry, dining room, and hall to reach the front door without making a sound. If she used any other, her father might hear her from his bedroom over the kitchen. She didn't know that her mother was lying awake and listening to every whisper of skirts, every creak of the boards.

Outside, with the moon and stars shining in a cloudless sky, it was lighter. The familiar trees stood grey and black like looming shadows. In the fields granite boulders glimmered white, mirroring the moon. Julia shivered in the cold, still air. She stepped off the porch. First the grass, then the thick carpet of pine needles, muffled her footsteps.

As she neared the stables, the horses whinnied a soft greeting. She stopped dead still, hardly daring to breathe, but she heard no movement from the house. She felt like a thief, stealing away from the house in the dead of night.

She felt even guiltier as she saddled Fancy. Papa had given her the horse for her birthday only last July. She remembered her joy and that of her father when she'd first seen the chestnut mare. Now she was using his gift to run away from him.

Still! It had to be done. She lifted her chin with determination. If only he wasn't so stubborn!

She tied her bundle on and checked the saddle and bridle as well as she was able in the moon-shadowed dark. Paying that she wouldn't clink or clank, she led the horse out of the stable over to the mounting block. Come first light, she'd have to check everything again, but for now it would have to do.

Once on the highway and around the bend, out of sight of the house, Julia felt easier, but when she reached the fork to Scargo Hill Road, she hesitated. Jason had said not to take the back roads. Yet Scargo Hill Road, though actually only a path, was shorter, and there'd be fewer houses to pass. 'Twas easy to get lost in the dark, but she knew the way well and shreds of moonlight filtering through the trees were there to guide her. Besides, there might be people about on the highway, fishermen going to their boats and such like.

She turned left and entered the dark tunnel of branches. She could just see the glimmer of sand that was the path. With that and trusting to the mare, she rode on.

Owls were hooting up on Scargo Hill, and the brush around her rustled with small night creatures. An occasional bird wakened and gave a small cry of surprise. Otherwise all was silent in this cold, windless world. She shivered inside her cloak, thankful for its warmth.

In the quiet of the night, she wondered what on earth she was doing here. Running away from Papa, from her comfortable home, the shipyard, and her family. Running to a stranger she hardly knew.

It still wasn't too late to turn around and go home with none the wiser. None except her mother and Cousin William and Jason.

Jason! How would he feel, standing on that early morning dock, waiting for her, waiting for a girl who would never come? Jason, who had promised to take her to sea. Jason, with his tall, lean body and his green eyes filled with promises. If she stood him up now, he'd not give her a second chance, and she would spend the rest of her life wondering what would have happened if she had gone through the dark night into morning and a packet that sailed to Boston for her wedding.

No, she couldn't go back. Before her lay her life. Behind lay childhood and nameless yearning. Only now it would have a name. Jason.

When she reached Bass River Road, she hesitated once again. She could follow it a ways, then cut round Dennis, avoiding the church and houses on the highway. But she wasn't all that sure of the lanes farther on. No. Through Dennis she must go and pray all the while that no one remarked her. If she hurried, it would still be dark by the time she reached the other side of the village.

Once she gained the highway, she urged Fancy on to a trot, and as they neared the houses, she pulled her cloak up to hide her face. If anyone noticed, they would just think she was keeping from the cold. Kicking the horse hard, she gave her free rein. They dashed through the village.

It was just growing light when they reached a copse of scrub pine. Spotting a fallen log, she reined Fancy in and dismounted. She checked all the straps and buckles. She'd done a pretty good job in the dark stable. Satisfied, she remounted and headed up the road at a more leisurely pace. She'd soon be in Yarmouth, then Yarmouth Port. She hoped Jason would be waiting for her.

Just as she figured she'd left Dennis behind and was entering the township of Yarmouth, a hidden horse whinnied in the woods ahead. A tall cloaked figure rode out to intercept her. Startled, she dug her heels into the mare and whipped her with the reins. They swerved when they galloped past the threatening figure.

"Julie!" he called.

Her heart, beating so fast with fear, seemed to stop. "Jason?"

"Julie!" He rode quickly after her.

"Jason. Is it really you?" She reined Fancy in.

"Of course, it's me. Who did you think it was?" He swept off his hat as he approached her. His dark hair tumbled over his forehead, and his face looked pale in the pre-dawn light.

"I don't know. You frightened me." She brushed her hood back so that he could see her face. "I didn't expect to see you here. I thought you'd be waiting at the landing."

"I was worried about you. Alone and the night so dark. I thought I'd best ride down to meet you." His green eyes were anxious as they searched her face.

She laughed. "You're always worrying about me being alone. I'm not afraid."

"No. But I'm afraid for you." He leaned from his saddle, put an arm around her and kissed her lightly on the lips. He held her motionless for a moment as the horses moved restlessly beneath them. "Oh, sweetheart, I was so worried about you, not knowing if you'd gotten safe away, wondering if your father might not have guessed and locked you in your room."

"No lock could keep me from you, Jason."

"I don't think it could." He smiled and released her. "Come. We'd better ride. We want to get on board the packet before the crowd gathers to see her off."

Afterwards, Boston and its people, its ships and wharves and stores, were all a jumble to Julia. But the wedding ceremony in the small oak-paneled chapel was not. That she would remember all her life. With Cousin William on one side and Jason standing tall on the other, she gladly repeated the marriage lines, plighting her troth to Jason in a firm, clear voice. And Jason's words had rung proudly strong through the sunlit chapel as though from a quarter-deck, and his green eyes were serious in a grave pledge when he slipped the narrow gold band on her finger.

Somehow, Cousin William had arranged it all. The

chapel, the minister, the friends' house where they had stayed the night. He had even bought the ring, taking her small opal one to match the fit, while she and Jason had gone shopping for her trousseau.

It was only years later that she was to learn that Cousin William had told the minister that she was "expecting" and that the young couple must be married at once, before Jason put to sea. It was not the first time the minister had heard that tale, and he had quickly agreed to perform the ceremony. When Julia did eventually hear of it, she forgave William the lie.

After the wedding they had only enough time for a quick lunch at the Bromfield House before rushing to Long Wharf to catch the packet home to Brewster. Julia's new sea chest and clothes had been sent down to the sloop early in the morning before the wedding party had set out for church.

Now, as they boarded, they were met by Captain Burgess, who welcomed them on board.

"Heard you'd come down to Boston, Will. Didn't expect to see you going back so soon."

"Just went down to get these young folks wed," William said, shaking his hand. "Now, we're for home to get them settled."

"Hear tell Ben Howard was over in Brewster, inquiring for his daughter. Looked black as a stormcloud, they say."

"Well, if he's still there, he'll find her soon enough. 'Course that depends on how fast you can move this bucket between Boston Harbor and Brewster."

"Reckon faster than you can move that big hulk of a ship you got lying idle over there," Captain Burgess answered with a chuckle, nodding at the *Belle of Canton*, who lay at anchor in the harbor. "We're just about to cast off."

Julia frowned. Captain Burgess's words reminded her of her father. For a while, she'd been able to forget him, but all the way down to Boston she'd been a little frightened. Although they'd had a favoring wind and fair weather, she hadn't been able to properly enjoy them. Every time a sail had appeared behind them, she'd ducked below to the richly paneled cabin, sure that her father was chasing them in a faster boat.

In Boston, with its hundreds of buildings, its crowds, and its bustle, she'd felt safely hidden. 'Twould be hard to find anyone there.

But now, she was afraid again. Afraid that she would find him, smoldering in anger, on the pier at Brewster. It was strange to be afraid of her father. She never had been before. Not really.

"Maybe we should have stayed in Boston," she said as she watched the crew setting the sails.

"No need to worry," Cousin William said, guessing her thoughts. "You're properly wed and got the paper to prove it. There's not much your father can do about it now."

"He could still take me home, married or not." She stared out at the forest of masts they were leaving behind them.

"Don't think he'd try that. Not Ben." William pushed his hat back on his head. "We'll soon have you home safe and snug. He'll come round when he sees you happily settled and provided for."

"Cousin William." Julia tightened the blue satin ribbons on her bonnet as the wind caught at its brim. "I haven't thanked you proper for all you've done for me. Buying me a trousseau, giving me a home."

"No need for thanks, Julie. You're part of the family now." He looked up at the sails, critically noting their set. "The house will be the better for being lived in. Needs a woman to give it warmth. It's been a rare lonely place since Margaret died. Now when we think of it, Jason and me, we can picture you there. It'll be a comfort when we're away."

"I wish you didn't have to go," Julia said wistfully.

"You wouldn't have it otherwise, Julie." Jason's voice was strangely bitter. She looked at him where he stood leaning on the rail, staring at the green waves that rolled by them.

"No." She went to stand at the rail beside him. "I wouldn't have it otherwise for either one of you. It's just that I'd rather go with you on your ship than stay behind in your house."

"That'll come before you know it," William said heartily. Then he spotted an acquaintance aft. "There's Captain Aldritch. Didn't know he was aboard. Got a few things I

131

want to talk over with him, so I'll leave you two alone. You got better things to do than spend your time talking to an old codger like me."

Julia moved closer to Jason at the rail, but he made no move toward her. His cap was pulled low over his forehead and his tanned face looked stern.

"Jason." She took off her bonnet and shook out her hair. Then she laid her hand on his, which were clasped before him. "We're married. Really married."

"Yes." He took her hand and held it between his, but he continued to stare moodily at the sea. Julia was puzzled.

"Are you angry about something? Or worried about Papa?" She hesitated and bit her lip. Then she blurted it out. "Or do you regret having married me?"

"No, sweetheart." He straightened up and put his arm around her. "It's just that I hate to go to sea and leave you so soon. We have so little time."

"Then it's even more important to make the best of it," she said, "and not think about the time to come when you'll leave. Jason, let's live each day as if it were the only day that ever mattered or ever will matter, as though it were forever."

He looked down at her and his face softened into a smile. "You're right. There's no point in brooding about it. Maybe having so little time will only serve to make it better."

"I know it will. And I'm so happy now. Let's pretend that this is your ship, that you're her master, and that we're not going to stop when we reach Brewster. Soon we'll round Race Point and leave Cape Cod behind us. Then we'll keep going down the coast round Cape Horn till we reach Valparaiso on our way to China."

"I'd rather pretend that we're on our way home, where we'll have a wonderful life together, and that I'll never have to leave you."

"Well, that's partly true. We are going to have a wonderful life together, and once you're made captain, we'll never be parted for as long as we live. Not ever."

"All right." He smiled but there was no gaiety to it. "This is our ship, and we can roam the world together. But right now, we'd better move aft. You're getting soaked."

"And I love it!" she said exultantly, lifting her chin to the sea and letting the wind whip her hair into a black river.

"You look like a figurehead," Jason said, catching a strand of her swirling hair and kissing it.

"Ah, no. I'd rather be a living woman than a piece of wood."

As they neared the wharf the next day, Julia peered anxiously into the crowd that had come down to meet the packet. There was no sign of her father. "He isn't here," she said with relief.

"Didn't think he would be," William said. "He has better things to do than go chasing around the countryside after a wayward daughter."

"Could be he's waiting for us at your house."

"Could be," Jason agreed, "but I doubt it. Just forget about him, love. Think! We'll soon be home, our own home." And you'll be in my arms, he thought. Tonight you'll truly become my wife.

Chapter Eight

1836

"WHICH GOWN DO YOU like best, Jason?" Julia asked, delving into her new sea chest and bringing up two long white nightgowns covered with lace.

"Let me see." He pretended to examine them while putting one arm around her. Then he swiftly took them from her and tossed them at the chest as he swung her around to face him. "It doesn't really matter," he said hoarsely, his lips closing on hers. "You're not going to wear them anyway."

Then why did we buy them? Julia started to ask, but she forgot the question as she became aware only of his soft lips and strong hands and wild-pounding heart. She felt his fingers unbuttoning the neck of her dress, and soon they were probing to slip under the top of her corset. She trembled as they touched her bare breast. She felt wildly exultant and, at the same time, so faint she would have fallen if it hadn't been for his strong arm around her, holding her so close. And still his lips clung to hers, the tip of his tongue searched for hers.

Without releasing her, he picked her up and laid her on the bed, and she was grateful for its soft support under her weak body. When his lips left hers, she lay unmoving, unable even to open her eyes. All of her senses were centered on his fingers as they swiftly undid the rest of the buttons of her dress.

"Oh, sweetheart, you're so beautiful," he said, kissing her brow, her nose, her eyes, as he slipped the dress from her shoulders.

"Am I, Jason?" she asked, opening her eyes and seeing his so intent, so intense, and yet so languorously soft.

"You are, you are," he repeated as each garment came away.

She lay quietly in her happiness while he kissed the flesh so newly bared, but when he nuzzled her breasts, she was so violently shaken she reached up and gripped his thick, coarse shock of hair with her hands. Slowly his lips relinquished her breast and came hotly down on hers. His tongue was wilder now, probing, probing, and she heard the surf pounding in her head, enveloping her.

"Oh, Jason," she moaned as he left her lips for further exploration of her body. They were circling, circling in an ever narrowing quest toward the center. As first his fingers and then his tongue entered her, she was shaken by a violent spasm, her body arching to meet him. The surf was louder now and more demanding. Then suddenly he was gone. Gone from her, gone from the bed.

"Jason!" she called wildly. He mustn't, he couldn't leave her now.

"I'm here, sweetheart," he whispered, stroking her lightly. "I have to undress."

"Hurry."

"I will."

It seemed forever, but then he was with her, his naked body pressed tight against her, his skin so fresh and clean rubbing against her like satin, the coarse hair on his chest caressing her breasts. His lips and tongue were darting quickly now all over her body, returning again and again to hers. And while he held her in a long drowning kiss, she felt his fingers enter her once more, exploring that secret, hidden part.

Again her body arched, and he caught her hips and held them. She felt his large, hard maleness entering her, slowly at first, then faster and faster, and then there was pain

135

that flooded her. She tried to scream, but his lips held her fast. Suddenly she was lifted to new heights of wild glory.

Then she was no longer Julia. She was woman. The first and only woman. And he was no longer Jason, but the first and only man. And they were truly one.

Afterwards, she sighed and reached up to touch his face, his beloved face. "Oh, Jason, my love," she sighed her completion.

He took her hand and kissed it gently. Then raising himself slightly on one elbow, he brushed his lips lightly across her face as he bestowed benediction on every part.

They rolled over on their sides and slept in that close embrace. Twice more during the night, he wakened her, and each time, it seemed ever more glorious and beautiful.

When she awakened in the morning, the first thing Julia saw was Jason's face shining above her. He was propped on one elbow, his long green eyes staring down at her in wonderment.

"You're beautiful when you sleep," he said, playing with a long strand of her curling black hair.

"You're beautiful when you're awake," she said.

He laughed and hugged her to him. "You're also a hussy."

"Jason! That's a terrible thing to say."

"No, it isn't. It's what every man dreams of marrying. Unfortunately, most women aren't."

"I don't understand."

"Didn't your mother ever tell you that you must act maidenly in the wedding bed, that you must resist me and fight me off when I tried to take you. Or that you must submit quietly to the things I would inflict on you?"

"Oh, no! I love you. How could you take what was already yours? Did I do the wrong thing?" She looked up at him with a hurt, imploring look.

"Oh, no, my darling," he laughed. "You did exactly the right thing. Everything. You're so beautiful I can't believe it." He kissed her on the tip of her nose.

"It was wonderful."

"And it will be again." He kissed her long and deeply. Then he looked down at her sapphire eyes, her rosy cheeks and lips, her clear, fair skin. She was his, he exulted. Completely and forever his.

"Now," he said hoarsely and his lips were upon her again.

When they had bathed and gone down to breakfast, they found the house empty, though there were platters of warm food in the oven and a pot of tea warm on the stove.

They could not know that William, after having relived his own wedding night during the long, sleepless hours, had gone over to the cemetery to be with his Margaret.

After they had eaten, they played at keeping house, washing the dishes, straightening the kitchen. Jason, his shirtsleeves rolled up, pretended to help, but mostly hindered her in their game of love.

"Let's go for a walk," Julia said when they had finished.

"Do you really want to?" he asked, running his fingers lightly over her face.

"Oh, yes! I feel so glorious, so alive! Do you know, you are still within me?" She took his hand and pressed it against her. "I can feel you there, burning and warm."

"I hope I didn't hurt you." He was concerned.

"You did." She threw her arms around him. "But only at first and it was beautiful. I hope that, as long as I live, I'll feel you there."

"I'll try to make sure you do," he promised.

"Come." She pulled on his hand. "Show me your secret places."

"It's not a day for secret places," he said. "It's a day for sunshine and open fields. I want to walk down the road and tell everyone we meet that I love you and you love me and that you're mine. I want to ring the church bells and climb the steeple and shout to the world below, 'Julia is mine! Julia is mine!' "

She laughed at him. "Then let's go do it."

"All right. We will. But first, let's walk through the woods over to Freeman's Pond and tell the frogs about it. They're great gossips, and they'll tell everyone. Or would you rather ride over to the beach and tell the sea?"

"She already knows. She was there last night. Besides, I don't feel up to riding today." She smiled, wrinkling her nose at him. "You rather ruined that."

"Are you sore?"

"Yes. In a very nice way. Let's go explore the woods and find those frog friends of yours."

While they were gone, William returned to the house, and finding it tidy but empty, he smiled. Already Julia's presence had made itself felt. There was a warmth and glow about that had been missing since Margaret had died.

"Oh, we'll have beautiful grandchildren, Maggie," he told her portrait that hung in the parlor. "Perhaps a little wild, but beautiful."

He was musing over the future when he heard a horse ride up and then a man's heavy footsteps on the walk. A loud pounding came at the door. When William opened it, he found Benjamin, truly as Captain Burgess had said, looking black as a stormcloud.

"Well, hello, Ben. Come on in."

"I've come for my daughter," Benjamin said, standing as stubborn and still as a granite boulder.

"Well, come in, come in. She's not here just now. I left the house early, and when I came back, she and her young husband were gone."

"Where is she?"

"I'm telling you, I don't know. If you just come in and wait a spell, they'll be back. Can't have gone far."

"I'll wait out here."

"Now, Ben, be reasonable. There's no telling how long you'll have to wait. Might as well be comfortable about it."

"I'll not accept hospitality from the man who helped steal my daughter."

"Then I'll not offer you any, but you might as well sit in a chair as on the front stoop. 'Course the neighbors might enjoy watching you, if entertainment is what you had in mind."

"No, I'll come in. I want an explanation from you, anyhow."

He stomped in and paced through the rooms, as though expecting to find Julia hidden in one.

"You want to check upstairs, too?" William asked. "I tell you she's not here."

"No. I believe you," Benjamin said grudgingly. Then he

turned accusingly on his friend. "Well? What do you have to say to all this?"

"Not much *to* say," William said, stroking his golden beard. "We went down to Boston. Julia was properly chaperoned. They were wed there. And now we're home again."

"They would never have dared do it without your help!"

"Oh, yes, they would. They were set on it and likely enough would have gotten themselves in a peck of trouble if I hadn't been along."

Benjamin snorted and paced to a window that faced on the road. "I'm warning you. I'm taking her home with me."

"Too late to untie knots that are fast. What's done is done, and you'd do better to leave them the little time they have. 'Tisn't long, but the years ahead will be."

"May not be too late yet." Benjamin thrummed his fingers on the windowsill.

"That, not you nor anyone else will know for two, three months. And if you take her now, no matter which way it goes, she'll hate you the rest of her life."

"And you'll make sure she does!"

"No. That I won't. I'm still your friend, even though you're no longer mine. The two of you share a deep love for each other. But she's grown now, and she has an even greater love for her husband, which is only as it should be."

"We'll see about that!" Benjamin turned to glare at William, his blue eyes flashing fire and his bushy black eyebrows bristling.

"You'll see if you stay, but don't you think 'twould be better to leave? You may well spend years regretting the things you'll say now in anger."

"You and your fine young son! You take her from me, he takes his pleasure from her, and then you're both off to sea, leaving a girl, who's barely more than a child, to face alone the consequences of your actions."

" 'Twas no wish of *ours* that she be alone!" William was finding it harder and harder to control his temper. "She could have returned to you and her mother if you hadn't been so damn stubborn about it," he said, raising his voice.

"I know what's best for my daughter!" Benjamin began to pace the room. "While you've spent the years away looking in on us now and then, I've been raising her, guiding her, teaching her. *You* look and see a pretty, young girl. I look at her and see my own flesh and blood. When I say she's too young, I mean she's too young, and no one knows better than me. But you'll find out!" He stopped at the fire and held out his hands.

"No," he corrected himself bitterly. *"She'll* find out. For you'll be off to sea without another thought of her, and once Jason rounds Cape Horn, he'll have forgotten her except as a pleasant memory."

"Damn it! You know better than that!" William finally exploded, his green eyes blazing back at Benjamin. "He'll remember her and relive every minute they have together, over and over again. I did and I suspect you did the same! He'll provide for her and well, and what he's not able to come up with, she'll have from me. She'll be taken care of without any of your damned help!"

The two men were facing each other in belligerent silence as Jason and Julia came laughing into the house. When they saw their two fathers in the parlor, they stopped at the doorway and stared in at them. Julia's first instinct was to run far, far away from this angry stranger who was her father. Then she squared her shoulders, set her chin, and walked into the parlor.

"We're wed, Papa," she said defiantly.

"So this man was telling me," her father said in cold fury. "And now you can pack your things and come home with me."

"I'm staying with Jason."

"I . . . said . . . you're . . . coming . . . with . . . me!"

"And I said I'm not."

"You'll do as I say!"

"No!"

He reached out to grab her arm, but Jason quickly stepped between them.

"Julia's my wife, sir, and if she says she stays, she stays," he said firmly. The natural flush of his high-boned cheeks was mounting to crimson.

"Oh, *your wife,*" Benjamin said mockingly. "And where's the paper to prove it?"

"Upstairs and you're welcome to see it. But I'll not get it as long as you're down here threatening Julie."

"I'm not threatening her. I'm her father. I'm telling her what she'll do."

"And I'm her husband, and I'm telling you what she'll not do."

"Julia," her father said, looking at her beyond Jason's shoulder. "For one last time, are you coming home with me or not?"

"No," she said clearly. "I'm not."

"Then you're no daughter of mine! I have only two daughters now. If you choose to be a Thacher, be a Thacher, and let them take care of you. You'll soon enough find the misery of it, but don't come crying to me for sympathy. I'll have none of it. You've made your bed. Now you know what to do with it."

He stormed out of the room and slammed through the front door. Julia stood silent and watched him go, her head held high and proud, her eyes dry and her chin resolute. No one moved or spoke as they heard the horse's hooves quickly receding in the distance.

Benjamin's angry visit and threats left a tarnish on the bright day, but by evening, they had banished it from their happiness. There was no time for worry. They had to cram what might be two years into less than three short weeks. Only occasionally in the days that followed did the thought of her father creep in to sadden a moment or two.

They tried hard, too, to forget how swiftly the day was coming when Jason would sail. Usually they succeeded but sometimes Julia would see his face tighten and the shadow of impending loss darken his eyes. Or there would be times when he gazed at her too intensely, as though trying to memorize every line, every fleeting expression of her face. Then she knew what he was thinking and would try to tease him with laughter out of the future back into the present.

William, feeling an intruder in his own house and knowing that they would be happier alone, invented a tale about having to see to his ship and took the packet back to Boston.

After Julia and Jason had seen him off at the landing, they returned to the house, which seemed a little emptier without him. As Jason hung up their coats in the small entrance hall, Julia opened the parlor door and listened. There was only the ticking of the clock on the mantel.

"It's so quiet," she said.

"Yes," Jason answered, coming up behind her and putting his arm around her. "Now I don't have to share you with anyone, not even for a moment. I have you all to myself."

"I'll miss your father," she said softly, then turned to look up at him. She could see from the glow in his slanted green eyes that he didn't sense the melancholy that seemed to pervade the house.

Jason led her into the sun-filled parlor, then turned her around to face him. "Don't be sad, sweet Julie. I won't let you miss him."

"It's just . . . just that . . ."

"It reminds you that I'll be going soon, too?" The lines beside his mouth deepened and the laughter was gone from his eyes.

"Yes." She bit her lip and looked down so that he wouldn't see the tears that were threatening to come.

"Oh, Julie!" He pulled her close to him. "Don't, don't, my sweet. We still have two weeks left."

"I know." Then she laughed shakily. "And I'm always telling you not to think about the future."

"Sometimes it's difficult not to think of it."

"Well, if we must, then, let's think of the future when you'll have your own ship and we'll be together again." She suddenly shivered. "I'm cold. Let's go into the kitchen and make a pot of tea. Then we can talk about all those lovely voyages we're going to make together."

Jason sat at the large deal table in the middle of the room and watched Julia as she moved about. He saw how the blue blazed in her hair when she passed through the sun streaks pouring through the windows. He saw how graceful her body was as she went to the sink to fill the kettle and as she bent to shake up the coals. He tried to imprint on his memory every gesture she made, every expression that fled across her face.

"It seems strange to actually see you here in this kitchen," he said, "and yet it's something I used to try to imagine."

"Did you really, Jason?" She smiled over her shoulder at him.

142

"Yes, but now, it seems as though you've always been here."

She could see the contentment on his face as he sat with his long legs stretched out before him. She felt a surge of love rise up like the waters of a spring and she went to sit beside him.

"Well," she said, taking his hand, which lay loosely on the table, "from now on when you imagine me here, you'll know I really am."

"But I won't like thinking of you here alone," he said, raising her hand to his lips. "I've been trying to come up with some scheme so you won't be."

"I don't mind, Jason, I really don't." She smiled at him and pressed his hand, then got up from the table to scald the pot and pour boiling water over the tea leaves.

He watched in silence while she set the table, sliced the cake, and put some down in the center.

"About your father . . ." he began as she sat down again.

"Let's not talk about him," she said quickly and directed all her attention to the tea she was pouring.

"We have to," he said, sitting up straight and pulling his chair closer to the table, "because I know it's bothering you."

"There's no point in talking about him, because there's nothing we can do about it," she said firmly and put the pot down on the table in such a way that it reinforced her words.

Watching her add cream and sugar to their cups, Jason said, "You *are* upset about him, aren't you?"

"Well . . . yes, I am." She looked down at her tea and stirred it very slowly. "You see, we always used to be so close. I didn't think he'd act the way he did when he came here that day. I thought that, once we were married, he'd accept it and life would go on just the way it always has."

"Do you think, if we went and talked to him . . . ?" She looked so sad he took her hand, ignoring his tea.

"No. It won't do any good."

"But we could try."

"Jason." She looked up at him and her eyes were blue with candor. "I don't want *anything* to ruin the time we have left together. It's too precious. Besides . . . I'm not sure I can forgive him for some of the things he said."

"He's still your father, Julie."

"He says he isn't."

"That was just his anger speaking. I'm sure he still cares about you, loves you."

"Well, I'm not all that sure I still love him."

"You do. You know you do." There was compassion mixed with the love in his eyes.

"Yes, I guess I do," she sighed. "Well, maybe after you've sailed, we can make up. But," she added, sitting up very straight, *"he's* the one who'll have to make the first move."

"Do you think he will?"

"I don't know," she said, pushing the tendrils away from her forehead with her free hand. "If only he weren't so stubborn."

"I've been thinking of something else." He stirred his tea with his left hand while he held onto hers with his right.

"What?"

"Maybe you should sail with my father. He'd probably take you and then you wouldn't be here all alone."

Julia took a sip of her tea and considered it for a long moment. She thought about the *Belle of Canton,* the foreign ports, the many oceans of the world. The pull of the sea was strong. But there were other things.

"No," she said slowly. "I don't think so."

He looked at her in surprise. "Why not? I thought that's what you wanted more than anything in the world. To go to sea."

"It was, but now there are things I want more." She looked at his face, so dear, so beloved. "I want to be with you. What if, when you came home, I wasn't here?"

"I'd wait. It wouldn't be long."

"Even a day would be too long. Besides"—she toyed with her spoon as she thought—"if I go off now, Papa will never get over it. I have to give him time, and I have to be here when he decides to apologize."

"Then you really think he will?"

"Oh, he will, Jason." She smiled and squeezed his hand. "It is funny, though."

"What is?"

"When I used to go to bed at night, I'd lie there and

144

pretend I was on the *Belle of Canton*, seeing the world from her decks, and here I am, turning it down."

"Are you sure?" He looked at her intently.

"Yes. You see, I want you to be the one to show me the world."

"I will," he promised.

"You can start by telling me about Canton. About the first time you went there." She put her elbows on the table and cupped her face in her hands.

"Only if you give me another cup of tea," he said, holding out his cup to her. After she had poured it, he captured her hand. "And a kiss," he added.

When she rose to kiss him lightly on the lips, he laughed and pulled her into his lap. "Now I have you, and I want a proper kiss."

"That's not fair," she said when his lips left hers to find the hollow in her throat.

"What's not fair?" he murmured.

"You promised to tell me about Canton, and now you're thinking about something else."

"Are you sure you want to hear about Canton?"

"Well," she laughed. "I want to hear about Canton *first*."

"Will you give me your word that . . . *after* I tell you about Canton . . ."

"I promise."

"All right," he said, reluctantly releasing her. "The first time I ever went to Canton, I guess I was about fifteen. I remember it was a beautiful spring day because, when we traveled upstream from the Whampoa anchorage, the cherry trees were blossoming."

"What did they look like, the cherry blossoms?"

"Like clouds. Pink and white clouds, and the sky was light blue, about the color of Amelia's eyes."

"Was there much traffic on the river?"

"Yes. There's always a lot of traffic on the Pearl River, especially when you get close to Canton. Sampans, junks, boats with poor families living on them, and boats with rich mandarins and their retainers. Sometimes it's difficult to see the water for the craft that's on it."

"Oh, I can't wait to see it!" Her eyes were sparkling with excitement and all sad thoughts had vanished from her mind.

"With me." He suddenly wanted to go to sea, to take her with him, to see her face light up when they sailed into some new port.

"Yes, with you. Go on."

"Well, I was part of the captain's party, and he sat there in the stern looking grim." Jason smiled. "I thought he was watching every move I made, ready to jump on me if I made a mistake, but more likely, he was just thinking about the trading he was going to do."

"Did you make a mistake?"

"No. At least if I did, the captain didn't notice it. Well, when we got near the city, you could smell the spices, and there was music, if you could call it that. Gongs and flutes and red banners waving everywhere."

"And pretty girls?"

"I suppose there were. I didn't notice. I was only fifteen."

"Don't tell me you didn't notice, Jason Thacher. I know you too well. You could have been five and you still would have looked."

"Well, maybe I did,"—he smiled at her—"but none of them were as pretty as you. Anyway, we couldn't do much looking. We had to march behind the captain in landing party formation, eyes straight ahead."

"But you saw something."

"Oh, yes. There were shops with ivories and silks and jade, everything you could imagine, including food. And there were hundreds of people in the streets, but they made way for us when they saw we were marching to the American factory. That's what they call the trading houses, you know, factories."

"I know. Did you see Houqua?" She asked about the famous Chinese merchant.

"Yes. I've seen him since then, too. He's really a friend to the Americans. He advised the captain to wait a few weeks to sell our cargo, because its value was bound to go up. It was good advice, too."

"What did he look like?"

"Very wise. You know they all speak in Pidgin English, which makes them sound a little simple, but they're not."

"And you didn't get a chance to explore on your own?"

"Yes, but we only got a couple of hours' liberty, not long

enough to get into trouble, if that's what you're thinking about."

"All that way to China and you only got a couple of hours' liberty?"

"I got more later, but you know we didn't go to China to see the sights. We went to make money." He got up and stretched.

"And did you?"

"The ship did, but I didn't see much of it. Only enough to buy a few presents." He pulled her up from her chair. "Come along, sweetheart. I've told you about Canton, now it's your turn to keep a promise."

"You haven't told me very much about it." She pretended to pout.

"I'll tell you more upstairs."

They soon forgot that William had left them, that he had ever been there, that this had not always been their own private world. When shadows of the future appeared, they banished them with love and laughter. They were not aware of the hours, and the days blended from light to dark and back to light again, but the calendar did not forget.

The morning finally came when Jason said, "This is my last day here, Julie. Tomorrow, I'll have to go down to Boston."

"Oh, no, Jason. No! It's too soon." She rolled over and held him tight in her arms.

"I must, sweetheart. I've got to supervise the loading of the ship." He straightened her hair where it lay tousled on the pillow, shining with blue fire in a shaft of morning sunlight. "But there's no reason you can't come with me. It'll give us a few more days together."

"Can I? I won't be in the way?"

"Of course not, love. We can't load at night. How would I be able to sleep by myself in Boston knowing that you're so near?"

She kissed his chin, which was excitingly rough in the morning before he shaved. "It might be dangerous to take me to Boston. I might stow away, and you'd never find me until you're well out at sea."

"No." He smiled. "You won't stow away, but I'll carry you with me in my heart. Better than that, I'll have a miniature painted of you while we're in Boston. Then I'll be able to kiss your lovely face every morning and every night."

"And you'll have one painted for me." She delicately traced the scar that ran through his eyebrow.

"I won't have much free time."

"But you must!" She sat up and looked down at him in indignation. "It's not fair for you to have a portrait and not give me one."

"Then I will." He pulled her down in his strong arms and kissed her. "I'll find a way."

When they arrived in Boston, Jason took Julia to Chestnut Street, where the Whitticombs lived. Their son Tim, an old shipmate of Jason's, had often brought Jason home with him to spend the first night ashore when they were boys. Later, after his mother died, Jason spent the greater part of his shore leaves with them. They had become like second parents to him.

The Whitticombs gave Jason and Julia a warm welcome, insisting that they stay with them while they were in Boston, as Jason had suspected they would. In fact, the older couple were flattered that, now a full-grown man with a young bride, Jason had turned to them once again for help.

With both their sons at sea and their daughter married, they had plenty of room, and the thought of having young people around the house again was pleasant. But they saw little of them, for Jason left for the wharf early in the morning, soon to be followed by Julia, and they returned well after dark.

The time went quickly for Julia. Sometimes she spent hours sitting quietly on a barrel or crate on the wharf, watching Jason as he went about his duties. It excited her to see her laughing, gentle Jason, her ardent lover, suddenly become a ship's officer, strong, capable, and stern as he issued orders and commands. It brought a new respect for him, which added dimensions to her love, and it gave their nights greater depth.

Sometimes she posed for her portrait. She was even able to persuade the artist to come down to the wharf, where he sketched Jason as he went about his work. Jason's finished portrait would be much larger than hers. She would be able to hang it on a wall and see him while she worked around the house.

Sometimes she spent a few hours with Cousin William, who took her shopping, introduced her to friends, and tried to amuse her in a dozen small ways. But those hours dragged by, and she was always anxious to get back to the wharf.

With each passing day, the glimpses she had of him, those moments she spent memorizing his face, his movements, his body, became more precious to her. They both knew it wasn't proper for her to be hanging around the wharf, but they didn't care. Jason treasured her presence as much as she treasured his. As the time for parting came closer and closer, she refused to go anywhere without him.

And then came the night when there would be no more nights, and she wept in their love. Jason comforted her, telling her how quickly time would pass. But he wasn't very convincing, and when she put her fingers up to touch his face, his cheeks, too, were wet with tears.

At first light, they left the house, Jason carrying the few possessions he had not already stowed aboard. There were not many people in the usually crowded streets as they made their way to India Wharf, but they found William waiting for them, smoking his pipe and searching the skies of dawn.

"You sail with the morning tide?"

"Yes, sir."

"Two hours, I make it."

"Yes, sir, but as you know, there's a lot to be done. Captain Avery was generous to let me stay ashore so long."

"Not many would do the same for their mate."

"I know. It's given him less time at home. I'll have to make it up to him. I must go," he said, shaking his father's hand. "Take good care of her, sir. See she gets home safe to Brewster."

"That I will, and I wish you a good voyage. Perhaps we'll meet before we're home again."

"I hope so, sir. Julie," he said turning to her. "I'll have another chance to say goodbye to you before we sail. Will you wait?"

"Of course, I'll wait. I'll be here long after the *Katy*

149

Saunders is out of sight," she said, blinking back the tears. "But my heart won't wait. It'll be with you."

He kissed her lightly and sprang up the gangplank to report to Captain Avery.

She and Cousin William sat together on a plank laid between two barrels and watched the ship come to life. For a while, Jason was alone on the quarterdeck, shouting out commands to the second and third mates, who in turn ordered the crew about. Then the captain joined him, and Jason became the captain's voice.

On the wharf, a large crowd of wives, sweethearts, and families began to gather, forcing Julia and William to leave their comfortable seat. William used his bulky body to force a passage through to the edge of the wharf and drew Julia after him. Once there, he put a strong arm around her to keep her from being pushed into the dark, swirling water.

In what seemed to be forever and yet no time at all, the ship was ready to put to sea. Captain Avery spoke once again to Jason in his quiet voice, but this time, Jason did not relay the command. Instead, he leaped from the quarterdeck. As he jumped on shore, he caused the crowd to move back and make way for him. He caught Julia in his arms.

"We're casting off, sweetheart," he said. He held her close, the length of his body pressed tight against hers, and he kissed her deeply as he did in their moments of greatest passion.

Before she had time to speak, he was back on board, and the gangplank was being hauled up.

"Sheet fore and main tops'ls," Jason's voice rang out in the clear morning air, and his command was echoed through the ship.

"Let go aft." And the ship began to move.

"Ease away forward."

And as they warped her toward the end of the pier, the chanteyman, at Jason's command, began to sing.

"Oh Shenandoah, I love your daughter."

"Away you rolling river," a few voices joined in.

"Oh Shenandoah, I want your daughter." The voices now rang through the ship, strong and lusty.

"Away, I'm bound away, across the wide, wide Missouri."

Almost as though powered by the men's voices, the ship swung slowly out into the channel. As the ebbing tide caught her, sails fluttered up on her yardarms, and she sprang to life with the morning breeze.

Watching the stretch of empty water widen between them, Julia could suddenly no longer stand it. "Jason!" she cried. "Jason, come back. Come back to me." But her voice was lost in the crowd and the ship's song. Across the water, Jason couldn't hear her.

She saw his distant profile. Then his tall back was turned to her as he shouted out his orders to the crew. The crowd slowly dispersed, but Julia rigidly stayed where she was, staring after the ever-dwindling ship.

Much later, when it had finally disappeared over the horizon, William gently took her arm. "Come, lass. He's gone. There's no more to be seen."

"Oh, no. Not yet," she begged him.

"Be reasonable, Julie. You can't stay here until he returns. You need food and warmth. Your hands are frozen," he said as he chafed them.

"He's gone," she said, looking at William with eyes empty of anything but the surprised pain of loss.

"I know. I know," he said soothingly and put an arm around her to lead her up the wharf. "But he'll be back. It won't be as long as you think." But it will, he added quietly to himself. It will seem an eternity before you're finally through it.

Julia reluctantly let him lead her away, glancing constantly over her shoulder at the water that was filled with ships, but none of them Jason's.

The next day, they took the packet up to Brewster. Julia said little and clung to the rail where once she and Jason had stood together. Now there was only his portrait stowed safe in the cabin, Cousin William at her side, and the empty grey sea before her.

William kept her company in silence for a great while, but finally her sorrow was more than he could take.

"You mustn't grieve, Julie. There's a lot of time to be gotten through before he returns, and you've got to stay healthy for Jason. Your beauty's a precious thing to him. Don't let it fade while he's gone."

"Oh, Cousin William, I love him so. How will I ever get through all the months and years that lie ahead?"

"For that, you'll have to trust in God and His goodness. He wouldn't part you, so newly wed. Most ships eventually return. If they didn't, no man would go to sea."

"Jason doesn't like the sea."

"You're imagining things. Of course, he likes the sea. He's my son, isn't he?"

"No, he doesn't." Julia looked away from the water and solemnly met William's green eyes, so like Jason's and yet so unlike. "I wish that I could have gone with him to protect him."

"Protect him! How could *you* protect him? Protect him from what?"

Julia straightened her shoulders and held her chin high to keep it from trembling. She stared out over the water.

"From the sea," she said.

"You *cannot* control the sea!" William said in exasperation.

"I understand it."

"And so does Captain Avery and so does Jason and so do most of the men on that ship!" He shoved his cap back on his head and pulled it tight. "Do you think they spend their lives out there without gaining a little knowledge? You don't own the sea, you know, Julie."

"I understand it," she repeated stubbornly. "I think you do, too. But I'm not so sure about them."

"Julie, you're talking nonsense. Come. You'll catch a chill up here. We'll go below and get warm in the cabin."

"No. I'll stay here. You go if you want to. You don't have to keep me company."

William stared at her profile. For once, her hair was well under control, tucked beneath her bonnet, but wisps and tendrils escaped and blew around her face. Her soft features seemed to have sharpened overnight, and the laughter was gone.

"I promised Jason I'd take care of you and see you safely home, and that's exactly what I intend to do," he said. "If turned my back on you, I wouldn't be surprised

152

to find you'd jumped overboard and started swimming after him."

"No," she said quietly, her voice almost inaudible under the rush of water and the singing of the sails. "You can trust me. I told Jason I'd wait for him, and wait I shall."

The few days William was able to spend in Brewster with Julia were filled with activity on his part and a numb passivity on hers. She ate when she was told to, went to bed when he reminded her of the time. It was as though her soul were on the *Katy Saunders* with Jason, only her body remaining behind to inhabit the land.

William felt guilty about leaving the girl, but what could he do? He was helpless. More than once, he silently cursed Benjamin.

He did what he could. He arranged for the nearest neighbors to keep an eye on her. He hired a girl and a man to help around the place, and he trained them.

He changed his will to include her, but he didn't tell her about it. She would have guessed the reason. It provided for her as well as for Samuel in case neither he nor Jason returned.

He gave her a large sum of money to add to the funds Jason had left her and explained how to contact his bankers if she needed more. Julia listened silently and stoically to his advice and filed it away in her mind, never thinking to find a need for more money than she already had. The Thachers, father and son, were generous.

The day before he left, William went up to her bedroom and hung Jason's portrait for her.

"There. Now you'll have him with you," he said, "to keep an eye on you."

"It's nothing but paint," Julia said despondently.

"I think it a good likeness, myself," William said, standing back and looking judiciously at the picture.

"A *likeness*," she said bitterly. She turned her back on the portrait and walked to the door.

"Julie, you knew before you married him that he was going to sea."

"I didn't know it would be like this."

"Well, you should have."

"Perhaps." She lapsed back into indifference.

"There'll be another portrait coming from Boston, Julie. I told the artist to paint one of you the same size so you could hang it near Jason's."

"So a painted Julia can look out of her golden frame at a painted Jason in his, but where does that leave me?"

She looked at William and saw the grief and hurt in his eyes. She went to him and laid a hand on his arm.

"I'm sorry, Cousin William. I didn't mean to say that. I guess you think I don't realize all you've done for me, but I do. I'm sorry for the way I've acted since Jason left. I just can't seem to help myself."

"I know, lass," he said, patting her hand and thinking of the young girl who had once come dripping out of the sea, proclaiming herself a mermaid. "I hate to leave you when your spirit's so low. I'd stay if I could."

"But time and tide wait for no man," she said, smiling with her lips, but not with her empty eyes.

"All too true."

"No one should know better than me." She dropped her hand from his arm and went to stand before Jason's portrait. She looked at it searchingly. "Perhaps it's best for you to go. I might feel better knowing that you're out there. The sea might be kinder to him if you are."

This was a new fancy. William didn't know whether to humor her in it or not. Where she got her notions of the sea, he didn't know. After more than thirty years on ships of all kinds, he thought he'd heard them all, but Julie could come up with some whoppers. Well, if it comforted her to believe it, he'd let her.

"Perhaps it will," he agreed.

After William had gone, the neighbors, true to their word, tried to be kind. Too kind to suit Julia. Being the wives and mothers of sailors themselves, they understood her loneliness, but they couldn't heal the painful longing she felt for Jason or the growing ache she had for her own family. They tried to show her the way. They asked her to tea, to join the sewing circle, but after her repeated refusals, they left her alone.

They watched her as she walked or rode to the beach in all kinds of weather. They put their heads together and clucked their tongues. Noticing that she was growing thinner, they questioned the servant girl and found there was plenty of food in the house but that Julia ate very little of it.

They shook their heads and remembered how it had been when they were young, how so often it still was. But Julia Thacher went beyond the bounds of sorrow, somehow. They, too, knew the lost ecstasy of their husbands' arms and paced their barren, moonlit houses in lonely agony, but by day, they managed to fill the empty hours that ran in a string to months and years. It made the time pass more quickly. For many of them, it was hard-won knowledge, but they couldn't reach Julia to pass it on to her.

Then one day, a dray appeared at the door of her weathered grey-shingled house just as Julia was setting out to keep her vigil on the sands.

"Mrs. Thacher?" the drayman inquired of her. He was a stout, grey man. She had never seen him before.

"Yes. I'm Mrs. Thacher."

"Mrs. Jason Thacher?"

"Yes."

"Got a trunk for you," he said, indicating the one on his cart.

"For me? Are you sure? I'm not expecting anything." Jason? Could it have anything to do with Jason? She felt a moment of panic.

"Captain Benjamin Howard told me to bring it over."

"Oh." Not Jason. Thank God. "It's all right, then. Will you bring it in?"

"Yes, ma'am, but I'll need help. It's right heavy."

She called the hired man to help him and showed them the place to put it in her bedroom, where the two portraits now hung gazing at one another from opposing walls.

After the men had gone, she took off her cloak and threw it on the bed. Kneeling, she unlocked the trunk with the key the drayman had given her. Inside were her clothes, and from the look of it, all of them. She shook out the rose silk dress that lay on top, and a letter fell from its folds. She quickly opened it, but saw, in disappointment, that it was her mother's, not her father's, handwriting on the page.

My Very Dear Daughter Julia,

As you can see, your father has directed me to pack all your belongings and send them to you. It is the first time he has spoken your name since he went to see you at Brewster. Nor will he allow your name to be spoken in his hearing. It grieves me for we all miss you.

When he came home from Brewster, your father locked the door to your room, and he has both keys. Today he opened it for the first time. Sarah has asked if she might have the room for her own. That made him furious. When I have finished packing, the door will be locked again. I don't know, though I have pondered long upon it, whether this is a good sign or not. I hope it means that he wants it kept just as it is for the day you return.

Your father has changed since you left us. He is silent and angry most of the time. I have not seen him smile since you left.

I don't know what to tell you. I only pray that time will heal the rift between you as it does so many things. I wish you could come home, but I know he will not have it. At least, not at present.

I worry about you, but I have heard from those who have seen you that you are well provided for and have a good home. I remember the house and know that you are comfortable, for which I am grateful. Please take care of yourself.

I will send word to you if anything new arises.

> Your loving mother,
> Lydia T. Howard

Julia threw the letter in the trunk and slammed the lid. When she became aware that tears were trickling cold down her cheeks, she snatched up her cloak and flew from the room. Outside, Fancy still stood saddled and waiting for her. Brushing aside the hired man, Julia clambered up onto the saddle and cantered down the sandy road to the beach.

Once there, she drove the horse up and down the hard-packed sand at the water's edge. Suddenly she realized the chestnut mare's coat was sweating in the cold air. Remorse overcame her angry grief, and she turned the horse toward the dunes. There, in a sheltered spot, she tethered her to a large piece of driftwood.

"Poor Fancy," she said. She removed the saddle, then unfolded the blanket and threw it over the heaving horse. "I shouldn't have taken it out on you."

The mare snorted and nuzzled at her in sympathy.

"I know," she said, stroking the horse's nose. "You're my friend. Sometimes, I think, my only friend."

After she was sure the mare would be all right, she retraced her steps to the water's edge, where she could walk off the anger and the sorrow that still surged through her. But in rhythm with her steps, she heard her father's parting words: "You've made your bed. Now you know what you can do with it."

Until today, there had been the hope that Papa would come round, that someday he would come to her, ask her to come home. Her mother's letter had completely destroyed that illusion. Papa would never forgive her.

Chapter Nine

1836-1838

THE DAYS PASSED. THE radiant leaves turned brown and left the trees. The winter storms began. At times, gales raged so fiercely they forced even Julia from the beach. When the stinging sand bit into her skin and cut her clothing, when the wind loosened her hair and turned it into a wild, whipping scourge, she had to stay home.

Those were the worst times. She prowled through the house, listening to the wind tearing at the shutters, her agony doubled because she couldn't see the water on which Jason sailed. And those were the days when she thought of the snug office at the shipyard with the potbellied stove warming the coffee pot and her father, with a cup in his hand, talking to her about the business of building ships and sometimes telling her the tales of his youth.

As Christmas approached, she received a package from Boston, sent by the Whitticombs, with whom they had stayed. Mrs. Whitticomb wrote that Jason had left the package with them before he sailed and had asked her to send it to Julia in time for Christmas.

Julia carefully put the package away on the top shelf of her oak wardrobe. She would save it for Christmas Day.

From her family, she heard nothing. She didn't think she would.

She was alone on Christmas Day, since the servants were spending it with their families. When she awakened that morning, the clouds hung low and grey, and there was a damp, penetrating chill in the air. A dreary day to be alone.

She resolutely pushed away the memories that crowded in. Memories of Christmases with her family. The greens on the mantels. Her father laughing with the pleasure of giving. Her mother smiling with the happiness of having her family all around her. Amelia's dimpling giggles. Sarah entranced with her presents. The good smells of Christmas dinner coming from the kitchen.

But she had Jason's package. It was the only word she'd received from him since the day he'd sailed. She knew it had only been a few weeks, but it seemed an eternity.

She delayed opening the gift. Once she had, Christmas would be over. After lighting the fires, she fixed breakfast for herself and ate it slowly, all the while thinking of the parcel lying upstairs, waiting for her.

Finally, she could resist it no longer. She went to the bedroom and took the package down from the wardrobe shelf. Then she sat on the bed with it in her hands. Here she could see Jason's green eyes smiling down at her from his portrait. Slowly she stripped the paper away. Inside, she found a long black velvet box and a letter. With careful fingers, she opened the letter.

MY DARLING, DARLING JULIE,

You are sleeping in the bed beside me while I write this, but I will be far away when you read it.

You smile now in your sleep. Have I ever told you that you smile in your sleep? How many hours have I spent at your side, memorizing that smile, memorizing every precious contour and feature of your beloved face?

At the very moment you open this, I will be thinking of your face and your smile and you, and I will be beside you. No matter where my body may be on earth, my spirit will always be at your side.

My beloved, I would write more, but I cannot. I begrudge every minute that is spent without you in my arms. The clock is ticking all too loudly, whittling down the time that remains. If only I could stop all time and seas and ships and parting sorrow, I would, but since I cannot, I must wake you from your sleep to share this hour with me.

Need I say how much I love you, worship you, adore you?

Yr. devoted husband,
JASON THACHER

Tears had started at the first sight of his writing. Now they flooded unchecked down her face. Looking up at his portrait, she could see only a blur of color: green, black, white, red. She threw herself on the pillow, sobbing wildly.

Later, much later, when the spasms no longer racked her slender body, she got up and went to the washstand. The cold water soothed her hot skin and swollen eyes.

She returned to the portrait and stared into the painted green eyes. As she looked, it was no longer a portrait, but Jason himself who looked back at her with a smile grown warm. His skin was tanner, and his hair was longer than she remembered.

"Open the box," his eyes seemed to be trying to urge her.

She picked it up from the bed and, reluctantly lowering her eyes from his, opened it. Inside, glowing with pink and blue lights, lay a long strand of pearls.

She caught her breath. They were worth a small fortune.

"Oh, Jason," she heard herself saying aloud, "they're beautiful."

His white teeth seemed to flash in his tan face, the creases beside his green eyes seemed to deepen. Then there was only a painted portrait once again, and she was alone.

At the beach, she paced the sands, listening to the grey sighing sea. A few gulls kept her company, raucously crying as they swooped down over the waves in their hopeful quest for fish. Otherwise the beach was deserted. Only a few sails crossed back and forth on the horizon. The deep-sea merchantmen. A few setting out on their journey. Most of them returning, just missing Christmas by a day.

She wondered where Jason was now. He must be in

southern waters, blue as her eyes he had once told her, with the sky reflecting their brilliance, white foam cresting the waves and Sargasso weed trailing its golden fingers through the sea.

Suddenly the aching longing overwhelmed her and she stopped at the water's edge.

"Oh, sea," she called. "Sea. Take care of Jason. Bring him safely back to me."

The sea lapped softly, like a horse nuzzling, at the shore.

"Please. Please. You must." She lowered her voice. "Take care of him. For I love him. I can't live without him."

A large wave, glittering green in a shaft of weak sunlight, higher than any of the others, came traveling over the Bay toward the beach where she stood. She stepped backward over the pebbles and sea wrack to avoid the icy water. As the wave broke, she saw something large and white thrown onto the sand.

She ran down to it and found a glistening, unbrokenly perfect conch shell, its inner surface a soft rose. She had never seen one quite like it. None so beautiful.

It must have traveled many leagues to reach her. Perhaps it had even been tossed off a passing ship, but the sea of its birth was a southern sea. That she knew.

She caressed it, tracing its sweet curves with her fingers, and she smiled. This was the sea's Christmas gift to her. A pledge. Jason would be all right.

"Julia!" A man's voice called from the dunes behind her.

She whirled around, clutching her shell.

Striding across the sand toward her, the cold sea wind whipping his long cape around his burly body, was her father.

She couldn't believe it.

"Papa!"

She ran, stumbling over the pebbles and rocks that littered the beach, into the arms he held out to her.

"Papa. Oh, Papa."

He folded her in his arms and held her too-slender, sobbing body close in their protection.

"It's all right, Julie," he said, stroking her midnight hair. "It's all right now, sweetheart."

She clung to him, as though afraid that he would leave her as suddenly as he had appeared.

"Julia, my little jewel, it really is all right. I'm here. I'll take care of you."

"Oh, Papa, I missed you so."

"I know. I know. But no more than I've missed you."

His voice sounded strange and she looked up at him. Tears were running down his face. It shocked her. She had never seen her father weep before. He had always been the one who mopped away *her* tears.

"Papa, don't. You mustn't cry."

"It's all right. They're tears of joy." He smiled at her. "Will you come home with me for Christmas dinner? They're waiting for us."

She smiled back through her tears.

"Yes, Papa."

"And after that, you'll stay?"

"If you really want me."

"I've never stopped wanting you."

They walked together up the sand to their waiting horses. Her hand was tucked securely under his arm while her other held her shell.

On the far side of the dunes, as he stood ready to help her mount, she put her hand on his arm and looked searchingly into his blue eyes.

"Papa," she said gravely. "You understand that it's only till Jason comes home."

"I understand." His voice was equally solemn and his gaze unwavering. "But meantime, you must bide with me."

At the house, she changed from her damp, dark wool dress and put on a blue satin one. A Christmas dress. She brushed the tangles out of her long, curling hair and put it up on top of her head. When she looked at herself in the mirror, she saw a stranger. A woman looked out at her where, the last time she had really looked, she had seen a girl.

She wrapped her brush and comb and a change of clothes into the large wool shawl she had used once before for the same purpose. Then she had been running away from home. This time, she was running to it. Both were times of joy.

"I'm not leaving you, Jason." She looked up at his portrait and touched the pearls at her neck. "I'll be back for you tomorrow." She placed the conch shell carefully on the table beneath his picture.

"Julie," her father called up the stairs. "We must make haste or dinner will be cold. We don't want to vex your mother."

She smiled. How familiar that sounded.

"I'm coming, Papa." She tied the ends of the shawl together and ran down the stairs.

"That's a handsome dress, Julie. It makes you look like a pretty flower, just waiting to be picked."

"Jason bought it for me in Boston. He chose it."

"And I didn't even provide your trousseau."

"Oh, Papa!" She kissed him on the cheek. "That doesn't matter. What's done is done. What's important now is that you've come for me."

"Yes." He wrapped her cloak around her shoulders. "But it still troubles me. While riding over here, I came up with a plan. I want to tell you about it and get your advice on the way home."

"I'm not sure my advice is worth very much at the moment," she said as she mounted Fancy.

His face clouded.

"Aren't you pleased with your choice, Julie?"

"You mean Jason?"

"Yes."

"Of course, I'm pleased. I love him."

"And you've no discontent with him?"

"No. None." Her face lighted up. "You should have seen him on the ship, Papa. I'm so proud of him."

"A good mate?"

"Yes. The only trouble is . . ." She paused and glanced at the quiet houses on either side as they rode out of the village.

"Yes?"

"The only trouble is that I miss him so much. It'll be so long before he comes home."

"You still plan to go to sea with him if he gets a command?"

"Yes. Definitely. I'll never let him go without me again."

"Well, that's part of my plan."

"You wouldn't try to stop me again, Papa?"

He saw the worried hesitation in her blue eyes, her hand stiffening on the rein as though to check her horse.

He smiled reassuringly at her.

"No. I'll never try to stop you again. I know now I'll never be able to keep you from doing whatever you set your heart on. If I could, you wouldn't be Julia."

They rode for a while in silence through cold sunlight that filtered from the grey sky. Each was immersed in his own thoughts, but the silence was companionable, as it had been so many times before.

They passed a copse of trees with the snow lying in white pools beneath the black branches. It reminded her of the one where Jason had met her on that early autumn morning. It hadn't been so very long ago, Julia realized. It seemed an eternity.

"Well, Papa, what's your plan?" she asked to distract herself from her darkening thoughts.

"I've been thinking about it," he said. "Don't know just how to put it."

"Never known you to be at a loss for words before."

"No?" He looked at her and saw the twinkle in her eyes, the held-in smile. Looking more like herself all the time, he thought with satisfaction. He grinned back at her. "Guess it's because it's a new idea. Just came to me as I was riding over to Brewster. Let's see." He glanced up the snow-patched hill on the left side of the road as though he would find the words there. "When Jason gets home, we assume he'll be qualified to become master of a ship."

"Oh, he will."

"And you'll go with him?"

"Yes."

"And I've given you no dowry."

"That's not necessary, Papa. We're all right." She thought of the funds both Jason and Cousin William had given her. She'd hardly touched them.

"Well, I wouldn't feel right about it if you didn't have one. I gather Jason hasn't been promised a ship yet."

"Didn't mention one, but *he* won't have any trouble." Julia straightened her shoulders, sitting proudly in the saddle.

"Most likely not, but that's not the point. The point is, when you go to sea, I want you to go in the best vessel that can be built. A good, safe ship. And since I build them, there's no reason why I can't provide it."

"Papa!"

"When you're out there, I want to know that every timber in that ship is sound, every fastening properly fitted, the design both seaworthy and fast. I won't have you going to sea in some leaky old tub. I'll build your ship for you with my own two hands and with those of the men I trust."

"How wonderful! A new ship. Jason will be so pleased."

Benjamin smiled. He knew that, when she said Jason would be pleased, it really meant that she was pleased.

"Then you approve?"

"Approve? Of course, I approve. Can I help build her?"

"I'm counting on it. The owner should always be on hand when his ship is being built."

"Owner?"

"She'll be your dowry. Of course, we'll have to sell a few shares to any of our people who want them. But the rest, the controlling interest in the ship, will belong to you and Jason."

"Papa! A ship for a dowry? That's too much."

" 'Tis what I wish to give you," he said firmly.

"But what about Sarah and Amelia? You'll have to give them dowries, too. Can you give us all ships?"

"Doubt they'll want ships. I know Sarah won't. Don't know about Amelia. Too early to tell yet. I'll give them whatever they want, as long as it's within my means."

"It'll have to be something equal, Papa, and that won't be easy to do," she warned him, thinking about what she knew of her father's finances.

"No one but you, me, and Jason has to know how many shares you own."

"I don't know." She frowned. "You have to be fair."

"I don't have to be anything except what I want to be."

"Papa, you're getting stubborn again," she warned him.

"Am I?" He looked at her and smiled. " 'Twouldn't surprise me. They say it runs in the family. Seems to get worse with every generation."

When they opened the front door and Julia saw the dear familiar hall, the banister that just fitted her hand, the rack holding the family's coats and cloaks, the flowered carpeting that ran up the stairs, she almost burst into tears.

"Where've you been, Benjamin?" her mother called from the dining room. "We've been waiting dinner for you."

"Best set another place, then," he called back, flinging his cloak on the rack.

Lydia hurried into the hall. She hadn't heard Benjamin's voice sound so cheerful since Julia had left. Who on earth could he have with him?

"Oh, Julia!" At the sight of her daughter, she turned pale and held out her arms.

Julia rushed to her. "Oh, Mama, Mama. Papa came for me."

"And never a word to me! He went stalking off after church and told me to wait dinner for him," Lydia said, laughing shakily.

"Wasn't sure she'd come," Benjamin said gruffly.

"Did you go to church this morning, Julia?"

"That's where I found her." It all depends on what you call a church, Benjamin added to himself.

Sarah, hearing voices below, came slowly down the stairs to investigate.

"Well, hello, Julia. Merry Christmas."

"Thank you, Sarah."

Julia went to the foot of the steps to kiss her sister, who coolly turned her cheek and whispered in her ear. "I see the prodigal has returned."

"Julie, Julie!" Amelia, at twelve, had undergone a rapid change since Julia had last seen her. Where she had been straight up and down, the beginnings of breasts and a waist were now noticeable. Her pale blond hair was hanging loose over her cherry-red Christmas gown. Caught between childhood and womanhood, she had a breathtaking quality about her. She's going to be the real beauty of the family, Julia thought.

" 'Melia!" She hugged her sister, who was covering her with kisses. "You're so pretty! Let me look at you."

"Have I changed much?"

"Oh, yes. You're really growing up."

"I have a Christmas present for you. I've been trying to find a way to send it, but now you're here, I can give it to you." Amelia's cornflower-blue eyes were dancing as she raced up the steps. "I'll be right back," she called over her shoulder.

Julia looked apologetically at her family. "I don't have any presents for anyone."

"It's present enough to have you home, child," her mother said. Then she looked at her husband. "Thank you, Benjamin."

"I know you've been grieving for her."

"Yes, and with good reason. You're so thin, Julie. You haven't been eating right. Nor sleeping neither, I'd venture." She looked searchingly at the hollows in Julia's cheeks and the dark circles under her eyes.

Julia returned her gaze and thought, she's aged. So many more white hairs mixed in with the gold. Her face so haggard. In such a short time, she's grown older. Am I the cause? Julia wondered guiltily.

"Oh, dear Mama." She hugged her again. "Today we'll both eat well and tonight we'll sleep."

"You'll stay?"

"Yes, Mama. Till Jason comes home."

"We're going over to Brewster tomorrow to pack up her things and close up the house," Benjamin promised.

On the last day of the year, Julia dusted her hands and surveyed her room. She had rearranged the furniture so that her portrait could face Jason's, which hung in the place of honor over the mantelpiece. The fire burning on the hearth threw flickering lights into the late afternoon snow dusk.

The conch shell on the mantel, which she had washed and carefully waxed, glowed lustrous as it had when it came to her wet from the sea. Her new oak chest stood gleaming beneath the window that looked up the road toward Scargo Hill and the beach. The road down which Jason must come when he returned to her.

She looked up at Jason's portrait and wondered idly where it would hang next. Back in their bedroom in Brewster? Perhaps in the parlor, since she would have Jason himself in the bedroom with her.

The longing, that never completely left, now swept through her, a real and searing pain. She sat down quickly in the chair in front of the fire. She was glad that, though

Jason had once slept in her bed here, it had not been with her. Sleep came more easily without the pillows, every lump in the mattress, holding a memory.

Trying to distract herself with a fantasy of the future, she looked up again at the portrait. Maybe they'd hang it in a house of their own. But what need would they have for a house when they would be spending most of their lives at sea?

She was able to smile at the pictures that conjured. Jason, tall and proud on the quarterdeck, master and owner of his own ship. She would be standing beside him, watching the flying fish in the bow wave. The porpoise playing beside the ship. All the world lying before them.

She wanted to go down to the beach, but she knew it was too late. Supper would be ready soon.

It had been hard to fit back into family life. She had grown so used to living alone with her memories and her pain. Her parents didn't seem to know how to treat her, either. One moment, it would be as an adult, the next, a child.

With the new year, though, she would once again take up her duties at the shipyard. She stretched. It would be good to get back to work.

Tomorrow, with all the men on holiday, she and her father would be going over to the yard alone. They would start planning the new ship. The *Jewel of the Seas* would finally be built, even if they wouldn't be able to start laying the keel till fall.

She smiled as she thought of Jason and the joy he would have in the ship. She would write several letters, hoping that one would reach him, and tell him about it. It was a shame he wouldn't be here to see her keel laid, but how exciting it would be for him to arrive home and find her fitted out and ready for his command.

She sat down at her small carved teak desk and pulled out some paper, the crystal inkwell, and her quill pen.

In March, when it seemed that winter would never end, a letter finally arrived from Jason. On a day of lowering clouds and light snow, Julia was working near the potbellied stove in the office at the shipyard. She was trying to tally up a list of payments that would be due after they launched the next vessel, when her father came in, stomping the snow from his boots.

"Here's what you've been pining for," he said, handing her the envelope. "Jeremiah Kelley brought it over from Brewster just now."

She jumped up from the desk. "Is it from Jason?"

"Appears to be."

She snatched it from his hand and stared at the now-familiar handwriting on the travel-stained paper.

"I'll leave you to read it alone," Benjamin said gruffly, embarrassed by the open hunger he saw on her face. He shut the door quietly behind him and went out into the swirling snow.

Julia stood by the warm stove holding the letter unopened in her hand. So long. It had been so long with no word from him. Once she had read it, she would never have it to read for the first time again.

His Christmas letter was worn out from being read so many times, the creases torn from so much handling. Once she'd realized she knew it by heart anyway, she'd put it carefully away in her desk at home and limited herself to rereading it only on Sundays.

Though this one was smudged and water-spotted, it was still new and fresh, the words unknown and unguessed. She turned it over and over in her hands. Where had he been when he had written it? What had the weather been like? she wondered, tantalizing herself. Would the news be good or bad?

Finally summoning up courage, she broke the seal and opened it.

My Darling Julie, My Wife, My Sweetheart, My Love,

It is Sunday afternoon, and for the first time since this voyage has begun, I have the time to set down on paper the thoughts of you that have so constantly filled my mind.

No matter where we are or under what conditions we sail, you are always with me. I sometimes think, when all else is still, that I hear your voice calling me, talking to me in the bow wave, singing to me from the sails. Outlined in the stars above us, I glimpse

your face, the midnight sky your hair. The deep blue
of the ocean here is the blue of your eyes, and when
the sunlight sparkles off the water, it recalls your smile.
There are times in the dark of night, I fancy I hear
your laughter. Does it travel across all the leagues that
separate us? Or is it only your sister mermaids at play?

The voyage has begun well, though we have many
green hands to plague us. They will ripen with time,
I hope, though I misdoubt two of them.

Captain Avery and I get on well, which is a relief.
Never having sailed with him before, I was not sure
what kind of master he would be. No matter what appearance a man may have on land, at sea he becomes
a different creature. When the master and first mate
fall out, it is an unhappy thing for all the ship. However, Captain Avery is a fine captain, and we see eye
to eye on many things.

We shall not put in until we have rounded Cape
Horn and lay up the coast of Chile to Valparaiso. Of
course, much depends on how we weather the Cape.
I am writing this in the hope that we may meet a home-
ward-bound vessel that will take it to you. We have
met several, but none that were bound for Boston or
New York. Can you not conjure one up for me?

I picture you in bed beside me, on the sands watching the Bay, on the deck of the packet, and then you
are next to me on the quarterdeck, laughing at the
wind, your eyes sparkling with the rain, your long
black hair whipping out behind you, your chin lifted
to the pounding sea, and all is bearable once more.

Oh, my love, my sweetheart, my Julie, how vast and
lonely is the sea without you, and we are just begun.

> Your loving husband,
> JASON R. THACHER

Julie put the letter carefully down on the table and
stared out the window at the falling snow. Then she put
her face in her hands and wept. Oh, Jason, my Jason!
You're as lonely as I am. We had so little time together.
It went so quickly and now the hours drag by. Why did
you have to go to sea? What sense is there in all of this?

Then as though to maliciously wound her, words he had

spoken on the packet, words she had barely noticed at the time, returned to her.

She remembered him leaning on the rail, staring into the waves, the brooding look in his seaweed-green eyes, the tightness of the lines beside his mouth, the bitterness of his voice.

"You wouldn't have it otherwise, Julie," he had said.

But it's not my fault you went to sea. It's not *my* fault.

Benjamin, passing by, looked through a window and saw her weeping. Perhaps she would rather be left alone, but he couldn't bear it. He burst through the door and stomped over to the stove to stand beside her.

"Julie." There was a catch in his voice. Her distress and pain so easily became his. "Is it bad news?"

She lifted her tearstained face from her hands and looked at him as though he were a stranger.

"No."

"What is it, then?"

"Oh, Papa . . ." Her face crumpled as she rose and flung her arms around his neck. "He's so lonely."

"I know, lass, I know." He held her close and awkwardly patted her back. "The sea's a lonely place, especially if you've left someone you love behind you."

"I want to be with him. I want to be with him *now!*"

"I know. I know," he said soothingly.

While he held her, waiting for her sobs to subside, Benjamin stared out at the snow, now beating a flurry against the windowpane.

"We'll get no more work done today. Best get home before it starts to drift. I've already given the men word to leave."

"I don't want to go home. I don't think I can face it yet." Her voice was muffled in his coat. "Can't we stay here alone a little while longer?"

"Yes. A little longer. But first, let me take off my coat. Fix us a nice pot of tea. Then we can talk this over."

"Papa." Her face still held the pain of loneliness, but her hand was steady as she poured the tea into her father's cup. "I don't know how I could bear all this without you."

"You know you never have to do that," he said, his dark blue eyes grave as he looked at her. "Never again. I'm sorry

I wasn't with you when you perhaps needed me the most."
He sipped at the hot tea, thinking sadly of the time past,
for which he could never make amends. Then he thought
even more sadly of the future when he, being so much
older, would no longer be here to comfort her.

As though reading his thoughts pondering the mortality
of man, she said, "I'm so afraid Jason will never come back.
He was alive when he wrote this letter, but that was months
ago. How do I know he still is?"

His eyebrows gathered together, almost meeting, in a
frown, and he ran his hand through the thick black hair
that was now sprinkled with grey.

"You have your shell," he said quietly, looking down
into his cup of tea and avoiding her eyes.

"My shell?" Her eyes widened under their arched black
brows. "How did you know about that?"

"I was there when it was given to you."

"The whole time?"

"I heard you calling to the sea on Christmas Day." He
raised his eyes and looked at her levelly. "I saw what
happened."

"Do you believe it, Papa? Do you believe the sea pledged
me his safety?"

He got up and paced about the too-small room. Despite
his years away from it, he had never been able to lose the
habit of the quarterdeck. It returned whenever he needed
to think. He paused at a window and looked out at the
ships and buildings and piles of logs, all shrouded in snow.
Julia watched him, wondering.

"I don't know what to believe," he said finally. "Others
have warned me, ever since you were a small child, not
to encourage you in your strange notions of the sea. When
you were tiny, barely able to talk, you prattled about it. I
thought then that it was just a charming fancy of yours,
and because I loved the sea, I guess I did encourage it."

He came back to the warm stove and threw in another
chunk of wood. Then he sat down heavily in his chair.

"Yet as you've grown older," he continued, "I've often
wondered just how much was truth and how much fancy.
My mind tells me one thing. My ears and eyes tell me
another. In my heart, I just don't know." He picked up
his spoon and drew a pattern on the table.

"Papa, don't say any more," she warned him. She didn't like this talk of the sea. It was wrong. It shouldn't be spoken of.

"Julie, you've got to be more careful," he said, studying her defensive face, the stubborn set of her chin, while he sipped at his tea. "What's charming in a child becomes strange in a woman. There's danger in it. I'm afraid people will notice and start calling you a witch."

"A witch?" She laughed. "A sea witch? That's too ridiculous. Besides, what do I care what other people think?"

"They can harm you. Let that kind of gossip spread, and people will start being afraid of you." He got up and went to the window to watch the snow blowing across the shipyard. "What they fear, they often try to hurt, Julie. Never let anyone see you talk to the water again. You're no longer a child."

"I won't, Papa," she said, caressing Jason's letter with her fingertips.

The laying of the keel took place in early autumn. Already many of the ribs had been shaped on the mold loft floor and stood waiting. This time, there was no secret as to whom the ship was for. Everyone knew and many of the men in the yard had taken shares in her.

Julia watched her growth avidly and even gave a hand in some of the lighter construction. In the glowing days of middle autumn, when the marsh grass had turned golden and the creek was at its bluest, Benjamin watched her working around the ship. She was learning rapidly, he thought proudly. Already she was better than Josiah at his best had ever been.

If only he could keep her for just a few more years, she would match his own knowledge and capability. He sighed, for he knew she would be gone from him too soon. When the *Jewel of the Seas* was launched, he would lose his daughter.

With the laying of the keel, Julia's spirits picked up. Jason would soon be on his way home to her. He might already be homeward bound. He'd written that their trading was going better than they'd expected, and with luck, they planned to leave Whampoa in late August. They'd sail to England for their final trading. Then home.

He'd be here to see the final stages of construction and the fitting out, Julia thought happily, running her fingers along the newly fastened oak ribs that gleamed in the sun. We'll have to spend a few months ashore, but Jason will probably welcome that. Then the sea.

During the autumn, as she watched over the growth of their ship, she took imaginary voyages with him, sailing to the East Indies, to Canton, to Russia. There would be wine to be purchased in France and copra to be loaded in the Sandwich Isles.

In January, she received a letter saying that they were round the Horn and heading for England. Soon, soon, she thought, hugging Jason's letter to her.

Chapter Ten

1838

THE KNOWLEDGE THAT ONLY the Atlantic separated them now acted as a goad to Julia's impatience. Though the days were short, the winter weeks seemed to move like a sluggish icebound stream. By March, she was unable to concentrate on her work. At every opportunity, she mounted the dunes to watch the distant vessels pass, always hoping to catch sight of the *Katy Saunders* with her spyglass.

Then on a late March morning, when the sky was blue and a brisk southwest wind warmed the air, Daniel Sears came bursting into the office, his swarthy face alight and his brown eyes sparkling as they rarely did.

"Miss Julia! The *Katy Saunders!* The signals on the hill say she's been sighted from Provincetown."

"Oh, Daniel!" Julia almost spilled the cup of coffee she had been pouring. Despite trembling fingers, she set it down carefully and then threw her arms around the astonished foreman, hugging him in her excitement. Pausing only to grab her warm red cloak from a hook and the spyglass from its shelf, she ran out the door, leaving Daniel grinning yet bemused behind her.

By the time she had covered the distance to the sawyers'

pit, the news had spread through the yard and the men stopped work to smile at her as she dashed by them.

Benjamin joined her on the crest of the dune.

"Sight her yet?" he asked.

"No. Here, Papa," she said, handing him the glass. "See if you can find her."

"Nope," he said, after studying the horizon. "Too far away. After all, they just sighted her from Provincetown. Still a long way off."

"I'm going to go up Scargo Hill. Maybe I can see her from there." She turned to go, then whirled back. "But maybe I should go home first and get some clothes together so I can get the next packet down to Boston. Oh, Papa! He's coming home!"

She threw her arms around his big chest and hugged him. He held her close for a moment, then looked down at her radiant eyes, her rosy cheeks and lips, and he was as happy at her joy as she was.

"Hold on, now. Stop and think. If he gets into Boston and takes the first packet home, you might just pass him on the way. Best wait till he sends word."

"But he won't be able to come right home. He has to see to unloading the cargo first."

"You never know. Captain Avery may just let him come ahead, knowing what a short time you've been wed."

"Do you think he would?"

"Been known to happen. I arranged a couple of things like that myself when I was captain."

"Then I'll go on up Scargo Hill. Even if I can't see him, I can at least see his ship."

"Go ahead. You're not going to be any use around here, anyways," he said, grinning fondly at her.

Even before she was sure the *Katy Saunders* had docked in Boston, Julia watched every packet from her dune, but there was no sign of Jason. Then on the third day, when she sighted the schooner from far away, she was certain that Jason was on board. He had to be.

Half an hour later, her certainty was confirmed. That tall, lean body standing midships at the starboard rail was like no other body in the world. No one else carried his broad shoulders with quite that air of nonchalant ease. Then he had spotted her in her red cape on the dune and was waving to her. As she waved in return, crisscrossing her arms exuberantly back and forth above her head, she wanted to rush down to the beach, plunge into the cold water and swim out to meet him.

Instead, as soon as the schooner neared Sesuit Creek, she flew to the shipyard dock and flipped the bowline off her dory. It took only a couple of minutes to row across the water to the town wharf. After making the line fast, she found a path opened up for her in the crowd that had started to gather. People smiled as she darted through, but she had eyes for no one but that magic figure on the packet.

As the schooner swung into the creek, Jason climbed up on the rail and stood poised with one hand on a stay. His face was shaded by his visored tweed cap, but still she could see the happiness in those clear green eyes. Before a line had been cast from the packet, he jumped from the rail to the wharf and suddenly she was in his arms.

All thought of the world disappeared, and there was only his strong, lean body holding her, crushing her. The sharp, salty scent of his skin, the way her head just fit in the hollow of his broad shoulder, things she had almost forgotten returned now, so familiar and so dear.

Then he loosened his embrace just enough so that he could look down at her face.

"Julie," he breathed as he studied her features. "I couldn't believe you were as lovely as my memory, but you're even *more* beautiful."

"Oh, Jason, my love! How I've missed you." She raised her hands to frame his beloved face.

"No more than I've missed you, sweetheart." He gazed at her for a moment longer. Then he said, "Let's go home. I'll come back for my chest later."

"Someone from the yard can fetch it for you, but we have to take the dory back. Besides, Papa will want to see you . . . and you have to see your new ship!" Her eyes sparkled with anticipation as she thought of showing him the *Jewel of the Seas*.

"No, sweetheart." His green eyes were filled with a burning longing, but his words were tempered by a smile. "No

Papa, no ship. Not today. Nothing but you. We'll rent a couple of horses and ride directly over to Brewster."

"Jason, we can't just run off like that."

"Why not?" One peaked black brow rose quizzically, urgently, and the fingers he brushed across her lips were warm despite the coldness of the day.

"I don't know why not," Julia said, a little dazed. "I'll . . . I'll take the dory back and tell them to send your chest over to Brewster. My horse is at the yard. I'll ride over to the stables and meet you there."

He tightened his arm around her and smoothed the arch of her eyebrow with his long fingers. "I hate to let you go for even a moment."

"I know. I won't be long. I promise, Jason."

As they walked up the wharf to where her dory was tied, he looked across the creek at the shipyard.

"Which one is it?" he asked.

"The biggest one, of course. See." Julia pointed with her one free hand. "She's on that railway. Your ship, Jason!"

"Our ship." His eyes were full of promises as he held her for a moment longer before he handed her down to the dory. "Don't be long."

"I won't," she promised as she fitted the oars into the oarlocks.

He watched her as she flew across the creek, her eyes never leaving him until she touched the opposite dock. Daniel Sears was there, ready to take the line from her as she jumped out of the dory.

"Isn't Mr. Thacher coming over?" he asked, looking anxiously at her face to see if everything was all right.

"No. We're going over to Brewster," she said breathlessly. "Daniel, will you see that someone fetches his chest from the packet and brings it over to Brewster?"

"Yes, of course," Daniel said, smiling to see her happiness.

"What about your own things?" Benjamin, who had been waiting on the bank, asked as she climbed up to him.

"Oh, Papa, I don't have time. Besides, I have some clothes over there. I never brought everything home."

"Knowing that you were going back."

"I told you I was going back!"

"I know." Benjamin grinned at her. "You'd better hurry.

I see your young husband's walking up the road to the village."

As they entered the house, Julia could tell by the warmth and the freshness of the air that her instructions had been carried out. The morning after the *Katy Saunders* was first sighted, she had sent word to Brewster that the house was to be thoroughly cleaned and that low fires were to be kept burning every day and banked by night.

"Looks as though you were expecting me," Jason said as he followed her into the parlor. He took off his jacket and, tossing it on a chair, stretched his arms in the welcome warmth.

"Expecting you?" She whirled about and threw her arms around his neck. "Oh, my love! Expecting you, hoping for you, praying for you."

He kissed her on the forehead, then brushed his lips down her nose. With the barrier of his jacket gone, she could feel the movement of his muscles under his shirt as he embraced her.

"I'd best stop now," he said huskily, "and poke up the fire or it's going to be almighty cold in here before very long."

She watched him intently as he put more logs on and stirred up the fire. Her eyes had been so long hungry for the graceful strength of his arms, the lithe movements of his body.

He turned and saw her watching him, and the fire that blazed in his eyes was no less than that that blazed on the hearth.

"Julie!"

He caught her up in his arms and carried her to a large wing-back chair near the fire. Holding her in his lap with her head resting on his shoulder, he began to cover her face with kisses, pausing only occasionally to gaze into her eyes.

The tensions and frustrations that had mounted for over a year fell away as Julia relaxed under his caresses. Her dreams and memories of Jason were only pale shadows of his reality, and they were forgotten.

Listening to his strong heart beat, she felt her own pounding in unison. She wondered briefly if their hearts followed the same rhythmic perfection even when they were parted, then lost the thought as his lips brushed against hers, his tongue tickled the corners of her mouth and his hand found its way to her breast.

The winter sun had glided from one window to another and was shining in her eyes when she felt his trembling fingers unfastening the buttons at the neckline of her dress. Then his hand had found its way beneath her chemise and his long fingers invaded the top of her corset, pulling her breast above it. She arched her body to a more comfortable position and his mouth was on her breast, circling it with kisses that made shivers ripple through her body.

In her excitement, she tried to reach him with her lips, to fondle him with her hands, but his arms imprisoned her, holding her motionless. Then he had drawn her nipple into his mouth, flicking it with his tongue, and it was more than she could bear.

"Jason!"

And he quickly moved to silence her with a kiss while his hand continued the rapid fondling of her breast that his tongue had begun.

She struggled against him. It was too much. It had to stop! *He* had to stop! And then she was drowning, only slightly aware that he still held her, was murmuring to her. Lost in her own ecstasy, she didn't feel his fingers brushing the hair away from her face, didn't know that he was gazing at her with adoration.

"Julie, my darling, my dearest," were the first words she heard as she began to emerge from that ethereal world, and she could feel the kisses that fell gently on her eyelids.

She opened her eyes and smiled at him, so at peace with him, and she could see the hunger and satisfaction on his high-planed, tan face.

"Jason. My beloved," she murmured and languidly lifted one hand to run through his hair. She pulled his head down to her and kissed him on the cleft of his chin, running her lips up to gently caress his. Then she let her hand fall upon his neck and buried her face between his cheek and shoulder.

It was into this dark and loving eternity that the fall of the door knocker sounded, rudely startling them out of their enclosed world.

He held her tightly.

"Maybe they'll go away," he whispered.

"Maybe," she breathed. Then she remembered. "Jason, it might be your chest."

"They can leave it on the doorstep."

"No. You'd better go see. The neighbors will know we're home. What will they think if we don't answer the door?"

"I don't care what the neighbors think."

"Well, I do. They think I'm right peculiar, as it is."

"All right," he said, reluctantly releasing her and allowing her to get up.

He brushed his hands over his hair, smoothing it down, and tucked his loosened shirt into his trousers. Julia, watching him, was suddenly aware that her bodice was open and her breasts exposed. She pulled her dress around her and fled into the dining room.

In the mirror above the sideboard, she caught sight of her reflection. With her hair tumbled, her face pale as foam, and her pupils dilated, she hardly knew herself. She would have to hide in here or in the kitchen until whoever it was had gone, she thought, as she rearranged her underclothing and began to button up her dress. One look at her and anyone would know what they had been doing.

But he's my husband, she thought defiantly. We have every right to do as we please.

She heard the murmur of men's voices in the hall and finally the front door banged shut. Then Jason, with his long strides, was behind her. His arms folded around her and she could see the passion on his face.

"Don't button them," he said, catching her hands.

"Who was it?"

"You were right. It was my chest."

Holding her fast with one arm, he lifted her heavy hair and began nuzzling the nape of her neck.

"You should have given them something hot to drink. It's a long, cold ride from the yard and back."

"Don't fret about them. I gave them some money. They'll find a tavern." While kissing her ear, his fingers began to undo the buttons she had just fastened.

Julia watched his hands in the mirror, then remembered there were more duties involved in being a wife than just one.

"Are . . . are you hungry, Jason? It's well past noon."

"No. I'm hungry for only one thing," he murmured, and she could feel his breath hot on her skin. Then he turned her in his arms and looked down at her. "How beautiful," he said in a hushed voice. "How very beautiful."

"Am I, Jason?" She wanted so very much to be beautiful for him.

"Above all other women," he said, and holding her closely to his side, he led her into the parlor. She went, leaning her head against his shoulder, feeling that she had no will of her own. Nor did she want to have one.

He guided her to the wing-back chair and knelt on the floor in front of her. As he began to slip her dress from her shoulders, she shivered.

"Are you cold, my love?" he asked.

She couldn't tell whether it was the coolness of the room or the sight and feel of those long powerful fingers that sent the tremors through her body.

"I . . . I don't know."

He glanced over his shoulder.

"The fire's dying down. I'll get some more wood."

"Don't leave me," she implored him.

He pulled her dress back up around her shoulders, then held her and kissed the hair away from her face.

"I won't leave you, sweetheart. It will only take a moment. I don't want you to fall ill. You're too precious to me."

Feeling, not thinking, until he returned, she leaned back in the chair and closed her eyes. Even then, she opened them only enough to watch him at work.

Once the fire was blazing high, he took her in his arms and pulled her out of the chair.

"Come closer to the fire, sweetheart," he said in that husky voice she had for so long heard only in her dreams.

And it was like a dream to find herself stretched out on the rug before the fire with Jason placing a crewel cushion beneath her head.

"Are you warmer now?" he asked.

"Yes." She raised her arms to him, and he lay down with her, an elbow resting on each side of her body, cradling her head in his hands.

"I worried about you so," he said. "After we sailed, it

182

was all I could think about. You here alone with no one to protect you."

"You were here, Jason."

"No. Not the way I wanted to be. That first Christmas, I looked at your miniature and I thought I saw you crying. You looked so desolate. It broke my heart."

"I saw you, too, that Christmas, but you were smiling."

"Was I? Maybe that was before I saw your tears. Just before I looked at your picture, I was thinking of the present I had left for you, hoping you would like it."

"Oh, I did." She smiled at him and traced the fine white, jagged scar that ran through his eyebrow, the scar received from a storm-freed block when he was only a young boy.

"You look warmer now," he said.

"I am. Oh, I can't believe you're really here," she said in wonder, looking at the clean, sharp lines of his face. His eyes were the color of emeralds and his teeth flashed white when he smiled. "I love you so much."

"Ah, I know, sweetheart." He held her close, the weight of his body giving strength to hers.

They lay there a few minutes, feeling the warmth of the fire and the warmth of their bodies.

Then Jason rolled over and held her up, pulling the dress from her shoulders. Once her arms were free, she loosened the cloth around his neck, wanting to see and fondle the curling black hairs on his chest.

But as soon as she had bared his chest, he pushed her gently to the floor and was on her, kissing her, while his hand reached beneath her skirts, pulling them up as he stroked her long, lovely legs.

She tried to wiggle away from him so that she could loosen her chemise and corset, but he misunderstood her intentions.

"No," he breathed, pausing in his kisses, and he captured both of her wrists and held them firmly above her head with one hand while the other continued to work inside her thighs. Through the fine cloth of her pantalettes, she could feel his fingers caressing ever softer flesh.

Then he was loosening the waistband of her pantalettes, and he sat up abruptly, impatiently to pull them down.

When he tossed them from him and began to work on her stockings, she realized how soon she would be totally naked.

"Jason!" She sat up. "Not here in the parlor."

He paused for a moment, then laughter filled his eyes as he asked, "Why not? You expecting visitors?"

"No, but someone may come to call."

"They won't," he said, pushing her back down and covering her face with kisses. "Not on a sailor's first day home."

"Bessie might walk in to check the fire."

"I locked the door." He ran his hands through her curls, fanning them out on the floor so that they sparkled in the firelight around her face.

And then he seemed to be everywhere at once. Her clothes were gone and the clean smoothness of his skin rubbed across her body while his lips and hands were first one place, then another, and she could feel the excitement mounting higher and higher. She hardly realized that she was clutching, holding him, crying endearments, in wild abandonment.

As he slowly began to enter her, she raised her knees and could feel her inner muscles of their own accord caressing him, welcoming him back.

"Oh, Julie," he moaned, resting his weight on her for a moment.

"Don't stop. Please don't stop."

Then awareness of time and place slipped away and there was only love that went on and on through all its peaks and valleys. When she thought she could no longer endure it, he exploded inside of her, and she felt as though she were riding a waterfall into a world of thick fog where there was no sound or dimension.

When she finally opened her eyes, the room was shrouded in twilight except for the firelight flickering on Jason's face as he leaned on an elbow above her.

"Are you all right, sweetheart?" His face was filled with love.

"Yes." She smiled blissfully, lowering her legs to fit between his. She could feel him still within her, peacefully at rest.

"You're as pale as alabaster," he said, stroking her cheek with his knuckles.

"I feel wonderful," she murmured and drew him down in her arms, not wanting him to withdraw from her. "It's been so long."

"Too long, sweetheart, but we'll never be parted again."

"No . . . never."

It was dark, and in the hearth, only a few glowing embers remained when they simultaneously realized they were cold. Jason rose from her, stroking and kissing her as he left and went upstairs to their bedroom for towels and quilts. He returned quickly and wrapped her tightly in a quilt, rubbing warmth back into her.

"You'd better get in here, too," she said, starting to open the quilt.

"No. I want to, but I'd best get dressed and bring in some logs. I've never known a fire to burn so fast," he said, shaking his head ruefully.

"Or so hot," she giggled.

They didn't leave the house for four days, days of dreaming, days of planning, days of love. But then one morning, a man from the shipyard arrived at the door.

"What is it, Tom?" Julia asked when Jason ushered him into the dining room, where the dishes of a late breakfast still covered the table.

"Your pa asked me to carry this note to you," he said, handing her a piece of paper. "Said I was to wait for an answer."

"Oh, very well. Sit down and have a cup of tea, Tom," she said, taking the paper from him and indicating a chair.

She was half-exasperated as she unfolded the paper. After she had read it, she was fully so.

"What does he say?" Jason asked as he poured a cup of tea for their guest.

"He says our ship isn't going to get built if I don't come home and get back to work." She tapped the edge of the paper on the table impatiently.

"Your father . . ."

"He also says he thinks you'd want to take a look at her by now."

"Tell him we'll be over next week," Jason said.

"Capt'n Howard's gettin' right snappish," Tom said.

"How's the work going on the ship?" Julia asked him.

"It's going. I can't see nothin' wrong with it." Tom grinned. "The yard ain't the same without you, though, Miss Julia."

"Oh, well," Julia said, handing the letter to Jason. "I reckon we might as well go and get it over with. Tell him we'll be over later today."

"Yes, ma'am," Tom said, putting his empty cup down and rising from the table. "I'd best be gettin' on back. Capt'n Howard told me not to tarry long."

After Julia had seen Tom out the door, Jason exploded. It was the first time Julia had known he possessed such a temper.

"Your father! All he has to do is beckon and you go running to him."

That was too much for Julia.

"There was one time I didn't go running to him," she exploded back. "And you're a witness to the fact!"

"Well, he's not always going to have you around and he might as well get used to *that* fact right now!"

"We *are* building a ship, Jason!"

"You heard Tom. It's getting built without your help."

"I'd think you'd care more about that ship than anyone else. Don't you *want* to be a captain, Jason?"

"Damned right, I want to be a captain, but I don't have to build the damned thing. All I want to do is sail her."

"Well, if she's not ready for launching come fall, you're not even going to get the chance to do that."

Jason looked at the blazing dark indigo eyes in her white face and suddenly the anger left him.

"Oh, Julie." He put his arms around her rigid body. "It's just that I can't bear to share you. Surely we could have just a few more days alone."

She melted as she felt his strong arms holding her so gently.

"Oh, my dear." She leaned her head against his shoulder. "I want it, too, but we have to think of our future. If Papa gets too riled up, he might think twice about giving us the *Jewel*."

"Your father's the worst-tempered man I've ever seen on land."

"Not really. You've just seen him at the wrong times.

Besides"—she smiled impishly up at him—"it seems he's not the only man in the family with a temper."

"I'm sorry, Julie."

"Don't be. The master of a ship better have an occasional temper or he's not going to get very far."

"But not with you, Julie. I should never lose it with you." He looked down at her face. "You're the most beautiful, the most splendid woman in the world." Then he grinned and squeezed her. "In or out of bed."

"You been sampling?" She looked at him wickedly.

"No." He was suddenly serious. "Not since I met you. You know that, don't you?" he asked, tilting her slender chin up.

Her eyes danced sapphires at him. "It better be true or you're going to see a real temper around here."

As they rode down the lane to Toct Bridge, Julia's exasperation with her father rose again. Jason was right. Papa did think all he had to do was send for her and she'd be there anytime he wanted her. Well, she was going to set him straight. Today. He was just going to have to realize that she was a married woman and that she had more responsibilities than the shipyard.

But as they topped the rise of the hill and the yard across the sun-sparkled creek came into view, Julia forgot her anger. The familiar sounds rose to meet her, and she felt as though she were returning home after a long absence. Four days? It seemed more like four months that she had been gone.

The snow that had lain puddled in permanent shadows had disappeared, and she realized that it would soon be April. Only a few months to complete the *Jewel* and have her ready for launching on the high fall tide. Julia felt the press of time and was suddenly impatient to get back to work.

Benjamin was at the hitching post, waiting for them, when they rode into the yard.

"Welcome home, lad." His deep blue eyes were candidly amiable as he beamed at Jason. "We all missed you, especially this young lady," he said, helping Julia dismount.

"Thank you, sir." Jason swung down from his saddle and held out his hand to Benjamin, his clear green eyes as pleasant and guileless as his father-in-law's. "It's good to be home."

Julia, who remembered too well the last time these two men she loved had met, felt as though a weight had been lifted from her mind. After Jason's outburst of the morning, she had been uneasy about this moment, but here they were smiling and chatting together as though no unpleasantness had ever occurred between them.

"Mustn't keep you here talking, though," Benjamin was saying. "I want to hear all about your voyage, but I know you're impatient to see the *Jewel*. Plenty of time for talk later." He clapped Jason on the shoulder and steered him toward the largest railway. Seemingly as an afterthought, he called over his shoulder, "You comin', Julie?"

When she caught up with them, she heard her father ask Jason, "Well, what do you think of her?"

Jason nodded. "Very impressive."

Then, with his hands jammed in his pockets, he made a slow, thoughtful circuit of the ship, keeping well clear of the workmen who seemed to be everywhere. With each new angle, he would stop and study her critically, but Julia could read nothing on his high-planed face. The joy she had expected was missing.

"Well?" she asked expectantly when he had completed his tour.

"Beautiful work," he said, and to her ears, his voice seemed flat and noncommittal.

Surely he could show more enthusiasm than that! But Benjamin was pleased.

"Won't find any better," he said with a note of pride. "Julie, why don't you take him up and show him what's inside?"

"That's a good idea," she said, leading the way to a tall ladder laid against the scaffolding. Perhaps once he was aboard, he would be able to picture the completed ship more fully.

The decking was only partially laid, and there were catwalks and ladders everywhere.

"Isn't she going to be marvelous?" Julia stepped onto the forward decking and swept her arms aft, embracing the ship.

"She's got good stowage space," Jason said, looking below.

"She should! Six hundred fifty tons, one hundred forty-eight feet long, and over thirty foot of beam. You can't ask for much more than that."

"Julie, the beam of her midships . . ."

"What about the beam?" Julia suddenly felt defensive about the *Jewel*.

"Isn't it a little . . . radical?"

"Oh, Jason, you've been at sea too long. You haven't kept up with the latest developments."

"That's where you see ships. At sea. In the ports. I think her forward lines are too sharp." His eyebrows gathered sharply in a frown.

"Jason, this is the ship Papa's been dreaming of for years," she said impatiently. "Other people are just beginning to catch up with him. Why, he went down to St. Michaels in Maryland last summer to see one of the newest Baltimore packets being built. *They* haven't got their widest breadth of beam forward. It's midships, and you certainly can't call them slow."

"But they're smaller and don't have this kind of cargo space, Julie. Don't usually carry a ship's rig, neither, and they're not meant for the kind of seas an East Indiaman will meet."

She turned to look at him, and his face was stony with resistance.

"I just don't understand you, Jason. Here's a beautiful ship . . . and a fast one . . . being built just for you. Why, she'll make your reputation with the records she'll set."

"Sweetheart, I don't want to take you out there in a ship that's not seaworthy." His voice was soft, but his eyes were resolute.

"Seaworthy! Jason Thacher!" she said, putting her hands on her hips. "There's never been a vessel launched from this yard that wasn't seaworthy. You ever heard of a Howard-built ship being lost through faulty design?"

"No, but the Howard Shipyard never produced a vessel that looked like this one before."

"Do you honestly think my father would design a ship, knowing full well I was going on it, that wasn't the safest in the world?"

"I'm sure he wouldn't, love, but he could get carried away proving his ideas. Some men do."

"Well, if you're so skeptical about her, you can use her for the coasting trade." Julia tossed her hair back and looked scornfully at her husband. "Can't make much money that way, but you can't get in too much trouble, neither. Not if you're careful."

"She's built for the East Indies," Jason said, looking down at the cargo space, his face closed to her, "and you'd be miserable if I didn't take you there. It's all you've been talking about the past few days."

Julia looked at him where he stood apart from her. This wasn't a stony stranger. This was her Jason. He was here, close to her, just as she had dreamed he would be during those long, lonely months that had just ended. Why were they fighting? Anything he wanted . . . he could have anything! Just as long as he came back to her.

"No, Jason. I won't be miserable," she said softly, linking her arm through his. "Just being with you, sailing with you, anywhere would make me happy."

She could feel his lean body relax against her arm, and he smiled reassuringly down at her.

"I'll take you round Cape of Good Hope in her, but I doubt 'twould be harmful to make a couple of voyages across the Atlantic first, just to get the feel of her."

"I'd like that," she said, smiling mistily up at his beloved face. "To see England and France, maybe Denmark and the Mediterranean, but Jason, please don't let on to Papa that you have any doubts. Ever."

"I won't." He patted her hand.

"We'll just let him think it's my idea. That I want to see Europe before we go east."

By the time they had inspected the hull from stem to stern and climbed down the scaffolding ladder, the sun was low in the sky. Benjamin met them as they reached the ground.

"Well, lad?"

"She's beautiful, sir. A real jewel." Jason grinned at him. "Makes the *Katy Saunders* look like an antique."

"Think you can handle her?"

"I'm sure of it, sir. You've thought of everything."

"Good, good. We better get on over to the house now.

Your Cousin Lydia's been wanting to see you, to say nothing of the girls."

"Papa, let's wait till tomorrow. We want to get home before dark."

"Home to Brewster."

"That's right, Papa."

"When do you plan to start work?"

"We'll be over tomorrow morning."

"Bright and early!"

"Well . . . fairly early," she said, smiling at him. "Tell Mama we'll be there for dinner."

As March turned into April and April lengthened its days, Jason accompanied Julia to the shipyard each morning. At first, he enjoyed just watching her move gracefully between ship and woodshop, caulker's shop and office, but soon he found himself growing restless. Though interested in the building of a ship, the progress seemed slow and he had no skill to offer except that of an observer.

He found it difficult to cope with idleness after so many years of constant work at sea. Gradually he began to think about going back. A short trip to fill the months between spring and fall. The Atlantic was at her best now, quiet and well-behaved. He wouldn't be able to sign on as a master, but there should be no difficulty in finding a vessel in need of a first mate.

He didn't mention his restlessness to Julia. There was no need to till he came to some decision. He hated the idea of being parted from her even for so short a time, yet there was money to be made there. Money to buy her some of the many beautiful things he wanted to give her.

There were times, too, when he saw Benjamin's eyes resting on him with a question, and he knew that the same thoughts were crossing his mind. He felt that he was slipping in his father-in-law's esteem.

Then one day, Julia and Jason arrived at the shipyard to find Benjamin escorting Captain Avery on a tour of the vessels under construction.

"What's he doing here?" Julia asked, narrowing her eyes in suspicion. She had been aware of her husband's growing restiveness, although she had pretended not to be aware of it.

191

"I don't know. He should have put to sea a week or so ago. Maybe he wants your father to build him a new ship."

"Maybe," Julia said in a tight voice. "You'd better go find out. And it had *better* be about a new ship."

When Jason caught up with them, the two men were admiring the *Jewel of the Seas*. Benjamin turned to him as he joined them and said to Captain Avery, "Here's a lad you know."

"The very lad I've come to see," the short redheaded captain said.

"Glad to see you again, sir," Jason said, shaking hands with the older man. "Thought you'd be on the high seas by now."

"Nope. Planned on it, but that new mate wasn't worth shooting. Had to get rid of him. He got the cargo stowed all wrong. First storm we'd have hit, we'd have been in bad trouble. I had to restow the whole damn thing myself."

"What brings you up here, Captain?" Jason asked. "I'm certain you're anxious to put to sea."

"That your ship?" Captain Avery asked, ignoring Jason's question.

"Yes, sir." Jason was slightly embarrassed, knowing full well that the other man's ship was sixty tons smaller and a much older vessel.

"You're fortunate, lad. Not many get a ship like that for their first command. How soon'll she be launched?"

"On the full-moon tide in October."

"Long ways from now. Find time hanging heavy on your hands, do you?"

"Well . . ."

"That's what I've come about. How about sailing with me for one more trip? Just over to Liverpool. Should be back about August. You'll be home for the launching with time to spare."

"It's only three weeks that I've been home, sir. I'd planned on spending a little time getting acquainted with Mrs. Thacher."

"Thought she was going to sail with you on that," he said, nodding at the *Jewel*.

"She is."

"Well, you'll have time and plenty then. Nothing like a long voyage for getting acquainted with your wife. Mrs.

192

Avery and I were married five years before I convinced her to sail with me. When I got her there, made me realize we'd been practically strangers those first five years."

"Well . . ." Jason looked across the yard at Julia, who was standing beside the woodshop, apparently absorbed in her work; then up at the *Jewel*, unfinished on the ways. "When do you sail, sir?"

"I'll delay a couple more days if you'll sign on."

Jason rubbed the back of his neck as he thought about it.

"Let me talk to Mrs. Thacher," he said.

"I'll spend the night here with Captain Crofton. Old friend of mine and we've got a lot of catching up to do. Have an answer for me in the morning before the packet sails."

"It's a hard decision to make in one night."

"As I recall, you were always pretty quick when it came to making decisions aboard the *Katy Saunders*. I don't doubt but that you'll come up with the answer by morning."

When Captain Avery had left the yard, Jason wandered over the dunes to the water's edge in order to avoid the questions he knew Julia would be throwing at him. He wanted to do some thinking of his own, to have the answers before he talked to her.

Julia, however, had seen the direction he took and was not about to be forestalled by it. When she arrived on the beach, she found him staring out across the Bay at the sails that looked like low-flying scud in the misty April air.

"Well?" she said as she joined him.

Without answering her or looking at her, Jason bent and picked up a flat green stone. Aiming carefully, he skimmed it across the calm water.

"Jason?"

"He wants me to go to Liverpool with him," he said, his eyes still on the spot where the stone had sunk.

"You told him you're not going, of course."

"No, I didn't. I told him I'd give him an answer in the morning."

"Well, you don't have to wait for morning. Go tell him right this minute. You're not going with him."

"Julia," he said, turning and finally looking at her, his eyes serious. "I have to make my own decisions."

"I don't see what there is to decide," she said, lifting her chin stubbornly. "Come fall, you'll be in command of your own ship. It'd be terrible if you weren't here for the launching."

"I'd be here. We'd be home by August; at the latest, the first of September."

"Jason, you were gone for seventeen months. You've been home barely three weeks. Now you want to leave me again." Incipient tears turned her eyes into blue pools.

"I don't want to leave you, love!" He gathered her in his arms and kissed her eyelids to shut away the pain. "But I'm not used to being idle. You have your work to keep you busy while I'm looking forward to six months of unemployment. Every time your father looks at me, I feel as though I'm a lazy soger."

"Oh, Jason!" Her wet eyelashes parted in surprise. "I know Papa doesn't feel that way. He's as happy as I am to have you home at last."

"That may be, love, but it doesn't take away from the fact that I'm loafing while you're hard at work."

"I'll give up work then, Jason," she said, smiling with enthusiasm. "We could travel. Go to Boston or New York. We could have such fun together. Let's do that!"

"No. I can't let you do it." He brushed the curls away from her earnest face. "I've watched you at work for too long. I know how much you relish it."

"Not as much as I relish you," she said, putting her head on his shoulder and holding him tight. "Please don't go away, Jason."

"I don't want to, sweetheart."

"The work isn't that important. I'm going to leave it once the *Jewel* is launched, anyway," she pleaded with him.

"But you'll be involved in the rigging," he said, twisting one of her curls around his finger, "and then you'll be at sea, where you'll be happy. We're not people meant for idleness, love, neither one of us. You know you'd be feeling guilty every minute if you went off and left the work you promised to do."

"But I'd be with *you*, Jason."

"Julie." He tilted her chin up and looked tenderly at her. "If you were in my place, what would you do?"

She lowered her thick black lashes so that he couldn't see the expression in her eyes while she thought about it.

"I guess . . ." she said finally. "I guess I'd feel I had to go."

He took his hand away from her face and held her close to him. The answer wasn't the one he wanted, but it was the one he had expected. It confirmed the feeling he'd begun to have that, if he stayed home idle, he would gradually begin to lose her respect, too. Even though he had argued for it, he felt trapped by the decision that was being forced upon him. Couldn't they have had just a little more time together?

As if in echo to his thoughts, Julia said, her voice muffled against his chest, "Jason, I can understand. I really do. But can't you stay with me just a little longer? I won't spend so much time at the yard. We can do so many things together this spring."

"If I wait too long, sweetheart, there won't be time to make a voyage and return for the launching. This way, I'll only be gone four months. Then we'll never be parted again." He lovingly traced the line of her cheek with his long fingers.

"That's what you said the last time you sailed." She bit her lip and her eyes were dark indigo as they reproached him.

"I didn't realize then that I'd have to wait so long for a ship to be built. I thought I'd find a command shortly after I got home." He pressed his lips together in sorrow and the cleft in his chin seemed to deepen.

"We started building her as soon as we could," Julia said apologetically.

"I *know,* sweetheart, and I appreciate all your father is doing for us in giving her to us. She's a better ship than I had any right to expect as my first command. Still, sitting on the beach isn't what a sailor does best."

"Must you *really* go?"

"Yes, I must."

"How soon?"

"A couple of days."

"Oh, no! Jason, no!" She clung to him as she cried her pain of sudden parting.

He kissed the top of her blue-black curls and held her

195

close so that she wouldn't see the tears that were running silently down his cheeks. He took out a handkerchief and wiped them away before he turned her face up to blot her pale cheeks.

"Come, sweetheart," he said hoarsely. "Let's go home."

Of the two days left them, there was no time for anyone but each other, and though they tried to hold and memorize each swift minute, every passing second, yet the hours rolled by just as inexorably as the tide ebbed, flooded, swirled up the beach and ebbed again. This parting was harder than the first, for it was the parting that was never supposed to happen.

Julia tried to understand his decision, did understand, for if she had been a man she would have done the same. Still, it was difficult for her not to think he loved her less because of his ability to leave her. And Jason, watching the doubts that flickered across her face, wished that he were a landsman, a shipbuilder, the lowliest apprentice in her father's yard, so that the waves would not beckon him, command him, so that the sight of sails passing far out beyond the Bay did not wash him with guilt.

The afternoon before he sailed, they went to watch the sunset on the beach at Brewster. The spring sand glowed with golden life and the clean foam reflected the dusky rose of coming evening.

They walked beside the water's edge, their fingers intertwined, but they walked in silence. There were so many things to say, it was difficult to find the most important, and the silence bound them closer than any words could do, for then they could enter each other's souls where speech was only a barrier to their intermingling.

Yet words must be said, if only to lessen the pain of perfection.

"When I was gone, did you come here to think of me sometimes?" he asked.

"Yes. I came," she said quietly. "It was a long and lonely time. This isn't my favorite stretch of sand."

"I know."

The sea gulls rose in a flight and swooped across the water, searching for their last meal of the day. With coming evening they too were silent, even in their quest for food.

"Julie, when I'm gone, don't come back here. Go home to your family. Work on your ships. Walk your own beach when you think of me. It's a happier place for you."

"I will."

"When I see the morning star, I'll think of you, and when the sun sets in the west, I'll know that it is coming to you, and my love will come with it."

"I'll remember."

"It won't be long."

Julia tried to smile but it came out crooked. "Too long," she said. Then suddenly the restraint she had imposed upon herself disintegrated, and she flung herself into his arms. "Oh, Jason, don't go, don't go. I'll do anything you want. Just don't go away. Don't leave me." Her tears came as a cloudburst.

He held her and petted her, but he couldn't tell her what she needed to hear, for if he spoke, he, too, would break down, and one of them must be strong.

When she had begun to regain control, he gave her his handkerchief.

"I hate to take it," she said between lapsing sobs. "You're leaving so suddenly, not all your clothes are clean."

"It doesn't matter," he said. "The steward will see to them."

"He'll think you have a terrible wife."

"No one thinks that." He took the handkerchief with which she had been ineffectively dabbing at her eyes and gently wiped her wet face. "Julie, sweet Julie, don't cry for me while I'm gone. Don't think of the days as taking me away from you. Think of them as bringing me back to you. Each day that takes me eastward is one day closer to my return. Will you remember that?"

"Yes. I'll remember."

"And you'll keep busy?"

"Well, I've got to get that ship built for you, don't I?" She tried to laugh. "If she's not ready when you come home, you might just turn around and leave me again."

"No, don't think that." He tilted her chin up, and though he smiled, there was pain in it. "I'll never leave you again. That I swear."

The next morning, Julia stood on the wharf and watched the packet bearing Jason away from her sail out of Sesuit Creek into the Bay. He had refused to let her come with him. The *Katy Saunders,* since she was already loaded, would sail almost immediately after he arrived in Boston, and he didn't want her to be alone in the city. Still, they both knew that she would be watching from the top of Scargo Hill to see the sails of his ship set for England.

Chapter Eleven

1838

THE SUMMER PASSED SLOWLY, then swiftly, then slowly again. The fog rolled in. The nor'easters blew. The sun shone bright and clear. In late summer, Julia mounted the dunes to watch the distant ships, always hoping to catch sight of the *Katy Saunders* with her spyglass.

Then in August, a day dawned grey and orange, and though the sun rose high in a cloudless sky, it gave a filtered yellow light. There was a sticky pressure in the air. The barometer fell rapidly.

The men worked quickly at the shipyard, stowing everything they could move into the sheds and buildings, tying down the unfinished vessels with long ropes made fast to giant boulders and deep-driven stakes. There was a frantic quality to their movements, and the gulls soared, screaming excitement, over them. The air was calm and still, but the birds seemed to be playing in a high wind aloft. No one knew what was coming, but it was coming. A gale and, perhaps, worse.

As Julia worked beside the *Jewel of the Seas*, securing a line to a high thick timber that was driven into the sand, the haze became thicker and more oppressive. It was hard to breathe. She looked up and saw the sky now a mass of turbulent grey clouds. She took another turn on the line and ran to pick up the next rope that was being flung from the ship.

In the late afternoon, when everything was secure, Benjamin sent the married men home to look after their families and with them sent the boys. He kept only the strongest single men with him at the yard. The women had brought quantities of food and water to them as they worked, and now they were provisioned to wait out the storm.

Then Benjamin looked for his daughter. He found her checking once again the lines on the *Jewel*. Her rough grey dress was torn, her face was smudged, her hands grimy, and strands of hair had escaped the pins and fallen curling down her back. She looked exhausted, as though she had kept going on nervous energy alone.

"You go on home, Julie, and take the horses with you."

"I'll stay here with you, Papa."

"No, the horses will be safer at home, and your mother and the girls will need looking after." Running his hand through his rough salt-and-pepper hair, he thought about what else would have to be done, even while he spoke.

"Are you sure you'll be all right?" she asked, reluctant to leave him.

"I'm sure," he reassured her. "Now you get on home."

The horses were nervous and jumpy as she saddled them. Once on the path across the marsh, a gust of wind stirred the leaden air and flattened the tall reeds and grass. Baron shied, and she had to struggle with him to keep him on the path. Eddies of sand played all around them, like miniature whirlpools. There was fear in the air, and the two horses communicated their nervousness to her. She was glad to get them home and turn them safely over to Ezra.

The big white house looked strangely withdrawn with the black shutters bolted in place. She went in by the pantry door to find everyone in the kitchen, cooking by lamplight. It looked like a cave, and the heat was stifling.

"Where's your father?" Lydia asked, looking up from the stove and mopping her face with a towel.

"He's staying at the yard."

"He would." Lydia shook her head. "Now we'll have to send some food down to him."

"No. He has plenty. It'll take them a week to eat everything they've got." Julia sank down in the rocking chair. She hadn't realized how bone-weary she was. All day, she had carried loads beyond her strength and had worked as hard as any man. Then the struggle with the horses. She could feel the results of it all now.

"You look weary, Julia," her mother said. "Go up and get out of your clothes. Amelia will bring you some hot water for a bath."

"It's too much trouble," Julia said, feeling that it was more than she could do just to get out of the chair.

"Do as I say or you'll feel worse in the morning than you do now. Have a nice hot bath. Then you can have dinner in bed."

"I'm not sick, Mama." Julia just wanted to go on sitting in her chair.

"You will be if you don't do as I say."

"Come on, Julia," Amelia said encouragingly. "Stand up and put your arm round my shoulder." She put her own around Julia's waist and tried to pull her up. Feeling her sister's young strength, Julia drew from it and managed to stand up.

"I don't know what's the matter with me," she said groggily.

"Exhaustion," snapped her mother. Benjamin had no business letting the girl get overtired like that.

After the hot bath, Julia lay down while her sister went downstairs for a tray of food, but when Amelia returned, she couldn't rouse Julia from her deep slumber. She put the tray on the dresser, tiptoed out of the room, and left the door open. I'll hear her if she calls, she thought.

Although Julia's first sleep was the immobile sleep of exhaustion, she later began to turn from side to side as though there were no comfortable position for her tired body. The sheets tangled around her, and they were soaked with her perspiration.

She dreamed that she stood on a quarterdeck beside Jason. It looked like the *Katy Saunders*. A strong wind was blowing. The topmasts were snapping. The ship was rearing and plunging deep among the mountainous waves. She kept trying to tell him that they were on the wrong ship. They should be on the *Jewel of the Seas*. Then the ship gave a tremendous shudder as though it had struck a rock, and Julia woke up.

It was the house shuddering under the impact of the gale. She got up and lit her lamp to look at the time. Half-past-two.

She thought about her father at the shipyard and wondered how the vessels were surviving this gale. Then she remembered her dream and thought of Jason. Strange how real dreams could be. But he would still be far out at sea. His ship would likely escape this storm altogether.

She paced around her room, listening to the roaring wind that almost drowned out the sounds of broken branches, sheets of water, and light stones beating against the sides of the house. Suddenly there was a crash above her, as though something heavy had struck the roof. The house shuddered more violently than ever.

When the crash came, Julia instinctively looked up at Jason's portrait to make sure it was safe. It was, but as she looked, the large white conch shell that lay under it seemed to be moving with the tremors that shook the house. She ran to the fireplace to steady it, but before she was able to reach it, the shell tilted over the edge of the mantelpiece and struck the stone hearth below.

She swooped to pick it up and found that one side of it was smashed. She knelt and let the chips trickle through her hand. Then the realization of what had happened hit her. She threw back her head and screamed. It was only one word repeated over and over. "Jason! Jason! Jason!"

She ran to her wardrobe and frantically yanked out her clothes, throwing them on the floor, until she found an old dress. She pulled it on over her nightgown. She thrust her feet into a pair of rough shoes and ran down the carpeted stairs, buttoning only enough buttons to keep the dress from falling off.

As she reached for the oilskins that hung in the front hall, she could faintly hear her mother and sisters upstairs, awakened by the crash. Their voices were muffled by the sweep of the storm.

She doused her lamp and tried to open the front door. As soon as she started turning the knob, it was jerked out of her hand and flung back against the wall with a crash.

The force of the gale knocked her back against the newel-post.

She pulled on the door, fighting it as though it were a living thing. Finally, the wind relaxed its hold just long enough for her to slam it shut behind her, and she was in the outer darkness with the roaring tempest. She struggled to the end of the porch by pressing herself flat and clutching at the wall and windows as she went.

When she staggered off the porch onto the grass, something heavy hit her shoulder, and she was knocked to the ground. She got up and pushed three short steps into the gale only to be knocked down again. She fell on her back. Sobbing with fury, she rolled over and started crawling through the littered grass to the road.

Her long skirt caught at her knees. She could gain only an inch at a time. Impatiently, she caught it up and bunched it at her waist.

When she lifted her head, she could barely see through the sand-thick, driven rain. Sticks and branches and strange hard shapes rushed through the air all around her. They pelted her body. She kept her head lowered and her eyes open only a slit, feeling her way down to the sandy road.

Here she was able to stand up. Pressing close to the woods on her left, she passed from tree to tree, clutching at them as the wind tried to tear her away. Branches of great trees snapped and fell around her. At times, the wind would blow her backwards, and she would lose in a minute what it had taken her fifteen to gain.

Bent double, she forced her way through it. All the while, she was screaming in her head the words she could not open her mouth to say.

"Jason! Jason! I'm coming!"

It took hours to reach the path that led over the dunes to the Bay. When she turned onto it, she was knocked flat again. There was no tree here to hold on to. She could hear the roar of the surf now, louder than the wind. She lay flat on the sand, entwining the fingers of one hand in the roots of a bush. With the other, she clawed at the underbrush.

It was calmer here on the sand behind the dunes. There was a tree nearby. She scrambled for it, wildly screaming above the storm, "Jason! Jason! Where are you?"

The surf roared in a never-ending, deafening tumult, but somewhere over or under it, she could hear his voice calling.

"Julia! Julia! Help me!"

"I'm coming. I'm coming, Jason. Hang on! Swim! Don't give up. I'm here! I'm coming! Hold on, Jason!" she screamed.

"Julia . . ." His voice seemed fainter.

"Hang on! Jason! Hang on! Oh, please, dear God, give him the strength to hang on."

She felt a blinding pain smash through her body, and then there was blackness.

Lydia missed Julia shortly after she'd gone. She ran frantically through the house, sending Sarah and Amelia in opposite directions, into the attics and cellar, but they could find no trace of her.

Checking Julia's bedroom, Amelia found the broken shell and the heap of clothes on the floor by the wardrobe. She rushed downstairs. In the hall, she knew what she would find, and when she looked over the oilskins and saw the wet, twig-strewn carpet, her fears were confirmed.

She went to the kitchen, where she found her mother. Lydia was staring helplessly at the outbuildings, as though she hoped for a glimpse of Julia there.

"Mama!" Amelia said, bursting into the room. Her light blue eyes were wide with fear. "I think Julia's gone to the beach."

"Oh, no!" Lydia snapped. "She couldn't have. It's impossible."

"Her shell's broken."

"What shell?"

"That big one on her mantel. The one she won't let anyone touch. I think she connects it with Jason somehow."

"That's ridiculous," Lydia said, pressing her lips tight together and looking back through the window of the pantry door.

"Her oilskins are gone, and the carpet by the front door is soaked."

"Oh, no!" Lydia sank down in the rocking chair and

buried her face in her hands. Then quickly she dropped them and jumped up. "We'll have to go after her."

"We can't, Mama. We can't go out in that storm. Listen to it."

"But Julia's out there. Maybe lying hurt. She could be just outside the door. I'd never forgive myself if I didn't try to find her."

"Mama." Amelia put her arm around her mother's waist and spoke to her as though she were a distraught child "Julia's probably all right, but we won't be. We don't have her strength."

"We can't just sit around and wait, not knowing. Why isn't your father here? His family should be more important to him than a shipyard."

When the eye of the storm passed over them, Benjamin and his men took advantage of the momentary calm to go outside and inspect the damage.

He was looking sadly at a large tree that had crushed an almost-completed fishing schooner when young Robert Sears came running down the hill into the shipyard. "Captain Howard! Captain Howard!" he shouted. "It's Miss Julia."

"What is it, boy? What's the matter?" Benjamin's eyebrows shot up and his face paled in alarm.

"She's lying up on the road near the beach with a big tree across her," he said, panting. "They're trying to get it off her, but they need help."

Benjamin yelled to his men to follow him. Then he ran up the storm-littered road in the direction Robert had pointed.

It was a long run for a man of any age, and Benjamin thought he would never get there. When he arrived he found three elderly men trying to lift the tree from his daughter's body.

"Wait," he shouted, seeing the limbs start to rise and then fall back. "You'll hurt her more that way! My men are coming."

He hurried to Julia's side and saw her rain-washed face, deathly white in the grey light. He knelt beside her to check the pulse in her outflung wrist. There seemed to be a flutter, but he wasn't sure. Perhaps it was only because he wanted to find it there.

He put his hand to her lips. He was sure he could feel a small whisper of breath there.

"Captain Andrew," he said to one of the elderly men who lived nearby, "can you fetch a shutter off your house? I think she's still alive."

"Certain." The three older men moved off as the young men from the shipyard gathered around Julia.

Benjamin looked at them. "Now what we have to do is lift this off in one heave. If we let it fall back, it'll kill her. Everyone station yourselves at even spaces around it and get a good firm grip on the trunk, and for God's sake, make this perfect."

The fourteen men, used to working together, quickly grouped themselves around the tree.

"Is everyone ready?"

"Aye-aye, sir," came a chorus of voices.

"Then," Benjamin said, grasping the torn roots at the end, "one . . . two . . . three . . . *heave!*"

The big tree rose as lightly as a sapling in their strong hands, and they threw it into the brush at one side.

"Good! Now some of you go over and see if you can help Captain Andrew with that shutter." He knelt beside Julia's body, touching it carefully, feeling for breaks and bleeding.

Daniel Sears came up to stand beside him, then saw the tears running down Benjamin's face.

"If I can borrow your horse, sir, I'll go for Doctor Willett."

"The doctor." Benjamin looked up and was reassured by the honest concern in Daniel's dark face. "Yes. Go get him. Bring him to the house."

"Yes, sir."

Daniel ran down the road through the rain-heavy sand, as fast as any man despite his limp.

Benjamin himself gently lifted Julia as the men slid the shutter under her. Then he placed the blanket Captain Andrew handed him over her wet body.

Eight men grasped the shutter and lifted it in unison. Benjamin walked beside them, constantly watching Julia's face. Every step they took jolted him. He was afraid they were injuring her even more, but it couldn't be helped. They couldn't let her lie there on the soaking sand waiting for the doctor. The storm would be on them soon again, how soon nobody knew.

Lydia, Sarah, and Amelia had started out in search of Julia as soon as the wind abated. They first checked all around the house and outbuildings, calling her name. Then they walked slowly up the road, searching on either side as they went. It was near Scargo Hill Road that they met Daniel running toward them.

He didn't pause when he saw them. "They're coming now," he panted as he passed them.

"Who's coming?" Sarah shouted, but Daniel's answer was lost if he gave one.

"Maybe it's Julia!" Lydia said. Picking up her skirts, she started running up the road, Amelia and Sarah following.

As they came around a bend, they saw the procession, the body on the shutter litter.

"Julia!" Lydia screamed.

"I think she's still alive, Lyd," Benjamin said softly. "Don't touch her. Daniel's gone for Doctor Willett. Sarah, Amelia, run home and get her bed ready and make up a fire. Hot water, too."

His daughters, frightened by the ashen, crumpled look of their sister, turned and hurried down the road toward the house.

When the storm hit again, Julia was safe in bed, and the men had returned to the yard, but Daniel and Doctor Willett had not arrived.

Benjamin and Lydia sat the long hours through, one on either side of the bed, watching her frail breath, wondering how much longer it would continue.

"I wish I knew what made her do it," Benjamin said.

"Amelia thinks it was the shell." Lydia pointed at it. Now, though broken, it was resting once again below Jason's portrait. "When the tree crashed through the roof, it shook the house. Could have knocked the shell off. A lot of things fell on the floor."

"The shell?" Benjamin got up and examined it. He looked at it sadly. "Yes," he said, "her pledge was broken."

"Pledge?"

"It doesn't matter. The only thing that matters is that

Julia has to live." He returned to his chair by the bed and gazed at his daughter's face. Her black hair was fanned across the pillow, making her face paler by contrast. There was no flicker of life behind her closed eyelids, and her lashes lay still on her cheeks. She looks drowned, he thought. Then he pushed the thought roughly away from him.

"I wonder if she can hear anything," he said.

"Not likely."

"No. I suppose not." He rose from his chair and walked to the other end of the room. "Come here, Lydia," he said softly.

Lydia was startled. She pushed back her chair and went to him.

"We don't know whether she can hear us or not. There's no point taking chances."

"What is it, Benjamin?" she whispered back.

"I have a feeling Jason's been lost in the storm. I hope not. Without him, I don't know what her chances for recovery are."

"You can't know! There's been no time for word of any wrecks."

"No. I don't know. I hope to God I'm wrong." He looked at Julia's face across the room and clenched his fists. "But we must be prepared for it. If Jason's dead, Julia mustn't be told. Not till she's well. She's very close to death herself now, Lydia."

"I know. You're right. *If* he's dead, she mustn't know." Lydia pushed her tangled, heavy hair back from her forehead. "We'd best caution the girls."

As the storm abated, their long vigil ended. Doctor Willett had almost reached them earlier, but had been forced to take refuge in a house only a mile down the road to wait it out.

He chose Amelia to fetch and carry for him, while her anxious parents stood by. Finally, he banished them from the room. He decided Amelia was level-headed, so he let her stay.

"You in school?" he asked, peering at her over his spectacles.

"No. I finished last year."

"Good. You can nurse her then. Your mother can't do it. Too frail to tend your sister without damaging her own health. You look young and sturdy."

"I am."

"How about Sarah?"

"She'll help, too."

"Don't know how much help she'll be. She looked mighty pale when she let me in."

"Sarah will be all right. It's just that Julia looked so awful when they found her." Amelia thought of the massive black bruises that covered Julia's body and the blood that seemed to come from everywhere.

"Well, you're chief nurse. I'm putting you in charge. Think you can handle it?"

"I'll handle it." The quiet determination in her voice left the doctor with no doubts about her ability.

"You'll do," he said, clapping her on the shoulder. "Now, it's not going to be easy to pull her through. I'm staying here till I'm needed elsewhere. After this storm, I expect to be right busy, but I'll stop in every chance I get. Have a bed made up for me."

"I will."

"Now, this leg's broken in two places, here and here," he said, touching the splint on her right leg. "Her ribs are busted on this side, too. That's dangerous. I've got them taped up, but till they start to mend, one of them could pierce her lung. Don't think any did, but could. So if she starts thrashing around, keep her still. Like this." He laid one hand on Julia's left shoulder and the other on her right arm. "Right collarbone's broken, too, so you can't touch it. Have you got that?"

"Yes."

"All right." He looked levelly at Amelia, wondering how much truth the girl could handle. A steady calm that came from deep inside masked the pain in her light blue eyes, and she stood motionless while she waited for him to continue. Dr. Willett nodded his head in approval.

"That's not the worst of it," he said. "She has a bad concussion. Don't know yet what other damage there may be inside. Can't locate any, but it might show up later. The concussion, though, that could mean anything."

"Is she going to live? Do you know that?"

209

"No, I don't. We're not safe ashore yet. Not by a long shot. She could go at any minute. Don't blame yourself if she does. Now, I want you to make sure she stays warm and dry. Keep those blankets on her even if she wants to push them off. If she runs a fever, she'll try to, but you keep them on."

"Yes."

"If she runs a fever, she'll sweat. Keep the linen changed and fresh."

"But if we can't move her . . ."

"I'll show your father how to slide her. You'll have to get the bed made under her fast. She shouldn't be exposed for long."

"Yes. I'll get Sarah or Maryanne to help me."

"That's right. You take command and tell the others what to do. How old are you now?"

"Fourteen."

"Hmpf! Thought you were older, but age don't mean nothing. Important thing is to keep a level head. Don't panic. Never. No matter what happens."

"I won't."

"If there's any change. *Any.* Good, bad, or indifferent. You send me word, describing the change exactly. Send a good tracker, 'cause he'll have to follow my trail."

"Ezra will find you. He'd do anything for Julie."

"Good. Now if she regains consciousness, give her one teaspoon of this," he said, handing her a bottle of thick green liquid. "Nothing else until I see her. Not even water. I'll get here soon as I can after I get word from you."

"I understand."

"Good. Now, send your parents in. You go wash up and lie down for a while. I'll send for you when I need you. You're goin' to need all the rest you can get. Try to sleep."

Julia remained in a coma for three days, and though Amelia, with a little help from the other members of the household, watched over her constantly, there was never any reason to send for Doctor Willett. He dropped in several times a day while on his constant journeys back and forth to tend the sick and injured, but there was nothing he could do except change a few bandages.

The day after the storm, the rumors started. Vessels of

every description were reported wrecked and lost. Some said thirty, some said fifty, had gone down. Throughout the village, everyone waited tensely for confirmation or denial of the various rumors. There was not a family that did not have at least one man or boy at sea. Most had several.

Day after day, reports came in. All along the ocean shoreline, around the tip of the Cape and down the Bay side off Truro, ships and boats were lying wrecked on sand and rocks. Pieces of others were washed ashore.

Part of a gig, some timbers, and one body, all identified as belonging to the *Katy Saunders,* were found on the beach at North Truro. Nothing else.

When Benjamin heard the news on the second day, he went into Julia's room and peered hopefully at her for signs of life. She lay just as she had the last time he had looked, but he thought her breathing seemed a little stronger. He glanced his question at Amelia. She shook her head.

Benjamin paced about the room, picking up Julia's silver brush and comb, the small curios that stood upon her dresser. He examined each in turn, as though in them he would find an answer, before he put them down. When he picked up the broken shell, he had an urge to smash it against the hearth. End it for once and all. But he put it down on the mantel again, carefully turning it so that, from the bed, it would look whole.

He was present the next day when Julia's eyes fluttered, then opened. She looked directly at him.

"Jason?" Her voice, usually so clear, was a slurred murmur.

"He's still at sea," Benjamin answered.

"Oh. Dreamed he was dead." She seemed to have a hard time focusing as she searched his face.

"Here. Take this," Amelia said. She lifted Julia's head gently so that she could swallow from the teaspoon. "Now, lie quiet and don't talk. We have to send word to Doctor Willett."

"I'll get Ezra started," Benjamin said and gratefully left the room. It was almost impossible to lie to Julia, she seemed to know the truth.

"How long . . ."

"Three days," Amelia answered quickly. *"Please* don't talk, Julia! You mustn't."

Julia's hand fluttered on the blanket, and Amelia covered it with her own. She looked at her sister gravely. "Doctor Willett will be here in a little while. He'll decide if you can talk, but till then, you mustn't."

When the doctor came, he examined Julia once more. As he'd suspected, the concussion was severe, but there were no signs of internal injuries. He ordered some broth brought and watched with interest as Amelia fed her. When Julia had finished, she fell into a deep sleep, but it was not a coma. He nodded his satisfaction, the light sparkling off his spectacles.

"You're a good nurse, Amelia. Your patient's round the bend now. Least I think so."

Amelia's smile was weary when she heard the good news, but for the first time in days, the trace of a dimple appeared in her left cheek.

"Not saying she won't need careful tending for some time to come. Almost more important than it was before, and it'll take a lot more effort on your part."

"It's all right. I'll take good care of her."

"I know you will, lass." He got heavily to his feet. The long, sleepless hours and constant journeyings in all weather were beginning to tell on him. Amelia watched him sympathetically as he left the room. She hoped he would be able to sleep soon.

It was October before Julia was able to move from her bed and spend a part of each day in her chair before the fire. She sat and looked at Jason's picture for hours without stirring. Every day she asked for him. Her constant questions and her talk of him grated on everyone's nerves. It was a hard lie to live. Yet so necessary.

One afternoon, it was Sarah's turn to keep an eye on Julia and see to her needs. It was one of those vibrant golden days of autumn, and Sarah stood looking out the window, resenting the time she must spend in the sick-room.

"Sarah, why don't you go on out?" Julia said, understanding her sister's longing. "I'll be all right for a while."

"What? And have everyone blame me if anything happens to you?"

"Nothing will happen," Julia said quietly. "I'm sorry you're so tied down because of me. When Jason comes home, he'll take care of me and you'll be free."

"He's not coming home," Sarah muttered, still staring out the window.

"What do you mean?"

Sarah whirled around and faced her. "He's dead and at the bottom of the sea. That's what I mean. He's *never* coming home."

"You're lying," Julia protested, but the faint color she had regained during her convalescence drained from her face as though she knew Sarah spoke the truth.

"I'm not the one that's lying, and I don't approve of everyone else lying to you. They say it's to protect you, but you don't need any protection. You just enjoy playing invalid. Now you know the truth, you might just get up and do something for yourself."

"No! You're lying." Julia put up a hand as though to protect herself from her sister's words.

"Am I?" Sarah went to the mantel and picked up the shell. She held it toward Julia, showing her the broken side. "Am I lying, Julia?" she mocked her.

Julia pushed herself weakly out of her chair. She tried to snatch the shell from Sarah. Sarah retreated slowly across the room, just out of reach, holding the shell enticingly out to Julia.

It took all of Julia's strength to follow her.

"Give it to me," she pleaded.

"All right." Sarah tossed it at her. Julia staggered under the impact as she caught it. She turned it over in her hands. Sarah returned to the distant window to watch her curiously.

"How could they?" Julia said quietly, looking down at the shell in her hands. "How could they lie to me?" She paused. Then she screamed at Sarah, *"How could they lie to me?"*

She was shaking as she made her way across the room. She steadied herself against the wardrobe. Then she opened the door.

"What are you going to do now?" Sarah asked. It was

simply a question to satisfy her own curiosity. Sarah really didn't care what Julia did.

"What the hell do you think I'm going to do?" Julia yelled and threw the shell at Sarah. It hit her face. "I'm going to Jason."

"You hit me!" Sarah's grey eyes narrowed as she wiped blood from her cheek.

"Good!" Julia struggled into her petticoat. "And I'll hit you again if you don't get out of here."

"It's not *my* fault he's dead."

"Get out, get out!" Julia screamed at her.

Lydia and Amelia had been in the kitchen together when they heard Julia's screams. Now they came rushing into the bedroom.

"Julia!" Lydia said sharply. "What are you doing getting dressed? Get into bed."

"You get out of here, too," Julia yelled at her mother. "You lied to me. You *all* lied to me." She glared at them, her blue eyes turning to dark sapphire in her fury.

Amelia, who had been standing in the doorway, flew to Julia and put an arm around her. Julia shook her off in a rage. "You're no better than the others. You lied to me, too! Get out of here! All of you get out of here!"

"Amelia, go get your father," Lydia commanded.

"*He* can't help you! He's a liar, too!" Julia yanked her dress down over her tousled hair.

Calling for Ezra to come and saddle Sarah's horse for her, Amelia raced from the room down to the stables. Impatient with the hired man's slow movements, she put the bridle on and buckled the bit into place. Then she sprang up into the saddle and raced for the shipyard. In Julia's room, they could hear the horse pounding up the hard sand of the road.

"Come, Julia." Lydia tried once more. "Get back into bed."

"I'll never get back in that bed! You can have it, Sarah. You've always wanted it!" She made her way to the door. Lydia tried to stop her.

"Sarah, help me. We can't let her go."

"I wouldn't touch her with a ten-foot pole. She's hurt me once already," Sarah said, lifting a self-pitying hand to her cut cheek.

Lydia tried to bar the door, but Julia knocked her aside. "Liars!" she said venomously. She almost fell down the steps, clutching at the stair rail as she went. With every movement, however, she seemed to be gaining strength.

She made it to the stables and threw the bridle on Fancy. She led the horse from the stable and tried to mount her, but without the saddle, she fell at her first attempt. The second time, she succeeded, and kicking the horse wildly, she urged her into a trot, then a canter.

"Jason!" she called as they tore down the road. "Jason, I'm coming!"

Lydia ran out of the house in Julia's wake. There were no horses left, so she had to follow by foot. Julia had disappeared long before she gained the road. She hurried on, hoping that she might be in time to prevent some disaster.

A few minutes later, when Benjamin and Amelia reined in, only Sarah was left standing on the porch, watching the road. Benjamin jumped off Baron and threw the reins to Amelia. He ran up to the porch to confront Sarah.

"Where is she?" he demanded. His face was red with fury.

"You mean Julia?" Sarah moved uneasily behind one of the pillars that supported the upper porch. "How should I know?"

"Answer me!" he thundered at her.

"All I know is she headed for the beach," she said apprehensively.

"You spleening bitch!" Benjamin started toward her, then thought better of it. Instead, he hurried back to Baron and, taking the reins from Amelia, tore off up the road to the beach.

Amelia tried to keep up with him, but with her slower horse, the distance soon began to open up between them.

Halfway there, Benjamin saw Lydia weakly running up the road. "Go home with Amelia," he shouted as he raced by her. "Don't follow me." And he was gone around the bend, leaving a cloud of sand hanging over the road behind him.

When he came to the end of the beach path, he saw Fancy standing patiently alone and untethered in the lee of the dunes. He brought Baron to a halt beside her and quickly hitched him to a stake, dreading what he would find . . . or not find . . . on the beach. In her weakened condition, it was a wonder Julia had made it this far.

Upon reaching the top of the dunes, he saw her standing stark and lonely at the water's edge, surrounded by the vast expanse of sand and sea. She was screaming at the roaring surf, and as he approached her, he could distinguish the words.

"You murderer! You liar! You promised and broke your promise! You killed him! You murdered him! You're cruel and vicious! I hate you! You murderer! Murderer! Why don't you take me, too? Are you afraid of me? I won't make it easy for you, but come and get me! Get me or give Jason back to me! You beast! You bloody beast!"

Benjamin raced down the sand and tried to grab her, but with an amazing burst of strength, she shook him off, then stumbled and fell into the water. She lay there, the sand eddying around her, resisting him as he tried to pick her up.

"Liar!" she yelled at him and choked as saltwater filled her mouth.

A large wave was fast approaching. He had to get Julia away before it broke. As she continued to struggle with him, he doubled up his fist and tapped her lightly on the chin. It was enough.

He dragged her now limp wet body up to the safety of the soft sand. He sobbed and the tears fell from his face to hers as he rolled her over. He pumped the small amount of water she had swallowed out of her lungs. Then he picked her up and staggered through the sand, rocks, and sea wrack back to the horses.

He laid her across Baron's pommel and mounted behind her.

The tears were still running down his face when Benjamin carried Julia up to her bedroom. Lydia and Amelia stripped off her wet clothes, rinsed her with fresh water, and rubbed her cold body with large towels.

When they had dressed her in a fresh nightgown, they called Benjamin to come and lift her into bed. Sarah slid into the room and watched from the doorway.

As Benjamin straightened up from his daughter's body on the bed, he caught sight of Sarah.

"Did you tell her?" he demanded. His anger was mounting.

"Yes, I did," Sarah said defensively. She lifted her head and looked at him levelly with her cool grey eyes.

"Why? Why the hell did you do it?" His face was red with rage and the veins at his temples visibly pulsed with his anger. He strode over to confront her, but Sarah refused to be completely intimidated.

"*I* wasn't going to lie to her. It's a sin. The Eighth Commandment forbids it."

"And what about the Fifth Commandment?" he roared at her. "What about that, you meeching bitch?" He slapped her and sent her reeling into the room. "Thou . . . Shalt . . . Not . . . Kill! You're always citing the Bible, you mealy-mouthed whore. What about this one? 'And the Lord said to Cain: What hast thou done? The voice of thy brother's blood crieth to me from the earth'!"

"I didn't touch her. She's the one who hit me," Sarah said, cowering against the wall. "I can't help what she does."

"When I asked you where she was, you said, 'How should I know?' " He advanced on her. " 'And the Lord said to Cain: Where is thy brother Abel? And he answered, I know not: am I my brother's keeper?'

"Cain!" he said and slapped her again, knocking her up against the wall. "So you would kill your sister, would you?" He grasped her arms and threw her on the floor. "*You spleening bitch!*" he roared and stomped from the room.

"Mother!" Sarah wailed, crawling across the floor to Lydia.

"You'll get no sympathy from me," Lydia said and pulled back her skirts with distaste.

"He called me Cain," she said, crying. "He called me a spleening bitch."

"That's what you are." Lydia's voice was cold and merciless. "Now get up off that floor and out of this room."

Amelia slipped from the room and ran after her father.

"Papa, shouldn't we get Doctor Willett?"

"Yes. My God, yes!" He slapped his forehead. "You're the only one who's got any sense in this family. Send Ezra for him right away. I've got to get back to Julia. I don't dare leave her. She's not in her right mind. No telling what she'll do next."

"Yes, Papa," she said and ran down the stairs.

"And you go down to the beach and get Fancy," he called after her. "She's up near the end of the beach path. Ride Baron over and lead her home."

Chapter Twelve

1838-1839

WHILE DOCTOR WILLETT WAS examining her, Julia regained consciousness.

"Liar," she muttered at him.

"Don't recall lyin' to you, Julia," he said calmly.

"You knew! You're like the others. You knew he was dead and pretended he wasn't."

"I don't recall any such thing," he said while he pulled up her eyelid and peered into her eye.

"Yes, you did!" she said, knocking his hand away.

"Calm down now," he ordered sternly. "There's nothing you can do about the matter except rest and eat and get well."

"Oh, there's plenty I can do," she said as she sat up and pushed the bedclothes away from her.

"Unless you do what I tell you, you're going to kill yourself," he warned her.

"That's just what I had in mind." She slipped her legs over the side of the bed.

"No, you don't," the doctor said, pulling her back.

She struggled violently with him, writhing and biting and striking out. Benjamin went to his aid, and together they got her, panting and disheveled, back on the bed. They held her down as she continued to struggle against them, yelling, "Liars, liars!"

"Lydia, go get some sheets and towels," the doctor ordered. "We're going to have to tie you in this bed if you don't behave," he warned Julia.

She surged against them with a new burst of energy. "No! No! Let me go!"

"Hold her tight, Benjamin," the doctor said as he tried to wind a sheet around her.

She struck out with both arms, and when her father grabbed them, she kicked wildly at the two men.

"There's no help for it." The doctor shook his bald head sadly. "We'll have to tie her to the bedposts."

"No! No!" she screamed. "Jason, help me!"

"Oh, my poor child," Benjamin said, his heart breaking as he helped the doctor make her fast.

Lydia could stand it no longer and ran sobbing from the room. As she reached the end of the hall, she saw Sarah in her own bedroom laying clothes out on a chair.

"What do you think you're doing?" she asked her daughter coldly.

"I'm leaving," Sarah said and turned her back on her mother.

"And where do you plan on going? I don't know of anyone who'd have you."

"Uncle Josiah and Aunt Harriet will have me. *They* care, even if no one in *this* house does."

"We'll see what your father has to say about *that*."

"You can't stop me."

"I don't even want to," Lydia said wearily. "The sooner you're out of this house, the better, as far as I'm concerned, but I don't know that your father will let you go to Josiah."

"He don't have anything to say about it, not after the way he treated me."

"According to the law, he has everything to say about it." Lydia shuddered as Julia's screams rose again in a new crescendo.

"Well, I'm not going to stay and listen to that crazy thing in there."

"Neither would I if I was you. My conscience would drive me away."

"I don't have anything on my conscience," Sarah said coolly. "I only told the truth, and for that I was beaten and cursed."

"I suppose you must believe that. Otherwise you wouldn't be able to live with yourself." She sighed. "I don't know where I failed in raising you, but fail I did."

Lydia crossed the hall to her own room. After shutting the door, she lay down on the bed. She was so weary. Every bone in her body ached and the pain in her head was unbearable.

Only a few minutes later, there was a knock on the door. What now? she thought.

"Come in," she said.

Doctor Willett quietly entered the room.

"Oh," she said, sitting up and pushing back her disheveled grey-gold hair. "I thought it was Benjamin."

"That's all right. Stay where you are. I want to examine you."

"Me?"

"Yes. You've been through a lot. Too much. You look worn out and you've got a hard road ahead of you." He felt her pulse. "Just as I thought. Pounding like a hard sea in a tempest. If you're not careful, we'll have two invalids on our hands."

"How can I be careful with that going on?" She nodded in the direction of Julia's room. "She's my child, my very own child. Can you understand what that means?"

"Yes, I understand, Lydia. I know what it's doing to you, and I'm worried how well you're going to bear up under it."

"I'll manage. I'm not sick."

"You looked at yourself in a mirror?"

"No."

"You're not strong. If you don't take care of yourself, we might have to make other arrangements for Julia. Find a place where they'll take her in and care for her."

"Never!"

Benjamin came into the room and sank down wearily in a chair. He ran his hand through his vigorous hair.

"Think the sight of me upsets her more than my absence will."

"You didn't leave her all alone?" Lydia asked in alarm. She got up from her bed.

"She can't hurt herself, Lyd."

"Might be better off alone," Doctor Willett said. "Might calm down if no one pays any attention to her for a while."

As if to give lie to his words, Julia's screams rose again to a new high. Lydia started for the door, but the doctor placed a restraining hand on her sleeve.

"Leave her alone, Lydia. If she keeps it up long enough, she'll exhaust herself. Then she'll go to sleep. Best thing for her."

"But it's so hard," she said, biting her pale lips.

"I know, but it's for the best. You still got any of that tonic I gave you?"

"Yes."

"Well, take a double dose of it. Then lie down and try to rest. And you keep taking it," he admonished her. "Next time I ask if you've got any left, I want to hear you say no."

"Something wrong with Lydia?" Benjamin asked. His full black eyebrows drew together.

"Not yet. But there will be if she don't get some rest. You watch her, Ben. Don't let her see Julia for more than half an hour a day. That's all she's allowed." He snapped his black bag shut. "Nothin' more I can do here now, so I'll be gettin' along. Send for me if you need me. Otherwise, I'll see you in the morning."

Benjamin started to rise, but the doctor waved him back.

"No need. No need. I can find my own way out."

After he had gone, Lydia said, "Sarah's packing her clothes."

"If I knew where to send her, I'd pack them for her myself!"

"She's talking about going to Josiah and Harriet."

"That's too much!" he exploded. "She'll go crying to them with some tale about how I've abused her. It'll be all over the township by morning."

"Well, you better stop her then. She's bound and determined to go."

"Oh, let her go, let her go," he said wearily, sinking

down on the bed beside her. "I'm too tired to stop anybody from doing anything."

"Oh Benjy." She took his large, warm callused hand and held it in hers. "What's happened to us? One daughter screaming like a madwoman. Another packing her clothes to run away from us."

"Far as I'm concerned, I've only got two daughters now. Their names are Julia and Amelia."

"You can't disown Sarah, Benjy. She's still a child. She didn't know what she was doing."

"Didn't she?"

"Maybe she did, but I don't think she realized what kind of effect her words would have on Julia."

"I think she did."

"Oh, Benjy," she sighed and rested her forehead against his strong shoulder. He stroked her back, then leaned his cheek against her silver-streaked hair.

They heard Sarah's door open and her footsteps in the hall. Benjamin got up and went to the door. Sarah was heading down the stairs, a large wicker basket in her hand.

"And where do you think you're going?" Benjamin asked.

Sarah, startled by his voice, paused and looked back over her shoulder.

"To Uncle Josiah's."

"And when do you think you're comin' back?" His deep voice was ominously quiet.

Sarah clutched at the stair rail. "I . . . I don't know."

"Well, you better plan on a long visit, because if you go to him now, you'll never set foot in this house again."

"After the way you've treated me, I'm not so sure I want to," she said defiantly.

"If you leave this house after what you've done to your sister, I don't want to set eyes on you again."

"She deserves whatever she gets."

"Get out!" He raised his hand and started down the steps after her. "Get out of my sight! Get out of my house! You're no daughter of mine!"

Sarah turned and scuttled down the narrow stairs.

The weeks went by and rumors spread about the doings at the Howard house. Some said that Benjamin had beaten both his daughters, had driven one out of her home and the other out of her mind.

Doctor Willett went his rounds, trying to quench the vicious gossip by telling the truth. Reverend Lamson, thundering from the pulpit, condemned rumor-mongers, preached of ungrateful children, and protected the Howard family as well as he was able.

Ezra and the maids, Maryanne and Janet, entered the fray and fought the family battles where they could. None of them liked Sarah with her imperious, sly ways. They were glad of the chance to put her down.

It was hard for the rumors to die a natural death, though, for Sarah and Josiah fed the flame. Sarah was highly visible and loudly vocal as she went around the village displaying her cut cheek and bruises with a pious, martyred air. For once, she was getting all the attention she so desperately wanted, and she made the most of it.

No one else in the Howard house was particularly visible, however. Callers were no longer admitted to the once warm, welcoming home, and Lydia and Amelia never left it. Benjamin went down to the shipyard for a couple of hours each day, but when he was there, he was taciturn and spoke only about the business at hand.

Most of the time there he spent closeted in the office with Daniel Sears. The years of training had paid off, for Daniel was now highly competent and able to run the yard smoothly and efficiently with only a few words of advice from Benjamin. His main problems lay in dealing with Josiah, who tried to countermand every order Daniel gave when Benjamin was not present. Fortunately the men respected Daniel more and usually were able to ignore Josiah.

Passersby on the road occasionally heard screams coming from the big white house. Some shook their heads sympathetically. Others raced into the village to tell everyone they met.

Inside the house, Lydia spent a greater part of the day in bed, lethargic from the strong tonics the doctor gave her. There were only Amelia and Benjamin to take care of Julia while the maids ran the house.

Benjamin moved into Sarah's vacant room so that he

could be closer to his daughter if she cried out in the night. Amelia often slept on a cot in Julia's room.

Doctor Willett, on his frequent visits, watched Benjamin turn greyer and more haggard, Amelia grow thinner and old beyond her years. His concern for them steadily mounted. He turned the problem over and over in his mind. Finally he came up with what he thought a likely solution.

On a cold, snow-rain morning in December, he examined Julia and found her to be steadily declining. He sighed when he snapped his black bag shut.

"I want to talk to you down in the parlor, Benjamin. I already told Janet to brew up some coffee and serve it down there."

Benjamin, more than a little alarmed, followed the doctor down the narrow staircase. They talked most every day, and the doctor had never found it necessary to use the parlor before.

"Well, what is it?" Benjamin asked impatiently as soon as Janet had brought in the coffee and left them.

"Want to tell you about one of my patients." Doctor Willett sipped the coffee appreciatively. "You ever know Tom Chambers?"

"Over in Orleans?"

"That's the one."

"Met him a few years back. Had some kind of accident, didn't he?" What did all this have to do with Julia?

"Yes. Happened up on the Grand Banks. His schooner got stove in on a rock. Sank. Most all hands got off in longboats or whaleboats, but Tom was last man overboard. When he jumped, he landed the wrong way and broke a few bones."

"Well?" Benjamin put his cup down and went to poke up the fire.

"Well, 'twas a couple of weeks afore they were sighted by another whaler and got picked up. Long enough for Tom's bones to set wrong. His shipmates tried to set them, but they didn't have much to work with. 'Twas mighty cramped in that longboat."

"That's a common enough story." The flames flickered and rose higher.

"Yes, but the worst of it was, he hit his head when he

landed. Delirious. Had a high fever. Wonder he lived at all. But he did. Crippled in mind and body ever since."

Benjamin put the poker down with a clatter and stared at the doctor. His brows were drawn menacingly together and his face was set. "You telling me Julia's going to be like this the rest of her life?"

"No, no." The firelight flashed on the doctor's spectacles as he shook his head. "This is about Tom. You see, he died last week."

Benjamin sighed with relief. So it wasn't Julia.

"Didn't know about that," he said.

"No reason why you should." The doctor poured himself another cup of coffee. "Point is he left a widow behind. She's managed to scrape by all these years, but she's got nothing left now."

"No children?"

"Two sons at sea. Too young to help. A daughter married down south somewhere. Martha don't want to leave the Cape."

Benjamin sat down again and picked up his cup of cold coffee.

"So you want me to give her a job?" he said.

"Well, that's what I was leading up to."

Benjamin shook his head. "Can't take on anyone else just now. Maryanne and Janet manage all right. I'll ask around, though. Might be someone who could use some help."

"You're wrong, Ben. You do need her. She's been taking care of Tom for years. Got a lot of experience along that line. I think she can handle Julia."

"No stranger's going to handle Julia!"

"Don't know why not." Doctor Willett studied Benjamin's set jaw. "She's a good woman. Pious. Cheerful beyond belief after what she's gone through. Strong. Capable."

"No!" Benjamin got up and began to pace around the room. "No strangers."

"You looked at Amelia lately? Seen what it's doing to her?"

"I know." Benjamin passed a hand over his face.

"Well, the fact that Martha Chambers *is* a stranger is all to the good. Julia can't claim Martha's ever lied to her. Might even eat better if Martha's doing the feeding."

Benjamin paused by the fire and stared into it. Hiring someone to care for Julia was an admission of defeat. The fog of depression thickened.

"You're telling me she's not going to recover. That it?"

"Now, Ben. I'm not saying anything of the kind." Behind his spectacles, the doctor watched Benjamin carefully, judging the effect of his words. "But she's not getting any better the way things are now. She might respond to a change. Anything's worth trying."

"I suppose so," Benjamin said heavily.

"You know so."

"Send her over. I'll talk to her, but I'm not making any promises."

"Good, good." The doctor got up and clapped Benjamin on the shoulder. "You're making some sense now. I'll bring Martha over when I stop by in the morning. You'll like her. She's a fine woman."

When Doctor Willett's carriage crunched through the snow the next morning, Benjamin heard it and went to the front door to peer through the narrow, vertical panes of glass beside it. Through them, he could see the doctor not only had a tall, plump woman beside him. There were two large trunks in the back of the carriage.

So the doctor thought he was going to put one over on him, did he? Figured Benjamin wouldn't turn her away if she arrived with her belongings? Well, they'd see about that.

He watched as the doctor hitched his horse to the hitching post near the road and helped the woman down from the carriage. When they reached the porch, Benjamin opened the door, looked pointedly at the trunks in the carriage, then turned the intensity of his hard blue eyes on the doctor.

"Mornin', Ben," Doctor Willett said, *his* eyes all innocence behind their steel-rimmed spectacles.

"Mornin'," Benjamin said, blocking the doorway with his bulky body, his eyes never wavering from the doctor's.

Doctor Willett smiled and turned to the woman beside him. "This is Captain Howard, Martha. Ben, Mrs. Chambers." He moved forward, forcing Benjamin to retreat into

227

the hall. "Now you two go on in the parlor and have a chat while I go up and check on my patients."

Benjamin was stubbornly silent as he watched the doctor mount the stairs. Then he turned to the woman who still stood patiently just inside the front door. "May I take your coat, Mrs. Chambers?"

"Thank you," she said, her calm, clear blue eyes forgiving him his rudeness.

He took the shabby black coat from her and hung it on the rack, then silently indicated the door to the parlor. " 'Twas good of you to come," he said, following her into the room.

"Not at all, not at all," she said cheerfully, looking around the large, high-ceilinged room. "Lovely house, Captain Howard."

"Thank you," he said formally. He indicated a comfortable armchair near the fire. "Won't you sit down?"

"Don't mind if I do. Right brisk out this morning." She rubbed her hands together and spread them out to the fire.

At that moment, auburn-haired Janet burst into the room with a tray bearing a tea set, three cups, and a generous plate of sliced cake. Her curiosity was obvious when she set it down on a table near Martha.

"Thank you, Janet," Benjamin said, more than a little annoyed. This wasn't a social call. "That will be all."

Janet left the room quickly enough when she saw his frown.

"Mrs. Chambers, will you pour?"

"Glad to," she said heartily, ignoring the captain's scowl. While she arranged the cups and poured the tea, Benjamin leaned back in his chair and studied her face. Despite himself, he liked what he saw.

Martha Chambers had good, strong features. Vigorous white hair tried to escape the neat black bonnet that framed her face. There were few wrinkles on her face, but those she did have were etched deep and sharp. He judged her to be in her late fifties.

Her hands, as she poured the tea, were large and square and capable. When she handed him a cup, she looked him straight in the eye, a trait he liked in anyone, man or woman.

"Mrs. Chambers, I'm afraid Doctor Willett brought you

here under false pretenses. Since I only agreed to an interview, I'm disturbed you brought your trunks along."

"That's all right," she said levelly. "He warned me it was just an interview. If you decide against me, he's got another place lined up. Not as fine as this"—she looked appreciatively around the room—"but still a place."

He nodded and took a sip of tea. "As long as you understand."

"I understand, but you see, I had to leave. In order to pay my bills, I had to sell the house and most of my worldly goods. They wouldn't let me stay any longer."

"You've lost a lot recently. I'm sorry," he said, quietly understanding.

"Yes, I have." She looked at him and knew that, through his own grief, he recognized hers. " 'Twasn't as though I didn't know 'twas coming, and poor Tom, he'll rest more peaceful now."

"Doctor Willett tells me you tended your husband for several years."

"Twelve in all." She sighed and looked down into her teacup. "Pour soul."

Benjamin got up and began to pace around the room. The sooner this interview was over, the better. It was too painful.

"The doctor tell you about my daughter?" he asked.

"Yes, yes. Swore me to secrecy, too. Have no fear that I'll go around repeating it."

"No," he said slowly. "I don't think you will." He stopped in front of her and searched her honest, open face. "She's completely out of her mind." It hurt to say the words. "We hope it's only temporary."

"I understand. Losing her husband like that and her so young. It's no wonder. Wouldn't doubt but that she'll recover, though. Time heals a lot of things, and at her age, she's got time on her side."

"I hope so, Mrs. Chambers," he said, coming to a sudden decision. "As far as I'm concerned, you'll do just fine. But it all depends on Julia's reaction to you. If you'll come with me, I'll take you up to her."

She put her teacup down carefully and got to her feet.

"Of course," Benjamin added, "there's always the possibility that, after you've seen her, you won't want the job."

"I get along with most people, sane or mad," Martha said complacently.

He led the way up the stairs and into Julia's room.

It was quiet in the sunlit, fire-warmed room. Amelia was sitting in a far corner, sewing, while the doctor was rearranging his black bag. Julia lay quietly on the bed, staring at the ceiling. Benjamin went to her side.

"Julia, this is Mrs. Chambers. She's come to nurse you till you're well."

"So now I need a keeper," Julia said bitterly, never moving her eyes from the spot above her.

"Land, no," Martha Chambers said. "Wouldn't know how to go about doing that. I'm just here to tend your wants and help you get well."

Julia, hearing the rich, warm voice, shifted her eyes to look at its source.

"I only have one want left to tend," she said coldly, "and I don't believe you'd help me."

"Well, what is it, child?" It hurt Martha to see that light in the sapphire eyes of what should be a pretty, young girl. She had seen it so often in poor Tom's eyes.

"I want to die."

"Well, you're right in that. I won't help you there, but I *can* make you more comfortable while you're living. I've had enough to do with dying, what with poor Tom gone just last week."

Benjamin glanced sharply at Martha. It was the first time a note of self-pity had appeared in her voice.

"Tom?" Julia said.

"My husband. Dead and buried. Now I have no roof over my head and no food on my plate."

"Did he die at sea?"

"No. More's the pity," Martha said with a sigh. She settled down comfortably in the chintz-covered armchair beside the bed and began to untie the ribbons on her black bonnet. " 'Twould have been far better for him if he'd gone at sea."

Benjamin went quietly to the door and was followed by the doctor. He beckoned for Amelia to slip out of the room behind them. The three went downstairs and into the parlor.

"Looks like we've finally found some medicine that

230

agrees with her," the doctor said, his eyes twinkling behind their spectacles. "Martha's staying, of course?"

"Of course," Benjamin said. "First time I've seen Julia take an interest in anything since she found out about Jason's death."

"Well, I hoped it might have *some* good effect. Didn't suspect it would be that good. But we mustn't congratulate ourselves too soon," the doctor cautioned. "Still have to keep a careful eye on her."

"If only Mrs. Chambers can get her to eat," Amelia said.

"I trust she'll have better luck than *you've* had." The doctor looked at Amelia. Even this early in the day, she looked tired. Her pale blond hair hung limply down her back as though she hadn't had time to tend it properly. Which, of course, she hadn't.

"What I want you to do now is start feeding yourself," he told her. "You're way too thin. Worn out, too. Lots of food and rest. That's what you need. That goes for you, too, Ben." He looked sharply at Benjamin.

"Well, it'll be a little easier, knowing Julia's in good hands," Benjamin admitted.

"From now on, you two are to stay out of that room unless Julia specifically asks for you. Give those two some time to settle down together."

"We can't ask Mrs. Chambers to do *everything*," Amelia said.

"That's what she's here for. You'll pay her well, Ben?"

"I may have my faults, but I'm not stingy."

"All right. Martha can tend all her wants. She's used to it. Spins a good yarn, too. Can you give her a room near Julia's?"

"I'll move out of Sarah's," Benjamin said. "She can have that. It's the closest."

"Good, good," the doctor said, rubbing his hands together. "Now, if we can get those trunks unloaded, I'll be on my way."

When Martha Chambers came down to get a lunch tray for Julia, she had removed her bonnet and put a white apron on top of her dark cotton dress. Already she looked as though she had already lived in the large white house.

Her tall, proud bearing impressed Maryanne and Janet so much that they cheerfully carried out her orders. It was good to have someone in command again.

When she crossed the dining room, carrying a tray loaded with enough food for two people, Benjamin heard her. He came out of his study and stopped her.

"How is she?" he asked.

Martha approved of the grave concern she saw in his tired eyes.

"Poor lamb, she seems quiet enough. I'm going to untie her when I get back upstairs."

"Think that's wise?"

"I'm pretty strong. I'll be able to cope with her, no matter what she tries. Right now, she don't seem to want to do much more than just lie there."

"She can be pretty devious," he warned her.

"I don't doubt it. Don't you worry about it. I'll hitch her back up again when I have to leave the room. I thought up more comfortable ways for poor Tom than what you've been using."

"Well, I'll have to trust your judgment, Mrs. Chambers." Benjamin ran his fingers through his hair. "I'm grateful to you for coming."

"Just call me Martha. I'm the one that's grateful to have a good roof over my head and food on my plate." She glanced at the tray. "I'd best be getting this upstairs before it gets cold. For the time being, I'll eat with her. Good company perks up a poor appetite."

Benjamin watched the big cheerful woman walk up the hall. He was already becoming fond of her. It would be comforting to have her around the house. Might perk Lydia up some, too.

Under Martha Chambers's care, Julia's violence, aside from an occasional outburst, seemed to subside. At times, Martha would capture her interest with some of the innumerable tales she told, but mostly Julia lay quiet and unmoving, staring at a spot no one else could see.

Martha was able to persuade her to eat a little. It took a lot of cajolery, but Martha had a lot of patience. As Julia's strength began to return and color once again appeared in her cheeks, Martha insisted that she get out of bed every morning and sit by the fire, where she gazed listlessly into the flames throughout the day, never raising her eyes to the portrait above them.

When Martha ran low on stories, she searched through the house for books to read to her patient. Anything would do. It was always the least expected that would rouse Julia from her lethargy.

The calm that had arrived with Martha was beneficial for Lydia. She felt more able to face each new day and depended less on her tonics. Rising early in the morning, she gave the maids their orders and saw that the meals were properly served. But her energies were still at a low ebb, and she took frequent naps.

Benjamin spent more and more of his time at the ship-yard, finding he could lose himself in his work. Yet even there, he was constantly aware of the empty place at his side where Julia had walked.

Sometimes her ghost seemed to haunt the yard, but he told himself it couldn't be her ghost. She was still alive. No, it was only his memories that haunted him. The bubbling child playing on the dunes and amongst the wood piles. The earnest, growing girl with her ink-stained fingers and tousled black hair. The excited young woman whose sapphire eyes sparkled each time she mastered a new piece of knowledge or conquered yet another skill.

Though Lydia and Benjamin urged her to visit her friends and join in their parties, Amelia stayed close to home. Her parents missed her lilting laughter, the dimpled smile, the radiance that had once seemed to shine all around her. The house was somber without that radiance. Amelia withdrew into her painting and played on the piano her parents had given her for her fourteenth birthday. It was a wonderful gift. She found she could wander down the spiral of notes into another world, from which she returned refreshed.

Sarah made no overtures to come home nor did they try to contact her. Benjamin paid Josiah a couple of dollars each week to take care of her board and clothes. He sometimes glimpsed her when she brought something to the yard for her uncle. Whenever he saw her, he felt his anger rise and turned his back. He could not and would not forgive

Sarah as long as her sister remained imprisoned in that nightmare world he could not reach.

The long dreary months of winter stretched into spring. Though Julia improved, it was at such an imperceptible rate her family was hardly aware of it.

"Where's Papa?" Julia suddenly asked one day.

"He went down to Boston on business," Martha said calmly, putting her finger between the pages of the book she had been reading to Julia.

"Here, give me that book." Julia snatched it away from Martha in irritation. "You don't know how to read! You drone on and on."

"Then *you* read to me," Martha said equably.

"No! I'll read to myself. If you want to read, go get yourself another book."

"I'll just get some sewing done," Martha said, settling back comfortably in her chair and reaching for a nightgown she was making for Julia.

"You don't have to stay here! I want to read alone."

Martha searched her ward's face carefully. There was anger, but there was something else. Something new. She decided to take the chance.

"All right, lamb, if you'll promise me two things."

"What?" Julia was surprised. She hadn't really expected Martha to give in so easily.

"First, that you won't try to hurt yourself, and second, that you won't try to leave the room."

"How do you know you can believe me, even if I give my word?" Julia lifted her chin and looked stubbornly defiant.

"I'll believe you," Martha said in her most comfortable voice.

"All right. I give you my word. Now go."

"Call me if you want me," Martha said cheerfully. She gathered up her sewing basket and the nightgown.

Martha left the door open behind her, but when she was halfway down the hall, she heard Julia close it. She hurried to her own bedroom, which was adjacent to Julia's, and picked up a waterglass from the nightstand. Then drawing a chair up quietly, she held the glass against the wall and put her ear to it. There was no sound.

She crouched there for an hour. It seemed an eternity.

Her body was cramped, but her doubts were the worst of it. She hoped she had been right in leaving Julia alone. Captain Howard wouldn't take it lightly if she'd been wrong.

Finally she felt she'd dared enough for the first time. She stood up and stretched her stiff limbs. As she did so, she heard Amelia coming up the steps. She went to the door and motioned the girl to come into her room, putting her fingers to her lips to caution her.

"Where's Julia?" Amelia whispered.

"In her room."

"Alone?"

"Yes."

"Is she all right?" Amelia asked anxiously.

"I think so." Martha told how Julia had snatched the book away from her. "First time she's tried to read to herself. I thought 'twas a good sign. Reckoned maybe it was time to let her be by herself a bit. Show we trusted her."

Amelia's eyes widened in skepticism.

"What I want you to do is go out on the porch," Martha said. "Pretend you're looking at the marsh or up the road. Then take a quick peek in her room. See what she's doing."

"I don't like the idea of spying on her." Amelia glanced at the chair drawn up to the wall and the waterglass on the floor beside it. "Why don't you do it?"

"Because she'll know I'm checking on her. With you, she won't be sure."

"All right," Amelia said reluctantly. "I'll try it."

She walked down the long carpeted hall and unlocked the glass-paned door at its end. She stepped through onto the wide porch that ran the length of Julia's room.

She breathed deeply of air rich with the scents of lilac and hyacinth. It really is spring, she thought, surprised that it should ever come again. She gazed across the road at the sun-warmed marsh turning green once more. Some robins were nesting in one of the horse chestnut trees that stood in front of the house. She watched as they flew to it with bits of straw and twigs in their beaks.

Then she remembered why she was there. Turning to walk farther down the porch, she was startled to see Julia standing pressed against the glass of one of the long windows, staring out at her.

"What are you doing?" Julia asked.

"Just admiring the spring." Amelia tried to keep her voice light.

"Spring?"

"Yes." Amelia hurried back into the house and opened the door of her sister's bedroom.

Julia still stood staring out the window, but as Amelia entered, she turned her head to look at her. "Is it really spring?" Her voice sounded lost and her face was bewildered.

"Yes. It's really spring." A dimple flickered when Amelia smiled at her.

"I wonder if I might go out. It's been such a long winter."

"Of course, you can," Amelia said. "Would you like to go for a walk in the garden?"

"Are the flowers blooming?"

"Yes."

"Then I'd like that."

As they passed one of the flower beds at the side of the house, Julia paused. Then she knelt to touch the golden petals of a daffodil. She gazed at it as though she had never seen one before.

"It's so fresh and new and perfect," she said wonderingly.

Amelia stood beside her and silently prayed that Julia was really beginning to return to them. She seemed so quiet now, so gentle. Julia had never been like this. It was as though she had been newly born into the world. Was she a new person?

They walked up through the carpet of dry pine needles, past the towering spruce trees. Julia paused to put a hand on one of their trunks. "Indians," she whispered.

Amelia was alarmed, but Julia continued up to the cutting garden. The sisters wandered through it, looking at the young plants pushing through the soil, trying to reach the sun.

Julia seemed calm enough and content in her enjoyment of the unfolding spring as they returned to the house. When they came to the lilac bush, bursting with fragrance and blossoms, she paused and touched one spray of half-opened buds.

Suddenly she burst into tears and ran weeping into the house. Amelia ran after her. She found Julia lying on her bed, sobbing as though her heart were breaking all over again.

Amelia sat on the bed beside her.

"What is it, Julie?" she asked.

"How can it? How can there be a spring without Jason?" Julia sobbed. "He's dead, dead in the cold sea, where he never wanted to go. It's always winter now. How can the earth be so cruel. How can it make a spring without him?"

"It has to go on, Julie. It sorrowed for him. All winter long. But now it has to go on for all the rest of us. For you, too."

"I can't bear it. I just can't bear it."

"I know," Amelia crooned. "I know. But you can. You've always been so strong, Julie. Bear it for Jason. See it for him. Live life for him. He would have wanted you to."

"He always worried about me being alone," Julia sobbed. "And I always laughed and told him I wasn't afraid. I lied. I *am* afraid of being alone. And I'm so alone without him."

"You're not alone, Julie," Amelia said soothingly. "You've got all of us. We love you."

"Do you know what he said to me once?" Julia asked, ignoring her sister's words, but quieter now. She rolled over on her back and stared at the ceiling.

"It was the morning I ran away from home. He was waiting for me in the woods. I didn't expect him to be there, but he was. The first words he said to me were, 'I was worried about you. Alone and the night so dark.'

"I've heard him saying that to me over and over all these long months of winter. 'Alone and the night so dark.' Even before that, in the fall. I knew he was dead, but no one would admit it. He came then and talked to me. It's my fault he's dead, but he never blames me.

"At night, in my dreams, he holds me safe in his arms. Then I wake up and he's at the bottom of the sea and I'm all alone here at the top and I'll never see him again." She rolled over on her stomach again and the sobs came louder.

"Julia . . ."

"Do you know what never means, 'Melia? It means

never, never, never. All I want to do is die. Go to the bottom of the sea and lie in his arms forever."

Amelia could feel the tears starting to trickle down her own face. She held Julia tightly and tried to keep her voice calm.

"Do you really think that's what Jason wants, Julie? Do you *really* think he wants you to die? There'd be no one left then to remember for him the happiness you had together."

"He keeps calling me."

"Not to die, Julie. Not to die. He's calling you because he still loves you. He still worries about you. You've been alone because you wouldn't let us be with you. You wouldn't let us share your sorrow."

"But Jason . . ."

"Jason wasn't the kind of man who'd call you to death. He's most likely been trying to call you to life. He wants you to live for him as well as for your self. He'll never really die as long as you live. Not as long as you remember him. He's part of you now, Julie. Don't let him die twice."

"Oh, Amelia!" Julia burst into fresh tears and buried her head in her sister's lap. "I miss him so. I miss him so."

Amelia said nothing, but continued to stroke her sister's hair. She sat on the bed and stared out at the young spring.

From then on, Julia's recovery was rapid. Her body, fortified by her youth and her natural good health, strengthened quickly, and her mind with it. Gradually, she found that she was able to get through a day without tears, although she often awoke in the night to find her pillow wet with them.

She spent her days reading and walking through the cutting garden, even venturing up to the grape arbor that held so many memories. Sometimes she would ask Amelia to play the piano for her. Then she would sit quietly, wandering the winding quiet rivers and the tempest-driven seas of music.

She rarely ventured beyond the grounds around the large white house, keeping well within the guarding grey rock walls that surrounded it. She, who had once not cared what people thought, found it hard to bear the smirks of some and the pity on the faces of others. She knew she now bore the label of madwoman. She heard the soundless snickers behind her back.

Chapter Thirteen

1839

JULIA WAS KNEELING IN the cutting garden, a trowel in her hand, her garden gloves thrown on the ground behind her. The fresh-turned soil felt warm as she crumbled it in her fingers. The garden was a healing place. The columbines, irises, and pinks already in bloom lent their perfume to the June morning and the earth smelled rich and fertile.

Here on a rising hill, screened from the road by the house and trees, Julia found a quiet peace. She was so alone with her thoughts she was startled suddenly to hear a voice just beside her.

"Julia?"

She looked up to see a large man, in a suit that seemed too small for his body, on the other side of the picket fence. He was removing his cap from a head of unruly dark blond curls.

"I didn't mean to frighten you," he said.

"I didn't hear you coming. Who are you and what do you want?"

"You don't remember me? I'm David Baxter."

She studied his face for a moment, trying to fit the man's broad, low forehead, his large jaw, his wide lips to the memory of the boy she had known years ago. An older boy, one of those who periodically came home from sea, then left again. The man her father had chosen to be master of the *Jewel of the Seas*.

"Yes," she said finally, "I remember you."

"There wasn't anyone at the house," he said apologetically, turning his cap in his hands, "so I came looking up here. I hope you don't mind."

"No," she said, pulling a weed out of the ground, "why should I?"

Glancing up at him quickly then, she dared him to answer, while she waited for the response she would see in his face. Yet in the grey-green eyes that curved slightly downward, in the mouth that held the suggestion of a smile, she found, not curiosity or pity, but only kindness.

"I . . . I've heard you weren't seeing anyone."

"I'm not," she said abruptly and threw the weeds into a pile.

"I haven't had a chance to tell you how sorry I am. About Jason." His voice was the low, warm voice she remembered in the boy, but it was richer. The note of compassion she heard there, however, bothered her.

"Yes. So am I," she said, refusing to raise her eyes to meet his. "If you're looking for my father, he went down to Boston to meet you. Took the packet as soon as we got word the *Jewel* was coming in."

David Baxter looked down at the too-slender girl with her earth-stained black skirts spread around her and her black hair bound up in a heavy knot on top of her head. She seemed pale and out of place amongst the soft, glowing colors of the flowers. He could see little resemblance to the laughing, rosy-cheeked child he remembered. If he had passed her on the road, would he have recognized her? Yes, he told himself, he would. She was still essentially Julia.

"In his letters, your father told me I was to come home to make my report."

"Well, I don't know anything about that. He just said he was going down to Boston to meet you."

She threw her trowel into a basket and rose, brushing the dirt from her skirts. Then she took a pair of scissors from the basket, and purposefully turning her back to him, began snipping a few of the flowers from their stalks.

"Was it a successful voyage?" she asked.

"Yes. Very."

"Good." She threw the flowers into the basket and picked it up, turning to look at him coolly.

"When my father finds you aren't in Boston, he'll most likely come directly home. You might as well wait."

"Guess that's the best plan."

"He'll send word. You're staying with your parents?"

"Yes." As she walked to the gate, he followed on the other side of the fence as though to open it for her. Instead, he put his large, square hand flatly on it. "Julia, I understand you're part owner of the *Jewel*. The figurehead . . . I've followed you for many a league."

"It was to have been my husband's ship," she said sharply, pushing at the gate.

He had no choice but to open it for her. "You don't hold that against me, do you?" he asked as she started to brush past him.

"I guess in a way I do." She saw a mixture of bewilderment and pain in the grey-green eyes that were rimmed with blue, and she softened her voice. "I know it's not your fault, but I can't help the way I feel."

"No, I guess you can't," he said gently. "Maybe if I were to tell you about the voyage, it would help."

"No! No!" She clutched the basket closer to her, as though it would stop the pain, and tried to rush past him.

"Julia . . ." He caught her arm and stopped her. "We were friends once. Can't we be friends again?"

"I don't have any friends!" She jerked her arm away from him and ran down past the spruce trees to the house.

David stood where she had left him, watching her black dress whirl across the dead needles on the ground until she had vanished into the darkness of the kitchen door. Then he made up his mind and followed her. He walked up onto the porch, the boards creaking under his weight. Well, at least he wouldn't startle her this time, he thought.

"Julia," he said through the open doorway. "I didn't mean to upset you."

He couldn't see her in the kitchen. He could only hear her voice.

"Go away!" she said.

"Please let me talk to you."

242

"You don't have to talk to me to keep your job as master of the *Jewel*." He could hear tears in her voice.

"That's not why I want to talk to you."

"Then why do you? I have nothing to say to you."

"I don't care whether you think you have friends or not. I've always been your friend. I still am."

"No. I was only a child when you knew me. A long time ago. I've changed a lot."

Talking to a disembodied voice finally became too much for David. Whether she invited him or not, he was going in. When he entered the kitchen, he found her on the far side of the sink, her hands clutching its cold edge, her head pressed against the wall. The flowers had been dumped heedlessly into the sink. There were tears trickling down her cheeks.

He wanted to touch her, to hold her, but she stiffened at his approach, and he let his hand fall.

"Julia, I remember you so well. When I looked at the figurehead, I thought of you. Skipping along the road on your way to school. Sawdust in your curls at the shipyard. Riding your father's horse all over the countryside. You were such a happy child."

"David, please don't." Her tears had stopped, but her indigo eyes carried such agony it pierced him.

"I want to see you happy again, Julia. You have a magic smile, like no one else on earth."

"Not anymore."

"You'll smile again."

"I've forgotten how."

"I don't believe it," he said. He wanted to wipe the drying tears from her face, to brush back the black tendrils that escaped from her hairnet, to smooth the tense lines away from her forehead. "Maybe it just takes a little time, but you will. I want to be here to see it when you do."

She looked at him, at the smile that only suggested itself at the corners of his wide lips, at the kindness and gentleness in his eyes. Despite his large body and the sun-wrinkles on his face, she saw again the boy.

"You . . . you always had a special smile for me," she said. "I remember, when I was little, I used to wish for a big brother sometimes, and I used to pretend that you were mine."

"Did you, Julia?"

"Yes. You seemed so much older and wiser. And you knew the sea. You were already going to sea."

"Can't you still pretend that I'm your brother? I'd like to be."

"No." Her eyes, which had softened with memory, now hardened. "It's too late for that now."

"Is it? Maybe you need a brother now more than you ever did before."

"Haven't you heard the stories about me, David?" It was the first time he had heard that bitter laugh come from Julia. "All the stories about crazy Julia?"

"No, I haven't," he said firmly. "I've heard that a tree fell on you during the hurricane and that you were ill for a long time afterwards."

"Well, the stories about crazy Julia . . . they're true."

He examined her face carefully for a moment, noticing the chin held high, her pale, strained look, the deep blue eyes daring him to disagree.

"I can't believe it, Julia," he said gently. "Don't do this to yourself."

"What do you want of me, David?" Her voice was hard, too hard for so young a woman. "If you're thinking about courting me for the sake of a ship, forget it."

"Why should I want anything of you, Julia?" His grey-green eyes were gentle, almost pleading. "I have the ship. I doubt your father will remove me from command."

"No. He won't."

"It's just that I like you very much. I always have. The only thing I want from you is to see your smile again."

She stubbornly pressed her lips together and just looked at him.

"I would have come courting you, Julia," he said softly, looking down at the cap he was turning in his hands. "If I'd known you were going to grow up so fast, I would have been here. You were still a young girl when I left. When I came back, you were married. You grew up while I was at sea."

This time when she looked at him, she compared him to Jason. David was only a little shorter than Jason, but he didn't have Jason's lean, beautiful body. Where Jason was agile, David seemed clumsy. He was well enough featured, but he didn't have Jason's sharp, upward-tilting bones or the penetrating green eyes.

She shook her head.

"It's just as well, David. Jason was the only man I ever loved, the only man I ever will love."

"I understand. I'm not courting you now. Just don't cut yourself off from life, Julia. You're still young and very beautiful. There are a lot of years ahead. You mustn't live out your life in sorrow. You have too much to give."

She pushed herself away from the wall and squared her shoulders.

"I have nothing to give," she said. "Not to you nor to anyone else. You'd better go."

"No, not yet." He stood his ground. "I have to convince you first, Julia. I'm not asking anything from you, only to be your friend . . . or your brother. Nothing more."

"Then I'll ask something from you. Go away and leave me alone."

"All right. If you really mean it, I'll leave, but remember what I've said, Julia. If you ever need me, send for me. If I'm at sea, write to me. You know how to reach me."

"I will," she said, willing to promise him anything just to be rid of him.

He paused by the door and looked at her reluctantly for a moment.

"I'll tell my father you were here," she said.

He nodded and put on his cap.

"Goodbye, Julia."

During the course of the next few days, David Baxter was apt to drop by the house in the evening to discuss ship's business with her father, but each time Julia heard his step on the porch or the knocker sound on the door, she fled upstairs and took refuge in her room. By leaving her door open, she could hear his voice, low and calm and steady. He always asked about her when he arrived.

A new emotion was being born in Julia, one she could neither understand nor handle. She did want David for a friend, someone near her own age whom she could talk to and confide in. Yet even that desire, she felt, was a betrayal of her husband. She couldn't open her heart, even that much, to anyone but Jason.

Still, at night after he had gone, she would sometimes think of his wide lips always about to smile, the grey-green eyes so startlingly outlined in deep blue, and she would hear the warmth of his voice. Then the loneliness would descend upon her, and she would cry into her pillow for Jason.

Soon the *Jewel* had sailed for England and David was gone.

Gradually Julia ceased to think of him at all.

The scent of pine resin was strong in the air and from the fields came the tangy odor of sweet fern mixed with bay leaves as Julia sat on the end of the low front porch, her feet on the grass before her. She was staring absently at an orange trumpet vine flower, which crowned her up-stretched finger, while a book lay forgotten in her lap. She felt the late morning sun on her face like a blessing, but her blue eyes were troubled and the beginning of a frown creased between her arched black brows.

Benjamin, returning home from the shipyard for dinner, saw her sitting there and started to go to her. Then he paused. He never knew quite how to handle Julia nowadays; whether 'twas better to leave her to her thoughts or try to bring them out of her. Still, he decided, best to have things out in the open. Brooding did no one any good.

"I remember when you used to make skirts for your stick dolls out of the trumpet flowers," he said, leaning against a white pillar.

"Yes," she sighed, and waggled her flower-capped finger, "and puppets on my fingers. Life was so much simpler then."

"As I recall, you didn't always think so," he said dryly, sitting down on the porch beside her.

"Guess I didn't," she admitted. "But I would have if I'd known what was coming."

"What's coming passes and then something else comes."

"Yes. That's what I was thinking about. More or less. I was thinking about Sarah."

"Sarah be damned! You shouldn't waste your time thinking about that one!"

"Well, what did she do that was so awful?" Julia stood the flower upright on his knee and looked up at him with

246

her compelling blue eyes. "Why should she be banished from her own home?"

"Don't you remember?" He tried to keep his voice gentle, to hide the anger.

"I only remember she told me about Jason."

"She did it maliciously. She knew very well what effect it could have on you when you were still so sick."

"Perhaps it was malicious," Julia admitted, "but I don't see how she could possibly have known what effect it would have."

"She was warned. We all were." His jaws tightened and his voice became harsher. "We knew that, until you'd fully recovered from the concussion, the shock could kill you."

"Sarah's so young . . ."

"Sarah was sixteen years old. If she couldn't understand plainspoken English at the age of sixteen, she won't now that she's seventeen, and never will."

"Papa . . ."

"No, Julie. You can't go round making up excuses for the girl. She's no good!"

Julia clasped her hands together loosely and looked down at them. "Papa, the Bible tells us we must forgive one another. That we must love one another. Don't you think it's about time she came home?"

"No. I don't."

"She's your daughter just as much as I am."

"Not that one, she's not."

"She is, Papa." She laid a hand on his sleeve, trying to erase the angry frown from his face. "You forgave me once. Now forgive Sarah."

"Ah, Julie, my love." He patted her hand. "It was you that had to forgive me, not the other way around. Sarah has no place in my heart. And none in my house. You . . . you never really left either."

"I know, Papa, but please let her come home."

"No! We're all happier without her around."

"I'm not." She squeezed his arm and tried to make him look at her. "I feel awful. It's my fault she's not here."

"It's not your fault!" He slammed his fist into his hand. "It's her own! Furthermore, *I* didn't banish her. She left of her own free will. Ask your mother. *I* told her not to go."

"But once gone, you won't let her come back."

"She hasn't asked to."

"Probably because she knows you won't let her. Why don't you ask her, Papa?"

"No!"

"Then let me ask her."

"No."

"Papa, please. What can I do to make you change your mind?"

"I don't know why you want that meeching troublemaker around here."

"I told you." Julia pushed her hair back over her shoulders. "She's my sister and she belongs here. I feel guilty because she's not."

With his jaw set and his blue eyes stubborn, Benjamin stared off at a patch of scrub pine at the bend of the road.

Julia, racking her brain to think of some way to convince her father, stared at the same spot. She left her hand lying idly on his arm.

Finally, he said, "I'll strike a bargain with you."

She looked up at him hopefully.

"What is it?"

"You come back to the shipyard with me."

"No."

"Listen to me. All you have to do is put in an hour or two a day to begin with, but I want you to come back and work with me."

"I can't!" She jerked her hand away from him and clasped it tightly with the other in her lap.

"Yes, you can."

"No."

"Why not?"

"Because . . . Because I can't face them. I can't face anyone. Everybody thinks I'm crazy."

"Then you've just got to face them and prove they're wrong."

"No."

"You can't hide here the rest of your life. Someday you've got to get on with the job of living. Might as well be now."

"Not yet, Papa. Please." She twisted her hands tightly together in her lap.

"Now."

"I can't!"

"Yes, you can! You were never one to hide. You always walked tall and proud, not caring what others said. You haven't changed all that much. You're still Julia Howard and you can do it."

"Julia Thacher." She bit her thumbnail.

"Julia *Howard* Thacher!" He took her hand away from her mouth and held it. "Your new name only gives you more reason to walk with your head high. It's a proud name. Did you ever see a Thacher hiding in the shadows?"

"No," she admitted. "Jason and Cousin William always walked proud." She remembered William's rolling, vigorous gait. Then, more painfully, she remembered Jason's long stride. He'd tried so hard to slow up to match her shorter one.

"Then live up to your names! Both of them."

"Oh, Papa. It's just too much to ask." She squeezed his hand. "I'm afraid I'll break and run. I couldn't stand it if I did."

"Which is precisely why you won't. Besides, I'll be there with you."

"And Sarah?"

"That's my part of the bargain. *I'm* not going to ask her to come back. But you come down to the yard with me for a few days, and you can ask her."

"I think you should ask her."

"No, but you can tell her I've agreed to it. Not that I know how I'll be able to endure the sight of that bitch in my house again . . ."

"All right, Papa. I'll go over to the yard if I can ask Sarah. But I'm not going to walk tall and proud unless you promise to act kind to her when she comes home."

"You're asking too much."

"Is it any more than you're asking of me?"

"No," he said gruffly. "I guess it's not. But I can't promise anything."

"Then neither can I." She turned her head away from him and looked intently at a small white cumulus cloud that was passing in the blue sky just above the last tall spruce.

Benjamin scowled at her. Then he suddenly threw back his head and roared with laughter.

"You minx!" he said and slapped his knee. "You strike a hard bargain. By God, you're my own daughter, all right. You just proved that. Maybe I taught you too well for my own good, but it was there to be taught the day you were born."

He hugged her to him. She looked up and smiled at him. A full Julia smile.

"Then it's a bargain? All terms to be met in full?"

"It's a bargain," he said, still grinning. "Here's my hand on it."

As they neared the yard, Julia reined in and stopped. Around the next bend, just beyond those pine trees, she would be fully exposed. Exposed to a hundred curious eyes. Already she could hear the sounds of saw and hammer, the ringing anvil of the blacksmith's shop. She could smell the tar and oakum and fresh-cut lumber.

Benjamin reined in just ahead of her. He twisted in his saddle to look back at her.

"Come on, Julia. You didn't come this far only to cut and run."

"I'm not running." Her face was pale, but she sat proudly in the saddle. "I'm just getting up my courage."

"Only way to swim in cold water is to plunge in without thinking."

Her blue eyes were enormous in her strained face, but she tapped Fancy with her heel, started forward, and passed her father. Ignoring him, she rode into the yard. Her chin was held high, her shoulders tensely set as she guided her horse to the mounting block beside the office.

The last time Julia had seen the shipyard the sky had been piled high with turbulent grey clouds sliced with lightning. The sand had swirled about in miniature tornadoes and the gulls had been screaming their warning overhead. There had been lines everywhere, holding down the ships.

Now the ships stood unfettered on the ways, a light south wind blew the blue water of Sesuit Creek into diamonds, and the gulls perched peacefully on docks and pilings. The men went about their work with purpose, but there was no sense of urgency. It was hard for her to believe that, after the storm, everything could return so quickly to normal.

Then she realized how many months ago that storm had come. Almost a year.

Daniel Sears stood waiting for her at the mounting block, his brown eyes crinkled in a smile, his swarthy face alight with pleasure.

"Miss Julia!" he said as he helped her to dismount. Despite his rough, stained clothes and his heavily callused hands, Daniel had as deep and inbred a gallantry as any courtier.

"Thank you, Daniel," she said, not wanting to face him, and yet, in the face of his courtesy, she couldn't run away.

"We're mighty glad to have you back, Miss Julia," he said with real warmth. "Now, maybe things'll go right again."

"What do you mean?" His honest pleasure in seeing her took her aback. It wasn't what she'd expected, although, she thought, she should have expected it of Daniel. "Has anything gone wrong?"

"Everything." When he frowned, his eyebrows met in a straight line. "Last shipment of oak came in late and it's still green. Won't be able to use it for months. We're just about out of copper and Hiram Brothers keep putting us off. All our supplies are low. And that's not the worst of it . . ."

"Tom Rawlings fell off the brig and broke his leg," Raymond Treat, who had drifted up behind Daniel, cut in.

The men gradually left their work and began to gather around them. Their voices came thick and fast, each trying to be first with some piece of bad news.

"Charlie Lewis cut his hand so bad Doctor Willett had to sew it up. Lost the use of two fingers."

"The ways rotted out and broke under the schooner."

"Fire started in the rope locker."

Julia looked at their faces. This wasn't the hostile crowd she had been expecting. These were her friends. The good, strong, gentle men she had grown up with. The men who had taught her so much, who had shown so much patience with her as she learned. Only Josiah, watching her with a narrow coldness, stood apart, and that didn't matter. She was used to hostility from Uncle Josiah.

Caught between tears and laughter, she laughed. They cared about her. They really did.

"Oh, thank you," she said. Impulsively, she kissed grizzled old Fred Goodson on the cheek.

"You're staying, ain't you, Miss Julia?" someone in the back of the crowd asked.

"Yes, I am. I most certainly am." For the first time in months, her smile was radiant. "It's so good to be back."

Benjamin stood grinning beside her. Watching her face come vibrantly to life once more, he felt like whooping and giving the men a half holiday.

But Daniel Sears had other ideas.

"Miss Julia," he said. "Want to take a look at the ships? Might be a good idea if you checked them over."

"Guess that's as good a place to begin as any," she agreed, looking up at the scaffolding beside the brig on the nearest railway.

"All right, men! Back to work," Daniel ordered, seeing that the men were still milling about them and showing no inclination to leave.

There was some grumbling as the men returned to their jobs, but it was good-natured. Leaving Daniel to escort Julia around the yard, Benjamin went into the office.

"I can't very well climb scaffoldings in this dress," Julia said apologetically. "I hadn't really planned on working out in the yard today. I was just going to look in at the office."

"Guess not." Daniel shook his head as he looked at her full-skirted black dress. "How about starting off with the small craft?"

"Yes. After all, that's where everything starts, isn't it."

They crossed the sandy, rutted road and climbed the hill to the sheds where the older, most promising apprentices worked on the small boats. There, on gigs, longboats, and dories, they acquired the knowledge and skill that would enable them to go on to the larger vessels, eventually becoming masters of their trade.

There were twelve of these small boats in various stages of completion, some of them ribbed skeletons, some receiving their final coat of paint. The familiar smell of wood shavings, linseed oil, turpentine, and beeswax was strong on the hill.

Julia went from boat to boat and inspected each in turn. Running her fingers lightly over the close-grained wood, she felt the texture and sweet curves of their hulls and found pleasure in the contrasting shades of cedar, oak, locust, and pine. Her well-trained eye was quick to find flaws, but she also appreciated work that was well done.

She was lavish with her praise, and the boys stood eagerly by to receive it. But when she came to a crude or haphazard bit of workmanship, she frowned and clicked her tongue. The offenders blushed or looked at their feet and tried to hang back so as not to be noticed.

Daniel tried to rush her by the last boat, the smallest of all, which was half-hidden in a far corner. Julia, however, was not to be rushed. She walked determinedly over to it. With one glance, she knew why Daniel hadn't wanted her to see it.

"That's awful!" she said. "The Howard Shipyard can't put out anything this shoddy."

"Oh, no, ma'am. We won't." A tall boy of about fifteen stepped up. "It's just Earl and Paul." He pointed to two small boys of about nine or ten, who were trying to hide in the crowd. "They're not even apprenticed yet, but they wanted to help. Mr. Daniel, he let them have some scraps nobody wanted."

"Well, in that case . . ." She smiled down at the two young boys. "Earl and Paul. So you want to build boats that much?"

"Yes, ma'am." They shuffled their feet and tried not to look too embarrassed.

"All right. You will. But you're going to have to do better than that."

She looked at their downcast faces and remembered what it had been like to be that age. Everyone else seemed to know how to do the things you wanted to do, and things that came so hard to you seemed so easy for others.

"I'll tell you what. I'll help you build a *real* boat."

"You will? Really, Miss Julia?" the red-haired boy, who she thought was Paul, asked eagerly.

"Yes, I will. First boat I ever helped build wasn't much

bigger than this one, and I've still got it. I might even take you sailing with me in it one day."

"You will?"

"Maybe," she said. "But first you've got to do something about this disaster. No point building a boat that won't even float." She pointed to the crooked, ill-fitting seams. "Not even out of scraps. Now, you two take this apart today. Every nail out! Tomorrow, I'll show you how to go about building a real boat."

"Yes, ma'am." Towheaded Earl picked up a hammer and started prying at a nail.

When they had left the filtered light of the last shed and walked out into the bright sand-reflected sunlight, Daniel said, "I appreciated the way you talked to Paul. He's my sister's boy."

"Oh? I didn't know. Doesn't look like you."

"No. Takes after his father. Maybe you remember him. Paul Kelley?"

"I think so. Tall, thin redhead about your age?"

"That's him. The boy's been pretty miserable these last few months. His father was second mate on the *Hope*. Went down in the gale last summer. Means a lot to Paul, being able to come down to the yard with me."

"The same storm . . ."

"The same."

Julia stopped. Beyond the low sandy crest of the next hill, she could see the blue waters of the Bay, placid in the still, early summer morning. Far out on the horizon, they were still there. The soaring sails and the low-lying clouds meeting and intermingling in their whiteness.

"Thank you, Daniel," she said and laid her hand on his sleeve. "Thank you for reminding me I'm not alone."

Daniel's hand covered hers and there was deep devotion in his brown eyes. "You're not alone, Miss Julia. As long as I live, you'll never be alone."

Julia quickly withdrew her hand. "I . . . I appreciate that, Daniel. I really do. But I was thinking about the storm. There were a lot of people besides me . . ."

"Yes, ma'am." Daniel's face flooded with color. "Hardly a one of us but didn't lose someone. Thirty-two vessels."

They strolled down the hill and across the road in an embarrassed silence. Daniel? Julia thought. That's impossible. I've known him practically all my life. And he's a lot older than I am. Must be about twelve years' difference. She glanced at him curiously as he limped beside her. No, she decided. I'm imagining things. He just meant that as a friend.

Then she thought again of what he had said. Thirty-two vessels. That meant hundreds of men. She had never asked. She had never cared enough to ask.

"Guess I've been pretty selfish," she said as they approached the upcreek railway, where a small schooner, destined to be the new Dennis packet, was building. "Acting as though I was the only one to lose a man."

"No, Miss Julia," Daniel said slowly. "No one thinks that. You were awful young. And you were happy. Everyone could tell when you'd got a letter from him. Your face lit up the yard."

Julia sighed and watched a soaring gull dive into Sesuit Creek. She didn't want to talk about Jason.

"You've never married, have you, Daniel?"

"Nope." He looked up at the schooner, avoiding her eyes. "Don't reckon I will."

"You should."

"There's a lot agin' it."

"Not your leg! That doesn't matter." Julia could have bitten her tongue.

"No. I never think about that." His smile was warm and understanding. "There's a lot of reasons. My sister, Paul's mother, is one. There's no one else but Philip and me to take care of her, and Philip's married."

"That wretched storm!"

"Well, at least we got *you* safe out of it."

"Did you help take me home that morning, Daniel?"

"No. I fetched Doctor Willett. Did help lift the tree off you, though. Right heavy. Wonder you lived through it."

"You've done a lot for me. So've a lot of the men," she added quickly. "Who else helped? I want to thank them personally. Should have done it a long time ago."

"No need for thanks. Having you back's what we need. 'Twasn't any joke when I said things wasn't going right."

"That bad?"

"Can't seem to lay a hand on anything round here that don't go wrong." Daniel looked with suspicion at the schooner, as though it might disintegrate before their eyes. "The men are starting to talk. Say the yard's jinxed. *I* don't believe it, but if *they* do, it's not going to get any better."

"We can't afford to lose them."

"No. Don't think we will now, though. If you stay."

"What've *I* got to do with it?"

"Don't know where it started, but someone got the idea that, when you came back, things would smooth out. Now they're all saying it."

A shiver ran through Julia as though a rabbit had run across her grave.

"That's ridiculous. Pure superstition," she said indignantly. "Where'd they get an idea like that?"

He shrugged and looked across the creek at the village wharf.

"Who knows? These things come out of nowhere. What men believe's got nothing to do with what Reverend Lamson preaches from the pulpit on a Sunday."

"And what do you believe?" she asked, looking at his dark face curiously.

"Don't know," he said and continued to stare across the creek. "Reckon I hope the men are right. Too much's been going wrong. Too much."

"They blame me for what's been happening?" She remembered her father's warning about people and fear.

"No. They lay it to a curse or a restless soul, I reckon. Something like that. But they believe it won't hang around once you're here."

"I still don't like it," she said, frowning.

The days slipped by more easily for Julia as she settled back into her old familiar routine of going to work with her father in the early morning and returning with him at twilight. Rather than avoiding the shipyard, she found herself looking forward to it.

She also found herself drawn more and more to the art of ship design. She talked for hours on end to her father about it and spent some evenings, as well as days, working on ship models. There was something soothing about carving the wood. The idea of building a ship the sea couldn't beat was compelling.

She walked up the road to the brow of the hill to Josiah's grey-shingled house, looking for Sarah, but her sister was never there. Or so Aunt Harriet said. Julia didn't know whether to believe her or not. Aunt Harriet acted strange. Never asked her in. Sometimes actually closed the door in her face when Julia was still talking.

Finally she wrote a note to Sarah, asking her to come to the yard. She stuck it under Josiah's front door. The next morning, when she was working alone in the office, she looked up to see Uncle Josiah staring at her, his lanky body propped against the doorframe.

"Sarah got your note," he said tersely.

"Is she coming?"

"No. She ain't."

"Why not?"

"Says she's scared of you. After what you did to her, can't say I blame her."

"Well, will she see me if I come up to your house?"

"Nope."

"Uncle Josiah, this is ridiculous," Julia said, putting down her quill pen. "Sarah's got no reason to be afraid of me."

"I think she does. Don't pay to mess around with a crazy woman, specially not one who's attacked you once. Could happen again. Then where would poor Sarah be?"

"I'm not crazy!"

"Can't prove it by me. You're loony, right enough. Always were."

"But I'm not!" Julia found her hands were beginning to tremble and she clutched them tightly together so her uncle wouldn't see them.

"Yes, you are," he cackled as he stepped into the room. "Cracked. Wild. I've heard you down on the beach talking to yourself. Or maybe the devil. Swimming with hardly a stitch to cover your nakedness. Tempting men with your lewd ways. You're either mad or an agent of the powers of darkness. Both, maybe, both."

"Uncle Josiah!" Julia gasped, seeing the wild light in his brown eyes as he advanced across the room toward her.

"The thunder of the Lord will avenge the wickedness you do, and He has appointed me His agent." He was

257

moving closer and closer to her, his thin body tense and threatening.

Julia stared at him in horror and pushed her chair back, away from him. "Leave me alone!" With her throat so tight, it was hard to raise her voice above a whisper.

"I'll leave you alone soon enough," he said, grabbing her arm with fingers like bands of iron. "After I've done with you, everyone'll leave you alone, you whore of Babylon."

"No!" Julia screamed as he jerked her to her feet. "Let me go!"

She struggled wildly to get away from his cruel, twisting grasp.

"Let me go!" she screamed again, her fight now pushing her voice to its top limits.

"Whore," he hissed at her and glowered, a red light flickering in his eyes. He raised his other arm and threw his weight into the hand that swung down on her.

Julia closed her eyes and tried to duck away from that descending arm, when suddenly the grip that held her loosened. She opened her eyes to see Daniel Sears standing behind her uncle, swinging the older man away from her by his own raised arm. Once clear, Daniel doubled up his fist and hit Josiah as hard as he could.

"What's going on here?" Her father rushed into the office just as Josiah hit the floor.

"He was going to hit Miss Julia," Daniel said as he glared down at Josiah's inert body.

"Oh, Papa, Papa!" Julia ran to her father's arms.

"Was he really going to hit you?" Benjamin asked in a voice of tempered iron.

"Yes," she sobbed. "Look at my arm." She held it up, showing the angry red marks that stood out sharply against her white skin.

"That does it!" he exploded. "Josiah, you better stay on that floor the rest of your life, because the minute you get up, *I'm* going to hit you. And I'll hit you so hard you may never rise again."

"And I'll hold him for you," Daniel said, his brown eyes still glaring and his muscles still tensed.

"Loony. Loony as your daughter," Josiah muttered from the floor.

I'll murder him, Benjamin thought. If I stay here any longer, I'll murder him.

"I'm leaving, Josiah," he said. "I'm giving you five minutes to get up off that floor and out of this yard. And don't you ever set foot in it again. You do and I'm not responsible for your life. Daniel, see him off the premises."

"With pleasure," Daniel said grimly.

"Come, Julia. We're going for a five-minute walk, and when we get back, the air around here'll smell a lot cleaner."

Benjamin put his arm around her shoulders, which were still shaking, and led her out of the office.

Walking up the creek away from the yard, they picked their way across rivulets that ran through the soft black marl, heedless of the sand-burred grass and the thorny, golden-headed weeds. The wind had risen with the day, and around the marsh, the tall grey windmills were spinning saltwater into the waiting vats.

The summer-green hills beyond, some pastured, some wooded, browsed in the hot sun. Across the marsh, in Quivet Village, the church bells chimed out a peaceful hour. Small black fish swam in miniature saltwater ponds, forgotten by some ebbing tide. Here the air was thicker with the damp, muddy, sea-bottom odor of newly exposed marl.

The creek, sparkling-voiced, never silent, leaving mussel shells and pebbles like jewels strewn on the marl, wound its way beside them. Wet rocks gleamed and dry rocks glowed in muted colors, ranging from seashell white to rich dark grey, lighted by dusky rose and earthy blue and all the greens there ever were.

From amongst the boulders that lay in the marsh like sheep grazing the rich green salt grass, Benjamin picked one that was flat. Clean granite, gleaming white in the summer sun. He led Julia to it, and they sat down.

Benjamin studied his daughter's face.

"You all right, Julie?"

"Yes, Papa."

Her face was tear-streaked, but it was calmer now .

"You want to tell me about it?"

"Yes." With her eyes, she followed the flow of Sesuit Creek up through the marsh to the point where it met

Quivet Creek. She couldn't really see it through the tall cattails, but she knew it was there.

"You see," she said, "it all started because I was trying to get in touch with Sarah . . ."

Trying to remember every detail, every word, trying to recapture the evil Josiah had radiated, she told him of her attempts to see her sister and ended up with the morning's scene in the office. Benjamin listened to her words intently and read the emotions that flickered across her face as she relived the story. When she had finished, he looked away, up at the signals fluttering from the highest hills, the signals that telegraphed news of inbound ships, carrying word to their owners in Boston. But for once, he was not reading the signals or thinking of the ships.

"That does it," he said finally in a low, firm voice. He had come to a decision. "I'll take no more nonsense from Josiah. He's becoming dangerous. I'm going to have to buy him out."

"Won't that be awfully expensive?"

"For the little he's got, yes. But he don't have much stock left in the yard. Josiah's always been a gambler. Puts his money into every crackpot scheme that comes along. Thinks he can get rich quick that way. Result is he's lost almost everything he ever had. Wish I could count the number of times I've had to bail him out. But for every cent I paid on his account, I've demanded some of his share in the yard in return."

"So you own a lot more than he does now?"

"I own most of it, but I'll probably have to pay him ten times what his share's worth to get rid of him."

"Think he'll sell to you?" Julia asked skeptically.

"Mmmm," he said, rubbing his chin. "After today, maybe not."

"I don't think he will. He'll hold out to spite you."

"There are ways. If Josiah don't know it's me he's selling to."

"How?"

"I'll have to get what they call a front man. Someone I trust. Someone who'll buy from Josiah and sell to me. Just on paper. It'll all be done with my money. Might get it a lot cheaper that way, too," he said. There was a delighted glint in his dark blue eyes and his mouth turned up ever so slightly at the corners.

Julia had to laugh at him.

"You know, you almost look like you're enjoying this."

"I am. I am." His smile deepened and he rubbed his hands together. "I'm going to enjoy the hell out of it. It'll be worth every penny."

"It might be at that." Julia's smile matched her father's.

"Now don't you go round saying a word about this to anyone," he cautioned her. "Can't let Josiah get wind of it. We'll just bide our time, wait till he's hurting for money. Make Josiah think that, by selling to an outsider, he'll be putting a burr under my saddle." He chuckled with pure, malicious delight.

When they returned to the yard, Julia went back to her desk in the office while Benjamin went to check on the schooner. However, she found it difficult to concentrate. She kept seeing her uncle with his arm raised against her and the madness in his eyes. She was a little afraid that he might come back and find her alone.

Instead it was Daniel who came.

"He's gone, Miss Julia," he said as he stepped into the room, "and I don't think he'll be coming back. Not for a long time."

Julia looked at Daniel's torn shirt. There was a smear of blood on one of the sleeves.

"Are you all right, Daniel?"

"I am." The warm concern he heard in her voice and saw in her eyes gave him a new confidence.

"What did you do to him, Daniel? You didn't hurt him?"

"Not so's he won't recover from it. Once word gets around, no one's ever goin' to touch you again," he said, looking at the bruises on her arm. There was a tight, controlled fury in his voice.

"I don't want you to get into trouble on my account," she said softly, looking at him with new respect.

"I won't get into any trouble over it, Miss Julia, and if I did . . . it would be worth it."

"I don't know how to thank you, Daniel," she said as she toyed with the quill pen she had laid down when he came in. It was difficult to meet the dedication she saw in his dark brown eyes. "I don't know what would have happened to me if you hadn't been here."

"No need to thank me. You know that, Miss Julia."

"It was lucky for me you were near when he came in."

"I wasn't," he said, coming closer to her. "I was up on the brig when I saw him heading for the office. I knew you were in here alone, and the way he's been acting lately, I thought you might need me, so I followed him. Didn't think he'd go so far as to try to hit you, though."

"It was pretty frightening," she admitted. "I guess I'm still scared he'll come back and try it again."

"Not while I'm around, he won't. Besides, I don't think he's goin' anywhere for a while."

After dinner when Julia and her father rode into the shipyard, they saw Sarah sitting daintily on her trunk in front of the office. She was smiling her most practiced smile at a young carpenter who stood beside her. He was obviously deeply entranced with Sarah.

"What's that creature doing here?" Benjamin muttered when he saw her.

"Now, Papa." Julia put a warning hand on his arm. "I asked her to come. Remember your part of the bargain."

"I remember. But I still don't like it. Specially now, right after our fight with Josiah this morning. Smells like a Grand Banks schooner coming into port. Fishy."

"Papa! There's bound to be some good reason. Maybe she's had enough of Uncle Josiah, too."

"Could be. But I don't believe it."

Chapter Fourteen

1839-1840

THE YOUNG, BLOND CARPENTER, seeing them approach, looked embarrassed. He knew he was loitering when he should have been working.

"I just helped bring Miss Sarah's trunk over," he explained defensively before either Benjamin or Julia had a chance to speak.

"That's all right, Charlie," Benjamin said. "You can get on back to work now."

"And thank you so much, Mr. Jones," Sarah said, fluttering her dark lashes over her dove-grey eyes.

"Yes, ma'am." The young carpenter blushed, then turned on his heel and hurried over to the carpenter's shop.

"Well, Sarah," Benjamin said.

"Well, Papa," Sarah said in a hostile voice.

"Sarah, I'm so glad to see you." Julia went to her and tried to embrace Sarah's unyielding body.

"I'll bet you are."

"But I am. I've been trying to see you for days."

"So Aunt Harriet mentioned," Sarah said coolly.

"We've all wanted you to come home."

"And now I'm coming, seeing as how I haven't got any other place to go, but it's not by any wish of mine."

263

"Then whose wish is it, Sarah?" Benjamin said roughly.

"Uncle Josiah threw me out. After the way you beat him up this morning, he said he wasn't going to support your daughter anymore."

"He never did 'support' you. Least not in any financial way. In other matters I could mention, I reckon he did. Like lying about your sister and spreading filthy rumors about your own family around the countryside."

"Well," Sarah said as she got down from her trunk, "I'll have to go and see if Miss Coombs will take me in. I can offer to earn my keep by helping her teach the lower grades." She turned and started walking away from them in great dignity.

"Sarah!" Julia blocked her sister's path. "Don't go. You know we want you to come home."

"I'll not go to a place where I'll be yelled and cursed at. I'd rather starve in a ditch first."

"Nobody's going to yell and curse at you. Are they, Papa?" Julia raised one black eyebrow and stared at her father.

"No," he said, while clenching his fists with the effort of his words. "I'll go get someone to hitch the ox up to the wagon and take her home." He turned abruptly and left them.

"Sarah." Julia's indigo eyes were wide as she pleaded with her sister. "Please don't take on so with Papa. You just antagonize him."

"If it hadn't been for you, Julia," Sarah said with narrowed eyes, "none of this would have happened. If you'd just stayed over in Brewster where you belong, I'd never have had to take refuge with Uncle Josiah. You think I enjoyed it?"

"I'm sure you didn't. And I didn't enjoy having you away."

"Don't put on any of your saintly airs with me, sister dear. I know all about you and your filthy tricks. That's one thing living with Uncle Josiah and Aunt Harriet did for me. They opened my eyes to a lot of things that've been going on. Things even I wasn't aware of."

"What are you talking about, Sarah?"

"Uncle Josiah says you're not really my sister. You're a changeling. When you were born, the sea nymphs stole my mother's child and put you in her place. He says that's why you're always down at the beach, because you really don't belong on land at all. You belong in the sea. You go down there and whisper to the waves, and the sea nymphs come and tell you secrets, like how to put a curse on people and how to bewitch men."

"Sarah!" Julia was really shocked by the hatred on her sister's face. "How can you say such things? You know they're not true."

"Aren't they?" Sarah drew a line in the sand with the tip of her apricot-colored parasol. "What about the spell you put on the shipyard so that everything went wrong until you came back? And when Amos Randolph broke his leg two weeks ago, Uncle Josiah said he saw you putting a curse on him."

"You'd better not let Papa hear you saying things like that. With his temper, I don't know what he'd do."

"Oh, I expect you'll contrive to tell him. Anything to get me into more trouble. You're an expert at that."

"Sarah!" Julia was completely dismayed. She sat down on Sarah's trunk. "How can I convince you that I have no wish to harm you? I only want to help you."

"You can't convince me of anything. After a lifetime of living with you, I'm on to all your tricks."

The big dark grey ox, dragging the yard wagon behind him, lumbered up to the office. Two men jumped down to load Sarah's trunk into it.

"I'm not going to ride in that filthy cart," Sarah said, drawing her skirts away from it.

"You can take my horse," Julia said quietly.

"I will. You owe me that much, anyway."

Julia pressed her lips together, afraid of what she might say if she opened them. She watched Sarah mount Fancy and ride out of the yard beside the wagon. Sarah's face became instantly vivacious as she smiled and chatted with the men in the wagon.

When the men returned, leading Julia's horse behind them, they drew the wagon to a halt beside the ship where Julia and Benjamin stood talking.

"Excuse me, Captain Howard, Miss Julia." It was Philip Sears, Daniel's younger brother, who spoke. "Mrs. Howard wants you both to come home right away. Says she needs your help."

"Do you know what it's about, Philip?"

"Yes, sir. I think it has something to do with Miss Sarah's room."

"Oh, my God!" Benjamin said, looking at Julia. "Aunt Martha's in there."

"Oh, no!" Julia put her hand to her lips. "We'd better go, Papa."

At home, they found the upstairs in a turmoil. Sarah was carting her clothes from the trunk in the hall to one of the empty servants' rooms over the carriage house. Martha was removing her possessions from the drawers in what had previously been Sarah's room. Lydia stood wringing her hands in the hall while Amelia sat glumly at the top of the steps, watching the scene.

"Now, what the bloody hell is going on?" Benjamin roared, his patience tried to the limit.

"Benjamin, don't swear," Lydia said automatically.

"I damn well will swear in my own house when every woman in it has suddenly taken leave of her senses."

"I am simply moving my things into the servants' quarters, where it seems I now belong," Sarah said coolly.

"You'll do no such thing. Put those clothes down."

Staring at her father haughtily, Sarah tried to think of the next shaft she would loose.

"Put them down, I said!" He ripped them from her hands and threw them in the trunk. "*I* didn't say you could move into the servants' quarters."

"Well, what else am I to think? I come home and find a perfect stranger has taken over my room." Her eyes took on the look of a crippled bird. "You certainly wouldn't let anyone use Julia's room when she was gone."

"Aunt Martha is *not* a perfect stranger. She's part of the family now." Benjamin hit the banister with his fist. "There's a very simple solution to all this, and if any of you had half the brains I've given you credit for, you'd have found the answer."

"I've told Sarah she could move in with me," Amelia said from her seat on the stairs.

"I'm going to have a room of my own. Even if it is the smallest in the house and the coldest," Sarah said, staring with contempt at Amelia. "I need my privacy as much as anyone else does."

"Amelia can move in with me," Julia offered, leaning down and putting her arm around her youngest sister's shoulders. "Aunt Martha can have Amelia's room then."

"Will you all shut up!" Benjamin shouted. "Just shut up and stop dithering." He glared them all into silence.

"Now that's better." He paced up and down the carpeted hall.

"You, Sarah." He stopped and pointed a finger at her. "Are going to move back into your own room.

"You, Aunt Martha." He turned and pointed at the tall, white-haired woman, who stood in the doorway of the disputed room with her arms folded. "Are going to move into my room. And *I*." This time he paused in front of Lydia. "Am going to move into your room."

"Then where will Mama go?" Amelia asked, troubled.

"Your mother will stay right where she is. If there's any sharing to be done, we're the ones who're going to do it."

Bewildered, trying to fathom the meaning behind his words, Lydia looked at him. He had never before suggested that they might once again share the same bed. Then she made up her mind and went to him.

"Oh, Benjy, I'm so glad."

"And high time, too," he said gruffly, then put an arm around her.

On a warm night in August, Julia wakened to find the full moon flooding her room. She lay and watched the shadows of branches as they played across the papered walls and painted ceiling. Soon, though, she found that she was as restless as they were. The bed was too confining. She got up and went to her window.

The world had softened into a thousand shades of grey, from rose to amber and silver to black. The low white moon spread its brilliance over the woods, the fields, the gardens, and the marsh. The birds were astir and restless, singing the night through, accompanied by frogs and locusts. It was a night to be shared.

She paced the room, aching for Jason. To hear his voice. To feel his hands caress her body. To see his eyes reflect the moon. She paused and looked up at his portrait above the cold fireplace.

As she watched, the stark and empty oil seemed to soften, quiver, come to life. His green eyes suddenly shone with laughter. His high-planed cheeks flushed to life. His teeth flashed white in his tan face as they had that Christmas Day three and a half long years ago. She stood before it, hypnotized.

Jason! Jason, you're not dead. You can't be. You're still alive. Somewhere, you're still alive.

His eyes seemed to be telling her something. She strained to read them. Once she and Jason had been so close! Thoughts had danced between their minds with no need for spoken words. Why couldn't she understand him now?

"Jason, what is it? Tell me. Please tell me," she whispered.

But even as she spoke the colors dimmed back to join the shades of grey and black that filled the room.

"Oh, Jason," she mourned. "Where are you?"

She stared at the portrait, compelling him to return. But it remained cold and lifeless.

Finally she turned away from it. Feeling even more bereft and alone than she had earlier, she went to one of the long windows that led onto the upper porch. Ducking her head, she went through into the night. Mosquitoes were singing somewhere nearby. Beyond the chestnut trees, the marsh grass rippled silver light under a gentle breeze.

Then she heard his voice calling from a long, faraway place.

"Julia. Julia. Come to me." He wasn't frightened anymore. It was his husky, yearning voice of night, of bed, of love.

"Oh, Jason," she sighed. "Where are you?"

"Come to me, Julia. Come to me." It came from the direction of the Bay.

"I'm coming," she said. "Wait for me."

She hurried into her room and threw on a dress. Then she ran lightly down the stairs, carrying her shoes in her hand. Once outside, she sat on the edge of the porch to put them on. As she tied the laces, she heard his voice again. It came to her from beyond the marsh, beyond the trees, beyond the fields, repeating only one word over and over again: "Julia."

She ran down the soft, sandy road that glimmered white in moonlight, following the voice that always seemed to be just around the next curve, beyond the far bend. When she came to the path that led to the beach, she was breathless and she hesitated.

She hadn't been down that path since the last time she had heard his voice. The night of the storm. The night a tree had fallen and kept her from him.

His voice was stronger now. More urgent. He was alive. Had to be. He was waiting for her on the beach they had walked together.

When she reached the top of the dunes, she saw him. A tall, shadowy figure standing near the edge of the placid, lapping water.

"Jason!"

She raced over the sand, stumbling in its softness, jumping over the sea wrack, putting the sand crabs to flight.

"Jason!"

She ran with her arms stretched wide, ready to embrace that tall, familiar shadow.

But when she reached the spot where he had stood, there was no one. There was nothing to cast a shadow.

"Jason," she sobbed in frustration. "Where are you? Don't hide from me. I love you. Where are you?"

Over the soft shushing sound of the water, the tinkle of pebbles, she heard his voice. So near. So close. Just a few feet out in the water.

"Julia." It was a whisper. "Come to me."

She kicked off her shoes and threw off her dress. She stepped into the cool black-silver water.

"Darling Jason, where are you?"

"Here." His voice came from the sparkling-bright moon-path. "I'm here."

She waded out. Deeper and deeper. She followed the voice. It was always just a little farther down the white lane.

Soon the water washed around her waist. She began to swim. His voice grew dimmer. He was moving away from her faster than she could follow.

"Jason! Don't leave me! Come back! Wait for me!"

She swam for what seemed to be an eternity, always following the fading voice.

Suddenly her hand struck something hard and cold. A large fish, drawn by the full moon, jumped beside her. She swerved away from it. When she turned her head to look down the moonpath, there was only the golden sparkling water. In the far distance was a shadow of land. The end of Cape Cod, where Provincetown . . . and Truro lay.

"Jason!" She treaded water. There was no answer. "Jason!" No answer. No shadow. No presence. No laughing, green-eyed face. Only the empty sea.

She looked back at the shore from which she had come. It seemed far away. The way it might look from the deck of a passing ship. The high dunes were merely a glimmer of white thread between the sparkling sea and the tall black sky. Had she swum so far?

She struck out for the land, keeping her eyes fixed on the tallest dune-line. The water, warm from the summer's heat, caressed her body and supported it. The salt tasted sweet on her lips. It was the first time she had been swimming at night for a long time. She had forgotten how luxurious, how restful, it could be. The worries of the shipyard and her life on land seemed to drop away. But Jason? Why had he called her? His presence had been so real, and now he was gone.

Before she knew it, the land rose up before her, and she rode a wave in to the shore. She shivered when she stood up. The night air was cold. Her clothes, which she had dropped at the water's edge, were now far up the beach, stranded by the ebbing tide.

As she ran up the beach to pick them up, she heard Jason's voice once again. This time it was just behind her. She stopped, but she didn't dare to turn and look. She was afraid he would flee from her again.

"Farewell, sweet Julia," he said. "My love will bide with you through eternity, but I must go."

She waited for more, but there was no more, and when

she turned, there was only a faint lightening of the sky in the east as a new day prepared to begin.

As autumn progressed into winter and the days grew shorter, the work in the yard became more taxing but more pleasant. Benjamin, through Captain James Chase, managed to buy Josiah's remaining shares in the shipyard, and with Josiah's departure there was an easing of tension. Josiah considered the money these shares brought him a fortune, and he enjoyed strutting through the village and wielding what he thought was power of wealth, but few paid any real attention to him.

Then one day, while Benjamin was in the carpenter's shop, Daniel Sears came bursting through the door. He was out of breath and his swarthy face was tense.

"Capt'n Howard, he's back."

Benjamin forgot the carpenters and his entire attention was centered on his foreman. Daniel was not an alarmist, and when he spoke, Benjamin now listened.

"Who's back?" he asked.

"Your brother, sir."

"Josiah?"

"Aye. He's over in the office goin' through your papers. Happened to see him through the window and thought I'd best come get you."

"That devil!" Benjamin strode through the door with Daniel immediately behind him. "Where's Miss Julia?"

"Over at the mold loft, last I knew."

"Well, go find her and tell her to stay away from the office."

"I'll come with you, sir." Daniel was panting and limping at the same time.

"I don't need you, but I don't want Julia anywhere near that man." The ground was slippery with morning ice, but Benjamin didn't shorten his stride for caution.

"I'll keep an eye out and head her off if she comes, but you do need me, Capt'n Howard."

"I can fight my own fights, Daniel."

"Yes, sir, but you might need a witness."

"A witness?" Benjamin glanced sideways at his foreman's sharp profile.

"Yes, sir." Daniel's face was set and his brown eyes determined. "A witness."

"Well, you may be right at that. Come along, then."

When Benjamin threw open the office door, the breeze caught papers that were piled haphazardly on desks, chairs and tables. Josiah, his thin rump sticking up in the air, was delving deep into one of the brass-bound chests that held the records of the year.

"What in the bloody hell do you think you're doing, Josiah?" Benjamin growled.

"Think you can trick me, do you?" Josiah straightened up with a snarl. "Well, you're not gettin' away with it. I'm lookin' for my rights and I intend to have them."

"What rights?" Benjamin's thick eyebrows came together over eyes that were filled with anger. "You don't have any damned rights around here anymore. Get out!"

"I've got my rights." Josiah clenched his fists and a defensive hatred twisted his face. "You stole this yard from me. Weren't satisfied with the first half you stole, you had to steal the rest piece by piece. I'm goin' to take you to court, Benjamin, and I'm goin' to get this place back."

"You're not getting anything, Josiah, except out of here. The first half I inherited, same as you did. The second half, you sold."

"Not willingly, I didn't. You forced me into it, and that's what will count in a court of Godfearin' men. You didn't give me half what it was worth."

"Half? I gave you one hell of a lot more than it was worth at the time. If it's worth more now, it's only because I've put my sweat and blood into it . . . and, yes, my money, too. And you've reaped the benefits, Josiah. You made quite a profit when you sold out to Jim Chase."

"Chase!" Josiah spat. *"Thought* I was sellin' out to Chase, but I wasn't, was I? I was sellin' out to you."

"Where'd you get that idea?"

"Obvious, ain't it? Three months after he buys, you've got the whole thing. Think I'm not smart enough to figure that out?"

"If you're smart you'll get your hands off my papers and yourself out of this yard. And if you're really smart, you'll never come back."

Josiah took one step back, as though guarding the ransacked chest. "You goin' to throw me out?" he challenged. "Or do you need a cripple to help you do it?" He looked pointedly at Daniel's lame leg.

"It would be my pleasure to do it with my own two hands." Benjamin moved toward him, his big shoulders twitching menacingly under his heavy coat.

"I'll leave," Josiah said as he edged away from the chest and around behind a tall desk, "but I'll be back. I'll get my rights, Benjamin. One way or t'other, I'll get my rights."

"Don't bother to come back, Josiah," Benjamin said as he watched his brother sidle toward the door. "The papers you're looking for aren't here. They're not in the house, either, if you ever get to thinking about breaking in there. They're tucked away in a good safe place where *you'll* never find them."

"The court will find them for me," Josiah said as he laid his hand on the doorknob. "You may be able to stop me from looking, but you'll never stop the law."

"I'd be delighted to produce them in court, but you know damned well that isn't why you were looking for them. You were looking for them to destroy them. You don't have the guts to sue me, even if you had the money to do it. You've already squandered and gambled away half what you got from Chase."

"Maybe not now, but someday, Benjamin. Someday you're goin' to get your comeuppance." He quickly opened the door, slipped through it, and slammed it behind him. The wind caught the papers and strewed them across the floor.

Benjamin shook his head. "Well, Daniel, want to help me clean up this mess?"

"Best I follow him." Daniel nodded at the door. "Make sure he leaves the yard."

"Yes, Daniel. Go ahead." Benjamin waited until the breeze had rearranged the papers once more in Daniel's wake before he started the methodical and calming work of sorting through them.

After Josiah's departure, the yard settled down once again to a relative peace, and Benjamin was not a man to worry about empty threats. The days of Julia's deepest, formal mourning ended. Young men, and some not so young, began to show an interest in her once more. It surprised Julia.

Knowing that strange tales and rumors still followed her like an evening shadow, she hadn't really expected any suitors. Not ever again. In a way, she wished those tales and rumors would discourage them.

She had no wish to marry again. Never anyone but Jason. There wasn't and never would be anyone who could measure up to him.

Still, the glint she saw in men's eyes when they looked at her, the small courtesies they showed her, made her glad. They saw her as a normal, even as a desirable, woman. A woman they might marry. She was no longer an outcast.

Julia treated her suitors with kindness. When the Mason brothers alternatively came home from sea, joking and laughing like schoolboys, she smiled at their unquenchable spirits. When Jonas Abney, quiet and solemn in his pursuit of a master's berth, arrived, she listened to his tales of woe and sympathized. But when they turned the conversation to more serious matters, she talked to them of Jason. She found a way to bring him into any conversation. She used him as a shield. For most, it was enough. But not for Aaron Martin.

Aaron Martin, long ago her mother's favorite candidate, now not only looked at her from behind his prayerbook in church. He also found excuses to pass by the shipyard and he spent a lot of time at the docks. Just on the chance of seeing Julia, he often dropped by the house. He was definitely paying court to her.

"Aaron came by looking for you this afternoon, Julia," Lydia said one night at supper. "Said he'd been over at the shipyard, but you weren't there."

Julia shrugged and looked down at her soup. "I was there."

"Then why'd he think you weren't?"

"He came when you were down at the beach, Julie," Benjamin said.

"Why didn't you tell me?"

"Didn't think you'd be interested."

"I'm not."

"Well, *I* would be if I was your age," Lydia said. "He's a good-looking young man."

"I suppose." Even Julia had to admit he was handsome with his rich auburn hair and his brown eyes made warm with amber. "But looks aren't everything."

"Maybe not, but he's rich to boot, what with his father owning one of the biggest saltworks on Cape Cod."

Julia just shrugged, but Lydia was not to be put off.

"And you can't complain about him not being smart. Not after he's been to Harvard."

"Not as smart as you might think."

"Julia! You just can't afford to be choosy." Lydia's patience was easily tried. "You've got to realize you're a widow. That puts a lot of men off."

Benjamin spluttered on a piece of fish that had gone down the wrong way. "Hadn't noticed it had that effect," he said when he regained control.

"I wish it did!" Julia said viciously, stabbing at an innocent piece of potato. "Aaron's too damned impressed with his looks and his education and his father's money."

"Well, I think he has a right to be," Sarah said.

"Then why don't you take him, Sarah?"

"Not me. I've got other fish to fry."

"Mother." Julia laid down her fork and looked imperiously across the table at her mother. "I want to get this straight once and for all. I am not going to marry again."

"You can't go on mourning Jason the rest of your life."

"Oh, yes, I can."

"Leave her alone," Benjamin said. "She's got the right to do as she pleases. If she don't want to see Aaron Martin, she don't have to."

"I don't mind seeing Aaron," Julia said. "I really like him. I just don't intend to marry him, and"—she looked at her mother again—"I don't want anybody trying to push me into it."

"You just like all those books he's always loaning you," Sarah said.

"Well, what if I do?"

It was true that Aaron had opened up whole new worlds to her. Some of the books he lent her were by authors whose names she had only heard mentioned; others by men she had read only once. She had become involved in the ideas and dreams of Thomas Carlyle, Jean Paul, George

275

Sand, and Schleiermacher. New and exciting ideas. Dreams of a better world.

"And those slim leather-bound books of poems he gives you!" Sarah raised her eyebrows suggestively.

"You been reading them?" Julia's eyes could now harden as threateningly as Benjamin's could.

"Reading them . . . and noticing what he underlines, too." Sarah gave her grey-eyed cat smile as she chanted:

> " '*This* breathed itself to life in Julia, *this*
> Invested her with all that's wild and sweet.' "

He left you *Childe Harold* by Lord Byron today," she added.

"It's none of your business what he underlines," Julia said.

"Maybe." Sarah daintily cut a piece of fish. "And maybe not."

What Sarah didn't know was that Julia gave those books back to Aaron after she had finished with them, and there were a few new underlines she had added herself. So far, it had been a pretty effective way of keeping him from speaking.

On a Saturday afternoon a week later, Julia was going through her wardrobe, packing away her lightweight summer clothes and bringing out the woolens she would need for the approaching winter. Rummaging through her chest for an old wool scarf that might do down at the yard for one more year, she glanced out the window and saw a horseman riding around the bend.

Even with a tall beaver hat covering his auburn hair, she could tell from the set of his solid body that it was Aaron. He was dressed in his usual elegant style. She sometimes had to smile at Aaron and his clothes. She was sure he spent more time and money on them than most girls did on theirs.

And here she was with her hair braided loosely and pinned none too neatly on top of her head. Her old black wool dress was covered with attic dust and she was sure her face was, too. Well, he must take her as she was.

The worst of it, though, was that neither Sarah nor Aunt Martha was home. They made the best chaperones.

Her mother would always agree to it, but after a few minutes she invariably drifted away with some vague excuse. She had to check on the laundry or the preserves. Lydia was definitely on Aaron's side and wanted him for a son-in-law.

Amelia was better, but not much. All Michael Adams had to do was to come whistling up the walk, and Amelia was gone. Julia didn't blame her. Michael, home fresh from the sea, was a tall, large-boned blond boy with black eyebrows and lashes. At the age of seventeen, he'd suddenly grown into a man.

He'd been on a deep-sea merchantman, but after his mother was taken seriously ill, Michael had come home. He'd found a berth on the East Dennis-to-Boston packet, so he was frequently ashore. And when he was, Amelia was with him. It pleased Julia to see sixteen-year-old Amelia's glowing happiness, but it made her completely unreliable as a chaperone. It was just as well she was off somewhere with Michael today.

Aunt Martha was good and stayed close when Julia asked her, but Sarah was the best. Surprising, too. Sarah had plenty of beaux of her own, but she'd stick tight as a burr until Aaron had given up and gone home. Julia didn't understand it, but she hoped it meant that Sarah was slowly becoming her friend.

Julia wiped the dust from her face with a damp cloth, made a pass at her hair with the brush, and went downstairs to meet Aaron, whom Janet had just let in.

"Hello, Aaron," she said, giving him a distant hand. "Glad you dropped by. I wanted to give *Childe Harold* back to you."

"Hello, Julia." He looked pointedly at her dusty dress. "I hope I didn't come at the wrong time. You weren't in the middle of anything, were you?"

"As a matter of fact, I was, and I have to finish it today. So I'm afraid you won't be able to stay long."

"I was hoping you'd go for a ride with me." His rich brown eyes were pleading.

"Not today, Aaron."

He followed her into the parlor, where she went to get

his book for him. When she handed it to him, she said, "Aaron, I want something understood between us. I appreciate your lending me your books, but I don't want any more you've gone through and underlined."

He took the book she handed him and managed to hold her hand when he did it. "I only do it for you. So you won't miss some of the better passages."

Julia withdrew her hand from his.

"I think I'm quite capable of judging which are the better passages. And they don't necessarily include my name."

His face was troubled and he looked down at the book.

"I just wanted to make sure you saw it."

Julia had to smile. Aaron had such a good, open, honest face. He would make a good husband. There were times when he almost made her wish she were someone else. Someone whose mind wasn't always two steps ahead of Aaron's. Someone who had never known Jason.

"Julia," he said earnestly, "there are things I want to say to you, but I can't always find the words. Not when I'm with you. But some men have said them before and have said them better than I ever could."

"They're better left unsaid, Aaron. I have to get back to work."

"I brought over a letter from Steve Logan." He pulled it out of his breast pocket and held it eagerly out to Julia like an offering. "Wouldn't you like to hear what he has to say?"

She sighed and sat down. She *would* like to hear the letter, and she could hardly ask Aaron to loan it to her. Stephen Logan, whom she had never met, had been a friend of Aaron's in college. His were the only letters Aaron brought that were really worth reading. When Aaron read them to her, he always left out some parts, and Julia was sure they referred to her.

"Well, let's hear the letter," she said.

"I'll explain some of the finer points of it to you."

"Read it to me first and then explain the finer points."

Aaron had an absolute genius for bringing her the fresh, blooming ideas that were springing up in Cambridge and handing her a dry and withered bouquet. He didn't even understand what he was talking about. His words were empty, nothing but a false echo of other voices he admired. The owners of those other voices, though! Those were the people she would like to meet.

Julia didn't want to settle for second best.

After dealing with Aaron's attentions, Julia found herself looking forward to seeing David Baxter. She thought more and more often of his unruly dark blond curls, of his not-too-handsome face, of his friendly grey-green eyes. Even his clumsy movements seemed more honest than Aaron's posturings. In her memory, he seemed rather like an amiable bear.

When they read in the hilltop signal flag that the *Jewel of the Seas* had been sighted homeward bound, she was almost excited. Yet a few days later, when she looked from the shipyard across Sesuit Creek and saw him stepping off the packet, she felt suddenly shy. At their last meeting she hadn't been exactly polite.

Then, too, had he really meant his offer of friendship as only that? He had also spoken of courting that day, even while denying it, she remembered. She so hoped he wouldn't be like the others. She desperately needed a friend.

It was late afternoon when he arrived at the yard. Hearing him talking to her father outside, Julia stopped writing and held the quill pen tensely between her fingers. What could she say to him? How should she act?

Maybe he won't come in here, she thought. Maybe he'll just talk to Papa out there and then go away. She hoped he would . . . and yet she couldn't bear it if he did.

When his body bulked large in the doorway, though, she felt surprisingly calm. With his back to the sun, it was difficult to see his face, only the light brightening his dark blond curls, but there was no mistaking the gentle warmth in his voice.

"Hello, Julia. Your father said you might not object to seeing me."

"Hello, David." She found her voice impersonally cool. "Did you have a pleasant voyage?"

"Aye. Summer's a good time in the Atlantic, though now it's September, I doubt it will keep so for long."

"And a profitable one?"

He chuckled as he entered the room and came to stand beside her tall desk.

"I can see you've been going over the ledgers. Well, you can add a few profits from the *Jewel* to your accounts this time."

"Most likely more than a few," she said, smiling at him. "You've done well on every voyage you've made for us, and you've proved Papa was right when he designed the *Jewel*. How many records have you broken?"

"Three so far." He tossed his cap at a nearby chair and leaned his arms on her desk. "Julia, it's good to see you smile again."

A polite smile, he thought, with none of her old radiance. Nevertheless, a smile. It was a beginning.

"Yes. You were right," she said. "I'm beginning to find pleasure in my work, the shipyard, a lot of things."

"Friends?"

"There aren't many of those," she said quietly.

"Will you let me be?"

"A *friend,* yes. I'd welcome it, David. But nothing more."

"I understand," he said, his eyes searching her face. "It's all I ever asked of you. You know that, Julia."

"Yes. I know."

"Will you be done with your work soon? I'd like to walk down the road with you when you go home."

"I'd planned on walking over to the Dennis beach later. I've been cooped in here all day, and I want to get some exercise."

"May I come with you?"

"If you wish. Perhaps you'll tell me about your voyage and about England."

"I'd like that."

"I have a few things to finish first."

"I'll wait for you outside."

By the time they had reached the path to the beach, leading Fancy behind them, Julia had begun to relax. It was just as it always had been with David, a calm, unhurried friendship. The years between might never have been, and now she wanted to tell him about those years.

"They tell me this is where the tree fell on me," she said, pointing to the spot.

"You don't remember?"

"No. It was a terrible night," she said, walking on up the path.

"What were you doing here, anyway?"

"Jason . . ." She found it hard to go on as the memories of that night came back to her. "Don't ask me, David."

"I won't. Are you sure you want to come here?"

"Oh, yes. I often do. I don't usually think about it anymore."

"You shouldn't."

She hitched Fancy behind the dunes while David went ahead to the top. He was standing there, watching the sails, when she joined him.

"When I heard the *Jewel* had been sighted from Provincetown, I brought a spyglass up here and looked for you."

"Did you?" There was more than just a suggestion of a smile on his lips as his face lit up with pleasure.

"Yes. You had her going well." She paused a moment, then went on. "It's the first time I'd seen her since . . . since before she was launched."

"You should come down to Boston to see her before we sail. She really is a jewel."

"Perhaps someday." She ran down the side of the dune, and David followed her more leisurely, his steps slow and considered.

When he reached her at the water's edge, he hesitated to ask the question, but it had been bothering him since June.

"Do you still resent my being master of the *Jewel?*"

She walked in silence for a moment. It was something she hadn't considered for a long time.

"No," she finally said. "I know you're a very able captain. One of the best. The *Jewel* won't come to any harm with you. I'm glad she's in your hands."

"That's good." The relief was obvious in his voice.

"Did it really worry you, David?" She looked at him wonderingly. "How I felt?"

"Yes. I thought of it often this last trip. I'd see you . . . your figurehead rising above the waves, and I'd think of you."

"Does it look much like me?"

"You haven't seen it?"

"No."

He studied her profile as they walked. She was no longer the pale and listless young woman he had seen in the spring. Summer had given her skin a light, vibrant tan, and the sea breeze had whipped glowing color into her cheeks and lips. She looked now more like the girl he had known, the radiant bride so lovingly portrayed in wood.

"Well, David?" she asked, pushing the escaping black curls back away from her face as she looked up at him.

"Yes. It looks very much like you."

They walked a few moments in comfortable silence before she spoke. The lapping of the waves and the cries of the gulls were happy, familiar background sounds to both of them.

"Do you know, I've sometimes wished that, instead of the figurehead, it could be me aboard."

David looked at her questioningly. He didn't quite know how she meant it. But her deep blue eyes held nothing but wistful innocence.

"Why don't you make a trip aboard her? She's your ship. Perhaps next spring, when the winter gales have died down."

"No. I don't think so."

"Why not?" He became enthusiastic over the idea. "I remember when you were a little girl, you were always saying how you were going to sea. Every time I came home, you were pestering me for sea stories."

Julia laughed. "Yes. I guess I did. Pestered you and everyone else in sight for a tale."

"I didn't mean that you were pestering, you know. I used to save up all my stories to tell you." He grinned down at her. "Even made up a few along the way."

"You didn't!"

"I did." He smiled at the memory of the boy he had been. "Julia, why *don't* you come next spring? You can have my cabin and I'll move over to the mate's. It was meant to be yours, anyway, the captain's cabin."

"Yes, I know. That's why I can't come, David. Even with Amelia or Aunt Martha along to chaperone, I still couldn't do it."

"No. I guess not. Maybe by spring, you'll feel different about it."

"I doubt it."

They had reached the end of the beach, and they stood for a moment, looking back at the way they had come. Julia, leaning against a dark grey boulder, looked up at him and saw there was worry in his grey-green eyes.

"Well, David," she said, "where's the sea story? I don't even mind if you make one up."

He shook his head and smiled, as though despairing of her.

"You still want one?"

"Of course."

"Well, did I ever tell you about the time, this was in the Mediterranean, mind you, the time we ran into the eight-headed, ten-ton octopus?"

The next morning Julia arrived at the shipyard soon after sunrise, hoping for a private swim before the world began to stir. Following her walk with David she had slept well with no dreams, and now she felt happy. Happier than she had for a long time. Something that had been wound very tight within her had relaxed.

She climbed the dunes, taking out the pins that bound the thick braids around her head. It was almost a day for singing. She looked out at the sparkling morning sea that still held a little of the golden rose of sunrise. Carefully descending the face of the dune, she was watching her footing in the tall beach grass when, from the corner of her eye, she caught a movement.

A man was there, his hair dark with water and his back turned toward her. She could just see the top of the crease between his buttocks as he pulled up his trousers. His shoulders were extraordinarily broad, as was his upper back, but there was no extra flesh on the muscle she could see rippling there.

She watched for a moment, holding her breath, then just as she was about to quietly slip away, he turned to pick up the white shirt that lay behind him on the sand. His movement was so graceful she couldn't believe, as he looked up at her, that it could be David.

He was as startled as she was, and for a moment, each

283

stood motionless, staring at the other. Smiling, he retrieved his shirt and straightened up. He made no effort to cover his naked torso as he looked at her, but held his shirt loosely in his hand. Julia couldn't stop staring at him. She had thought him too heavy before, but now she saw the powerful chest covered with thick, curling hairs turning blond as they dried, the strength that lay in those large arms.

"Good morning, Julia," he said quietly.

"Good . . . good morning." She felt the color suffusing her face, and she picked up her skirts to flee.

"You don't have to run away," he said, but by the time he had finished the sentence, she was already over the dune.

Her braids were swinging loosely, slapping her back as she ran across the yard to the office. Once there, she rushed inside and locked the door behind her. She sat down in a chair next to the cold stove and covered her hot face with both hands.

She didn't understand why the sight of his body should so upset her. She had often seen men in the shipyard stripped to the waist on a hot summer's day and had thought nothing of it. But David! Why? Was it the shock of surprise? There had been something comforting in what she had thought of as excess weight, as though he weren't really an eligible man.

She heard the door handle rattle, and then there was a knocking at the window nearest her chair. She peeked through her fingers and saw David peering in. She quickly covered her eyes again.

"Julia, please let me in."

She remained motionless.

"Won't you even tell me what's the matter?" His voice was pleading.

She slowly uncovered her face and looked at him through the dusty panes of glass. His wet curls were still clinging darkly to his head, but she could see the white of his shirt and the blue of his jacket.

"All right," she said and slowly got up, but before unlocking the door, she paused until her hands stopped shaking.

"Julia, I'm sorry if I upset you," he said when she opened the door.

"Yes. Well, you have as much right to swim there as I have." She was still not able to look into his eyes.

"I hope I didn't shame you."

With his shirt and jacket covering the splendor she had seen, she felt more comfortable. Still, it was hard to erase the memory of him as he had been on the beach with the early morning light glinting off his skin.

"No . . . no, you didn't." She moved back into the office and returned to her chair.

"I'm not ashamed, Julia," he said, entering slowly. "There's nothing to be frightened of."

"No. I suppose not. I . . . I just feel as though you might think I was spying on you."

"You?" He threw back his head and his even white teeth showed in his laughter. "If there was any spying to be done, most likely 'twould have been the other way around."

"David!"

"Didn't mean that quite the way it sounds, but it's what most would expect." He managed to control his laughter. "If you want to take a swim, go ahead. I'll stand guard for you."

"No. I've changed my mind. I don't feel like swimming after all."

"Julia." He was suddenly serious. "I won't look. You know you can trust me, don't you? I'd never take advantage of you."

She was touched by the sincerity she saw in his face.

"I know that, David, but the men will be coming to work soon. Someone'd be sure to spot me."

"I'm sorry I took your swimming time away from you. I know you used to swim there when you were young. I just didn't know that you still did."

"I guess I've never quite grown up."

"If that's what growing up means, then don't. Don't ever grow up."

"I never meant to, but it happened."

"Yes. It does to all of us. I don't regret it. I'm glad to have those years behind me, and I'm glad you grew up, too. You were a beautiful child, but you are much more

. . . " He saw the warning in her indigo eyes. "More remarkable as a woman," he finished lamely.

That night, Julia dreamed of David, found his strong arms holding her, felt the curly hair of his chest brush across her breasts, rested her head in the hollow of his powerful shoulder, rose to the kisses of his smiling lips. Then she awoke and she felt the pain, the aching emptiness of her loins. And she thought of Jason. She had betrayed him!

She rose from her bed and, guided only by starlight, began to pace the room. She saw David's grey-green eyes again, startled beneath pale brows, as he had looked up at her from the beach. She tried to think of Jason, but the image of David's body overpowered the memories of her husband, and she was frightened.

There was no more sleep for her that night, and by dawn she was exhausted. She went out onto the porch and watched the sunrise across the marsh. She wondered if David were swimming this morning.

David remained home for two days more before returning to Boston and the sea, but they could not recapture the relaxed companionship that they had found so briefly. Often he would look at her, puzzled, but the armor she wore prevented him from asking any questions.

On the last morning, he asked her to come see him off on the packet. They spoke only sporadically about unimportant things; the day, the wind, the *Jewel;* until they came to Toct Bridge. Then he swung his bag down on the weathered boards.

"We've a few minutes yet, Julia. I want to talk to you before I go."

"Yes, David." She leaned on the rail of the bridge and watched the narrow waters of the creek expand with the incoming tide.

"It's going to be a long voyage, Julia, to the Mediterranean, then on to France or England. Wherever there's a cargo." He lounged against the rail beside her and searched her face for a reaction.

"I know. I'll miss you, David." She looked up at him

and gave a small, tight smile. "You were right when you said I needed a friend."

"Will you think about taking a voyage on the *Jewel* in the spring?"

"Oh, David, I'd like to, but . . ."

"Just say you'll think about it," he quickly interrupted her.

"All right, David. I'll think about it."

He seemed to be about to say something else, but he changed his mind and picked up his bag.

"It will be warm in the Mediterranean this winter," Julia said as they walked along. "I'll think of you there when it snows."

"Aye. It'll be warm, but spring can be lovely in England."

"Yes. I promise, David. I'll think about it."

When they reached the wharf, the cargo was still being loaded, and David drew her aside.

"We're still friends?" he asked, looking down at her.

"Good friends," she said. Her smile of reassurance was more relaxed.

"Perhaps someday we can be more than friends."

"No, David." She felt uncomfortable under his gaze and looked away at the crates and barrels being swung aboard the vessel.

"I'm not talking about today or next week. I said someday."

"It can't be. Don't you understand?" There was pain in the pleading blue of her eyes. "It can never be. I can't feel that way about you. I can't feel that way about anybody ever again."

"You weren't meant to lead a lonely life, Julia."

"I'm not lonely. I have the shipyard to keep me busy," she said as she looked at it across the creek.

"It's a cold comfort."

"It's enough."

"What you're trying to tell me, Julia, is that it never can be *me* . . . even if it can be someone else?"

"I didn't say that."

"I think it's what you mean." He bent over and kissed her lightly on the forehead. "Goodbye, Julia."

As she watched him swing aboard the packet, she wanted

to call him back, to tell him that he really had misunderstood her, that if there ever could be anyone, it would be him. But already the lines were being cast off, and there was nothing she could do.

Well, he would be home again in the early spring. She would tell him then. She couldn't honestly say that she could ever love him, except as a dear friend. In honor, she could not lead him to expect what she might never be able to give. She had seen other girls lead men on, holding them against the chance that they wouldn't find a better man, but she couldn't do that. Not to any man. Especially not to David.

She wondered why she felt so depressed as she watched the packet sail out of Sesuit Creek. She shivered as though winter were already setting in. Then she squared her shoulders and waved to him.

He would be back and by that time, perhaps, she would know her own mind more fully. She looked across the creek at the shipyard. David was right. It was a cold comfort. Much as she loved it, there had to be more to her life than just that.

Chapter Fifteen

1840-1841

As THE YEAR PROGRESSED into golden autumn, Aaron
Martin became more persistent and Julia grew more impatient with him. She became increasingly adept at avoiding solitary meetings.

If he came to the shipyard, she always found some errand
that would take her to the busiest, and often the dirtiest,
part of the yard. At home, she made sure that either Sarah
or Aunt Martha was there. If they weren't, she pretended
she wasn't home, hiding until he went away.

But one day in early winter, he caught her alone in the
house with only the maids for company. The night before
had been one of those endless, restless nights of dreams
and longing, and Julia had wakened from a brief sleep
feeling listless and washed out. Deciding she would be no
good at the yard, she'd spent the day quietly reading in
front of the parlor fire. When Aaron came, he found her
there with a book in her lap, staring into the blue and
orange flames.

"I'm glad I've found you alone at last," he said, taking
possession of the wing-back chair next to hers. "I stopped
by the shipyard, and your father said you weren't feeling
well today."

"I'm all right. Just tired." Julia wished he would go away and leave her alone.

"Well, you have a right to be!" Aaron crackled with indignation. "Your father works you too hard down at that shipyard. It's no place for a girl. It's too much! After we're married . . ."

"Aaron!" Julia broke in bluntly. *"We* are *not* going to be married." Might as well have it out in the open, she thought. She'd hate to lose him as a friend, but she was just too tired to hold him off any longer.

"Julia! You can't say that! You've hardly given me a chance."

"All the chances you're going to get, Aaron." Julia looked into the fire, stubbornly avoiding his eyes.

"I won't press you." He got up and went to drape himself with an elbow on the mantelpiece, standing between Julia and the fire. "I'll understand if you say you need more time, that you have to think it over."

Julia couldn't stand that sympathetic, paternal, almost patronizing air, the stupidity on his handsome face, his absolute refusal to believe her.

"No, Aaron!" Her eyes flashed blue fire at him. "The answer is no! It's no today. It'll be no tomorrow. The day after that and the year after that, the answer will still be *no!"*

"I just picked the wrong time." Aaron was not going to be shaken from his smug certainty. His smile was full of understanding patience. "I spoke too soon. I'll wait."

Julia pushed the escaping black tendrils of hair away from her face. "There's nothing to wait for." She turned her voice to steel.

"I think there is. You'll marry again someday, and I'd just as soon it be me."

"No!" Julia got up impatiently and, swishing her black skirts in her long stride, walked to the far end of the room. Leaning against the windowsill, she turned to face him. "No! No! No! No!"

"I love you, Julia." As he walked across the room toward her, the sunlight coming between the velvet curtains touched his hair and turned it to copper. His face was earnest but not pleading. "I always have loved you . . . as far back as I can remember. And you could do a lot worse. I've got a lot of money. I can give you anything you want. We like the same things. We have a lot in common."

"Not nearly enough."

"Then what *do* you want, Julia? The moon?"

"No." She looked across the room at the fire. "The sea and a man I *really* love beside me."

"Once we're married, you'll learn to love me. Women do."

"Oh!" Julia flung back her head and stared at the ceiling. Then she glared at him. "We have absolutely nothing in common. I was interested in what you had to say about Harvard, but I'm getting awfully tired of your hackneyed words and your stupid mind. *If* I ever marry again . . . and I doubt it . . . it'll be to a man of the sea. A man who understands why I love to build the ships that sail on it."

"My salt comes from the sea!" Aaron was finally beginning to get mad, but he was still stubborn. "And it brings in a lot more money than the fish some men catch."

"You couldn't catch anything if you tried."

"You're hard, Julia. Really hard." He looked at her as though he were seeing her for the first time, examining her as though he were looking at a glass-encased specimen under a microscope. "What makes you so hard, Julia?"

"Can't you guess?" She laughed bitterly. "I'm pickled, Aaron. Pickled in brine, in the salt that you steal from the sea."

"If only you weren't," he said sadly. "You have everything. Everything except the most important thing of all."

"I never noticed anything was missing." She set her chin and looked at him coldly.

"You have no heart."

"*What* a pity."

He was halfway across the room when he turned. "No heart. No feelings. You should be more like your sisters. *They* feel."

"Well, if *that's* what you want, why don't you go court one of them and leave me alone? *I* didn't ask you to come buzzing around me," she taunted him.

His face was stiff with anger as he went to the door.

When he reached it, he turned to look at her one last time.

"I might just do that, Julia. I might just do that."

A few days later, Aaron Martin rode down to the wharf on Quivet Neck. The early afternoon was sparkling bright and clear after a morning snow. From the icy, wooden wharf, Aaron could look across Sesuit Creek to the shipyard and see Julia without having to speak to her. He reined in his horse, a dark sorrel to match his hair, and sat patiently in the sunshine, watching for her.

It wasn't long before he spotted her tall figure striding down the hill from the blacksmith's shop to the office. He smiled and wheeled his horse around. With Julia hard at work at the shipyard and likely to be there for hours, it was safe to go to the big white house with the long porches, tie up his horse under the bare-limbed chestnut trees, and find a welcome inside from Sarah.

As he rode his horse down the winter-hardened, ice-puddled sand of School Street, Aaron thought of Sarah. At eighteen, Sarah was fulfilling her early promise of beauty. She had a quiet, restrained elegance which he enjoyed. Where Julia was flamboyant, even in black, her sister was graceful and lilting with laughter. Where Julia argued with him and enjoyed the winning, Sarah looked up at him with admiration and took his every word as gospel truth. Maybe he'd picked the wrong sister. Right from the beginning.

At first, he'd been amused. Later he'd been touched by the signals Sarah had flown behind her sister's back when he was courting Julia. He hadn't really taken her seriously. She was so much younger than he was. She'd always seemed like a child to him. But she was certainly no child now.

When he reached the highway, Aaron urged his horse to a trot. He hoped none of Sarah's other beaux were hanging around this afternoon.

That would teach Julia! He laughed in the crisp winter air. That would really teach Julia.

As the long, dark winter days dragged on, Julia found that she did miss Aaron's company. Not that she didn't see him. He was always around the house in his ardent pursuit of Sarah. And Julia had to admit it did rankle. Especially when Sarah dropped all her other beaux in his favor and sparkled at the very mention of Aaron's name. They seemed to have an understanding, but no one knew exactly what it was.

Julia tried to stay away from them because she noticed that, whenever they became aware of her presence, the tone of their conversation became more feverish, their laughter higher pitched and somehow false. It was almost as though they were mocking her.

Not that she cared, she told herself, but it made her uncomfortable. Whenever they met, Aaron was stiff and remote. He spoke to her only when courtesy absolutely demanded it. His eyes were as hard as warm brown eyes can ever be.

Sarah had taken to looking at Julia sideways with her dove-grey eyes slitted in mocking triumph, a complacent smile on her lips. All pretense of friendship had disappeared.

In her loneliness, Julia turned toward others her age, but most of the girls were married and occupied with thoughts of their husbands and babies. Those that weren't bored her. Even Aaron, with his secondhand thoughts, had been more stimulating company. Julia realized that she had never really had many friends.

Once in a while a young man, rising through the ranks, came home from sea, and she enjoyed talking to him of his travels. They would discuss the books he'd read on his long voyages and the polyglot peoples he'd met. But like the ebb and flow of the tide, they came and they went, leaving her standing on the shore.

She found her thoughts turning more and more to David Baxter and the spring. At night when she went to bed, she would think of him rather than of Jason, and she no longer felt guilty about her feelings. Jason was dead. She accepted it. Their love would never die, but it was a part of the past.

She could hear David's low, gentle voice saying, "You're still young and beautiful. There are a lot of years ahead," and she would curl up in the warmth of her quilts and smile. There was a warmth inside, too. It was comforting to think that, somewhere, alive in this world, there was a man who loved her; who, perhaps at this very moment, was thinking of her.

Rather than trying to forget the vision of his body as she had seen it on the beach, she would purposefully remember it, and she would wonder how it would feel to be loved by him. With mental fingers, she would trace the path of the muscles on that powerful back, brush lightly through the thick curls on his chest. Then she would drift off to sleep, pretending that his arms were holding her, that her head lay nestled in the hollow of his broad shoulder. If her dreams assigned him a more vigorous role, they no longer embarrassed her.

Sometimes in the morning, she would awake and smile. How amazed David would be if he knew the nature of her dreams!

As winter set in and the days grew longer, a nervous excitement mounted in the house. Amelia and Sarah seemed constantly to be running up and down stairs, in and out of doors in a steady round of evening parties, sleigh rides, skating parties on the lake. Their rooms were mounded with laces and curling papers, and a rainbow of ribbons was strewn all around.

It crystallized in the first week of March. First Michael approached Benjamin and asked him for Amelia's hand. Then Aaron, not to be outdone, followed the very next day and asked for Sarah's. Benjamin gave his consent immediately to each of the young men. He seemed to be relieved that it was settled.

The next night at supper, with only the family and Aunt Martha present, Lydia looked around the table and thought how sad it would be to lose her daughters. Just when they were growing up and she was really beginning to enjoy them. Then a brighter thought occurred to her.

"Wouldn't a double wedding be lovely," she said.

"No," Amelia said.

"No," Sarah said.

"But you'd set each other off so nice. And since you're both going to be married soon, it seems an awful waste of time and money to have two weddings." She sighed and leaned back in her chair. "I'm sure I don't know how I'm going to handle two in one year."

"I am going to have my own wedding," Sarah said. "And I'm sure that, if you and Papa don't want to go to the effort of giving me a proper one, Aaron's parents will."

"Now, I didn't mean that at all, Sarah," Lydia said.

"I think you did."

"I know you didn't mean it that way, Mama," Amelia said, "but I really do want my wedding to be my very own. Nothing elaborate or expensive. With Michael's mother so sick, anything else would be in bad taste. Michael and I just want a very simple, quiet wedding."

"Well, I don't," Sarah said. "I want the grandest wedding anyone ever saw. Years from now, when I'm an old lady, I want people to still be talking about Sarah Howard's wedding."

"Now hold on," Benjamin said. "I'm not sure I can afford that."

"You didn't have to pay for Julia's. Surely you have enough saved up for mine."

"Julia may be getting married again," Benjamin said.

"I doubt it," Sarah said.

"Nonsense!" Lydia exploded.

"Anyway, we're talking about Sarah and me," Amelia said. "It would be nice to get that settled. I want to be married right away. Next month."

"Don't you think that's rushing things a little, dear?" Lydia said. "It doesn't give us much time."

"We don't really need much time. Michael's mother isn't getting any better. She says she's going to die soon and she wants to see Michael and me settled before she does."

"What a morbid way of looking at it," Sarah said.

"I don't think so. It just means we don't have much time. And Michael says that, after she dies, he's going back to sea. He's always telling me there's no money in the packets."

"There isn't," Benjamin said. "Not for a mate."

"Well, he wants to go back to sea to make our fortune. I don't know how long I'll have him ashore. You understand, don't you, Julia?"

"Yes." Julia knew that Amelia was remembering how short were her own days of happiness. She thought Amelia right to claim as much as she could for her own. "I understand."

"Well, I'm not going to rush into things. I need at least five or six months to get ready for it," Sarah said. "I'm older, so I should get married first, but at least I'll get a little practice for my wedding in yours. You do want me to be your maid of honor, don't you?"

Amelia looked down at her plate, then across the table at Julia. "I'd thought of asking Julie to be my attendant," she said quietly.

"Why that's ridiculous!" Sarah said. "She's a widow."

Amelia turned to look at Sarah. Her light blue eyes were very cool. "I don't see as how that makes any difference. When Julie was married, she didn't have a nice family wedding. I want her to be part of mine."

"For once, Sarah's right, Amelia," Julia said. "It wouldn't be fitting for me."

"Fitting or not, I want you. Please, Julie?"

Julia knew, from Amelia's expression, that there was some other reason she wasn't mentioning. Whatever it was, it was important to Amelia. Julia smiled at her youngest sister.

"All right, 'Melia. If Mama and Papa agree."

Lydia frowned. "That takes some thinking on. Anyway, it's not the most important thing. The important thing to figure out is how we're going to get you married in a month."

As Julia watched her sisters and listened to them making their plans, she wondered if she would ever marry again, and she thought about David Baxter. But did she really know David well enough to even consider it if he did ask her? If? No, she was sure that, with a little encouragement, he would propose. After all, hadn't he been leading up to that last September?

Still, she had never known him for very long at one time. Six years older than she, he had been going to sea as long as she could remember. There had never been more than a few days or weeks between voyages. She would have to see more of him before she even let him guess where her thoughts were leading.

But how? He was always at sea.

She smiled when she thought of the obvious answer. She would do as he had suggested. Come spring, she would sail with him on the *Jewel of the Seas*. Even if she found David wouldn't do as a husband, she would, at least, finally go to sea.

The next morning as they were riding over the ice-puddled sand road to the shipyard, she approached Benjamin on the subject.

"Papa, I'd like to go away for a while."

"Go away!" He turned in his saddle to look at her. "Where would you go?"

"To England."

"Why would you want to go there?"

"Well, it's not just wanting to go to England. I'd like to sail on the *Jewel*. You know, we always planned to build her so *we* could go to sea, and neither of us ever has."

"Can't say I blame you for wanting to get out of the house with all the fuss and feathers about weddings goin' on there, but the *Jewel* won't be back for a month or so."

"I know." She pulled her cloak tighter around her body as they rounded a curve and felt the full blast of the north wind. "I wouldn't want to miss Amelia's wedding, anyway. But after that . . ."

"A trip down to Boston do just as well? I'll find it hard to spare you in the yard."

"Papa, it's something I need to do."

"Need?" He looked at her speculatively from under his bushy brows. "You think you'll find it easy on the *Jewel*? If you want to go to sea, why not sail on another vessel? I can arrange it."

"No. It has to be my ship."

"You sure you can face it?"

"That's one of the things I have to find out." Despite the wind whipping at her face, her head was held high.

"One of the things? There are others?"

"A few." She smiled at him.

"Young Baxter seemed right attentive to you last time he was home."

"I remember."

"Hmmm." They rode on in silence for a few minutes while Benjamin thought it over. "Goin' to have to have someone with you. Can't go alone. Too many idle tongues just waiting for a juicy bit of gossip to make them wag."

"That I know too well. I'd thought about Aunt Martha."

"Got it all thought out, haven't you? But it's goin' to be hard to spare her with all the weddings goin' on."

"Amelia'll be married by then, and I think Sarah can manage her own. She likes to run things, anyway."

"Run them, but not do them. Well, I can't see any other way. If you want to go to England, you'll go to England. The others will just have to take second place. We'll see how Aunt Martha feels about it. I can't order her to go."

"I know, Papa. I hope you don't think I'm being selfish."

They reined in, as they always did when they reached the crest of the last hill, to look over their domains, the shipyard and the Bay beyond the dunes.

"No. I don't think you're bein' selfish. It's the first time you've asked for anything for yourself in years. Probably do Aunt Martha some good, too. A little sea air. That's what you both need."

"Papa!" Julia turned to him, her eyes sparkling sapphire in the morning sunlight. "Why don't you come instead of Aunt Martha? I think a little sea air might be just what *you* need."

"Nope. Time for that's past." He urged his horse on to a walk, but not before Julia had seen the edge of sadness in his eyes. It showed in the sudden gruffness of his voice, too. "You talk to Aunt Martha about it, but don't let on about your plans to anyone else for the time being. You might change your mind, and your mother's got all she can handle just now."

Amelia's wedding day, as she had wished, was in the early spring when the first haze of green appeared to gild the world. It was still cool, but you could feel the warmth like a promise from the sun. As Julia, Lydia, and Aunt Martha helped Amelia dress, Julia thought how perfectly the day matched Amelia with her fair blond hair, her sparkling cornflower eyes, and her cheeks that were glowing above her dimples.

Aaron had already called for and taken Sarah to the church and Benjamin was pacing the hall below before Amelia was finally ready. At last, satisfied, the three women stood back to admire her.

"You really are a beautiful bride, Amelia. Michael will be so proud of you," Julia said.

"I hope so," Amelia laughed. "Though I really don't think he notices *how* I look most of the time." She whirled in front of the pier glass, watching her white reflection. "And you look beautiful, too, Julie. That's another good thing about my wedding. I got you out of black."

Julia smiled and glanced down at her own silver-grey silk dress with its discreet trimming of blue ribbons.

"I guess it was about time," she admitted.

"Amelia!" Benjamin called up from the hall. "You're goin' to be late for your own wedding."

"Hold your horses, Benjamin," Lydia called back. "We'll be down directly."

When Sarah arrived at the church, sweeping through the tall double doors in her new red velvet dress, she managed to turn a lot of heads. She had designed the dress carefully, deciding that, if she had to be the last daughter to marry and if she couldn't be Amelia's maid of honor, then she was going to be the most beautiful of the Howard girls at this wedding as well as her own.

As she went down the aisle on Aaron's arm to the front pew, she decided she was just as glad she wasn't involved in the wedding party. If she had been, she couldn't have had Aaron beside her. Aaron was one of the richest and certainly one of the most strikingly handsome men on Cape Cod, and he was hers. Or soon would be. It was pleasant to walk down the aisle with him, knowing that everyone was whispering about what a handsome couple they made. She gave Aaron her most charming dove-eyed smile when he handed her into the pew.

But when Amelia came down the aisle on her father's arm, no one could match her fair-haired radiance. Julia, preceding them, could see how Michael's square face lit up and how he smiled as he looked over her shoulder at his bride. She knew that, for him, there was no one in the church but himself and Amelia.

As she stood beside them at the altar, Julia could feel the fringes of the golden glow that surrounded them, it was so real. She wondered if this was how she and Jason had looked in that quiet, empty chapel in Boston.

It all seems so long ago, she thought, as though it's already become a part of history. Four and a half years. Six weeks of love, two years of marriage, two and a half years of mourning. I hope Amelia has more. Much more. I hope his mother lives for a long time yet and keeps him on the packet.

Sarah, standing next to Aaron in the front pew, listened carefully to the marriage vows. In a few months' time, she would be saying them herself. She glanced up at Aaron with a smile, but he was staring straight ahead at the altar.

He was staring at Julia! The yearning she saw in his face made her shiver. It was so open! To distract him, she tucked her hand under his elbow, and he looked down at her and smiled. But the smile was almost an apology.

Sarah managed to smile guilelessly back, but when he turned his attention back to the altar, this time to the right spot, she set her chin.

I'll get her, she thought. I'll get Julia if it's the last thing I ever do. I wonder if there's some way I can manage to keep her away from the church when I get married?

To comfort herself, she thought of the large beautiful house Papa was having built for her on the land Aaron's parents had given them. It was high on a hill on Quivet Neck overlooking the marsh and the creek and the salt-works, the fields and the rolling hills. The Martins had been generous in the amount of land they'd given the young couple. Sarah suspected it was because they wanted to keep their only son close to home and the saltworks. Still, all Julia got for her dowry was a few shares in some old ship she never saw, and Amelia was getting practically nothing.

Amelia might be pretty, but she wasn't very smart. Marrying a penniless young seaman. Going to live in a small cottage with a dying woman. Telling Papa she could wait for her dowry until after he had taken care of Sarah's. That was pretty dumb.

It was only right that Papa should consider her, Sarah

first, since she was older than Amelia. But if their positions had been reversed, she would have fought for her share. Amelia just didn't have much gumption.

No. All in all, Sarah wasn't dissatisfied. Once she and Aaron were married, she'd see to it that he never went near Julia again.

Not long after Amelia's wedding, the *Jewel of the Seas* was expected home, and Julia began to consider what clothes she would need for the voyage. She and Aunt Martha had quiet conferences about it, but they kept their silence in front of the others.

Then word came that the *Jewel* was in Boston. David Baxter was on his way home. Julia thought about meeting the packet, but immediately discarded the idea. It would be best for him to come to her.

When Julia saw him riding down the road to the shipyard that afternoon, she left the schooner she was inspecting and ducked into the office, where there would be more privacy. If her face gave her away, she didn't want the men to see it. She sat down on the tall stool behind her desk and waited, remembering how he had found her here the last time he had come home, how tense she had been. But that had been last fall and this was spring. And last time, Jason had stood between them. Now he was gone.

The door opened and he was there, looking huge in his bulky clothing. Once again, the sun glimmered in his dark blond curls, and he held his cap in both hands, turning it as he looked at her. Julia left her perch and went to meet him.

"David," she said, holding out her hands, "how glad I am to see you."

"No more than I to see you," he said. Now that she was close she could see that his grey-green eyes were troubled, his wide lips were serious, and there were lines in his low, broad forehead.

"I've thought a lot about you while you were gone," she said, trying with the warmth of her smile to clear his eyes, to make the corners of his mouth peak up. "I've thought about our last conversation."

He looked at her for a moment, saw the smile, the blazing magic sapphire smile that he hadn't seen for years, and it was almost more than he could bear.

"Julia, before you go any farther . . ."

"David," she said, cutting him off, "you were right. You always have been right and . . ."

"Julia, I'm married."

How long they stood frozen, staring at one another neither one could later tell. Finally, Julia was able to find her voice.

"How . . . how wonderful, David. Congratulations."

His eyes were an anguished murky green as he looked at her suddenly pale face.

"Thank you," he said quietly.

"Who is she?"

"You don't know her. She's a girl I met in England."

"Oh? What's her name?"

"Cynthia. Cynthia Fielding."

"Cynthia," Julia repeated as though it were an alien word she had never heard before. "Why didn't you write and tell us?"

"I couldn't do it in a letter. I . . . I had to tell you in person. To explain to you."

"You don't have to explain, David." She wanted him to go away, to leave her with this pain so that she could examine it.

"She's going to have a child, Julia."

"How nice." It was hurting more and more. Oh, David, go away. "Is she at your parents' house?"

"No. She didn't want to leave England and her family. She says she'll be able to see me as much there as here."

"Is . . . is she pretty?" How could they stand here, talking so politely?

"Not as pretty as you."

Oh, no, David, no.

"Is she a nice girl? A sweet girl?"

"Yes. Her father's a shipmaster. Are you all right, Julia?"

The pounding of a storm-driven surf, that had been rising in a whirling crescendo in her head, now grew louder and louder. It drowned out his words. If only he would go.

When she regained consciousness, she was lying on the

floor, and David was covering her, putting her cloak on top of his own.

"Julia?" he said when he saw her black eyelashes flutter.

"What?"

"You fainted."

"Don't be silly." She tried to sit up. "I never faint."

He held her then in his arms and they were as warm and strong as she had imagined they would be. Laying her head against his chest, she could hear his heart pounding. If only she could pretend she had never heard those awful words.

"Can I get you some water?" he asked and his lips brushed across her forehead.

"No. Not yet." She wanted the security of his arms around her, to erase the name of Cynthia from the world.

"Julia." Her name was almost a moan on his lips and his arms tightened around her. "I didn't think you could ever care for me. I wouldn't have . . ."

"Don't say it, David. Never say it."

"No."

He held her quietly for what each of them wanted to be forever until they heard footsteps outside.

"Can you get up?" he whispered.

"I think so." Her knees felt weak, but with his help, she managed to stand.

Benjamin came into the office, glanced at the two cloaks on the floor, noted the anguish on David's face, saw Julia leaning weakly against a chair.

"Sit down, Julie," he said kindly and watched her as she did.

"You've told her?" he asked David and then wondered why he'd bothered to ask. The answer was obvious.

"Yes, sir."

"Then you'd better leave. I'll talk to you tomorrow about the ship's business. Be here at ten."

"Yes, sir."

"Papa, David is still master of the *Jewel*." It was not a question. It was a statement.

"Yes." Benjamin's blue eyes were serious but kind. "Of course, he is."

"Thank you, sir." David picked their cloaks up from the floor and laid Julia's on the desk, his fingers stroking it before he turned. Then for a moment, he looked at Julia as though memorizing her face. "Goodbye, Julia. I'm sorry."

"It's all right, David. I hope I'll see you again before you leave."

"Yes . . . I hope so." He stared deep into her eyes for another moment. Then he turned abruptly and walked out the door.

Benjamin took the chair across from her and sat down with his elbows resting on his knees. He, too, took a moment to study her face.

"What happened?"

"I fainted, Papa."

"Didn't know you cared that much about him."

"Neither did I. I probably don't. Just the shock . . ."

"I kind of hoped it would be him," Benjamin said.

"Did you?"

"Yes. He's a good man. Always worried about you when you were sick, wanted to see you every time he came home."

"But now he's married."

"Aye," Benjamin said heavily. "Those things happen."

"Did you know about it when I was making all those plans to sail on the *Jewel?*"

"No. He told me just before he came in here. No time to tell anyone sooner. After all, he was married only a couple of days before he sailed from England."

"But she's expecting a baby."

"Is she? That explains a few things, don't it?"

"Yes," she agreed. "I guess it does." It didn't help, though.

Then an awful thought struck her. "You didn't tell him I was planning on sailing with him, did you?"

"Nope. No need for anyone to know that except you, me, and Aunt Martha."

"Well, I'm thankful for that."

"Want to take a voyage on some other ship? Get away for a while?"

"I don't think so. Not now. Maybe later." She pushed her hair back from her face with both hands. "I don't want to see him again, Papa. Not for a long, long time."

"No reason why you should. You stay at the house tomorrow, and I'll see that he's gone the next day."

"Thank you, Papa. I think I want to go home now."

There was no letdown after Amelia's wedding, for Sarah kept the house in a turmoil, and Julia was grateful for the confusion her sister created. When Sarah wasn't going down to Boston to shop for her trousseau, her linens, and her furniture, she had materials laid all over the house and two seamstresses working on them.

Aaron, for his part, seemed to enjoy it all as much as Sarah did. He was in no great hurry to get married now that it was settled. Besides, it took time to do things right, and the best was none too good for himself and his future wife.

Also it fit in with his plans. He wanted Stephen Logan, his best friend from Harvard, for his best man, and Stephen was still at sea. He was sailing as supercargo on one of the Logan ships and was due to arrive home sometime this summer. Aaron didn't admit it even to himself, but he was looking forward to Stephen's visit almost more than to his own marriage.

In late June, when summer had really set in, earlier than Aaron had expected, Stephen Logan arrived. When Aaron got Stephen's letter, he was wild with delight. He had always looked up to Stephen. Now, at long last, he would be able to show his friend all the things that *he*, Aaron, had.

It was hard for Aaron to decide where to start. What would he show Stephen first? His father's vast saltworks with their windmills and modern vats? The new house his future father-in-law was building for him? Or Sarah?

Steve was sure to be impressed with Sarah. Once he heard her lilting laughter, once he saw her dainty head held high under its coronet of golden brown braids, once he saw those lovely black-fringed grey eyes, Steve was sure to be jealous of him.

The thought of it made Aaron smile. Steve jealous of Aaron. In the old days, Aaron had envied Stephen his easy manner, his sureness, his quick mind, but now the tables would be turned. When he saw Sarah, Steve would understand why she was the perfect choice to grace his big new house and his very elegant life.

305

On the day Stephen was to arrive, Aaron was ready long before the packet was sighted. His father's carriage was polished and the hardware had never shone so bright. When word finally came, as it always did by signals flown from the higher hills, that the packet would soon be entering Sesuit Creek, it didn't take long for Aaron to cover the short distance between his parents' house and the town landing. He was one of the first to arrive.

Even before the schooner, followed by a flock of gulls, swung into the wharf, it was easy to spot Stephen. He had an electric quality that made him stand out from all the others as he lounged at the rail in a sailor's easy stance, his blue cap pushed back on his sun-bleached hair. When the schooner luffed up to the dock, Aaron could see white wrinkles at the corners of his grey eyes. Steve looked older, a lot older than he had when Aaron had last seen him. And yet, as always, the slow, lazy grin that lighted his face made him seem impossibly young.

As soon as the lines were made fast, Stephen leaped ashore and clapped Aaron on the back.

"Well, you old cod, I see you've done yourself proud." He looked pointedly at Aaron's freshly pressed light tan suit, his highly polished boots, and his neatly barbered auburn hair.

"Steve, Steve! I can't believe you're really here," Aaron said, thumping his friend on the back in return. "I've got so much to show you, I don't know where to start. The saltworks? My new house? Let me take you over to meet my fiancée." Aaron's amber-brown eyes shone with innocent joy.

"Before we do anything else, I'd like to get washed up." Stephen's grey eyes touched with blue smiled lazily back at his old friend. "There was quite a crowd on board and light winds all the way."

"We'll go up to the house as soon as your trunks are unloaded."

"I've only brought one along." There was a touch of pride in Stephen's voice as he nodded at a chest being unloaded from the schooner. "My sea chest. It's over there."

"I'll have it put in the carriage." Aaron, with an air of great self-importance, detached a couple of men from the lounging crowd and had them cart the chest over to the carriage.

"After you've washed up, where would you like to go?" Aaron asked as he flipped the reins to get the horses started.

"I want to explore the Cape," Stephen said, stretching and taking a deep breath. "I've never been up here before, you know. Sighted it often enough from out there." He waved his hand at the Bay. "Outward bound and homeward bound, but I've never set foot on this pile of sand. I want to see if all those tall tales you used to tell me are true."

"They're true enough." Aaron grinned at his friend.

"And I've brought a few books along. Picked them up in England. I wanted to discuss them with you." Stephen had always found Aaron useful as a sounding board for his own ideas. When he struggled to make Aaron understand them, they grew and took shape in his own mind.

"We'll have plenty of time for that, but I want to show you around first."

After Stephen had washed up at the Martins' low, rambling grey house, he was ready.

"Let's walk," he said when Aaron started toward the carriage. "I want to stretch my legs."

"All right. The new house is just down the road," Aaron agreed.

"I don't want to see your new house yet. I want to walk and have a long talk with you."

"All right." Aaron frowned when he thought of his expensive new boots, but then he forgot them, he was so happy to have Stephen here at last.

"Do you know any shipowners around here?" Stephen asked as they started down the sandy road.

"Yes, of course. The woods are full of them," Aaron answered absently. He was watching one of the windmills that wasn't operating properly.

"I want an introduction to some of them."

The cold determination in his friend's voice made Aaron forget the windmill. Stephen was staring straight ahead, ignoring the countryside he had said he wanted to see.

"Good Lord! Why? Haven't you had enough of the sea?"

"I've had enough of being a supercargo. I want my own ship."

"But doesn't your uncle own several ships?"

"Yes. Plenty. And he's promised to give me a command . . . someday."

"Then I don't see where you've got any problem." Aaron idly flicked his riding crop at some tall-flowering Queen Anne's lace that grew beside a stone wall.

"I want that ship now." A note of bitterness had joined the cold determination. "I'm already better than most of his captains, but he keeps putting me off. Says they're good men and he won't relieve them of their command."

"Why don't you do something else then? Something on land?"

"It's all I'm trained for."

Aaron looked at Stephen incredulously.

"After your brilliant record at Harvard?"

"No money there. The only way I'm going to make my fortune is at sea. As master of a ship. It's what I do best."

"Fortune? But your family has plenty of money."

"My *uncle* has plenty of money. I don't have any. My uncle also has three sons and two daughters."

"I didn't know that."

"No reason why you should." Stephen pushed his cap still farther back on his tawny hair. "I was pretty well off when you knew me. My uncle did his best for me then. Brought me up as though I were his own son. Sent me to Harvard. Provided me with spending money while I was there. As soon as I was through with college, he put me on his ships as a supercargo."

"That sounds fair enough." Aaron was still trying to get used to the idea that Stephen wasn't rich.

"Fair?" Stephen looked across the blue streams that ran through the green marsh grass. "I suppose it was. I'm not sure he did me any favor, though. Maybe I should have sailed before the mast. Might have been easier to get a command if I'd tried coming through the hawse hole instead of through the cabin window."

"Hawse hole?"

"Sailing as a common seaman. Coming up through the ranks."

308

"That's not right!" Aaron was indignant for any slight that might have been done his friend. "*You're* a gentleman. With your education and brains, *you* should be given command before any of those clods."

"Maybe. Maybe not." Stephen, walking with his hands in his pockets, shrugged. "All I know is that I'm not going back to sea until I go as master of the ship I sail on. That's why I want some introductions."

Aaron's brow puckered in puzzlement as he tried to think of some owners likely to need a captain.

"I . . . I think it's usually the practice to give local ships to men from East Dennis. Or at least from Dennis, Yarmouth, or Brewster."

"Then I'll become a local man. I'll live with you. I'll be your brother," Stephen said, slapping Aaron on the back. "How would you like that, little brother?"

"I'd like it fine, but it won't wash. You've got to be born here."

"I knew you were provincial, but I didn't know you were so clannish."

Aaron shrugged and turned away. Stephen's words stung. Provincial! Clannish!

"Well, maybe there's a chance," he said finally. "My fiancée's father builds ships. I think he even owns a couple. I'm not sure."

"Well, ask her! Come on. What are we waiting for?"

"Go slow, Steve," Aaron warned him. "It doesn't pay to push things up here. Do what everyone else does. Sit around and yarn, tell sea stories with the greybeards, and sooner or later you might get an offer."

"It better be sooner or I'm off to better fishing grounds." The icy determination was back in Stephen's voice.

"Not before my wedding!"

"Need me to prop you up, do you?" Stephen laughed. "No, not before your wedding, little brother. But if nothing's turned up by then, I'll be gone on the very next packet. What's the date?"

"August twentieth."

"Two months." Stephen stretched his arms over his head. "Well, I need a holiday, anyway. Come on. Let's find that fiancée of yours and get to work. What did you say her name was?"

"Sarah. Sarah Howard."

"Oh, yes. Sarah of the deep blue eyes."

"No, that was Julia." Aaron's face flushed when he mentioned Julia's name, and Stephen noticed it with great interest. "Sarah's eyes are grey."

"That's right. You tacked right in the middle of courting one sister and went for the other. What happened?"

"Sarah's a lady. She'll make a better wife. You'll understand when you see her. Julia's wild. The next man that marries her is going to live in hell."

"And you've had a sample of it." Stephen laughed, enjoying his friend's embarrassment. "What do you mean by 'the next man'?"

"She's a widow."

"Not yet twenty-one and already a widow? She kills them off early."

"It's not unusual here on the Cape. A lot of men die young. It's the sea."

" 'The sea! the sea! the open sea! The blue, the fresh, the ever free!' " Stephen chanted.

"Who said that?" Aaron asked.

"Some damn fool who'd never set foot on a ship, obviously."

"You've changed, Steve."

"As you said, it's the sea. Come. Let's meet sweet Sarah, soon to be my adopted sister."

But when Sarah and Stephen met, there was nothing sisterly about her. Their grey eyes, hers soft and melting, his the color of steel touched by blue, locked and there was instant antipathy.

"So you're Aaron's famous friend," Sarah said. She smiled sweetly for Aaron's sake, but she was looking pointedly at Stephen's roughly cut sun-bleached hair and his travel-creased clothes.

"And you're his unknown lady." Stephen mockingly swept off his cap and bowed.

"It's nice to have you. I hope you'll be able to stay for our wedding." She was hoping he would leave the next day.

"Oh, I shall, I shall. I most certainly shall." He clapped Aaron on the back. "I'm fond of this old fellow, and I want to make certain he gets nothing but the best."

310

"Have you seen our new house?" Sarah asked, smoothing the golden-brown coronet of braids on top of her head. "When it's finished, it should measure up even to your standards."

"Only in passing, but I gather I will in good time." He turned to Aaron. "Now that I've met sister Sarah, Aaron, where is sister Julia?"

"Julia? What does Julia have to do with this?" Sarah demanded. Her eyes narrowed with suspicion.

"She's probably over at the shipyard," Aaron said. "That's where you'll usually find her, clambering all over the ships, smelling like tar and paint. Not like my sweet girl here." Trying to appease her, Aaron hugged Sarah to him. She fluttered her black lashes and smiled sideways at him.

Stephen lifted an eyebrow and smiled. "She sounds more interesting all the time. Come on. Let's all go find wild, wicked sister Julia."

"Go find her yourself," Sarah said. "I'm not going near that yard. And neither is Aaron."

"Aaron? Shall we go?"

"What's come over you, Steve? I've never seen you act like this before."

"Must be something in the air. Coming?"

"No," Aaron said. "Neither Julia nor her father would welcome us breaking in like that when they're working. We'll take you over to see the new house."

"How do you get to the shipyard, Aaron?" Stephen clapped his cap on his head and squared it precisely over his sun-creased eyes. "If you won't come, I'll go by myself."

"Oh, tell him, Aaron. Julia can take care of herself, and there's something I want to talk to you about."

"All right," Aaron said reluctantly. With Sarah still clinging determinedly to his arm, he led Stephen out to the road to point the way.

"I'll give Julia your best," Stephen laughed mockingly over his shoulder as he started down the sandy road. It amused him to see Aaron and Sarah standing like two well-groomed statues under the chestnut tree.

"Aaron!" Sarah said as soon as he was out of sight. "That can't be the same man you've talked so much about.

311

You *can't* let him be your best man. He'll probably spoil the whole wedding."

"I don't know." Aaron shook his head and continued to watch the empty road. "I wouldn't have believed it if I hadn't seen it. Steve was never like this. Something's changed him." He looked down at Sarah. "Sarah, I apologize for bringing him here."

"It's all right. If he's going to be here for two months, we'd have had to meet sooner or later." Then her face brightened and she began to laugh. "I'd just love to see Julia's expression when *he* rolls into the shipyard."

"She'll never forgive us for sending him there."

"Oh, come on, Aaron, you know it's funny, too."

Chapter Sixteen

1841

EVEN BEFORE STEPHEN COULD see the shipyard, he knew where it was. Around the bend, past the pines. The unmistakable odor of pitch and oakum, linseed oil, and lumber mingled with the thick clammy smell of the creek at low tide. He could hear men's voices, the ring of the blacksmith's anvil, the swing of hammers, and the rasp of saws.

He smiled and quickened his step. Something was going to come out of this shipyard. Something was going to happen today. It had to.

The first step was to find Captain Howard. He might have an inane daughter, but he had a shipyard. Maybe a couple of ships. Definitely contacts.

As Stephen strolled into the busy yard, however, he forgot his errand. There on the nearest railway, a great new ship was being built. He was drawn to her like a magnet.

Greater deadrise than most, he thought. And an elongated midship section. They'd flattened her bottom, too, like some of the Dramatic packets he'd recently seen, but she had sharper lines. He whistled as he walked around her, staying far away from the scaffolding and the hardworking men, so that he might have the best view.

Six hundred and fifty tons, he estimated. About one hundred forty-three, forty-four feet long and over thirty-one foot of beam. He'd love to get his hands on her. He looked up at the hollow lines of her wedge-shaped bow. Lean, he thought. Lean and beautiful. She'd slice through the water like a knife.

"Do you like her?" A girl's voice came from behind him.

"I'll say! She's a beauty."

"We think so."

He turned to see a slender, black-haired girl in a coarse grey dress standing behind him, her blue eyes sparkling with amusement. She was almost as tall as he.

"Who designed her?"

"We did. My father and I."

"You mean your father."

"No. She's the first ship my father's let me have a hand in designing. She's for the Canton trade, though she'll go just about anywhere."

"So you're the wild, wicked, infamous Julia."

"Which one of my enemies have you been talking to?" She seemed amused.

"Friends, not enemies. Former friends and family."

"And who are you?"

"Stephen Logan at your service, ma'am." He swept off his cap and gave her a mocking bow.

"Then you've been talking to Aaron Martin . . . and probably my sister Sarah."

"Precisely."

"Where are they?"

"Who knows the way of young lovers? Ask me where the bee goes after it leaves the marigold; ask me where the geese go after summer is gone; ask me where the wind blows after it ruffles your hair."

She laughed. "So you've come alone."

"Yes. I was bored with their company, and they promised I'd find some excitement if I came down here and bothered you in the middle of your work."

"Fireworks, no doubt."

"They didn't specify."

She looked thoughtfully at the lean young man who stood before her. His tan face with white crinkles at the

314

corners of his eyes and his windburned cheeks indicated that he was a sailor. His light brown hair was bleached blond on top from long exposure to the sun. His pale grey eyes just tinged with blue were impudently returning her scrutiny. She decided that she liked him.

"And what else do you do when you're not bothering people in the middle of their work?" she asked.

"Oh, I take them for walks at dawn and recite poetry to them, some of it of my own manufacture. I sit in the parlor and sing romantic ballads to them. And when I get bored with all that, I go back to sea."

"And the sea never bores you?"

"No. It aggravates, irritates, and tantalizes me. It's cruel, wicked, wild, tempestuous, beautiful, languid, soothing, parching, burning, freezing, and evil, but it doesn't bore me. Of course I'd just as soon never see it again, but it doesn't bore me."

"So you're the one."

"The one what?"

"The one Aaron got all his secondhand opinions from."

"*Madame,* my opinions, bad as they sometimes are, are *never* secondhand."

"I don't mean they're secondhand with you, but Aaron has never had an original thought since the day he was born. He *has* to live on secondhand ideas. I've often wondered where he got some of them. Now I know. You *do* realize that some of them are pretty bad?"

"*Were.* The advantage of thinking firsthand thoughts is that you can always change them. Secondhand, you're stuck with them until someone changes them for you. That's why I've come. To give Aaron some brand-new ideas. Make a new man out of him. You might even change your mind and marry him after all. My new thoughts are most interesting. Worth a lifetime of exploration. Poor Sarah, though. What will we do with her?"

"Sarah can have him. What gives you the idea that I ever gave a thought to Aaron?"

"Letters. They go back and forth over land and sea. When he wrote that he'd jilted you, I believed him." The mocking amusement on Stephen's face was replaced by a serious intensity. "But that was before I met you. Now I know who did the jilting."

Julia raised her chin and looked at him coolly. Imperiously, he thought.

"It wasn't a case of jilting. I never let it get that far."

"Didn't you?"

"I can't see what business it is of yours, whether I did or not. Now, do you want to see this ship or don't you?"

"If you'll be my guide. Otherwise I'd rather stay here and look at you." His slow, lazy smile made him look younger than he had before.

"Well, I'm not going to stay here. I have work to do."

"I'm still waiting for you to do something wild and wicked, like taking the rest of the day off, stealing one of those boats, and coming for a sail with me."

"If you want to go sailing, you can borrow my dory. It's right down there." She pointed at the floating dock. "But I can't come. Believe it or not, some people have to work for a living."

"Do you really, pretty Julia?" Stephen cocked his brow and looked at her skeptically. "I doubt it."

"Well, I do, or that ship you were admiring so much won't be ready for launching on the spring tide."

"Then I'll help you. Together we'll build her, and when she's launched, instead of stealing a dory, we'll steal her. We'll turn pirate and go roving the seven seas, wherever the picking is good. We'll let others do the work, and we'll take their profit. I'll dress you in silks and satins and cover you with diamonds and sapphires. With a few rubies thrown in for good measure."

Julia laughed. "I thought I was supposed to be the one that was wild and wicked."

"You are, my lady. I can tell it by the way you wrinkle your nose when you laugh. That's why you'll make an ideal partner in piracy. I can see you now, pacing the quarterdeck, ordering our prisoners to walk the plank just to feed your pet sharks."

"All the while in silks and satins, diamonds and sapphires?"

"Of course. How else? These things must be done with verve, you know. That's where most pirates fail. They have no style."

"And what will you wear?"

"Oh." He looked at the creek, then the sky, then the ship, as though seriously considering the matter. "Silver-buckled shoes and satin coats. With ruffled lace flowing from the sleeves, of course. I'll let my hair grow long and encourage moustaches to blossom."

"You sound very dashing."

"I am. I am. Just let me prove it."

"Aren't you ever serious?"

"Only when absolutely necessary . . . which I am now. I want that ship."

"Well, you'll have to wait till she's finished."

"Listen, Julia, I'm serious. I'm deadly serious. Has a master been chosen for her yet?"

"I'm not sure. You really mean it, don't you?"

"I was never more in earnest in my life," he said. His eyes had lost their twinkle and the blue lights had vanished. "Who owns her?"

"Captain Asa Crofton is having her built."

"A captain. Then he'll take command of her."

"I don't think so. He's been retired for a long time."

"Will you introduce me to him?"

"Yes. That's easy enough. He's always coming down to the yard to look her over. But do you have the credentials? You look rather young."

"I'm not. I'm twenty-eight years old and have yet to receive my first command. My uncle keeps me chasing around the world as his supercargo, but won't give me my own ship. As for credentials, I have letters of recommendation from my last two captains. If Captain Crofton would write to them, they'd verify that I'm extremely well qualified to be master of this ship or any other."

"With all the new ships being built, you shouldn't have any trouble finding one, then." Julia looked at him doubtfully. "I've heard that, if anything, there's a scarcity of men qualified to take command of them."

"It's my uncle who's standing in my way. Most owners feel that, if *he* won't give me a command, there must be something wrong with me."

"Is there?"

"No!" Stephen squared his cap impatiently. "He's just too cheap to build me a ship of my own. Even when he knows I'd make a good return on his investment."

"Hmmm." Julia looked him over once more, this time to see if he had the character so necessary for a deep-sea captain. He had a strong chin and a clear forehead. That was in his favor. He held himself well, and he was certainly blunt. "Let me see your letters."

"Are you thinking of hiring me?"

"I'll see what I can do for you, but first I want to see those letters."

"They're in my chest at the Martins' house."

"Then go get them."

"You don't shally around, do you, my lady?"

"No," she said levelly. "I don't."

"Then what were you doing encouraging Aaron?" His steady grey eyes challenged her.

"Listening to your opinions. Secondhand, of course."

"Of course."

"Don't you think you can trust me with your letters?"

"I think I could trust you with just about anything, my lady, including my life."

When he returned to the shipyard with his letters, Stephen found Julia deep in conversation with a tall, broad-shouldered man. His silver black hair and beetling eyebrows bespoke a man of vigor; his fresh complexion and clear blue eyes, a man of the sea. Captain Crofton, no doubt. Stephen squared his shoulders and prepared to make a good impression. So much could hinge on this meeting.

Julia glanced up at his approach and gave him a grave smile. "Did you find your letters?"

"Yes. I have them right here," he said, taking them from his coat pocket.

"Papa, this is Stephen Logan, Aaron's friend I was telling you about. Mr. Logan, my father, Captain Howard."

Benjamin offered his hand and gave Stephen a long appraising look before he spoke. "How do you do, Mr. Logan."

"At your service, sir." Stephen spoke deferentially as though he were addressing the captain of his ship.

"So you want a command?"

"Yes, sir."

"You certainly have a unique way of going about it."

"Actually when I came to the shipyard earlier, I was looking for you, sir. I felt you might be able to help me. Then I met Miss Howard, and she was kind enough to show me your new ship. She's a real beauty. I've already fallen in love with her." Stephen glanced up at the vessel that rose tall above them.

"The ship or my daughter, Mr. Logan?"

"Oh!" Stephen turned red. "The ship, of course, sir."

"You obviously haven't been properly introduced." Benjamin's eyes narrowed with sardonic amusement. "My daughter is *Mrs. Thacher*, Mr. Logan."

"Yes, sir." Stephen was acutely uncomfortable. What was the matter with him? He never made blunders like this. Julia was watching him curiously. Was Captain Howard deliberately trying to throw him off balance? A test? "I took the liberty of introducing myself. In his letters, Aaron's written so much about Mrs. Thacher, I felt we were already acquainted."

"Well, don't believe everything Aaron Martin tells you," Benjamin said dryly, glancing a quirk-mouthed look at Julia. "I believe the young man was prejudiced."

"No, sir," Stephen said uneasily. He didn't like the way this conversation was going. He glanced around the yard. "You turn out some beautiful vessels, Captain Howard."

"You expect us to be small just because we're not located in Boston or Salem or New York?"

"No, sir, but it's one of the largest shipyards I've ever seen."

"It's a far cry from the largest, but it'll do. Like to take a look around?" Benjamin said, relenting.

He didn't know why he was trying to embarrass this young man. He seemed likely enough. Benjamin wondered if it had something to do with the way Logan had looked at Julia. Nothing new in that. Plenty of men looked at her the same way. Well, it wasn't important.

"Yes, sir. I'd like that very much." Stephen started to put the letters back in his pocket, then thought better of it. "I've brought letters of recommendation from my last two captains, sir."

"Give them to Mrs. Thacher. She handles those details." Benjamin dismissed them with a wave of his hand. "Come along now."

319

"Yes, sir." Stephen handed them to Julia. "My lady," he said softly, "I give my life into your hands."

Then he reluctantly followed the captain's retreating back as the older man led the way up the creek to the smallest vessel on the ways. Stephen glanced back once to see Julia opening one of his letters. Captain Howard certainly had strange notions on what was important. Did he leave the hiring of *masters* for his ships in the hands of a young girl? More to the point, did he actually *have* any ships? There was still that important detail to be cleared up.

Well, whether he did or not, he was obviously a man of influence and one well worth cultivating. Stephen squared his shoulders and caught up with his guide.

"What do you think of these new steamships they're building in England?" Captain Howard asked him abruptly. "Seen any?"

"I saw the *Great Western* when she arrived in New York, sir, in the spring of thirty-eight."

"A record passage," Benjamin said and mused on that startling voyage. "Think they'll replace sail?"

"Never!" Stephen stoutly maintained. "They may be all right for a quick voyage across the Atlantic, but they'll be no good on the East India or Canton runs. The amount of wood alone required to stoke them makes it impractical."

"You make enough time, you can spare a little to put in for wood."

"Too dangerous. You never know when that wood's going to combust and turn the ship into a blazing inferno." Stephen shuddered inwardly as he thought of that most dreaded of all the perils the sea offered. Fire! "I'll stick with sail and so will everyone else who values his life."

"But speed's the thing." Benjamin scowled at the trig barkentine on the ways in front of them. "If you don't have a fast ship, you'll lose your market. You have to get there first."

"Aye, I know that, sir. Since I've been sailing as supercargo for several years, I know it only too well. But the sailing ships are getting faster all the time. Ever since the *Ann McKim.*"

"You take a good long look at our new ship?" Benjamin

stuck his hands in his pocket. Turning his back on the barkentine, he studied Stephen.

"Yes, sir."

"She'll beat the *McKim* hands down. I'm betting she'll beat the *Roscius* and the *Siddons,* too." He spoke of two ships that had set recent records.

"That's asking a lot," Stephen said, looking down the creek toward the new ship. "But I wouldn't bet against you, sir."

"Would you bet *with* me?"

Stephen glanced quickly at Captain Howard. Then he looked back at the ship. He saw that Julia was still standing beside it, reading his letters.

"Yes, sir. I would."

"Well, I'll see what I can do for you."

"I'd appreciate that, sir."

"Depends on what Mrs. Thacher decides."

Stephen looked at the captain in disbelief.

"You leave decisions like that to *her?*"

"Certainly." Benjamin looked ruffled. "She's got good insight. Good judgment. What's wrong with that?"

"Nothing," Stephen quickly backpedaled. This man said he would help him. "Nothing at all, sir. It's just rather unusual for a girl to be given that kind of responsibility."

"My daughter's a very unusual young woman . . . a very unusual *person,*" he corrected himself. "I've not met any men who can match her."

So the captain was warning him off. Why doesn't he just come right out and say: I might trust you with a ship, but not with my daughter, Stephen thought bitterly. Never mind. If he'll help me get a ship, he can keep his daughter.

Benjamin watched Stephen's face and was satisfied. Bright. He understood. Julia had had enough of sorrow, and Benjamin didn't think that this young man had anything to offer her but more grief.

"My ships are all in good hands at the moment," Benjamin said. "I'm not in the market for a master."

So he did own ships. But nothing for Stephen. The same old story.

"Yes, sir," he said.

"We've always hired local men to command our ships. Crew them, too. Men we know and trust."

"Yes, sir," Stephen said with a sinking feeling. "Aaron mentioned that might be the case."

"Well, don't let it discourage you. What with the boom in trade we're having, it's not all that easy to find well-qualified masters. This country's turning out more ships than men, seems like. Been tempted to go back to sea, myself."

"Then you think there's a chance?"

Benjamin began to stroll through the yard, watching the men at work, looking at everything but Stephen.

"Your uncle Brenard Logan?" he asked finally.

"Yes, sir."

"A good man. Shrewd if a little too conservative. I'll have Mrs. Thacher write him."

"I'm not sure just what kind of recommendation he'll give me," Stephen said uneasily.

"He's your uncle, isn't he?"

"Yes, sir, but he wants me to go back to sea as supercargo on his ships. We had some hard words on the subject just before I left Boston."

"Well, it's not a bad idea to have one of the family aboard to handle the business end. I can see his point." Benjamin paused by the sawpit and watched the sawyers at work with their long-bladed saws. "You've done pretty well in trading, I expect?"

"Perhaps too well," Stephen said. "I've made a lot of money for him, but it seems a waste to carry both a captain and supercargo when I can handle both jobs."

Benjamin noticed the bitterness in Stephen's voice. Just as well, he thought. Young men should be impatient.

"Never shipped a supercargo, myself," he said, and there was a note of pride in his voice when he continued. "My masters can handle anything that comes their way. All Cape men, born and bred to trade as well as to the sea."

"Then your captains are fortunate, sir."

"You ever sail afore the mast?"

"No, not technically, but I wasn't idle at sea. I've filled in for men who were lost or ailing. I've handled everything from reefing sails in a gale to acting first mate. On our last voyage, Captain Peterson came down with Yellow Jack. I brought the *Liza* round the Horn."

"As master?" Benjamin asked skeptically.

"As acting master. Captain Peterson was in his bunk for two months, delirious most of the time."

"And the first mate?" Benjamin began to stroll toward the caulkers' shop.

"A good mate, but not yet able to assume command."

"*That's* a mistake. The mate should *always* be able to assume command."

"My uncle didn't feel the need of it, sir, since I was aboard. The mate was his youngest son."

"Oh!" Benjamin stopped and looked carefully again at the young man. "So *that's* the way the wind blows. A son of his own coming up. That boy'll get a ship before you do."

"Yes, sir. I know. That's why I'm determined to part company with Uncle Brenard and his ships. I'll make my own way. Something I should have done a long time ago."

"Why didn't you?" Benjamin asked bluntly.

"Promises," Stephen said as he followed the captain up the path between the dunes. "He always promised me a ship after just one more voyage. When I got home, it was always just one more. I owed him a lot, too. He brought me up and educated me well."

"You an orphan?" Benjamin asked, scanning the sky and the horizon.

"Yes, sir."

"Any money?"

"None that I haven't earned myself."

"Enough to buy a share in that ship?" Benjamin pointed down to the large vessel on the railway.

"I don't know, sir. Depends on how much they want."

"You willing to put every penny you have in her?"

Stephen studied the ship and then the man beside him. All his savings? He thought of the long years, hard years, stretching behind him that those meager savings represented. Then he thought of the even longer ones stretching out ahead. He *had* to have a ship! Otherwise, he'd never make it. He made his decision.

"I'd be willing to put everything into a ship *I* commanded."

Benjamin clapped him on the shoulder. "Good man.

Come along now and let's take a look at those letters of yours."

They found Julia in the office seated on a high stool. She had a piece of paper in front of her and a pen in her hand.

She really is a beauty, Stephen thought, as the two men entered the room. Too bad her father's warned me off. His fingers itched to brush those crisp black curls away from her clear forehead.

"Come to any decision, Julie?" Benjamin asked.

"It's worth making further inquiries," she said tersely.

Benjamin turned to Stephen. "You ever sailed with anyone from around here?"

"Yes, sir." Stephen tried to keep his eyes away from Julia and concentrate on her father. "I've known some from Dennis, but I think they're all at sea. None of them were masters, though."

"Too bad," Benjamin said. "It would help if you could come up with someone we know to vouch for you."

"You built the *Belle of Canton*, didn't you?" Stephen asked.

"Yes."

"You're probably acquainted with her captain then, sir. He's from Brewster. Coming home in the *Liza*, we sailed around the Horn in company with the *Belle of Canton*."

"Captain William Thacher?" Benjamin asked.

"Yes, sir."

"My father-in-law," Julia said quietly.

"Oh, I didn't know," Stephen said, embarrassed. What else could he say? Should he offer her condolences on the loss of her husband? But according to Aaron, that was a long time ago.

"He in port?" Benjamin asked.

"We parted company. He went on to London while we put in to Boston."

"Still, he should be home soon. It's been a long time. Have you or your mother heard from him recently, Julie?"

"Not since his letter about the attempted mutiny," she reminded him.

"That's right. I remember now. Think he'll put in a good word for you?" he asked Stephen.

"I believe he will. I beat him round the Horn."

Benjamin laughed. "And you expect him to say something *good* about you after that?"

Stephen relaxed a little and smiled. "Well, he called me every name in the book, but I don't think he'll hold it against me."

"I'll write to him," Julia said, taking a fresh sheet of paper. "Cousin William's word is better than most."

Cousin William's reply came a few days later, not by letter but in person. Big, bluff, hearty as ever, if a little greyer, he sailed up in the Boston packet and hailed them from the landing across the creek to come and get him. As usual, he hadn't bothered to let anyone know he was coming. He just came.

Julia, hearing his voice, came out of the office just in time to see him jump from the small gig and confront Benjamin. She smiled as she watched the two men going through their ritual greeting. Clapping one another on the back. Both shouting at the tops of their voices simultaneously. Hugging each other in a giant, pummeling embrace. They reminded her of two big happy bears dancing around. They seemed to have forgotten their last bitter words.

When he saw her there, William strode across the yard to meet her. With her, his greeting was more gentle, though he did give her a robust kiss on the cheek.

"I'm sorry, Julie," he said softly. His eyes, sad and concerned, looked older.

"Oh, Cousin William!" She hugged him tight and felt the tears start up in her eyes. This was the first time she'd seen him since that long-ago day in Brewster when he had left her.

"I'm sorry I wasn't here when it happened. We could have been a comfort to one another."

"Yes," was all Julia could say around the awful lump in her throat.

He held her a little way from him and looked at her soberly, seeing that the young girl had become a woman. "You know I still consider you my daughter, Julie? With all it implies."

"I know, Cousin William." She smiled through the tears that glittered on her black lashes.

"And you always will be. No matter what happens."

"I know."

"I mean it. Someday you'll remarry . . ."

"No!"

"Yes, you will. You should. Jason would want you to. I just want to make sure you know that, when that day comes, I'll still consider you my daughter. Always! Whenever you want something, all you have to do is ask. I'm holding Jason's share of my money for you. It's yours. Let me know whenever you want it."

"No. That's not fair to Samuel. It should all go to him now. It's not as though . . . as though we'd had a child."

"Don't you worry about Samuel. He's master of the *Robin* now. He'll do all right. There's plenty for the both of you. Besides, it's not just money I'm talking about. *Anything* you want. All you have to do is ask. I want to make sure you understand that."

"I understand, Cousin William," she said quietly.

"You sure?"

"I'm sure." It was getting harder and harder to hold back the tears as she looked at his dear face, the eyes whose green reminded her so of Jason's. "How about the moon, Cousin William?" She tried to laugh. "I was accused of wanting it not long ago."

"The moon? I think I can arrange it." He smiled back at her, his strong white teeth flashing between the silvered gold of his mustache and beard. "Anything else?"

"Nothing at the moment. But if I put my mind to it, I'm sure I'll come up with something."

His smile faded when he said, "How about coming over to Brewster with me for a few days?"

"I . . . I don't think I could. Not yet."

"Not yet? It's been well over two years, Julie. Three come August."

"I know, but not yet. Please."

"Well, it was just an idea. Thought it might be easier for both of us if we went back for the first time together." He looked around the yard and noted the work in progress. Then his eyes stopped when he saw the large ship on the ways nearest the mouth of the creek.

"Looks interestin'," he said.

"It is."

"Let's go take a look. I want to talk to your father about building me a new ship." He put an arm around her slender waist and drew her along with him. "The *Belle's* getting pretty tired. Nine years old and not as fast as she used to be. We got soundly whipped coming round the Horn. Didn't dare push her as hard as I used to. I'm thinking of selling her."

They joined Benjamin where he stood, critically watching the men who were driving caulking into the seams.

"Want to build me something like that, Ben?"

"What's the matter with the *Belle?*"

"Now, don't get touchy. I know she's one of your children, but like all of us, she's beginning to show her age. Old-fashioned, too. She had her day, though." William chuckled as he thought of some of the records he'd set in her, now long since broken. "What I had in mind was something even more rakish than that one."

"You'll not do better than this."

"Maybe. Maybe not. What I want is a vessel that will *beat* that one." William paused to light his pipe.

Julia noticed that there seemed to be some trouble at the barkentine and left the men to go investigate. Once launched into an argument about ship design, they could go on for hours without missing her.

Benjamin shrugged. "I'll build you whatever you want, but you'll have to wait in line same as anyone else."

"You got much lined up?"

Benjamin ran his hand through his rough hair. He looked harassed. "Never seen anything like it. Where I used to go begging for work, now I'm turning it down. I hate to let it go, but it seems everyone and his brother wants a ship."

"Don't turn it down, for God's sake, Ben. Take it. Take all you can get. Grow with the times."

Benjamin shook his head. "Look around you, Will." He waved his arm around, including in its sweep everything from the piles of wood seasoning near the dunes, across the yard and up the hill to where the blacksmith's shop stood next to a variety of smaller sheds and buildings, down again to the creek and the vessels standing on the ways.

"We got three vessels on the ways now. When they're launched, there'll be another three to take their places.

The models for them are already, finished. There're only four of us to supervise the yard. Daniel and Philip Sears, Julia and me. Might have been different if Josiah had been any use or if I had sons, but I don't."

"By the way, where is Josiah?" William asked as he glanced around the yard.

"Out. I bought him out. Never was any good. Now I think he's unhinged to boot."

"You're well rid of him."

Benjamin nodded. "I think so."

"Well, if you need foremen"—William drew on his pipe—"why don't you train them same as you trained the Sears boys."

"Got three likely lads coming along, but they're not ripe yet. And look at the land. Where am I going to put more railways?"

William studied the shoreline and nodded. "You got a problem. Not much left but marsh. Can't build a ship in the marsh."

"Nope. Can't launch them, neither. Not with only two tides a year high enough to launch on. You launch two on the same tide, and you got problems. The creek's too damned narrow. I wake up with nightmares some nights, dreaming about launching day."

William nodded and puffed on his pipe.

"Glad they're your problems and not mine. When you figure on starting my ship?"

"Be three years before we can even lay the keel. If you don't want to wait, if you want to find yourself another shipyard, I'll understand. There're other good shipyards, Will. They're springing up all over New England." Benjamin paused to inspect a knee four men were carrying to the ship.

"Nope. I'll keep it in the family. Put my name down. I want the big railway, but we can figure what we'll build on it later. Might change my mind and want something different by then."

When the two men reached the top of the dune, they stopped to look out at the water shading from green to blue with a froth of white breaking on the bar.

"You say you got Julie overseeing now?" William asked.

"Yes. Had to put her in charge of a lot of the work."

William squinted to watch the far-flung ships with his seaman's clear-sighted vision. "Too bad. Thought she might like to take a trip with me. Say over to England and back."

Benjamin jerked his eyes away from the horizon to look at William, but his friend's face was all innocence behind his beard.

"You mentioned it to her?" he asked.

"Not yet."

"Then don't."

William took his pipe from his mouth and laughed mockingly. "Afraid she might go?"

Benjamin pressed his lips together. "I can't get along without her." He saw no reason to mention David Baxter.

"Julie'll be twenty-one next month. A married woman to boot. You won't have much say in it."

"Did I ever?" Benjamin started walking down between the dunes to the beach.

"That still riling you?" William asked as he followed him.

"I don't know. Maybe it is. One of the blackest days of my life was the day you brought Jason into my house."

"It was bound to happen sooner or later. If it hadn't been Jason, 'twould have been someone else."

"You don't know what she's been through." Benjamin clenched his fists. "What we've all been through."

"Lydia wrote."

"Words won't describe the hell we lived in. For months." Benjamin began to pace the hard-packed sand and left deep footprints behind him.

"They were happy, Ben. They had more of happiness in those few weeks than most people could even believe existed."

" 'Twould have been better if she'd had it spread a little thinner. And more time to enjoy it in."

"Don't ever recollect seeing Julie spread things thin. It's not her way."

"No."

William shook his head and looked down at the glistening pebbles on the edge of the waves.

"You really got her tied down now, don't you, Ben? Made it impossible for her to leave you without feeling guilty."

"Work's good for her," Benjamin said defensively and scowled. "She came back to life when she came back to the yard."

"Did you have to give her so much responsibility?"

"Yes. She wanted it. She's got to learn how to handle it. Someday this will all be hers, and I won't be here to keep it going."

William paused to light his pipe again and studied his friend's face over the flame.

"You been sick?"

"No, of course not."

"Didn't think so. You look healthy enough. I make you out to be forty-seven. Probably got another twenty, thirty years ahead of you."

Benjamin shrugged.

"And I could drop dead tomorrow. Known men my age who did."

"Doubt it."

Benjamin decided to change the subject.

"Young man named Stephen Logan's been here looking for a job. Said you might vouch for him."

"Don't know as he'd be any good in a shipyard. Right fair on a ship. I've run into him a few times over the years."

"He doesn't want a job with me. He wants command of a ship."

"You could do worse. He beat me round the Horn. Showed uncommon good judgment. Carried as much sail as he could handle and not an ounce more." He made a wry face. "Course *Belle*'s slowing down, or I'd have shown him my heels."

"Know anything else about him besides the fact that he can beat you?"

"Yes. Shrewd trader. I've heard a couple of deals he's made I wouldn't have believed possible. Surprised his uncle's willing to let him go."

"Won't give him a ship, so he says. Wants to keep him on as supercargo."

William, studying the vessels out on the Bay, critically watched the set of their sails while he reflected on the young man. Finally he said, "If I had a ship needing a master, I'd give it to him. Could do worse."

"You be willing to tell Asa Crofton that?"

"If he asks."

"I think he will. That's his ship I'm building back there. He doesn't have anyone in mind for her yet. Logan wants her."

"That's a rare treat for a first command. I'd put him on something older first."

"Well, that's where we started. On the old ships. But there's no reason *we* couldn't have handled the newest and the best."

"Guess not. Those were happy days, though, weren't they, Ben?" William's green eyes softened with memory. "In those old tubs."

"Yes. That they were." Benjamin took one last look at the scattering of white sails on the blue-green sea, then turned his back on them to return to the yard.

"All of life lying before us like an oyster," William said, following him, "and all we could think of was how we'd make our fortunes fast and leave the sea."

"And you never have."

"Nope. Made my fortune. Two or three times over. But I've never left the sea. Wonder why?"

"Life ashore's too tame for you."

"Maybe. But I'll be fifty next year. You'd think I'd have better sense by now. You were smarter than me."

"Smarter?" Benjamin raised his bushy eyebrows skeptically. "Maybe."

Chapter Seventeen

1841

It took less than two hours from the moment Captain William Thacher stepped off the packet at the town landing for word of his coming to spread through the village. News traveled faster in the sun-filled days of summer than it did during winter's confining cold.

Stephen Logan heard about it that night over dinner at the Martins'. The next morning, he was at the shipyard early. Too early. William and Benjamin, having talked over many a brandy the night before, were sleeping late. Only Julia was at the yard.

He found her in the office, braiding her damp black hair. Stephen stood in the open doorway and watched her for a moment before she became aware of his presence.

"Why don't you leave it down?" he asked. "It'll dry faster."

She looked at him coolly and went on braiding her hair.

"It gets in my way," she said.

He pushed his cap back on his sun-bleached hair and smiled.

"How did it get wet?"

"I don't think that's any business of yours." She coiled one long braid around her head.

"Swimming?"

"No. I walked through a heavy fall of dew."

"Swimming at dawn? You should have let me know, my lady. I would have joined you. Then like Wordsworth, I could say 'Bliss was it that dawn to be alive . . . .'" The blue in his grey eyes deepened as he settled down to enjoy himself.

"I swim alone." Julia slipped the last pin into her hair, securing it firmly.

"Don't you know that's dangerous?"

She straightened her shoulders and her deep blue eyes showed no warmth when she looked at him.

"Not for me," she said.

"No?" He cocked a tawny eyebrow at her. "Why are you so very special? What's different about you?"

"Nothing." She gathered some papers from the desk. "If you're looking for Captain Thacher, you're too early. Come back later."

"I'd rather stay." Solidly blocking the door, he leaned against the doorframe. "I want to find out what it is that makes you so special, my lady. I knew it the first day I saw you, but I don't know why. Every time I see you, I think I've found the answer. But then, when I see you again, it disappears."

"Maybe it's because I'm immune to your very obvious charms. If you'll excuse me, Mr. Logan, I have to get to work." She walked to the door and confronted him, her eyes and the determined set of her chin telling him to move.

He didn't budge. He just smiled his laziest smile.

"Can't be that. Dear Sister Sarah has an inborn immunity to me, wouldn't you say? And I find absolutely nothing special about Sarah."

Julia smiled when she thought of Sarah's scathing remarks about Stephen.

"Sarah doesn't have an immunity to you. She hates you."

"Really?" He *had* made her smile. "That's gratifying. I've been able to arouse an emotion in at least one member of your family."

"Mr. Logan, I know why you're here, and it has nothing to do with me." Julia was definitely becoming impatient.

She could hear the men at work, and with her father late this morning, she *had* to get out there. "Captain Thacher had a talk with Captain Crofton yesterday afternoon."

Stephen straightened up. There was no laughter in his eyes.

"About me?"

"I assume so."

"Well?"

"Captain Crofton will be over here to meet you later on this morning. If you hadn't been so impatient, I'd have sent you word."

"Do I get the ship?"

There was the barest hint of a smile on her lips as Julia looked him over, her eyes traveling from his tawny hair to his straight nose to his narrow lips and his hard, square chin.

"I think that depends on you."

"But there *is* a chance?"

"There's a chance. Daniel," she called over his shoulder, "I want to talk to you."

"Stay or go as you please," she said to Stephen as she slipped past him in the doorway, "but be here at ten-thirty."

Daniel's face was grave with concern when she joined him.

"That fellow botherin' you, Miss Julia?" he asked.

"No. He's all right, Daniel."

"He's been idling around the yard for a week now, trailing after you."

"He just wants someone to give him command of a vessel."

"Well, I hope he gets it and gets out of this shipyard." His limp became more pronounced as though to underline his feelings.

"Why, Daniel!" She looked at him in surprise. "What's the matter? Is he interfering with the work?"

"No. Not directly. I just don't like to see him strollin' around the yard with his hands in his pockets and nothin' to do. Gives the men ideas."

"Well, he probably won't be around much longer," she said soothingly. "My father won't be in till later this morning. How's the work lined up for today? Have all the men reported in?"

When Stephen returned to the yard at ten-fifteen, he found Julia as well as Benjamin and William waiting for him. They all towered over the wiry, bandy-legged, white-bearded man who was with them. A committee, Stephen thought.

"Here he is," William hailed him. "Good to see you again, lad."

"And it's good to see you, sir." Stephen tried to keep his hand as firm as the one that was crushing it.

"So after beating me round the Horn, you think you're qualified to get your own ship?"

Stephen returned his grin. "There's not many that could do it."

"That's the spirit!" William clapped him on the back. "Asa, this is Mr. Logan. Wants to be Captain Logan. What do you think?"

The short, spry old man glared at Stephen as though he were an enemy. "That's a lot of ship for a young man."

"Yes, sir, but I can handle it." Stephen was deferential, but he stood his ground.

"You ever been to Canton?"

"Yes, sir. Twice."

"Calcutta?"

"Yes, sir."

"Cronstadt?"

"No, sir, but I can find the way."

"Ever sailed a ship like that one?" He pointed his white beard at the ship.

"There aren't any ships like that, sir, but I've sailed the nearest thing to it."

"All right." The old man was still glaring at Stephen. "You're hired."

Stephen couldn't believe the swiftness with which the captain had come to his decision.

"Yes, sir."

"You start work today. One hundred dollars a month. That's your ship. The *Crystal Star*. She's your responsibility now. I expect a report from you every day. Check every timber that goes in her. Inspect every fastening. You see anything you don't like, you tell Captain Howard. Then come report to me. Understand?"

"Yes, sir." Stephen still couldn't believe it. "Thank you, sir."

"Don't thank me," Captain Crofton growled at him. "Make money for me. I want that ship paid for her first voyage. Think you can handle it?"

"I'm sure of it, sir."

"Don't care how you do it, long as it's legal. Least within the laws of *this* country. Out to China first. Then England. If you don't have her paid for by then, don't come home. Keep going till you've got the price in hand. That ship's being built to be driven, and you drive her. Get me?"

"Yes, sir."

"Now." A crafty gleam flickered in the old captain's watery blue eyes. "Captain Howard tells me you want to buy a share in her."

"I'm willing, sir."

"Good. Then you'll be working for yourself as well as for me. Make a better master of you. How much you got?"

"About twenty-five hundred dollars, sir."

"That all?"

"It's all I've been able to save."

"All right. That'll buy you four sixty-fourth shares. I want that money in hand before we settle with the Howards for the ship."

"You'll have it, sir."

Captain Crofton stuck out his hand. "We'll go into more details this evening. Report to me after dinner. Eight bells."

"Aye, aye, sir," Stephen said as he shook the old man's hand.

"Now, what are you doin', standing around here gabbing?" Captain Crofton grumbled. "Get to work."

"Yes, *sir!*" Stephen grinned at his new employer. He saw the twinkle the old man was trying to hide. Then he turned and strode off to the ship. *His* ship!

Asa Crofton pulled on his white beard as he watched him go. "Hope I'm doing the right thing. Rather've had a man from East Dennis, Dennis. Might've even considered one from Brewster." His eyes glinted as he looked sideways at William. "But there's none to be had."

"Captain Crofton, not everyone can be born on the Cape," Julia said with mocking amusement. "Might be *some* good men born west of Sandwich."

"Might. Hard to credit it, though." His smile was hidden in his beard. "That one better be. Boston! Any of his family come from around here?"

"I don't know."

"Have to find out. Feel easier in my mind if he's got some good blood."

Through the hot days of summer, Stephen was often the first to arrive at the shipyard in the morning and the last to leave at night. Though Julia had seen many masters concerned about the construction of their vessels, she had never seen one as anxious as Stephen Logan. She would look up to find him watching the fitting of a ceiling plank or the installation of a cedar stopwater only to find that he had disappeared, and a few moments later, she would hear his voice at the other end of the ship. His energy seemed inexhaustible.

At first, he watched each step with quiet intentness, but after a month, he began to find fault with detail after detail. He brought his complaints to Julia and she found them increasingly annoying.

One day as she was overseeing the placement of the midships hold flooring, he approached her. She tried to ignore him and moved closer to the carpenters. However, it was like trying to ignore a bolt of lightning that was about to strike.

"Miss Julia," his voice rang out. "I have to see you at once. There's a problem with one of the standing knees."

"Can't it wait?" she asked, looking up at him impatiently. "I'm busy."

"It will only take a minute. Of course"—his grey, steady eyes were compelling her to look at him—"if you can't spare the time, I'll have to take it up with your father."

"He's not here. You know he's gone down to Boston."

"Then I'll have to go find Captain Crofton. I know *he'd* be concerned about the quality of his ship."

"Oh, very well," she said as she dusted the sawdust from her hands onto her skirt.

"Tom," she called to one of the apprentices, "go see if

you can find Mr. Small." Jack Small was one of the finest master carpenters in the shipyard, and she knew that he was capable of supervising the installation of the flooring, but heaven only knew what important job she would be dragging him away from.

"Well, *Captain* Logan," Julia said after Mr. Small had arrived to relieve her of her duties. "What was so important it couldn't wait an hour or two?"

"I told you." His impatience matched her own. "A forward standing knee. It's not properly fastened." He led the way below.

Julia picked up her skirts and followed him, stepping high over the heavy timbers of the bilge. Stephen, having reached the questionable knee before her, looked back, appreciatively noting the graceful shape of the legs her lifted skirts exposed. Even in the dim twilight below decks, Julia could see the smoldering blue in his grey eyes.

"All right, Captain Logan. Show me."

"It should be obvious. The wooden trunnels are all driven in, but there are no bronze spikes to give it strength. Just give us one good gale, and that knee's going to loosen."

Julia, with her lips pressed tight together, knelt down beside the knee and ran her fingers along the curve of the wood as she inspected it. There was no doubt about it. There were no spikes driven between the trunnels.

Stephen, leaning close behind her, laid a hand lightly on her shoulder, and she could feel his warm breath on her cheek. His loose, flowing sleeve brushed her hand as he pointed out the trunnels and the empty spaces between.

Jerking around, Julia pushed him away from her.

"I can see without any help from you."

He stood back and calmly crossed his arms, his amusement obvious from the satisfied curve of his lips and the glimmer in his eyes.

"Did you know that, in this light, your eyes look black with just sparks of blue in them . . . like your hair in sunlight?"

She stood up and faced him, her chin lifted high so that she appeared to be looking down at him.

"We're here to discuss fastenings, not my eyes and hair, Captain Logan."

Now his grin, slow and lazy, broadened. Here comes the boyish charm, thought Julia.

"Why is it you never call me by my first name?" he asked softly. "With you, it's always *Captain* Logan."

"I thought you rather liked the title. You seem arrogant enough about it."

"Not arrogant. Just proud to have finally attained it. Why should you object, my lady? Without your help, I might still be plain Stephen Logan without a vessel to call my own."

"Well, to my mind, you've yet to earn it. Standing around a shipyard watching others work isn't what I call being a shipmaster."

"Oh, I'll earn it, pretty Julia. Don't you worry about that. Just worry about building her. That knee"—he pointed down at it—"is poorly fastened."

"Did it ever occur to you, *Captain* Logan, that this vessel has not yet been completed? It's still in the process of being built, which means that a lot of items are not finished. If you would stop quibbling over every little detail and leave me and my father and Daniel to get on with our work, you'd have a better ship. The next thing you'll be finding fault with is the flooring we're laying now, and you'll be to blame, taking me away from it when I'm needed."

"That still doesn't explain why every other knee down here is properly fastened and not this one. I think it's been overlooked and it never would have been noticed if I hadn't chanced to come upon it." His face, like his voice, was cold. All amusement had vanished. "Incidentally, this work was done before I arrived on the scene."

"I'll have it attended to at once. Now, if you'll excuse me, Captain Logan"—she picked up her skirts—"I have work to do."

Stephen caught her arm as she brushed past him.

"It's not just the knee. I wanted to talk to you."

"I'm busy. *If* you'll be so kind . . ." She stared down at the hand that held her, then looked coolly into his eyes.

"What do you have against me, Julia?" he asked without relinquishing his grip. "When I first came here, you were generous, spoke well of me to Captain Crofton. Now you freeze me out every time I come near you."

"I have nothing against you. I thought then, as I still do, that you'll make a good master. But you're interfering with the work."

"I'm doing exactly what I'm paid to do. Following Captain Crofton's orders."

"You're badgering us constantly over the most insignificant items. I have enough on my hands without this steady stream of disruptions from you."

"That knee is not an insignificant item."

"No, it's not, but it could have waited a few hours. If you want to see this ship launched come the spring tide, you'll have to stop it. It's not just me. Stop harassing the men with your constant questions and objections. They know a lot more about building a ship than you do."

"I know." His voice softened and the beginning of a smile flickered on his lips. "That's why I question them. How else am I to learn? Will you teach me, my lady?"

"You plan on applying to my father for a job?"

"No."

"Then it seems to me you know just about enough."

"I'll never know enough. You wouldn't want to think of me out there, the ship storm-torn or rock-damaged, without the knowledge I'd need to repair her, now would you, pretty Julia?"

"I reckon you've seen it done before. All it takes to make repairs is a little common sense."

"For a makeshift, yes, but I never do things halfway. If I promise not to bother you too much in the meantime, will you teach me after church on Sunday?"

"We have dinner after church."

"After dinner, then? We could take a walk and you could explain a lot of things to me . . . things I'd like to know about you."

Julia searched his face. The grey eyes serious and compelling with the hint of blue laughter behind them, his face from the clear brow to the strong chin disarmingly innocent. She knew from past experience that he would persist until he got what he wanted. She was just about to give in when she heard the ladder creak.

They both looked up to see a pair of legs descending, and Stephen dropped his hand from her arm.

"Miss Julia?" Daniel peered through the rungs of the ladder into the dimness of the hold.

"Yes, Daniel."

"They told me you were down here."

"I'm coming right up." She lifted her skirts and went to the foot of the ladder. "Captain Logan has discovered that there are no bronze spikes in one of the forward knees."

As she started to climb the ladder, she looked down at Stephen. "If you'd be good enough to make a list of your complaints and give them to me at the end of each day, I believe the work would be performed to your satisfaction . . . and to mine."

Once on deck, she turned to Daniel. "Is something wrong?"

"No. I just came by to check on a couple of things and the men told me you were below with that fellow. Reckoned you might want an excuse to get rid of him."

Julia smiled at the swarthy foreman. At least with Daniel, there was no guile behind his earnest expression.

"Thanks, Daniel."

"He's always after you about something. Maybe you ought to talk to your pa about him."

"It's all right. I can handle him. What do the men think about him? Are they complaining?"

"No. They like him well enough. He's always got a joke for them, and they respect his rights, seeing as how he's goin' to be master of the *Crystal Star.*"

"But you don't like him? Is that it?"

"I don't like him bothering you, getting you off alone down in the hold or some other odd place."

"Think I need a chaperone?" Her lips were soft as she smiled at his concern. "Don't worry about him, Daniel. He's harmless. Just another master worrying about his vessel."

"Better be."

Julia saw the threat behind his scowl and remembered the power of his arms when he had attacked Josiah.

"Well, Daniel, if he steps out of line, all I have to do is yell, and I know that you'll be there."

"Just remember that, Miss Julia. I'll be there."

Between the long dawn-to-dark days at the shipyard and the flurry of preparations for Sarah's marriage at home, the summer passed quickly. Stephen would often manage to come to the house with Aaron on a Sunday or sometimes for a quiet evening, but Julia managed to avoid being caught alone with him.

Then suddenly, it was Sarah's wedding day, a soft day of summer haze and no breeze. The church was hot, but Sarah, in her long white gown, was serenely cool.

Julia, watching the ceremony from a front pew, thought how well Sarah had planned everything: the church banked with flowers, the gowns of the friends who attended her, and above all her own appearance.

Her hair was done in the most elaborate fashion to be seen. No one would ever know the hours Sarah had spent perfecting the fall of ringlets on either side of her face, the smoothness of the full bun on top of her head with the wreath of wax orange blossoms and real roses woven around it.

The folds of the wedding veil of Alençon lace flowed behind her from just below her bun to within an inch of the floor. Her shoulders were delicately bare above the deep lace Bertha collar that covered her arms almost to the elbow, and the tight satin bodice emphasized her slender body and small waist just above the voluminous skirts of flower embroidered muslin.

Aaron, who had seemed nervous when he appeared at the altar in his elegant mulberry tailcoat and embroidered vest, had broken into a proud smile when Sarah had appeared with her father. It was obvious that he gloried in her beauty. Julia hoped the look was one of love as well.

While she was studying Aaron, it was impossible for her not to notice Stephen, who was standing beside the groom. She tried to ignore him, but it was difficult when he was staring directly at her with just the hint of a suggestive smile at the corners of his lips. Really! The man was impossible.

Later, at the wedding breakfast, the crowd flowed out

of the house onto the broad lawn. The tables that had been set up under the trees were decorated with flowers and favors tied with white satin ribbons. It seemed that every man present had to propose a toast, and by early afternoon, the champagne was still flowing in unbounded quantities. Julia wondered how everyone would manage to hold out until evening, when the dancing would begin on the wooden floor laid out in the back beyond the cherry trees.

She felt light-headed already, and the still air seemed even more stifling in the midst of the large crowd. Perhaps, she thought, there would be a little breeze on the beach. No one would notice if she were to slip away for an hour or two.

As she went into the house to fetch her bonnet, she found Sarah, surrounded by admirers, at the foot of the stairs. She tried to pass by her unnoticed, but Sarah, despite the champagne, was alert as always.

"Running away, sister dear?" she asked.

"No, of course not, Sarah," Julia said quietly. "It's just a little hot in the sun."

Sarah simply smiled her grey-eyed cat smile. Turning back to Aaron, she touched him lightly, but possessively, on the arm.

As she left the house, Julia wondered why Sarah would bother to embarrass her in front of so many others. It was her day of triumph, and Julia had done her best to remain unobtrusive and quiet. She shrugged. Well, she would just stay out of Sarah's way for the rest of the day.

Once on the beach, Julia sat in the little shade cast by a tall dune, unmindful of her good grey silk dress. It was quiet here, the sand deserted with practically everyone in the village at the wedding feast. Julia drew a deep breath of the cooler air coming off the water. It helped clear her head.

"That's a big sigh. Are you regretting that you turned Aaron down, after all?"

Julia looked over her shoulder and saw Stephen standing behind her. In his blue tailcoat with its brass buttons and his buff vest, he looked different from the workaday man of the shipyard. Even his sun-bleached hair was carefully cut and combed.

"You look like a Boston dandy," she said.

"As best man, I guess that's what I am." He laid his top hat carefully on a patch of beach grass and sat down next to her.

"You following me?" she asked him.

"I heard what Sarah said to you. You shouldn't have left the feast, you know. Now everyone *will* think you're running away."

"It really doesn't matter to me what people think."

"Not even when they're saying that Aaron jilted you and that you're jealous of Sarah?"

"They may say it, but I doubt there's a one that believes it."

"Oh, there are those who'll believe anything. A rich young man like Aaron. Good-looking, too. Why didn't you take him, Julia?"

"It's simple enough." She picked up a handful of sand and poured it between her fingers. "Aaron isn't a man I'd want to be tied to for the rest of my life. Besides, he'll be much happier with Sarah."

"Will he?" He cocked one tawny eyebrow at her. "I wonder."

"She'll make him a good wife."

"Do you really believe that? You know, Julia, I don't think you like Sarah any better than I do."

"Like her!" Julia looked up at him in surprise. "She's my sister. Of course, I like her."

"Really? Well, let me put it another way. Sarah doesn't like you any more than she likes me."

"You have to understand Sarah," Julia said as she looked across the sand at the water that caressed the pebbled beach with only the barest of ripples. "Being born in the middle made growing up a difficult thing for her. I was the eldest, so Papa always paid the most attention to me, and because Amelia was the youngest, she was always Mama's pet. Sarah got left out. And . . . there've been some other problems for her along the way."

"You mean like the time your father threw her out of the house?"

"He didn't throw her out. She left of her own accord, and it was really my fault anyway," she said sadly. Then she looked at him sharply. "How did you find out about that?"

"I've been here over two months now. There are a lot of wagging tongues just waiting to be loosened." With his finger, he began to sketch the lines of a vessel in the sand. "How was it your fault?"

"That's something I'd rather not talk about," she said firmly.

Stephen leaned back against the sand on one elbow and looked up at her. She was gazing out at the Bay and her clear profile against the tall dune stood out like a cameo.

"Well, let me tell you something about sister Sarah," he said. "She's not neglected and never has been. She doesn't even understand the meaning of the word. Look at the wedding your father's giving her. Look at the house he's built for her. I know what it means to be neglected, but Sarah couldn't even begin to comprehend it."

Julia looked down at him. The lock of hair that never would stay put had fallen over his forehead. Somehow it made him look vulnerable, something she had never noticed before.

"How old were you when your parents died, Stephen?" she asked gently.

"Young. Too young. And that's something *I'd* rather not discuss."

"Don't you think it might help to talk about it?"

"What good does talking do? It won't bring them back. It won't give them to me when I was a boy and needed them. You can't look back, Julia. You have to look ahead. You have to carry so much baggage through life, you don't need the added weight of a grievance . . . or a grief." He looked up at her suddenly and pointedly.

"I'm *not!*"

"Yes, you are. Why else do you avoid me?"

He sat up and took a hollow reed. Splitting it between his fingernails, he waited for her answer. She noticed his hands. Square, capable hands, clean and well-manicured. Looking down at her own hands with their work-shortened nails, she suddenly felt self-conscious and hid them in the silken folds of her skirt. Then she was angry over her own embarrassment.

"You are the most conceited . . ."

"No. That's not the reason, Julia. You're afraid of me.

Afraid that you could like me . . . very much. And you're afraid of being hurt again."

"I am not. Just because I don't fall all over myself every time you look at me, which is what I presume you're used to, doesn't mean that I'm afraid of you."

"Not every man who goes to sea dies there, Julia." He ignored her statement as well as her eyes. All of his concentration was on the reed. "Look at Captain Asa. Look at your father. Look at Captain Thacher. Look at half the men at Sarah's wedding feast. A lot of them are old, tired of the sea perhaps, but they spent a good part of their lives on it."

Julia looked down at the reed he was splitting, then out over the cloud-sprinkled water. No, they don't all die, she thought. But some men sail away on it and never come back. At least not to you. Then she realized Stephen was right. She *was* afraid of him. Not just because of Jason. There was David, too. She couldn't let another David happen to her, even if his name was Stephen. She stared out across the Bay to the sea. The next time she had to be very sure before she let herself think seriously of someone, and she didn't think she could ever be sure of Stephen. Once he had his ship, he, too, would sail away and leave her.

Then Stephen laughed.

"Don't brood, pretty Julia. It's not a day for brooding. It's a day of joy and glad tidings. Aaron and Sarah are wed. Let the bells ring out and all the earth rejoice."

"I think I like you better when you're serious . . . the way you are when you're working."

"Then we'll be serious. What shall we talk about?"

"I think we ought to go back to the house."

"Why? It's much more pleasant here."

"We'll be missed."

"Not by Sarah. Let's leave her to her glory, sweet Julia, and find our own right here."

Julia started to rise, but then realized that she still felt light-headed, and she sank back down on the sand. Stephen was right. It really was much more pleasant here away from the crowd and the impossible toasts.

"Why don't you tell me about some of your voyages," she suggested. "The places you've visited, what they're like."

"There's not much to tell that you haven't heard from a hundred men before me."

"You might have seen some things they haven't or you might have noticed some things they didn't. Every man looks through his own eyes, and every man sees something different."

"You're becoming very philosophical."

"It must be the champagne."

"So you like sea stories, pretty Julia?"

"Yes." Her eyes were a dreamy sapphire as she looked out at the gulls and clouds and sails. "When I was a little girl, I was always going to run away to sea and become a sailor, but then I grew up, and now I know I'll never see all those wonderful places. I'll have to make do with stories from those who've been there instead."

Stephen watched her face soften with longing, and he saw the other Julia she had always kept hidden from him beneath her efficient and often cold facade. He had caught only glimpses of this Julia before. Now she was here the way he had dreamed.

"I'd like to have known you when you were a little girl."

She knew that he was staring at her with a smoky intensity, but for once, it didn't bother her. She just smiled.

"I don't think you would have. I was a dirty, bedraggled child who was always getting into trouble. I tried to do all the things the boys did. I guess I would have worn britches if my mother had let me."

He smiled lazily back at her and she saw the boy that he once had been.

"You haven't changed much." He picked up her hand and looked at her nails. "Were you as beautiful then as you are now?"

"Let's talk about the *Crystal Star*," she said as she quickly withdrew her hand.

"Oh, no. Today let's *not* talk about the *Crystal Star*. That's all we ever talk about every other day of the week. Let's talk about a little girl named Julia Howard . . . and about a young lady named Julia Thacher and how she got to be the way she is."

"Is that how you seduce all your ladies? Get them to talk about themselves?"

"Damn it, Julia!" He straightened up and threw the torn

347

reed away from him. "I am *not* trying to seduce you. You're the most unseduceable woman I've ever seen in my life . . . and the most maddening."

"You don't have to swear at me!" she said primly, drawing herself up in an imitation of her mother.

Stephen fell back on the sand and roared with laughter at her imitation prudery.

"I've heard you swear often enough," he said as he gasped for breath, "when you thought no one was listening. It's *very* improper language for a lady."

"Well . . . maybe I'm not a lady," she said, irritated by his laughter.

"Oh, yes, you are. You're every inch a lady. Why do you think the men respect you so much? No one would dream of taking advantage of Miss Julia." Then he laughed again. "Who ever would have thought an aspiring sailor boy would grow up to be such a lady?"

"Oh, stop it, Stephen. You've had too much champagne."

"I'll stop on one condition." He sat up and, in doing so, managed to edge closer to her. "That you tell me about little Miss Julia."

"No. Not unless you tell me about young Master Stephen."

The lights withdrew from his eyes and their dark grey was that of low-hanging clouds before the rain.

"No. I'm not going to talk about that."

"And you told *me* not to carry a grief or grievance around."

"That's precisely what I'm trying not to do."

"I've changed my mind." She looked at him curiously out of the corner of her eye.

"About what?"

"I've decided I like you better when you're not serious."

"Then let's take a walk down the beach," he said as he got up and dusted off his clothing. "I'll tell you a sea story, but it's not going to be one about the past. It's a sea story that has yet to happen . . . but it will."

"I didn't know that, amongst all your other talents, you could see into the future."

"Ah"—he reached down for her hand to help her up—"there are a lot of things you have yet to learn about me, my lady."

"Well?" she said when they had reached the hard-packed sand left by the ebbing tide. "Where's the sea story?"

"Well . . . once upon a time, there was a princess. She had long hair the color of a clear night sea that curled to her waist and her eyes were the blue of the deepest ocean. Her father was a mighty king who ruled over many men and ships in a narrow, water-bound kingdom. The princess had everything a princess might desire . . . gold and jewels and power . . . except for one thing."

"Her own ship?" Julia interrupted.

"No. She could have had a ship if she'd wanted one. All she would have had to do was ask her father, for he gave her everything she ever desired. But the princess was under a spell cast by a wicked witch, and her father didn't know it. Neither did the princess."

"Now, how's that possible? If she was under a spell, she'd certainly know about it."

"Not at all, for, you see, spells are invisible things. They can surround you like the mist and you don't know they're there. You're not even aware that the world looks hazy."

"Well, what was the spell?"

"She couldn't see happy things. All life was very serious for her, and it made her sad."

"I'm not certain I like this story. Tell me another one."

"But I haven't even begun this one yet. Don't you want to hear about the handsome captain prince who comes to rescue her?"

"I don't think so, Stephen. I already know how that story ends. Let's go back to the house before they send out a search party."

He looked down at her and his eyes were strangely gentle.

"Is that what you really want, Julia?"

"Yes, Stephen, it's what I really want."

"Very well, then, my lady. We'll return to the festivities. I should have known that spells can't be broken in one day. But never believe you know the end of a story before it happens."

Once Sarah and Aaron had departed on their wedding trip to Boston and the gifts had been dispatched to their new home, the large white house settled down to a strange, echoing quiet. Bedrooms that had once seemed not enough now stood empty, and there were usually only four at the dinner table.

Aunt Martha, bustling everywhere, tried to keep their spirits up, but Julia found herself spending more and more of her free hours outdoors. Stephen had a way of appearing just as she was becoming restless, and she gradually found herself looking forward to seeing him.

As they walked, he told her about his college days in Cambridge, and he did finally tell her about some of the adventures he had had in foreign ports, while she spoke of the only things she knew, the shipyard and the people who populated her world.

Julia withheld large portions of herself from him and tried to keep their conversations on a neutral subject, but anger had a habit of flaring between them. It was not unusual for Stephen to leave her abruptly in the middle of a path. At such times, she wondered why he sought her out and why she put up with him, yet when they met again, it was always as though they had parted on only the most pleasant terms.

On a green-gold day in early autumn, Benjamin and Julia were riding home together, taking the longer road and skirting the marsh. It was the route Benjamin always took when he had something on his mind. Julia knew she'd hear about it before she reached home, and she was content to watch the evening light burnish the thick goldenrod to an even richer shade.

Finally, Benjamin came out with it.

"Julie, I don't want you working on the *Crystal Star* anymore. You concentrate on the barkentine and the schooner."

"But, Papa!" Julia looked at him in amazement. "The *Crystal Star*'s *my* ship. I helped design her."

"And with young Logan hanging around her all the time, you're neglecting your work."

"I am *not* neglecting my work!"

"Every time I come on board, I find the two of you together, talking away to beat the band."

Julia didn't like the way he set his jaw and avoided her eyes.

"We're both working. He's acting for Captain Asa. What

do you expect me to do? *Not* speak to him? Besides, if you'd stop to notice, we're mostly arguing."

"About what?"

"What do you think?" Really, he could be exasperating. "The way the ship's being built."

"Strange he don't find so much to argue with *me* about," Benjamin said. "You ever stop to think he might be arguin' with you because he likes to see you get mad?"

"That's ridiculous!"

Benjamin glanced at her.

"Ha!" he said.

"Papa, what's *really* on your mind?"

"Nothin'." He looked up at the reddening trees. "Just want to get a few vessels built."

"If it's about Stephen, you can just forget it." Julia glared at him. "Our relationship is strictly that of owner's agent and builder."

"Then what's he doin' hanging round the house come evening and Sundays?"

"Maybe we're friends, too. Lord knows, I have few enough people to talk to in this God-forsaken place."

"Your mother hears you swearing like that, she's going to be mighty upset."

"What Mother doesn't hear isn't going to upset her."

"First you tell me you have strictly a working relationship. Next you tell me you're friends. I'm waiting for the rest of it." His face was set on the road ahead of them, but Julia knew he was looking sideways at her from under those bristling eyebrows.

"There isn't any rest of it. That's it."

"Don't get too interested. Come spring, he'll be gone."

"I . . . am . . . not . . . interested," Julia said through her teeth. "Can't you understand that?"

"He's not the marrying kind. Poor, too."

"Well, if he's not the marrying kind, then there's nothing for you to worry about, is there?"

"Just don't want you gettin' hurt again."

"I won't be."

The silence between them as they rode along was not friendly. Finally, Benjamin said, "He's clever, that young man. Got a lot of charm. Kind you've got to be careful about. He gets what he wants."

"I hadn't noticed."

"Haven't you? Look at the way he got Asa Crofton to take him into his own home. Next thing you know, he'll be adopting him."

"Well, where else was Stephen supposed to go? After Aaron got married, he couldn't very well stay on at the Martins', and Sarah certainly won't want him around her house when she and Aaron get home."

"You know what Asa told me?"

"I'm not sure I want to hear it." She pointedly looked away from him at a blazing patch of cranberries growing on the edge of the marsh.

"Told me that he only hoped Logan could handle a ship as well as he can handle women."

"What are you talking about?"

"Well, you know that widowed daughter of his, Bertha?"

"I know her."

"She's got a sharp tongue, but Logan's got her eating out of his hand. Asa says Logan handles her nice and easy, but never really gives way."

"Well, Bertha's a little old for him, isn't she, Papa? She must be near forty."

"Old or young, makes no difference."

"That's nonsense!"

"Nonsense or not, you stay off the *Crystal Star* when he's aboard."

Julia's eyes flashed blue anger as she whipped up her horse and took off down the sandy road ahead of him, her grey cape billowing out behind her.

Benjamin watched her go, his eyes narrowed thoughtfully.

Chapter Eighteen

1841-1842

JULIA HAD NO CHOICE but to follow her father's orders. The next day, when she didn't appear on the *Crystal Star*, Stephen came looking for her, and from the tightness of his lips and the set of his jaw, it was obvious that he was angry.

"Are you trying to avoid me?" he asked her without preamble.

Julia, who had been checking through some papers in a brass-bound chest, straightened up and looked at him in surprise.

"Avoid you? What are you talking about?"

"Daniel says you're not going to be working on the ship any longer, and he's looking pretty smug about it!" He whipped off his cap as though to emphasize his words.

"You think *I'm* the one who doesn't want to work on the *Crystal Star* anymore?" She slammed a sheaf of papers down on the desk. "I'll have you know, Stephen Logan, that it's all your fault. If you hadn't been at me with your everlasting quibbles every time I turned around, I'd still be able to work on her."

"This is your father's shipyard. You can work on anything you damn well please, and you know it."

"You just said it yourself! This is my *father's* shipyard, and he gives the orders. I don't! And he says I'm wasting too much time on the *Crystal Star* because I'm always talking to you."

"Which does he object to . . . the talk or me?" His eyes had narrowed to dark grey glimmers between the lighter eyelashes.

"Maybe you'd better ask *him* that question. For myself, I'm none too sure which *I* object to most, especially when you come bursting in here attacking me."

"Well, what do you expect?" He moved closer to her, his muscles tense. "One minute you're warm and friendly, the next you're giving me a wide berth. If you enjoy playing games, *Miss* Julia, I don't."

"Don't you really, *Captain* Logan?" She drew herself up and looked at him imperiously. "I thought you invented them."

"If your father thinks I've been finding too many flaws when you're aboard, he or Daniel or whoever's in charge of the *Crystal Star* is really going to hear what faults I can find . . . constantly . . . until you're back at work on her."

"You might just as well forget it, because I have no intention of going back to work on that ship. Life is much more peaceful without running into you every time I turned around. I'll be glad when we get the *Crystal Star* launched and you out of this shipyard."

He looked at her indigo eyes flashing sapphire, her cheeks red with anger, and her black curls tumbling around her face. He wanted to grab her and kiss her, but he only smiled. It wasn't a pleasant smile.

"I'm not that easy to get rid of, my lady. Every voyage has its end, and you'll find me right back here every time I return."

"Well, don't expect me to be waiting to welcome you. Now, don't you think you'd better get back to work, Captain Logan? Captain Asa might get just a wee bit upset if he found you loitering around here when he's paying you good money for your time."

"I'm going, and I'm going to find your father and have this out with him."

"I wouldn't advise it. Remember, this is *his* shipyard and what he has to say goes a long way with Captain Asa."

"We'll see about that." He strode out the door and slammed it behind him.

Hoping to see a confrontation between Stephen and her father, Julia went to the window. That would really be a sight! Unfortunately, her father was nowhere to be seen, and Stephen eventually returned to work on the *Crystal Star*.

The next Sunday afternoon, Stephen turned up in front of the house just as Julia was starting out for a walk. When she came through the door and found him standing there in a green tailcoat and fawn trousers with his top hat tilted to one side, she had to admit she was glad he had come. Although they could hardly avoid one another at the shipyard, the few words they had spoken were cool and noncommittal. Her work had seemed dull without his constant presence, and the evenings at home even duller.

He had an air of great patience as he leaned with arms folded against the iron hitching post beside the road. She wondered how long he had been waiting.

"Have you come to apologize?" she asked as she approached him.

"I'd be happy to"—he straightened up and took off his hat—"if you'd tell me exactly what it is I'm supposed to apologize for."

She started down the road before she answered.

"Why, for causing that scene in the office the other day. What else? Or do you have other things on your conscience?"

"Julia, you know you're as much to blame as I am." He easily matched her stride. "Let's call a truce."

Julia looked at him sideways from behind the brim of her grey bonnet with a slight smile.

"I'm not accepting any responsibility for your temper," she said, "but I'm open to a truce."

"I've missed you these last few days, my lady. Discussing things with Daniel isn't half the fun that disputing them with you is."

"Well, I must say life has been a lot more restful."

"And boring?"

"There's no time to be bored."

"I've seen you looking over at the *Crystal Star.*"

"Just checking to see that Daniel hasn't done you any violence yet. He's capable of it, you know."

"So you do care about me."

"Well, I wouldn't want to see Daniel get into trouble."

"I thought we were going to have a truce."

"Now what did I say that could have upset you?" she asked innocently. Then seeing the frown gathering on his face, she decided to change the subject to one which she knew he enjoyed. "Tell me, have you heard anything more about this man, Emerson, you're always quoting?"

They resumed their walks and conversations, and as the weather grew colder, Stephen would occasionally call at the house to sit in front of the fire and entertain Lydia and Aunt Martha as well as Julia with his tales of Boston and Cambridge. Benjamin, not so easily charmed, would invite some of his retired sea captain cronies over to talk of their days of glory that grew with each telling. He seemed to tolerate Stephen's presence, but when Julia asked to resume supervision of the *Crystal Star,* he remained adamant in his refusal.

In early January, however, Benjamin came down with a cold. As it grew worse and he could no longer make it to the yard, it was necessary for Julia to go back to work on the *Crystal Star.* As always, the shorter days and the coming of the spring tide pressured everyone into working harder.

It was snowing, muffling the sounds of the men working within the hull, when Julia entered the captain's cabin of the *Crystal Star* one afternoon. She found Stephen, standing with his hands in his pockets, staring through a porthole.

"Getting the feel of it?" she asked mockingly.

"More or less." The flatness of his voice surprised her. He didn't turn to look at her.

"What's the matter? I thought you wanted this cabin more than anything in the world."

"I did."

"Little late to change your mind, isn't it?"

"I've not changed it." He turned then, but it was hard

to read his expression in the snow-wrapped cabin. "I'm just thinking about what this cabin really needs before I'll be happy with it."

"There's still time to modify it."

"I wonder."

"Well?"

"Julia." He left the porthole and came to her in the middle of the cabin. "What it needs is you."

"Well, I'm not part of the contract."

He looked at her levelly, his smoky-blue eyes too serious.

"Don't tell me that, when you got me command of this ship, you didn't intend to come along."

She backed away from him. "I did no such thing."

"Are you coming?" His voice was harsh in its demand.

"You certainly do have a strange way of going about things." She drew herself up very straight so that she could look directly into his eyes.

"You know you're sailing with me. I'm not leaving you here, my lady."

"Stephen!"

"And don't say, 'This is so sudden.' It's not and you know it's not." He took one step forward and grabbed her by the shoulders. "Don't you?"

"Stephen, stop it!" She tried to pull away from him, but he was too strong for her.

"Not until you say you'll marry me."

"No! All we do is argue. That's no basis for a marriage."

"Why not?" He smiled, but only with his lips. "It'll liven up a dull voyage. Besides, who will you argue with when I'm gone?"

Julia bit her lip and looked away from him at the polished bulkhead. She couldn't let him guess how often she had thought of the day when he would sail away and leave her standing on the shore alone. Always alone.

"All right, Julie." He didn't loosen his grip, but his eyes were softer now. "I'll say it the way you want me to say it. I love you. I want to marry you. I want you in my bed and on the quarterdeck beside me."

She could feel the strong surge of his desire in the hands that held her, could read it in the tensed muscles of his strong jaw. She lowered her eyes to avoid its impact.

357

"If you won't come," he continued, "I'll tell Captain Asa to find himself another master."

She was horrified. "You can't do that! It's . . . it's unthinkable."

"I can't live without you. That's even more unthinkable."

"Papa will never give his consent."

"You turned twenty-one last summer."

She shivered. She felt cold. So cold.

"I went against him once. I won't do it again."

"Yes, you will. No one's ever headed you in, and I doubt anyone ever will." He smiled and it was his gentle, lazy smile, though there was something different in his eyes. Something she had glimpsed once or twice before and which he had been careful to hide. "Though I warn you, I'll try."

"You're too opinionated and domineering and stubborn."

"So are you, my lady. That's why we understand each other. We'll get on well together."

"Or kill each other, one."

"Not when we love each other."

"I . . ." She couldn't say it. She couldn't say, "I don't love you," because it wasn't true. She did. She knew now that she loved him, wanted him, desired him.

In that love she felt a twinge of betrayal of Jason, a fear of rejection like David's. Yet she knew that this was right. Jason was gone. She had lived with his death for a very long time. Too long. Stephen was alive. Electrically, excitingly alive as no other man she had ever met had been. He lived life as though each moment were a new experience; he began each day as though the world had been created anew. To live with him, to see life through his eyes, would be a constantly stimulating adventure.

She knew that it was really she who had originally rejected David, and now she understood that what she had rejected had not been the man but the element of pity which she felt underlay his affection. With Stephen, whatever else his feelings for her, pity was not one of them.

Stephen watched the thoughts flicker through her sapphire eyes. "Go ahead and say it," he challenged.

Instead, she yielded to his arms, leaning her forehead

against his cheek. "You can speak to Papa," she said in a voice so low he could hardly hear it in the quiet cabin.

He closed his arms tight around her and brushed her cheek with his lips. "Tonight," he whispered.

"No. His cold's worse. Wait till he's better."

"I'll wait a week. One week! And I don't care if he's on his deathbed then. I'm going to speak to him."

"You won't find him easy," she warned.

He smiled and bent his head to kiss the hollow in her throat. "Nothing in life worth having is ever easy."

Stephen ran her father to ground on a Sunday afternoon a week later in the small office at the house. When he knocked and asked to come in, Benjamin knew what he had come for. Why did every young man who came along in pursuit of his daughters have to choose this room? He suspected his daughters put them up to it.

"Well, what is it?" he asked Stephen impatiently. "Something *else* wrong with the *Crystal Star?*"

"No, sir, it's not." Stephen closed the door firmly behind him. "I want to marry your daughter."

"They're all married," Benjamin said and turned back to the newspaper he had been reading.

"A widow is no longer married. I want to marry Julia."

Benjamin swiveled around in his chair and inspected Stephen as though he were a jury-rigged wreck.

Then he growled at him. "Why?"

"Why?" Stephen was dumbfounded. "Because I love her, of course."

"Love her or love the money you think she'll bring with her?" Benjamin's frown displayed his bristling eyebrows at their best.

"Captain Howard," Stephen said, his grey eyes turning to flint. "I love your daughter, and I intend to marry her. If you choose to disinherit her, as I hear you did once before, that's all right with me. I'll take care of her."

"Where'd you hear that?" Benjamin growled.

"It's common gossip."

"And you figure, if I disinherit her, I'll take her back like I did before?"

"Believe it or not, as you will, I'm not interested in your

359

money." Stephen steadfastly refused to retreat before the threat in Benjamin's eyes.

"No? I find that hard to believe. Here you are, a penniless young man, going into your first command, thanks to me, and you expect me to believe you don't care about money?"

"Captain Howard." Stephen folded his arms. "I don't give a damn what you believe. I want Julia. Go ahead and disinherit her. But I'm taking her . . . with or without your consent."

Benjamin leaned back in his chair and coldly surveyed the young man who stood before him.

"So you're putting me on notice. Is that it?"

"If that's the way you want it. I'd rather have your consent."

"I'll think on it," Benjamin said, turning back to his newspaper. "Now get the hell out of here."

"Not yet."

"What do you mean 'not yet'?" Benjamin thundered at him. "I told you to get out!"

At the sound of her father's raised voice, Julia, who had been standing just outside the room, opened the door and came in.

"And what do you want, miss?" her father asked.

"The same thing Stephen wants," she said calmly, standing tall in her pride.

"And how do you propose for me to run the shipyard while you go gadding off to sea?"

"You'll manage."

" 'How sharper than a serpent's tooth it is to have a thankless child.' "

"Shakespeare, *King Lear*, Act One. I believe Lear was crazy at the time."

"Don't get sarcastic with me, miss."

Julia stood silent and waited for him to continue. Benjamin, staring back at her, refused in this silent battle of wills. Their deep blue eyes, so much alike, were locked in stubborn combat.

Finally Benjamin brought his fist down on the desk with a mighty crash. "You went against me once, my fine lady, and look what it got you."

Julia lifted her chin even higher.

"It got me the love of a good man and more happiness than *you'll* ever know about."

"And more sorrow and regret."

"Papa! No matter who I wanted to marry, he wouldn't have been good enough in your eyes. I'd have died an old maid if you'd had your way."

"Never said Jason wasn't good enough. You were just too young."

"I was too young. Stephen's too poor. I'm sure that, if I'd encouraged Aaron, he would have been too stupid."

"And you would have been right."

"But he's good enough for Sarah. And Michael, with poorer immediate prospects than Stephen, is good enough for Amelia."

"Aaron will do for Sarah, and Michael will make his way, given time. He's of good stock. Known him since he was a boy."

"There's nothing wrong with my family," Stephen said.

"Didn't say there was, but they certainly didn't provide for you before they died. And look at your uncle. A skinflint. Didn't think enough of you to give you a ship."

"Papa." Julia's blue eyes were smoldering. "You promised me once that you'd never stand in my way again."

"That was when I thought you had a little sense. If you want to go to sea so bad you'll marry anyone, go with William. He wanted to take you along when he was here last summer. You don't have to marry *him* to get your way."

"He didn't tell me."

"No. I discouraged him. Didn't think you were in a mood to go to England."

Julia flung back her head. A few black curls fell down beside her face, and she pushed them away with an impatient hand.

"You really do delight in meddling in my life, don't you?"

"I'm your father."

"That's no excuse."

Benjamin studied his steepled fingertips in a pretense of indifference.

"Will sails again for Europe next month, I believe. Get your sea chest packed and go with him. He'll be glad to have you."

"If I'd known earlier, I probably would have, but now I'm going with Stephen."

"You still haven't got a grain of sense in that hard head of yours, have you? I'd think you'd have learned a mite of caution by now. You know nothing of Mr. Logan, and yet you're ready to rush into marriage on a whim."

"It's not a whim!" Julia moved closer to Stephen and took his hand. Together they were stronger than either one apart. "I know Stephen as well as I need to know him."

"Wait then. Wait till he proves himself. A successful voyage to Whampoa and back . . . that'll be proof of the pudding. If he don't make it, you've lost nothing. If he does, then he'll have his captain's share of the profit and be able to provide for you . . . which, as I read it, he can't now."

"I can provide for Julia," Stephen said as he held her hand tight within his warm one. "Captain Asa's been paying me full wages these past few months, and I've spent very little of it."

"You'll need every cent of it to buy cargo to fill the master's space in the hold. If you don't have your own goods to sell, you'll not be making the fortune you'll be needing to take care of a wife and family."

"I have money of my own, Papa," Julia said, her chin lifted defiantly. "We don't need yours."

"You're forcing me to say things I'd just as soon not mention." Benjamin studied his nails.

"Then don't!"

"You heard what Sarah said," he continued in a low voice.

"You know good and well Sarah doesn't like Stephen. She'd say anything."

"But Aaron didn't disagree." He looked up piercingly at Stephen. "You consider Aaron Martin to be a friend of yours?"

"I always have," Stephen said icily.

"Then you'll be interested to hear he told his wife that the only thing you want out of life is money, and that you'd go to any lengths to get it."

"That's a lie!"

"Not according to your friend Aaron."

"I want money, all right," Stephen said, his face stony

with anger. "I'll not make any secret of that. Only a fool doesn't want it, and I'm no fool. But I have *never* told anyone that I would go to any lengths to obtain it."

"Heard another story, too. Came from another source," Benjamin said calmly. "Seems there was a girl in Boston. Had a good bit of money. You remember that?"

"There are a lot of girls in Boston who have money."

"But this particular one. You asked her to marry you, and she was willing, but her father didn't like the cut of your jib. Bought you off, so I hear."

"Then you've heard wrong."

"The name Nancy Honeywell means nothing to you?"

"I know her and her family. She married a friend of mine."

"*After* her father paid you a few thousand dollars."

"I've heard the story, but this is the first time I've heard my name attached to it."

"Well, I'm offering you the same thing, Mr. Logan." Benjamin ignored Julia, who was seething, and looked pointedly at the angry young man beside her. "Five thousand dollars to go away and leave my daughter alone."

"Papa! How can you do such a thing? It's . . . it's absolutely unspeakable."

Stephen stiffened. Then he put his arm around Julia. "Come on, Julia. There's no reasoning with your father. I won't stand here and listen to insults."

"Five thousand dollars. Think it over, young man."

Julia, looking over her shoulder, blazed her father a look of pure venom and slammed the door behind them.

By unspoken consent, they put on their cloaks and went out into the frosty winter afternoon. Automatically their steps turned toward the shipyard.

When they were halfway there, Julia could contain herself no longer.

"I can't believe it! My own father. To insult you that way!"

"The insult was aimed at you, too. Five thousand dollars? That's an exceedingly low value to set on you."

"Low? That's a small fortune."

"I'd set the price a lot higher. Say . . . five million?" He grinned at her.

363

"Well, I needn't worry then. I don't know of anyone who has that much money."

"Nor I." He hunched his shoulders against the cold and pulled his cloak tighter around him. "But we will, my lady. Between the two of us, we'll amass a fortune that will make your father's head spin."

"I don't care that much about money."

"I do." There was a hard passion in his voice.

Julia looked at him curiously and wondered just how well she knew this man she had promised to marry.

"The only thing left to do," he continued after a few minutes, "is to lay our plans. You want to be married here or do you want to wait till we get to Boston?"

Julia took a deep breath of the cold air. In her anger, she hadn't really been thinking.

"I don't know. I'd rather be married here, but I want to see the *Crystal Star* finished and launched. I've put a lot of work into that ship, and if we marry now, Papa might ban me from the yard. It's only a couple of months. Let's wait and see what happens."

"I don't like to wait . . . for anything."

"I know," she sighed. "Nor do I."

The shipyard lay in Sunday quiet. Only the lonely wind and the gulls, shrieking at the edge of the half-frozen creek, broke the stillness. Inside the office the cold was bitter as the north wind fingered through the shingles. After Stephen had the fire started in the potbellied stove he held out his arms to Julia. She went to them and savored the comforting warmth and strength of his body.

"Have you thought about it?" Stephen stroked the fallen curls away from her face and tucked them beneath the hood of her cloak.

"That's all I've been doing . . . thinking. Best wait till the ship's in Boston."

"No! There's nothing to be gained by waiting. I want you now!"

"Where would we live meantime, Stephen?" Julia asked softly.

"Don't you own a house in Brewster?"

"It's not mine. Belongs to Cousin William."

"Couldn't we use it?"

364

"No!" She was horrified that he would suggest living in a house so rich with memories of Jason.

He smiled at her gently, glad that she didn't want to return to that house.

"We'll find something," he said, tracing her eyebrows' delicate arches with his fingers, soothing her, calming her.

"You can't afford to buy a house, Stephen, even if we could find one."

"I thought you said you had some money put by. Is it enough?"

"I don't know. It's tied up, anyway."

"You don't know? How much *have* you got, Julia?"

That angered her. Her father's words came back to her, and she tried to push him away.

"You're beginning to make me wonder if Papa wasn't right, Stephen! Just exactly what is it you want to marry me for?"

He tightened his arms around her resisting body, and kissing her deeply, he forced her lips apart against her will.

"You know damned well why I want to marry you," he murmured huskily against her cheek.

"Well, I'm surprised you don't take that five thousand dollars and go find yourself a Boston heiress." She refused to be placated, although his kiss had shaken her. "With that money and all your charm, I'm sure you can snare a likely one."

He smiled at her, amused. "Some inane little goose who can only embroider, paint on china, and flutter her eyelashes?"

"You can always get away from her by going to sea."

"That's not a joke, my lady," he said, suddenly sober. "Some men do, you know. They go to sea year after year, wear out their lives, die of Yellow Jack, get eaten by cannibals, all because they can't stay in the same house with the woman they married. That's not my way."

"What is your way?" she challenged him.

"My way," he said as he pushed back her hood and nibbled on her ears, "is to search the earth for the stubbornest, hottest-tempered, most maddening and most beautiful woman ever born and marry her before someone comes along and tries to take her away from me."

"You're impossible," she started to say, and then his lips

were on hers, and one hand had reached beneath her cloak to stroke the long, soft lines of her body. She clung to him then, letting the magic happen.

"We'll go talk to Reverend Lamson tomorrow," he whispered a few minutes later. "It's going to be impossible to wait until Boston."

Julia pushed back the tawny lock that had fallen across his forehead and felt the rich thickness of his hair between her fingers.

"What's Captain Asa going to say about your taking me to sea with you?"

"Why should he care? It's the master's privilege." Stephen brushed his lips across her cheek from her mouth to her ear. "Anyway, he's a good old man underneath that crusty shell. It's just an act he puts on so no one will guess how soft-hearted he really is."

Julia sighed. "I wish I could think of some way to bring Papa around. I'm getting tired of eloping."

"He seems pretty set."

"I don't know. I really don't. Like Captain Asa, it may be all an act."

"Five thousand dollars is no act."

Julia stiffened.

"You keep thinking about that money, don't you, Stephen?"

"Yes, I do. You'll have to admit, it was an extraordinary offer."

"Then why don't you take it?" She whirled out of his arms in sudden anger.

He let her go.

"For the same reason you're not going off with Captain Thacher."

"I think you're going to take it."

"Stop it!" He took her by the shoulders and shook her. "I am not going to take the money and that's final. You're going to marry me whether your father likes it or not. Whether you like it or not. Don't try to get rid of me by pushing me at that money, my lady. It won't work."

Julia, though shaken by the passion of his fury, spoke coolly.

"I hear you're a shrewd trader. You figure to get more by marrying me than by not marrying me?"

"You're the most infuriating woman I've ever met." His fingers were biting into her shoulders. "I'll never touch a penny that belongs to you. That I'll swear!"

She studied his face for a long moment. Behind his anger, she glimpsed a ruthless truth.

"I believe you, Stephen," she said quietly. Then a flicker of white on the night-blackened window beyond his shoulder caught her attention. "It's dark and it's starting to snow. I think we'd best go home."

A nor'wester had swept the sky clear during the night, and though it was cold, the crisp air had an intoxicating effect on her horse as well as it had on Julia. As she rode to the yard, eager to see Stephen, the boulders in the winter fields, the grey, chinked stone walls, the filigreed leaf-stripped trees on the high hills were cleanly etched in the crystal light. The gulls, moving inland in their search for food, soared over the marsh and fields. Their harsh cries were everywhere as they fought for chance morsels.

Julia hadn't left the house until mid-morning, allowing her father to be well on his way before she appeared downstairs. She had no desire to see him after the inexcusable way he had acted yesterday. In fact, her desire was *not* to see him. At the shipyard, amidst the bustle of work, she would be able to avoid him. But Stephen would be there!

As soon as she rounded the curve of the hill and could see the yard spread out below her, she scanned the decks and the ground around the *Crystal Star,* but she didn't see Stephen. He must be below somewhere, she thought.

She peeked into the office window as she passed by, and saw her father, favoring his lingering cough as he worked, ensconced beside the stove. Then she went across the yard to the ship. Stephen was sure to be aboard.

Checking the men and the progress of their work, she delayed the meeting with Stephen and savored the moment when she would come upon him in his concentration. However, an hour later, she had covered the entire ship, and there was no sign of him.

Finally, she began to question the men. No one had seen him since Saturday. With her brow furrowed in a frown, she climbed down the ladders and hurried across the yard to her horse. Perhaps he had fallen in the snow and freezing rain after he had left her last night. He might have broken some bones. Or could he have caught the grippe that was beginning to decimate the work force?

After she had clattered across Toct Bridge, she urged her horse to a trot. Something awful must have happened. Else he would have sent word.

From the look tall, rawboned Bertha gave her when she let her into the low-roofed cottage, Julia knew something really was wrong.

"Is Mr. Logan here?" Julia asked.

"You'd best see my father," Bertha answered, and the pity in her voice made Julia's heart plummet.

She found Captain Asa sitting in front of the fire in a shelf-lined room that was dominated by books and models of vessels.

"Captain Asa," she said as soon as Bertha had gone to make tea. "Where's Stephen?"

"Gone." The old man evaded her eyes by gazing into the low-burning fire.

"Gone?" Julia stared at him and sat down. "Gone where?"

"Caught the packet to Boston early this mornin'."

"But he couldn't have!"

"Did."

"Was it business? Did you send him?" Julia asked desperately trying to find a reassuring answer to Stephen's abrupt departure.

"Nope."

"When's he coming back?"

"Can't rightly say."

"Well, was it his family? Is someone ill? Why did he go?"

"Didn't ask him."

The wiry old man fidgeted in his chair, and it was evident he was trying to conceal something.

"Captain Asa!" If he wouldn't look her in the eye, at least he would get the full impact of her voice. "You know something about it. Else you'd be storming around here raising hell."

"It's none of my business."

"I think it is. You hired him to be master of the *Crystal Star*. Are you telling me he's not coming back?"

"Told you," he said with a determined look in his watery blue eyes. "None of my business."

"You looking for another master?" Julia watched him suspiciously.

"Nope. Not yet."

"What do you mean 'not yet'?"

"Just what I said."

"Captain Asa," Julia pleaded. She was on the point of tears now. "Did Stephen tell you we were talking about marriage?"

"Were you?" He lit up his pipe and puffed on it. "That's interestin'."

"Don't you think I have the right to know where he's gone and why?"

"Think he would've told you if he'd wanted you to know."

"He didn't leave a note for me? Anything?"

He considered a moment while he puffed on his pipe.

"Nope," he finally said.

"You've always been my friend, Captain Asa."

"Still am."

"Then why won't you tell me?"

"Don't believe in interferin' with other people's lives." He got up and went to the brass ship's clock that hung on the wall. "Just stir up a brew of trouble that way."

"You're already in trouble as far as I'm concerned," she glared at him while he hunted through a drawer for the key to wind the clock.

"Sorry to hear that, Julie. Now why don't you just go on back to the shipyard. You're bound to hear from him sooner or later."

Julia sat on for a moment, unable to move, but after observing Captain Asa's closed expression as he wound the clock, she knew she would get nothing more from him. And *nobody* ever got anything from tight-lipped Bertha.

"Very well, Captain Asa, but you'd better come up with an explanation pretty soon or else!"

"Else what?" Captain Asa looked suddenly interested.

"I'll think of something."

Chapter Nineteen

1842

JULIA BROODED OVER IT as she rode slowly back to the
yard, and the more she thought of it, the more she blamed
her father. His meddling had something to do with Stephen's departure. Of that, she was sure. Her anger at him
turned to a fine fury.

It was almost noon, the clean, sharp shadows disappear-
ing into themselves, when she stormed into the shipyard.
She saw her father coming out of the carpenters' shop, deep
in conversation with Daniel Sears.

She waited until he had neared the office and then she
called to him in a cold, tight voice.

"Papa! I want to talk to you."

He strolled casually across the yard to her.

"Little late gettin' to work, aren't you?"

"I want to talk to you in the office!" Her chin was set
and her eyes were flashing blue lightning. He could almost
see the sparks crackling in the air. She pointed to the
office door.

Benjamin shrugged and preceded her into the building.
She followed him and slammed the door so hard the windows shook.

"I've just been over to Captain Asa's house," she said.

Benjamin opened the grate to the stove and peered in.

"Wondered where your beau was this morning. He afraid to face me again?" he asked as he added a chunk of wood.

"No! Thanks to your meddling, he's gone."

"Gone?" Benjamin turned and looked at her in blank innocence.

"What do you know about it?" She narrowed her eyes at him.

"Me? Not a thing."

"Did you give him the money?"

"Nope. Haven't laid eyes on him since you two went slamming out of the house yesterday."

"You drove him off!" She strode up to him accusingly, her skirts whirling in anger. "Why do you persist in trying to ruin my life?"

"*I'm* not trying to ruin it. I'm trying to keep *you* from ruining it."

"Offering a man money to go away and leave me! What will you think of next?"

"I was only trying to make sure you knew your own minds. Looks like he didn't." He tested the coffee pot that stood on top of the stove. "Want some coffee?"

"No!"

She took off her cloak and threw it over a chair. Then she sat down on it and stared coldly at her father. He poured two mugs of coffee and handed one to her. For a moment, he thought she was going to throw it at him, but then she took a sip from it. He sat down in the chair opposite her.

"Why did you make up that story about a girl in Boston?"

"I didn't make it up. Captain Dodge told me. Even your young man said he'd heard it."

"Then why did you have to bring it up? If it ever did happen, it was in the past and you don't even know the circumstances of it."

"Nope, but I figured we'd better know what kind of man he is. If he'd do it once, maybe he'd do it again."

"You never gave him a chance."

"Yes, I did. Gave him the chance to fight for you. Any man worth his salt would have. Look at him. Turned tail and ran."

"Thanks to you."

"The only thing that perplexes me," Benjamin said as he sipped his coffee thoughtfully, "is that he didn't wait around for the money."

"You never intended to give him any money."

"Oh, I'd give it to him just to make sure he stays away." He shrugged. "Guess he'll be back or send for it. One thing sure is that he's not going to let it slip through his fingers."

Julia slumped in her chair and felt the first full impact of the pain that seared through her body.

"You don't have to give it to him. If he'd leave me for it, then I don't want him."

"I gave my word."

"You can't afford it."

"It'll mean selling off some things I'd rather not part with. Still, I said I'd pay it, and I'll pay it."

"It's not fair." Julia put her mug on the table. "Amelia hasn't even gotten her dowry yet."

"Amelia's not pushing me." Benjamin drew a pattern with his finger on the table. "I give her money from time to time to help out, and she's happy. She'll get a big chunk after we settle up at launching this year. Even earlier if some of the vessels I've got shares in make port with a good profit."

"Take the money for Stephen out of my shares in the *Jewel.*" She leaned her head back and closed her eyes, as though it would shut out the pain. "I don't need them. Not now."

"Nope. You keep what's yours, Julie. Don't go handing it out to anybody, not even to me. Invest it. Make it work. You may need it someday."

"I still can't believe it. Not Stephen!" she said as she got up and went to look out the window. The snow-patched yard was quiet now, the men at their noonday meal. She could see the *Crystal Star,* so nearly completed, on the large railway. She felt nothing but sorrow at the sight. "There has to be some other explanation. He wouldn't just go off and leave me like that. He wouldn't leave the ship."

Benjamin put the coffee cups back on their rack.

"It's time for dinner, Julie. You ready to go home?"

"No. I'm not hungry. I'll come along later."

When Benjamin had gone, Julia went once more to sit by the stove. She had to think this out, if only to stop the agonizing turmoil in her mind. He'd said he loved her. She *knew* he loved her. Else she would never have been able to care so much about *him*. Ever since he'd arrived, he had been after her. Or had it only been a game to him? A game into which he'd suddenly found he had gone too deep? Yet just last night, he'd said that today they would go and see Reverend Lamson together.

The money? She couldn't believe that he would take it. Yet why had he left so suddenly with no word to her? Had he gone to Boston to see if he could do better? Find another girl with more money to offer in marriage? Then he could come back and take her father's bribe and have a wealthy wife to boot.

The only thing Captain Asa had told her was that she was bound to hear from Stephen sooner or later. There was hope in that. Or was there? If it was going to end, she wanted it to end now. She couldn't bear the thought of ever seeing him again.

Still the thought of not ever seeing him again was even worse.

She buried her face in her hands, trying to stop all thoughts. She didn't notice the tears that were trickling between her fingers nor did she hear the door quietly open.

The first thing she was aware of was a gentle touch on her shoulder.

"Miss Julia."

She looked up to see Daniel standing beside her, his trousers brushed with snow and his bulky jacket damp with it.

"Is there anything I can do to help?"

She didn't know how it happened, but suddenly she had jumped up and was in his arms, sobbing her sorrow against his moist shoulder.

He held her stiffly at first and then more tenderly while he murmured all the comforting words his mother must have used with him when he was a boy.

"There, there, Miss Julia. It'll be all right. Everything'll be all right. You'll see. I'll fix it for you. Whatever it is,

I'll fix it for you." He awkwardly patted her on the back while he spoke.

The soothing repetition of his words and the gentleness of his wiry arms soon worked their spell and her sobs tapered off to soft hiccups. When he gave her his handkerchief, she looked at him through a glaze of tears.

"Oh, Daniel, what must you think of me?"

"I'm only glad I was here, Miss Julie," he said, his brown eyes peaked in deep concern. "What can I do?"

"I don't think there's much anyone can do," she sniffed.

"Is it Captain Logan?"

"Yes. He's gone away."

"I might have known." He pressed his lips together.

"Why? Why would you say that, Daniel?"

"Don't know. I just didn't like the way he looked at you, the way he was always at you."

"Is there anything else . . ." She wiped her eyes against the soft cloth. "Anything I should know?"

"No. Nothing."

"Papa offered him money to go away and leave me alone."

Daniel shook his head. "Captain Howard's a good man, but he oughtn't to have done that."

"But Stephen didn't take it. Not yet, anyway. He just left."

"Maybe he had a good reason. Something besides money."

"But why didn't he tell me?"

"Maybe he didn't have time."

"Captain Asa knows something. I'm sure he does. But he won't tell me."

"Wonder why?" Daniel said pensively. "He's a cantankerous old man, but he's not what you'd call harmful. Wonder if he'd tell me?"

"Do you think he would, Daniel?" Julia brightened at the idea.

"I'll try." He scratched his head as he thought. "I'll take a jug of rum over to his house this evening. Pretend I've come to talk about the ship. If I don't press him, maybe he'll tell me somethin' about what's going on."

"Do you think it'll work?"

"Don't know. Never gone calling on him before, but anything's worth tryin' if it makes you feel better."

"Oh, thank you, Daniel." She kissed him lightly on the cheek, not seeing the adoration in his brown eyes. "You're the best friend I've ever had."

"I'll always be your friend, Miss Julia," he said earnestly, "no matter what happens. You'll remember that, won't you?"

"Yes." Her words were soft. "I'll remember, Daniel."

That night there was no sleep for Julia, and the room was too cold to pace in. She lay huddled miserably under the covers and watched the red coals of the dying fire. Slowly the night passed into the first light of a new day.

In the morning, she went to the shipyard only long enough to see Daniel. He climbed down from the schooner as soon as he saw her ride in and came limping agilely across the snow and ice-ridged yard.

Julia dismounted but waited for him to come to her with the reins held loosely in her hand.

"Did you find out anything?" she asked expectantly when he arrived.

"No. I'm sorry, Miss Julia," he said in a dejected voice. "Think he knew what I'd come for, but he went into one of his acts. Kept pretending he thought I'd come to court Bertha."

Even though the news was not good, Julia had to laugh at the mixture of disgust and chagrin on Daniel's swarthy face. Then she asked him soberly. "Did he mention Captain Logan at all?"

"Not till I asked. The jug was half gone by then, and I thought he might let something drop."

"But he didn't."

"No. Only that he'd gone off to Boston. After that, he clamped his mouth shut and sat there lookin' ornery."

"Well, it was worth a try," she said glumly.

"Want me to hitch up your horse?" he asked as he reached for the reins.

"No. I'm not going to stay today. I'm quite . . . tired."

As Daniel helped her mount, she asked, "What are the men saying?"

"Nothing. Told them Captain Logan went down to Boston on business for Captain Asa. I think, though . . ." He looked down at the ground, embarrassed.

"Yes, Daniel?"

"Be best if you come back to work tomorrow," he blurted out. "If Captain Logan don't come back, it'll keep them from talkin'."

"Yes." She pulled the hood of her cloak around her face. "You're right, Daniel. Work's the best thing for whatever ails you."

"That's right, Miss Julia."

Time passed slowly as Julia went to the shipyard with her father each day and spent the empty evenings in the parlor with her mother and Aunt Martha. She tried to act the part of herself, but found it difficult to concentrate on her work. The world around her seemed to be nothing but a grey haze. Her sleep was the sleep of exhaustion made restless by bad dreams. Yet when morning came, she found it difficult to get up and begin another pointless day.

Five days after Stephen had disappeared, Julia was picking at her dinner under Lydia's anxious eyes when there was a knock at the front door. Julia hardly noticed when Janet went to answer it, so lost was she in her misery. Then a note in the voice she heard distantly through the closed dining room door caught all her attention. She was sure it was Stephen!

She stared tensely at Janet when the maid returned to the room.

"It's Captain Logan here to see you, Captain Howard. I put him in the parlor."

"That's fine, Janet," Benjamin said. He laid his fork on his plate and looked searchingly at Julia. "You want to see him?"

"No. You see him first, Papa. He asked for you."

"You leaving it in my hands? Is that it?"

"No! Yes!" She twisted her napkin between her fingers, torn between the desire to talk to Stephen and the dread of what he would say. "Find out what he wants. Then come tell me."

"I'll do that." Benjamin left the table and went through the door that connected the dining room and parlor. Before the door closed, Julia caught a glimpse of Stephen standing in front of the fire. Their eyes met for a fraction of a second, but she could read nothing in that fleeting glance.

She wanted to get up and go listen at the door, but she sat still, immobilized by the fear that a financial transaction was taking place.

"Well, sir, what do you have to say for yourself?" Benjamin asked brusquely after he had closed the door behind him.

"I have a letter for you, Captain Howard." Stephen's face showed no trace of emotion as he handed the envelope to Benjamin.

"I'm not interested in a letter. I want an explanation." His bushy brows lowered in anger over his eyes.

"The letter contains the explanation," Stephen said firmly.

"Very well." Benjamin broke the seal on the envelope and pulled out the pages written in a precise, masculine hand.

He glanced once more at Stephen before he read the letter.

DEAR CAPTAIN HOWARD,

I am disturbed that a certain story has reached your ears at all, and more than disturbed that you name my young friend, Stephen Logan, as the villain of the tale. Please be assured that it was not my friend, but a blackguard from Virginia named Stephen Langley who was at fault. I can understand your confusion, since the two names are similar, but believe me, sir, the two men are not.

I have known Mr. Logan since he was a boy, and indeed, was a good friend of his father before him. I cannot think of a finer young man than Mr. Logan, and I assure you, I would have been most happy if he had paid court to my daughter, as I believe you should be.

I trust this will clear up the misunderstanding and I beg you not to broadcast this tale, since it might mistakenly cast aspersions on my daughter, who is a lovely young woman. As a father, yourself, I am sure you understand my feelings in this matter.

> I REMAIN YOUR
> OBDT SVT
> NOAH HONEYWELL

"So this is why you disappeared so suddenly?" Benjamin said after he had read the letter twice over.

"Yes, sir."

Benjamin whacked the folded pages against the palm of his hand. "Looks like I owe you an apology."

"Yes, sir, I believe you do."

"Then will you accept my apologies, Captain Logan?"

"I will," Stephen said, accepting the hand that Benjamin offered. "I want you to know, however, that I still intend to marry your daughter."

"Still putting me on notice, that's what you're doing."

"Yes, sir."

"Well, you have my permission," Benjamin growled, but there was no menace in it. "My blessings as well, for all the good they'll do you. The rest is up to Julia. I'll warn you, though, she's a handful. You sure you're man enough to handle her?"

Stephen's face, which had remained rigid throughout the conversation, broke into a grin. "I'm sure I am, sir."

"I'll go get her for you, then."

Returning to the table, Benjamin silently handed the letter to Julia. She sat very still while she read it. Then she put her face in her hands as waves of relief washed over her.

"He's waiting for you, Julia," Benjamin said gently. "I've just given him my blessing. Told him it was up to you, though."

"Thank you, Papa," she said very quietly. Then she rose from the table and went into the parlor.

When she entered, he was standing waiting for her, his eyes riveted to the door.

"Stephen?"

And then she was in his arms. The anguish of the past few days disappeared and there was only joy in his nearness.

"Why didn't you tell me you were going?" she asked a few minutes later.

"It was too early in the morning when I left."

"Have you forgotten how to write? You could have left me a note," she chided him. Then when she saw the withdrawal in his eyes, she clung to him. "Oh, Stephen, I was so worried. I went to Captain Asa, but he wouldn't tell me anything."

"I didn't sleep that night, Julia," he said quietly. "I had the feeling that you doubted me, too. That you would never be sure of me until I disproved that lie."

"Oh, Stephen, no." She was aghast and yet she knew he spoke the truth.

"When I went, it was on the spur of the moment. I caught the packet just as they were casting off her lines. There was no time for an explanation." He traced her features lightly with his fingertips as though he had forgotten them in such a short time. "I couldn't let another day go by with your suspicions between us and your father building them higher every time he spoke of me. Julia, I don't want any walls between us."

He examined her face for the answer as he asked, "Didn't you know that I would come back to you? Did you doubt me on that, too?"

"I . . . I didn't know what to think. We were going to see Reverend Lamson and then suddenly you just disappeared. What was I supposed to think?"

"That you should trust me."

The coolness of his voice chilled her. She pulled away from him and went closer to the fire.

"We haven't known each other very long, Stephen." She rubbed her hands and looked into the flames.

"Over seven months," his voice came from behind her.

"But how well? We saw each other, worked on the same ship, but that isn't knowing." She turned to face him. "Don't you see?"

"The only thing I see is that you promised to marry me," he said implacably. "Are you doubting the wisdom of that, too?"

"No, of course not. But Stephen, what if I had been the one who suddenly disappeared, leaving no word, no explanation? What would you have thought?"

"I would have followed you."

"You're a man. You can do that. I can't. I'd be laughed off the Cape."

"You've said you didn't care what people thought."

"I don't because I know that what I do is right. But that wouldn't be right." She tried to read his thoughts in the slate-grey eyes that looked at her without emotion. "Would you really have wanted me to follow you, Stephen?"

He thought about it a moment. Then he said reluctantly, "No. I guess not."

"And if I had, wouldn't that have proved doubly that I doubted you?"

"Perhaps."

"Yet you would have followed me."

"Not out of doubt."

"Stephen." There were tears in her eyes when she went to him and took his hand. "These past few days have been terrible for me. I thought that you might be angry with me, angry with my father. Maybe you'd decided your life would be better without me and my family. I've hardly slept since you left. Please don't be upset with me now. I just can't bear any more."

His eyes softened into a blue-grey haze as he stroked her hair, then pulled her with him to the brocade sofa. "I'm not upset with you, pretty Julia, but you must never doubt me again."

"I won't. I promise."

"Other men will speak against me someday."

"I won't believe them. Never . . ."

He stopped her words with a gentle, undemanding kiss. Then he pulled her head onto his shoulder and held her in silence for a few moments.

"I've been thinking about our wedding, Julia. Not an elopement. Not a rush to the preacher. I want it done properly, like Sarah and Aaron's."

"That took months of planning and work," she said doubtfully. "Besides, I'm a widow."

He put his hand over her lips.

"Never use that word again. You're my betrothed, my beloved. You'll soon be my wife."

"Nevertheless . . ."

"We have a few weeks left before the launching. If we were to be wed the week before, there'd be ample time to plan something suitable, wouldn't there?"

"Whatever you want, Stephen."

She reached up to push the stray lock of tawny hair back from his forehead, and then his lips were on hers again. Any differences they might have had fell away, leaving them only closeness.

The days before their wedding and the launching went swiftly by, and the great ship came closer to perfection. Working from sunup to first night, Stephen and Julia were usually too tired to see much of each other except at the shipyard and on Sundays. But working together had its compensations.

Julia climbed down the rickety scaffolding ladders one day to find Stephen standing on the hill a little distance from the *Crystal Star*. He had forgotten his cap and the winter sun gleamed on his hair. Even from this distance, she could see the joy in his face as he surveyed his ship. He seemed oblivious of the men working around him, carrying timbers, pots of tar, hanks of oakum, and tools.

"I've seen masters admire their new ships before," she called out as she approached him, "but I don't believe I've ever seen one with quite that expression."

He smiled when he saw her and radiance was added to the joy on his face.

"Isn't she beautiful?" he said. He held out one arm to her and she went to its shelter.

"I think so."

Together they stood and admired the *Crystal Star* from her glittering copper bottom to her clean, bleached decks. Her elongated hull with its wedge-shaped bow gleamed with fresh black paint, the white waist standing out in sharp contrast.

"Well, Captain Logan, you think she'll float?"

"She'll float," he grinned. "Around the world and back again, my lady, with all the treasures of the earth filling her holds."

"She'd better or it'll be your fault," she teased him.

"How many times have you checked every knee and fastening? Three times or four?"

"Oh, no." He gave her a squeeze. "You won't get off that lightly. After all, you're the one who built her. How's the saloon coming? Did you have the carpenters put in those extra shelves?"

"There's not an inch of space left. That ship's going to be a floating library. I thought we were going to sea to trade, not to read." She pushed back the black curls the north wind had loosened.

"Those are big oceans out there, my lady. You'll be thankful for the books. Did you have them put your special plank aboard?"

"What plank?"

"The one we're going to have our prisoners walk when you feed your pet sharks, of course."

She laughed. "Of course. I'd forgotten all about that. It's the one I'm supposed to use when I'm wearing satins and laces and sapphires and diamonds?"

"That's the one."

"No. It'll have to wait till we turn pirate. Too bad we can't steal the *Crystal Star*, but here Captain Asa went and gave you command. Spoiled everything. Now we'll never get a chance to be pirates."

"Well, if I don't make the price of that ship on our first voyage, we may have to do just that. Captain Asa'd hang me from the yardarm if I came home without it."

"Legally, Stephen. He said you had to get it legally."

"That's right. The old codger goes around spoiling everyone's fun. Now I'll have to get you your silks and satins and jewels honestly." He shook his head ruefully. "It's just going to take a little longer."

"I can wait."

"But that does bring up something I've been waiting to talk to you about," he said more seriously.

"What?"

"Your clothes. You need a whole new wardrobe. I want to clothe you in every bright and shining color of the rainbow. Throw out all those dark grey and drab browns you've been wearing. They look terrible on you."

She glanced at him, then out at the sparkling blue waters

of the creek. He hated any reminder that she had been married before and that he was not the first. Still, she couldn't wear gay colors before they were wed. Her wedding dress was going to cause enough scandal, as it was.

"All right, Stephen, but we'll have to wait till we get to Boston. I just won't have the time for fittings and all that fuss before the launching."

"But your wedding dress. You promised it would be blue satin. A bright, rich blue as radiant as your eyes."

"Yes," she smiled at him. "Blue but it can't be too gaudy."

"I didn't say gaudy. I said radiant. I want this wedding to be perfect."

"It will be, Stephen. Mama and Aunt Martha are working hard on it. But it has to be simple. There's not much time."

"No. I wish there were. I hate the thought of Sarah and Aaron lording it over us."

"What difference does that make?"

"A lot. I've got the most beautiful ship and the most beautiful girl in the world, and I want everyone to know it."

Julia laughed at his exuberance. She often wondered which he loved best. The *Crystal Star* or her? But it didn't matter. They weren't in competition.

The simple wedding was not as small and quiet as they had planned. When Julia, dressed in her blue satin dress, arrived with her parents, they found a crowd milling around the lawn in front of the graceful, white-spired church. She had hoped that some of the men from the yard would come, but she hadn't realized what would happen when they brought their wives and families. In addition to them, it seemed as though half the village had turned out to stand in the cold, frosty air.

Captain Asa was waiting for them in the street in front of the church. He had commandeered five of the huskiest men from the yard to help clear a path for the wedding party. Now as Benjamin helped Julia from the carriage, Captain Asa laid about him, flailing his arms and shouting, "Lay back there. Avast ye lubbers, give way."

Julia laughed. "Captain Asa, you're supposed to be in the church with Stephen."

"He's there, right enough, waiting for you, but he sent me out here to make sure you got to the altar. Said he wasn't taking any chances you'd run away."

She smiled. Stephen had asked Captain Asa to be his best man, a fact which Aaron Martin resented. Yet their friendship would never be the same. Not after Aaron had allowed Sarah to say detrimental things about him to Benjamin. In fact, Stephen had told Julia, he'd decided he really liked the crusty old captain a lot better than he liked Aaron. Julia had to agree with him on that score.

Furthermore, the old man had given Stephen and Julia five hundred dollars as a wedding gift, an act that so startled his widowed daughter she spent one entire day throwing pots and pans and kettles around the kitchen according to the neighborhood gossip.

Now as they advanced up the path to the church, Julia laughed at the old man's proprietary air of command, and she waved to the friends who were calling out, "We've come to see you launched proper" and "Fair winds afore ye."

She was glad of the commotion and the launching day air of festivity. It distracted her from the memories that kept flickering through her mind. She kept seeing that old, quiet church in Boston with only William, Jason, and a shipmate at her side. She was glad William had put to sea and couldn't be here today. It would have been more than she could bear.

To reassure herself, she looked up at her father. He pressed her arm tighter to his side and answered her with a grin. He was obviously enjoying himself.

"Prettiest daughter I've towed to the altar yet," he said in a low voice.

Once inside the church, it was quieter. While she and her father waited for Asa to escort Lydia up the aisle, she could see through the inner doors. Sunlight was streaming through the many tall windows, lighting up the altar banked with greens and a few early crocus. Stephen, standing before the altar with Reverend Lamson, was looking down the aisle at her.

Julia tightened her grip on her father's arm. The man

with the light-struck, sun-bleached hair was a stranger. He was no part of her. Her life did not belong to him. Reverend Lamson, with his black book open, was ready to pronounce those words that would bind them together.

Until death do us part, she thought. She shivered. Was it the future or the past that haunted her? she wondered.

"Julia?" her father whispered.

"Yes?"

"It's time to go. They're waiting."

She nodded and, staring straight ahead with her head held high, she walked beside him down the aisle.

When she joined Stephen at the altar, he gave her a quick, nervous smile. She tried to respond. She didn't realize how white her usually flushed cheeks were or how large her deep blue eyes looked between their black lashes.

When Reverend Lamson cleared his throat and began to speak, they turned together to face the altar.

Yet when he came to the words, "Will you, Julia, take this man to be your lawful wedded husband?," she knew this marriage was right, and all thought of Jason disappeared. He was banished from her life.

She looked at Stephen, dear Stephen, with his clear forehead and his square chin, his air of gaiety that could turn into the deepest seriousness, his love of the sea and of ships, his love for her.

"I will," she answered with a firm clarity.

With every vow she repeated aloud, she made another spoken only to herself. These vows would never be broken. Not even in her thoughts.

Stephen's voice, when he spoke, rang through the church. There was no one who didn't hear him, and Julia knew that he brought to the words the same dedication she felt, solemn and deep.

When he bent to kiss her, he was strangely protective and gentle. His hard lips were soft on hers. His smoke-grey eyes promised quiet strength.

"You're mine now, Julie," he whispered.

She wanted to go into his arms, to have him hold her, but the first notes of the organ rang out and Stephen swept her down the aisle. He smiled at her and his face, struck by shafts of sunlight, was as radiant as hers.

After they had signed the register, it was almost impossible to leave the church. The crowd was greater than ever, enlarged by the people who had been inside when they'd arrived. They found it simpler to stand on the church steps and let the people come to them.

One after another, the men from the shipyard, their wives and children, her schoolmates, old cronies of her father's, lone women separated in one form or another from their husbands by the sea, pressed forward to congratulate Stephen and shake hands with Julia. They grinned as they called her "Mrs. Logan." Tomorrow, she knew she would once again simply be "Miss Julia."

When they were finally able to reach the ground, Amelia came up to them. With her Michael beside her, she was even more glowing than she had been on her own wedding day. She hugged her sister and said, "Oh, Julie, I hope you'll be as happy as we are."

"I hope so, too, 'Melia," Julia said, returning Amelia's hug with warmth.

Sarah, who had been coolly waiting her turn, kissed Julia on the cheek.

"You have quite a variety of names now," she said. "Julia Howard Thacher Logan. Wonder how many you'll collect before the end?"

Stephen, standing beside Julia, overheard her quiet words. He gave his new sister-in-law a look of sharp, cold steel. "Julia's name is Logan, dear sister Sarah, and there will never be another."

"Don't count on it, Stephen." Sarah's laughter was delicately lilting but filled with mockery.

Benjamin glared at his middle daughter and moved toward her, but she saw him coming. She neatly evaded him and took Aaron's arm.

"Don't bother, Papa," she said with a defiant toss of her head. "I won't stay around to ruin your pet's second wedding, and don't bother looking for us at the house. We've better things to do, don't we, Aaron?"

Aaron looked apologetically at Benjamin and Stephen. The look he gave Julia was filled with misery. Sarah saw it and quickly steered him away from the family group over to the road where their new carriage stood waiting for them.

The rest of the family gathered close around Julia, as

though to shield her, but over Michael's tall shoulder, she saw Sarah's flourishing departure.

"Don't pay her any mind, Julie," Lydia said quietly. "She's just having a bit of trouble adjusting to married life."

When Julia and Amelia looked at her strangely, she added nervously, "Some women do."

The two sisters glanced at each other, then quickly away, trying to repress their bubbling laughter. The same thought was in both their minds. "*Adjust* to living with the man you loved?"

"Come along now. No dallying. Martha'll never forgive me if you're late and the food's all cold," Captain Asa called from the road.

He was waiting for them with his open carriage, which he had insisted on driving, despite everyone's nervous pleas to let someone else do it. The captain was famous for his erratic driving, and most people got off the road when they saw him coming.

However, he had stubbornly dug in his heels and said *he* and no one else was going to drive the bridal pair and be damned to anyone who interfered. Finally, after much negotiation, a compromise had been reached. He had agreed to let Daniel Sears ride up front beside him and act as footman. Daniel had quiet instructions to take the reins away from the old man if necessary.

Stephen helped Julia into the carriage and winked at Daniel. "Don't mean to take your job away from you, but today, she's mine."

Daniel smiled back, but when he looked at Julia, there was a question in his brown eyes. Then Captain Asa had clucked up the horses and Daniel quickly turned, alert for the moment he would have to take over the reins.

However, Captain Asa fooled them and soon had the horses going in a smooth and steady trot. As they swung down South Street past the edge of the ice-streaked gold of the marsh, Stephen put one arm around Julia.

"Think she'll float, my lady?" he asked.

Julia knew he was speaking of their marriage.

"I know she will," she answered, her eyes sparkling with joy.

"The wind's ruining your hairdo."

"It always does." She lifted a hand to push the black tendrils away from her face.

"Don't." He took her hand. "I like it that way. Makes you look more like my wild and wicked Julia."

"I'm not . . ." she started to say, but in one swift movement he had pulled her closer and his lips were on hers. He had never kissed her with such passionate depth before. There was an urgency to it that made her tremble. It had been so long.

"I wish we didn't have to stay with your family," he whispered. "I wish we could go straight to a place of our own."

"I wish so, too"—she smiled—"but launching's not far off. Only a week away."

"Too long," he said huskily.

"Didn't think I could do it, did you?" Captain Asa cackled, looking back over his shoulder at Julia and Stephen. Lost in their own world, neither of them had realized that they had arrived and that the carriage was stopped in the oystershell driveway.

"I never had a doubt in my mind, Captain Asa," Julia said, her blue eyes wide with innocence.

"Well, I did," Aunt Martha said from beside the carriage. She had left the church with the two maids right after the ceremony so that all would be ready for the wedding breakfast. "I've seen you careening along with never a thought to the poor innocent souls who might be in your way."

"Never killed one yet, Martha," he said dryly with a twinkle in his eye. "When you goin' to come keep house for me?"

"Never." She put her hands on her ample hips and looked him over. "Don't think I'd have any more luck keeping you in line than that poor daughter of yours does."

"You wouldn't. I can promise you that. But you might be a heap more comfort on a long winter night."

Martha snorted. "Get down from there, you old bag of bones, and come in and warm yourself on some of my rum punch."

"That I'll do," he said, throwing the reins to Daniel and jumping to the ground with a spryness that belied his age.

Julia was pealing with laughter when Stephen lifted her down from the carriage. He held her for a moment.

"Stay like that always," he said.

After the wedding breakfast, which despite the smallness of the party, had had the usual excess of toasts, Julia turned to Stephen. "Let's ride down to the beach and get a little fresh air," she suggested.

"Going to tell her you're married? Introduce her to your new husband?" Benjamin had had far too many glasses of champagne.

"Papa!" Julia glared at him.

"*Who* are we going to visit?" Stephen asked.

"The sea, who else?" Benjamin slurred. "Julie always tells her everything."

"Papa please! Don't start on that now."

"All right, all right. Least you don't have to worry, lad." Benjamin leaned confidingly across the table toward Stephen. "Julie'll never reveal your secrets to anyone else, and the sea tells no tales."

Julia, to get away from this, threw down her napkin and left the table. She ran upstairs to change her clothes.

When she entered her room, she knew there was something wrong. Something different. It wasn't just Stephen's sea chest that now stood beneath a north window. Something else.

When she looked above her bureau, she knew what it was. Her portrait was missing. Yet it had been there when she'd dressed this morning. In its place hung the painting of a ship that had been in her father's study.

She whirled around to look above the mantelpiece. Her own painted eyes were smiling down at her. Jason's portrait and the broken shell were both gone. They might never have existed.

She started to rush from the room, then stopped when she reached the door. How could she go down and ask about them? How could she demand their return when Stephen was sitting there, waiting for her?

Then she understood. Someone with more forethought than she had removed them before Stephen might enter the room and find them there.

She shivered when she thought of Jason's presence, even in a painted picture, on her wedding night with Stephen.

It would have been terrible. And Stephen. He wouldn't have appreciated those ever-watchful green eyes when he brought her to bed.

Still, the place where it had hung was like an empty ache. She changed quickly from her new blue satin wedding dress into a rougher one that the wind and sand could not destroy and quickly left the room.

At the foot of the stairs, Aunt Martha stood waiting for her alone. Julia stopped on the bottom step and looked searchingly at the white-haired, clear-eyed older woman.

"It's in your father's study, Julie," Martha said quietly.

"And the shell?"

"Wrapped in an old linen nightgown in the bottom drawer of your dresser."

"Thank you, Aunt Martha." Julia hugged the large, big-bosomed woman.

"It had to be done. No point making a fuss about it." Martha hugged her back, then quickly released her. "You got a fine man, Julie, and don't you ever let them think otherwise. You got a good life ahead of you if you don't look back."

"I won't." She gave Martha a light kiss. "I'll try not to."

Julia walked lightly down the hall to the dining room. "Are you ready, Stephen?"

"More than ready," he said as he rose from the table.

The bar lay bare, its rippled sand exposed to the thin, late-winter sunlight. The few gulls walking on it flapped their wings from time to time as though in an effort to keep warm.

Julia and Stephen rode down the soft sand between the dunes toward the edge of water where pebbles shone like jewels amongst the jade-green seaweed. Even here, protected by the bar from the force of the waves, the north wind blew a mist of salt spray on them.

They wheeled their horses to the right and rode over the cold, wet sand. Gleaming thin but clear, ahead of them lay the white protecting arm of land. Provincetown and Truro and the quiet depths of rocks and wrecked ships.

Beyond the land lay the North Atlantic and from it came the high-soaring, white-crested ships returning to their homeland, crossing the wakes of their outward-bound mirrored images.

They rode in silence. There was no need for speech. Hearing the roaring beat of the waves, each thought of the *Crystal Star* riding those waves, her sails full and pulling. Pulling them on to new worlds, new lives.

When they reached the spill of boulders that marked the end of the beach, Stephen came to a halt. After watching the far-flung ships for a moment, he fished his watch out from under his cloak.

"It's raw out here, and the day's wearing on. Let's go to the yard and take a look at the *Crystal Star*."

Julia gave him a wicked smile and said, "I don't know who you care most about. Your ship or me."

He grinned back at her. "I could no more make that choice than you could if I asked which you preferred, the sea or me. It's all one, isn't it?"

She looked at him and suddenly knew that she had, for a long time, been picturing him as master on the quarter-deck of a powerful ship, able and sure of all he commanded. How much did that have to do with the love she bore him?

And how did he picture her? Were their images the persons they really were or were they projections of their desires? She shivered. Those were no thoughts for a wedding day.

"You're right," she said. "It is cold. Let's go see the ship. At least, we'll be sheltered from the wind there."

Chapter Twenty

1842

When they reached the deserted shipyard, Stephen reached up and swung Julia down from the saddle. He held her closely as they surveyed the great ship, whose black paint and copper bottom gleamed in the afternoon sun.

"She is beautiful, isn't she?" Julia said as she looked with pride at the vessel she had helped design, had helped to build, and which now was complete save for a few small finishing touches.

"Yes, but not so beautiful as she'll be under sail," he said, leading her toward the scaffolding.

She laughed. "You sound impatient."

"I am, my lady." He pulled her to the foot of a ladder. "Impatient to be gone, impatient to have you to myself and not have to share you with others. Let's go aboard."

"We should go back to the house. They'll wonder where we are."

"No. This is *our* day. We can do as we please." Then seeing her brows beginning to draw together in a frown, he relented. "While you were changing, I told your father we would be coming here."

Once on board, Stephen, with his arm around her, guided

her aft to the companionway, which led to the officers' cabins below the quarterdeck. Barely able to squeeze down the narrow passageway together, and yet unwilling to be parted even by a few inches, they came to the saloon.

"Welcome home, my lady," Stephen said as he flung open the door with a courtly bow. Then before she could enter, he picked her up and carried her into the room. When he put her down on the settee, she looked around in astonishment. Everywhere there were vases of bayberry filling the saloon with their pungent fragrance.

"Oh, Stephen," she smiled. "How lovely."

He tried to keep his face impassive, but it was impossible to hide the delight in his eyes. "I picked them for you this morning not long after the sun was up."

"Then you wakened early, too?" She took a piece of bayberry from the small vase on the table in front of her and drew it lovingly through her fingers.

"I hardly slept last night," he admitted.

"Not tempted to run away again, were you?" she asked with a gamin smile.

"Oh, no, my lady. From now on, where I go, you go, too."

Julia pushed back the hood of her cloak, then realized how warm the saloon was. She was alarmed when she saw the small cabin stove glowing. A fire could so easily have swept through the unattended ship, destroying her.

Stephen followed her glance and read the thoughts so clear on her face. "Don't worry," he said. "I wouldn't endanger our future. I bribed the watchman to come and light it. He was here until just a few minutes ago."

"So that's why you looked at your watch. You had it all planned."

"I have everything planned, pretty Julie," he said, tossing his hat through the open door of the captain's cabin. It landed on the bed. "There's even some of your favorite sherry aboard."

"I think I've had enough to drink," she protested as he went to the carved walnut liquor locker.

"It's bad luck not to toast each other alone on your wedding day," he said, bringing out a flat-bottomed crystal decanter.

"That's one I never heard before." She sniffed the bay-berry in her hand.

"It's an old Ombedian custom," Stephen said as he flourished the decanter in the air. "If you don't drink the good spirits, bad ones will come to haunt your marriage. You wouldn't want that, would you?"

"Ombedia?" She looked at him suspiciously. "Where's that?"

"In my head, my lady," he said, putting two tumblers on the table beside the decanter and smiling at her in a way that made him look years younger, "where so many good things are."

"With all the countries of the world to choose from," she said, laughing, "I wouldn't think you'd have to invent new ones."

"Ah, but sometimes those are the most exciting ones." He poured the sherry into the glasses and then looked up at her. "I'll take you to them, the new, the unexplored, where we can make our own rules. This"—his gesture included the entire saloon—"is Ombedia."

He handed her a glass and raised the other in a salute. "To the king and queen of Ombedia," he said. "Long may they rule."

Julia smiled as she raised the glass to her lips. "To the king and queen, the princess and the pirate."

"To my queen"—he sat down next to her—"greater than any queen who ever ruled a country, whether invented or real. You'll see some of them, Julie. Queens of little islands, queens of many islands. Perhaps someday the Queen of England. But none of them can outshine you."

"Can you believe it, Stephen?" Julia's eyes sparkled at the thought. "We're really going. To all the places I've only heard or read about. One man would tell me about the colors of a land; another described the smells; another, the people. I put all the tales together and tried to make it real, but it never *truly* was."

"Other men may have told you a few yarns"—he kissed the palm of her hand—"but I'm the man who will show you. I can't wait to take you shopping in the bazaars of Calcutta, to wander with you through the orange groves of Barcelona, to show you the apes on Gibraltar. There are small islands where it's likely no white man has ever been before. Large countries with their processions and riches and music."

"And dancing girls?" she teased him.

"Some," he admitted. "Perhaps you'll be permitted to see them."

"Permitted!"

"When given by the wealthy, ladies aren't usually welcome at such entertainments, and the taverns are too dangerous . . . often even for a man."

"Well, just remember what you said a little while ago, Stephen," she warned. "Where you go, I go, too."

"Not on business, my sweet, but then you'll probably be glad enough to see me off for a few hours after spending months alone with me."

"Alone? With a whole ship full of men?"

"You know the captain's wife can't make friends of them any more than the captain can. It's a lonely life, Julia."

"Not in Ombedia." She raised her glass and smiled at him over its rim. "No one is ever lonely in Ombedia."

"No," he said, laying an arm over the back of the settee behind her. "Not when there's a queen to share the king's solitude."

"I certainly hope not."

"Julie," he said, playing with the curls that had escaped down her back. "It's going to be a lovely voyage."

She twisted the gold ring on her left hand, unaccustomed to its weight. It was much wider than the slender band Jason had given her.

"Tell me about the seas," she said. "I don't know which I look forward to more, the water or the foreign lands."

He took another sip of his sherry and his hand grew still across her back. "The sea is not always kind, Julie."

"I know, but tell me about it. I want to hear about the winds and the doldrums, the dolphins and the whales. Tell me about flying fish and phosphorus."

"You want to hear about all the pretty things, though the doldrums aren't pretty. I'll tell you the most important thing, and you must never forget it, my sweet. The sea does not love a man . . . or a woman, either. We are there on sufferance, and when the sea decides to play her games with gales or ice fields or torrid heat in a flat calm, she doesn't care whether a few puny men in wooden ships are riding her waves or not. She plays her games. And if a few men die, what is that to her?"

"I know," she said quietly, "but there are some men she favors."

"No. There are no favorites, but she does not suffer fools gladly. It's the wise men, always alert to her whims and her treachery, who survive."

"Then why do you go to sea?"

"Why?" He stared out the aft windows for a moment at the sun that was sinking into harsh red and gold clouds. Then he looked back at her and his smile returned. "To take you there, of course, my lady. So that I can empty all the treasures of the world into your silken lap."

"You said it would be a lovely voyage."

"It will be," he said, pulling her closer to him and kissing the hollow of her neck. "You'll see. I'll trace our route for you."

His lips lightly touched hers. "This is Boston. And this" —he kissed the tip of her nose and the corners of her eyes—"is the North Atlantic. We sail halfway to England before we turn south." Pulling her cloak back from her shoulders, he kissed her more deeply, compelling her lips to open with his.

The saloon had grown dark except for a little glow cast by the stove when Stephen found his way through her layers of clothes to her breasts. "At last, the first sight of land," he said, fondling them. He bent low to press his lips against each in turn. Then he looked deep into her half-closed eyes. "They're lovely, Julia. More lovely than I guessed."

"You've been thinking about them?" she asked with a lazy smile.

"Of course, I've been thinking about them"—he grinned at her—"longer than you might suspect."

"And other things?"

"Yes. Definitely other things. I think we should go to the capital of Ombedia and continue the exploration of our kingdom."

"The capital?"

"Yes." He nodded at the captain's cabin. "It lies just beyond that door."

"The horses. They're standing out in the cold."

"No, they're not. The watchman has seen to that."

"But we should go home."

"This is our home, sweet Julia," he said, lighting the oil lamp that hung from the overhead.

"That's right. It is, but we can't live aboard while the men are working on her."

"Perhaps not, but this evening, there are no men working."

"No, there aren't, are there?" she said dreamily. "Do you always think of everything?"

"Always, my love. Come," he said, pulling her up off the settee. "To the capital."

The feather bed, which had been covered with rough cloth the last time Julia had seen it, was neatly made up, the wedding gift quilts piled high. The sight of it suddenly made her feel shy. She wondered at herself. She didn't think she had ever been this way with Jason. But had she forgotten? Or had the years spent repressing the longings of her body changed her?

Then Stephen's arm was around her, and the warm, sensuous feel of his fingers cupping her breast overcame her reticence. As he helped her undress, he was gentler than she had expected. He treated her as though she had never known a man before.

And she felt as though she never had. He was the first man, the only man, she thought, as his sure hands traveling slowly over her body, he whispered to her of southern seas and halcyon days.

He shed his clothes so deftly while he caressed her she was not even aware that they were gone until he slid beneath the covers and she smelled the rich fragrance of his skin and felt its smoothness against her own.

She reached a hand up to his face, but he took it and guided it beneath the covers to curl around the hard pulsation that was his while he fondled her secret softness.

"You're so big!" she gasped when he entered her slowly.

"Be gentle, my lady," he whispered.

His rhythm was the rhythm of the sea, with times of calm moonlight shining on the water in the intervals between winds that shook her from every direction, sometimes in gales, sometimes in sweet breezes. Then suddenly the tempest, where tingling lightning struck her every pore.

Then nothing but the white-hot blaze of light so blinding she reached the outer limits of the universe.

Returning slowly, she felt him covering her, surrounding her, within her, and she did not know which hands were his, which warm whisper of breath his, which heartbeat his and which her own.

After a while, he kissed her so lightly it was like a touch of windblown spray on her lips. "Cape Horn was never like this before." He barely breathed the words.

"Cape Horn?" she murmured. "I thought we'd circumnavigated the globe."

"No, my lady," he said, pushing the damp tendrils away from her face. "Only Cape Horn. We've hardly begun our voyage."

The large white house was dimly lit when they arrived, but Ezra slipped out of the carriage house door and took the horses silently from Stephen. They tiptoed up the stairs in a path of moonlight. There was no sound in the house, but Julia could picture those lying behind their closed bedroom doors awake and listening for their return. In her room the fire was burning, lately tended by someone, perhaps by the same person who had left a tray of food on her dressing table.

"Oh, I'm starved," she said, lifting the napkin that covered the dishes. "Did you plan this, too?"

"No." Stephen looked over her shoulder and smiled at the tray. "But I'm glad that someone did. Obviously someone who knew what would be needed."

"Most likely Aunt Martha."

"Aunt Martha?"

"I reckon she was quite a woman in her day," Julia said thoughtfully.

"You're quite a woman," he said as he put his arm around her, "and your day has just begun."

She turned and searched his face feature by feature, from his tawny hair and wide forehead to his straight nose, his wide, thin lips, and his hard, square chin. Then she looked long into his eyes. "I love you, Stephen," she said quietly.

"And I you."

They stared at each other for a few minutes and found

the people they didn't know were there. Then Stephen roused himself. "You said you were starving."

"I am!" she said and picked up the tray to carry it to a small table in front of the fire. "Let's eat here."

Julia, half wakening in the light of false dawn a week later, reached over in the bed to touch her husband, but although the sheets were still warm, he was gone.

"Stephen?" she murmured.

"I'm here, sleepyhead." He sat on the bed beside her and began to nuzzle her between her neck and shoulder. "Wake up. It's launching day."

"Oh, no," she said, curling deeper into the warmth of the bed. "Come back to bed. Launching's a long way off."

"Come on, Julia." He got up and flung the covers off her. "You may have seen many launchings, but I haven't and never one of a ship under my command. I don't intend to miss a thing."

"It's too early and it's cold, Stephen," she said, sitting up and reaching for the quilts, which he held away from her. "Give me back the covers."

"No," he said, pulling her out of bed. "How can you sleep on a day like this?"

She stood up and stretched, then shivered in the chilly air. "How can I not sleep after a night like that? The least you could have done was build a fire."

"If you dress quickly, you won't be cold." He pulled his tailcoat on over his satin vest. "I'll light a fire in the dining room. It'll be warm by the time you get downstairs."

"Well, you better hurry, because it's not going to take me long." She shivered again as she reached for the clothes she had laid out the night before. "Not in this cold."

When she reached the dining room, she found Stephen impatiently pacing around the table.

"Those maids are as bad as you. They'd hardly gotten the kitchen fires started when I got down here. Lord knows when we'll have breakfast."

Julia opened her hands in front of the blazing fire, which had not yet spread its warmth through the room. "Well, I told you you were starting the day too early. I'll bet Aunt Martha had something to say when she saw you in the kitchen, bothering the servants."

Stephen stopped his pacing to grin at her. "She threw me out."

"Physically?" Julia raised one delicate eyebrow at him.

"No. She used her tongue, but I wouldn't put it past her to have done it physically if I hadn't gotten out of there in a hurry."

"Well, if you ever need a first mate, you'd do worse than to consider Aunt Martha. She runs a taut ship."

Stephen made a wry face. "She argues with the captain, though."

"You're not the captain," Julia laughed and turned around to warm her back at the fire. "You're just another passenger as far as she's concerned. Like me. I found out a long time ago there was no point in disputing with Aunt Martha."

"Well, I hope she sees to it that we get breakfast soon." Stephen pulled a chair away from the table and sat down. "I want to get on over to the yard."

"Stephen, nothing's happening yet."

"But it will soon," Benjamin said as he came into the dining room, rubbing his hands. "Glad to see I'll have company at breakfast."

"I don't think Stephen slept all night." Julia moved away from the fire to give her father a kiss on his clean-shaven cheek. "He's as bad as a child before Christmas."

"Well, there aren't many children who get a present like that for Christmas," Benjamin said, winking at his son-in-law. "You all packed? Ready to go?"

"I am, sir, but I don't know about Julia," Stephen said, impatiently drumming his fingers on the table. "I had enough trouble just getting her out of bed."

"Most of my things are ready," Julia said airily. "Aunt Martha will see to the rest of it and bring my bag down to the yard. Our sea chests are already on board."

"What are you going to do when you don't have Aunt Martha to look after you?" Stephen teased her. "Julia's been trying to convince me to sign her on as first mate," he explained to Benjamin.

"Why, you'll be there to look after me, won't you, Stephen?" she said, opening her eyes in wide blue innocence.

"I'll be there," he promised her, "but you're going to have to learn how to pack your own bags."

Benjamin chuckled. "That's right, young man. Don't let her get away with anything. She'll try, but don't you let her. Looks like you've met your match, Julie."

"We'll see about that," Julia promised her father.

When the three of them arrived at the yard, some of the men were already hanging the bunting and putting up the flags under Philip Sears's watchful eye. Others were stringing ropes around the *Crystal Star* to keep the spectators away from danger. Stephen, seeing Daniel Sears with a crew of men on the deck of the ship, went to investigate, leaving Julia alone with her father.

"Well, Julie, you're finally going to get your wish," Benjamin said.

"Funny," Julia said, "I'm excited about it, but not as much as I thought I'd be. It seems so . . . so normal now, and it's rather sad."

"Sad?" Benjamin cocked one bristly black eyebrow at her.

"Yes. To be going away." She looked around the shipyard wistfully as though trying to memorize the familiar scene. "To think I won't see this again for years. I'll miss you, Papa. I wish you were coming with us."

"Now what good would I be to you?" he said gruffly. "A ship can have only one master."

"Yes, I know." She saw a sadness in his eyes that matched her own. "Papa, when the *Jewel* comes home, why don't you take her on her next voyage? David can always find another ship, or he might like to spend a little time with his wife in England."

Benjamin looked at her in surprise and rubbed his chin. "It's too late, Julie."

"No, it's not. You're still younger than a lot of captains."

He looked away from her and at the people who were beginning to filter into the yard.

"I'm tied to the land now," he said. "Tied to this shipyard. Tied to your mother. I can't leave."

When she heard the anguish in his voice, she was almost sorry she had brought up the subject. Still, she pushed on.

"The *Jewel*'s the ship you always wanted to build. The ship that was going to set you free. The one you dreamed about. Then you gave her to Jason and me. But she's still yours. She's part of you."

He found it difficult to speak and shook his head. Then he said, "Dreams have a way of coming true, Julie, but not always the way you'd planned."

"They still can, Papa," she said, urging him on. "Daniel and Philip can run the yard for a few months. Mother's had her way. Kept you home for seventeen years. Now it's your turn."

"No. It's not possible." He took off his top hat and rubbed one hand over his face as though to smooth away the pain. Then he clapped his hat firmly on his head and put an arm around her shoulder. "You'll go for me, Julie. Write and tell me everything that happens. What you do. What you see. How you feel."

"Oh, I'll write you often, Papa."

"That a promise?"

"Of course, it is."

"Then we'd better get to work and see about this launching or you won't be going anywhere." He smiled at her, though there was still a remnant of sadness in his eyes. "Come on, miss. Your job isn't finished yet."

Soon the crowd was filling the yard and the banks of the opposite shore. Rich and poor, young and old, they were dressed in their best. Elegant hats and bonnets, tall beaver hats and leather-billed caps, they jostled together in an excitement that mounted as the water level rose on the banks of Sesuit Creek.

Children raced around underfoot, the younger ones playing tag, the older ones climbing the giant boulders where they would get a better view. Dogs followed in their wake, barking wildly, while the shipyard cats hid under the buildings or in the trees.

Bets were made amongst the men. What would be the exact moment the ship hit the water? Would she enter cleanly or would she careen? Would anyone be injured?

Tales were told of other launchings. In the days of old Captain Howard, Benjamin's father, a man had been killed. They nodded wisely and spoke of disaster: broken arms, crushed legs, concussions. Caught between the land that gave her birth and the sea that was to be her home, a vessel could do strange, unpredictable things.

The retired captains, some old, some middle-aged, had taken over Toct Bridge, up the creek a ways. They knew it afforded the best view and none disputed their right to it. There they stood, high and dry, all their voyaging over and their fortunes safely tucked away. Smug that it was now someone else's turn to wager his life against the sea, they still felt a twinge when they looked at the *Crystal Star*. How they would love to get their hands on that one. Sail her round Cape of Good Hope over to the East Indies. One more voyage. They shook their heads and smiled ruefully at one another.

This was a day of muscle, a man's day, and there was little Julia, dressed in her satin dress and best caped coat, could do. When her mother arrived with Aunt Martha in the carriage, Julia went to sit with them.

"Well, Mama, I have my soap and you didn't have to pack me a lunch this time," she said as she joined them.

"I should think not," Aunt Martha said. "You got enough food on board to take you across the Atlantic."

"Well, hardly that"—Julia smiled—"and it won't be as good as though you'd just cooked it, but it'll see us to Boston."

"You'll take care not to catch cold now, Julia?" her mother said.

"Of course, Mama." She patted her mother's hand. "You have to stop worrying about me. What are you going to do when I'm half a world away?"

"That's what worries me," Lydia said, her green eyes misty. *"Why* do you have to go to sea, Julie? With no sons, I'd hoped I'd never have to go through this again, this worrying and waiting."

"Mama, you promised me you wouldn't talk this way."

"I know, but it's difficult when it's what I'm thinking."

"Well, just think about something else. After all, you're coming down to Boston before we sail. Just think what fun we'll have when you do. We'll go shopping together and to the Athenaeum. We'll have lovely dinners in elegant restaurants."

"It won't be the same, Julie," her mother began when Amelia's rosy face appeared beside the carriage.

"Julie!" she said as she bounced into the carriage, her

blond curls swinging, "I've been looking everywhere for you."

"Glad you found us," Julie said, looking at her sister's smart new coat and beribboned hat. "Where's Michael?"

"Oh, he's down there somewhere, discussing ships and sailing with Stephen and Captain Asa and about twenty other men. Didn't think they had any particular use for a woman around, so I came to find you. I wanted to say goodbye to you in private, anyway, before the launching."

"Have you seen Sarah?" Julia asked.

"Yes. She and Aaron are down near the water." Tiny lines appeared between her fair eyebrows. "They're with Uncle Josiah."

"Oh, dear," Julia said. "Well, I don't think even they can spoil anything today."

"Now, Julia," Lydia said. "That's no way to talk about your sister."

"You're right, Mama." Julia smiled and squeezed her mother's hand. "They'll be launching soon now. We'd better go on down and get our places before it begins."

Once they were in the area near the ship reserved for the family and special guests, they found conversation difficult over the din of the crowd. Soon Stephen and Captain Asa joined them, followed by Benjamin, who nodded to the Reverend Lamson.

Julia hardly heard his words as she watched the south wind driving the surface waves down the creek in foaming opposition to the rising tide. But despite the wind, the water was rushing in amongst the gold salt grass, the rocks, and the marl. It seemed to be laughing as it lapped at the miniature coves of grass, chuckling over the cracks in the marl. The gulls were everywhere, as they soared and fished with shrill, excited cries.

Before she knew it, the minister had finished and husky men, with their steel-faced mallets in their hands, had stepped up to the ship in pairs. Julia, in rising excitement, slipped her hand through Stephen's arm and clung to him. As the blocks were sundered two by two, she felt his hand gripping hers tensely, but she had eyes only for the *Crystal Star*.

When the last pair of blocks had shattered and the men had scrambled under the lines for safety, the ship still stood as though imprisoned by the land. Julia held her breath. If the vessel did not slide down the ways of her own accord now, they would have to help her, and innumerable dangers lay in that, both to the ship and the men who worked her.

Suddenly, with no previous warning noise or motion, she shot down the railway and into the water. She rolled on one side as she shot sideways down the creek, and people raced back from the opposite shore. Just before she reached the far bank, she righted herself and slued around, facing directly downstream. Men posted along the water's edge swiftly took in her lines, tethering her to the land.

Cheers rang out from both sides of the creek and Julia found that her voice was one of them. She looked at Stephen and discovered that he was grinning at her.

"And you accused me of being like a child at Christmas," he said as he looked at her glowing face.

"Oh, Stephen, look how beautiful she is, how proud she sits in the water."

"Like a swan," he agreed. "If you want to say goodbye to anybody, you'd better do it now. We'll have to board soon."

"The captain speaks?" she teased. He smiled and his grey eyes were almost blue with happiness.

"Mama. Papa." She kissed each in turn. "We'll meet in Boston. Amelia, can you come, too?"

"I don't know," Amelia said, then gave her sister a hug and a kiss that disregarded their clothes and hair. "It depends on how Michael's mother is doing. Anyway, Julie, you know I'll be thinking of you and praying for you. You'll write?"

"Yes, often." She turned to her dainty sister, who was dressed in the height of fashion. "Sarah, I'll miss you."

"I know," Sarah said with a quiet smile and held out her hand. "Goodbye, Julia."

After she had shaken hands with Aaron and Michael, she looked for Uncle Josiah, but he had disappeared into the crowd of workmen who were now converging upon her.

She glanced out in the creek to see that men were launching gondolas half-filled with water and racing with them out to the *Crystal Star*. Once there, they lashed them across her stern. Working quickly, they bailed the gondolas, raising the ship's stern just enough to carry her over the bar.

Her husband stood impatiently beside her as she shook hands with each workman. Then when Daniel Sears, who had gone aboard after the launching, rowed in to shore, Stephen took her by the elbow.

"Come on, Julia. It's time to go."

"Yes." She looked out at the ship and then at the faces that surrounded her, and she felt torn between two loyalties and two loves.

"Julie, Julie," her mother said, kissing her once again. "Take care."

"I will, Mama," Julia said as Stephen towed her away from her family toward the boat that stood waiting for them.

As she approached it, she regretted having worn her best clothes, but then she mentally shrugged. She'd best get used to it, for this would be her life from now on. Then she found herself looking into Daniel's dark brown eyes as he helped her into the boat and she saw an unexpected sorrow there.

"I'll take you out," he said.

"Thank you, Daniel." It was a courtesy, for he, as chief foreman of the yard, was not required to row people about.

In only a few strokes they were there, and before Julia turned to take the rope ladder that hung over the side of the ship, she held out her hand to Daniel.

"I won't forget you, Daniel," she said softly.

"Nor I, you," he said and blushed underneath his swarthy tan.

As soon as they were on board, Stephen guided her to the quarterdeck, where he began giving orders to the makeshift crew that was to take the ship to Boston. Julia took a quiet spot next to the helmsman and watched, in turns, her husband transformed into a captain and the sails being hoisted on the jury rig. Then the short lines were cast off and the pilot schooners set off before the wind, hauling the ship behind them.

Once they had sailed past the mouth of the creek and were clear of the bar, Julia looked up on the dunes that lay to port of them. Standing alone was a tall, husky figure in a top hat. She went to the rail and waved to him, and her father took off his hat and waved back. Then she turned and looked at Stephen, whose entire concentration was on the working of the ship. His hat gone, the sun shone on his tawny hair and, even though his eyes were narrowed in their search for imperfections, she could see the blue-grey that was the only sign of happiness in his serious face.

She smiled and, after one last wave to her father, she faced forward toward her new life and the sea.